BETRAYED SKIES

BETRAYED

A Novel by

Translated from the German by

SKIES

Rudolf Braunburg

J. MAXWELL BROWNJOHN

DOUBLEDAY & COMPANY, INC.
GARDEN CITY, NEW YORK   1980

Library of Congress Cataloging in Publication Data

ISBN: 0-385-15183-7
Library of Congress Catalog Card Number 79-7860
English Translation Copyright © 1980 by Doubleday & Company, Inc.
English edition published by arrangement with Franz Schneekluth
Verlag, München.
Originally published as Der Verratene himmel
Copyright © 1978 by Franz Schneekluth
Verlag, München
ALL RIGHTS RESERVED
PRINTED IN THE UNITED STATES OF AMERICA
FIRST EDITION IN THE UNITED STATES OF AMERICA

For A.B.

Ah, Mother, in my dreams
I saw a white-winged angel
stripping rifles,
smashing guns,
setting them all aflame,
burning them to ashes.

Ah, Mother, in my dreams
I saw a white-winged angel
take the ashes in his hand
and scatter them throughout the land.
And suddenly the ashes came alive
and soared like doves in the eastern sky . . .

Gasub Sirkhan, age fourteen,
from the Arab village of Qfar Yaffia.

Foreword

Autumn 1944 . . . In the west, the Allied invasion is under way. In the east, Soviet troops stand poised to do battle for East Prussia. Königsberg, the East Prussian capital, has already been attacked by a force of two hundred British bombers. The terror raids on Germany are nearing their climax.

Jagdgeschwader 99 never existed. The Polish township of Grojecko is not identical with the scene of this novel. What did exist was the generation of young German fighter pilots whose commanders flung them into a lost battle and vainly pitted them against the overwhelming superiority of Allied bomber formations. What are real are the murderous air duels and the fear of death that haunted the cockpits of the Luftwaffe's single-seat fighters. The author flew one himself, and this book represents the sum of his experiences.

Where mention is made of persons still alive today, there is no intent to vilify or glorify them. The verdicts passed on these men do not lay claim to objective truth. They are, however, authentic insofar as they convey the mood of the time, which was rife with rumor and dissent.

The author is grateful for the moral support of many friends who—in contrast to that small band of bemedaled aces whose numerous "kills" remain their passport to public esteem— were always on the losing end. Like them, he came to know the darker side of war; in his view, there is no other.

Translator's Note

During World War Two, Luftwaffe ranks, appointments, and formations had no exact counterparts in the USAF and RAF. They have therefore been retained in the text but are listed in the Glossary at the end of this book together with their Anglo-American approximations.

In all the world's armed forces, airmen are dapper, dashing types. They enjoy a special status dependent not only on the expense of their training but also on the romance, the occasional daring, and, in many instances, the unmistakably "sportsmanlike" nature of what they do and are.

Heinrich Böll

Fliers consider themselves an elite. . . .

Georg Leber

Hitler thought fighter pilots led a grand life. They lived in their messes for the purpose of flying from time to time and periodically engaging in chivalrous duels with the enemy.

General Milch to Adolf Galland

A fighter pilot stays put until he has expended his ammunition, shot the enemy down, been shot down himself, or until his aircraft has been disabled.

Royal Air Force Manual of Combat Tactics

Twenty thousand and one examples of the Focke-Wulf 190 single-seat fighter were built in the course of the war.

The Luftwaffe lost 44,065 aircrew personnel during World War Two. A further 28,000 pilots were wounded and 27,610 taken prisoner or reported missing.

Prologue

In fifteen minutes at most I'd be crossing the front line. The Geschwader was strictly forbidden to venture within fifteen miles of it.

The airplane under the seat of my pants was a Fieseler Storch. I'd flown a Storch only once in my life and exactly a year ago, so I skimmed through the operating manual and took off. I was fifty feet up before I'd decided whether to unstick. You simply couldn't keep a Storch on the ground.

Beneath me lay the serried foothills of the Lysa Gora. A range of clouds like frozen cascades echoed the conformation of the mountains.

We made a clumsy pair, the Storch and I. The map kept slipping off my knees. Whenever I bent to retrieve it the little machine bucked as though she'd abandoned flying in favor of seven-league boots.

The reason for my unusual mission: Lenz was missing— he'd crash-landed far behind the lines.

I hadn't heard the grim news until we touched down after our latest combat patrol. Only Wehrmann claimed to have seen Lenz pancake.

"It couldn't have been that far behind the lines," I snarled at him. *"Didn't you even circle the spot and pinpoint it? Could you see if he was hurt or not?"*

"I wasn't close enough for that." Wehrmann had just enough tact to keep a malicious smirk off his face, but he couldn't resist adding, *"We'll have to write him off, I'm afraid. Too bad. That's the last we've seen of poor old Lenz."*

Now I was hedgehopping over treetops, rooftops and rivers in the hope of crossing the lines unscathed. The Lysa Gora looked mottled, like the coat of some mangy beast.

If Lenz had any chance at all, the Storch was it. Laboriously groping my way over the same stretch of countryside I had crossed at ten times the altitude and almost ten times the speed only an hour before, I scoured my mind for any lecture-room snippets that might have stuck.

The Fieseler Fi 156 Storch, a high-wing monoplane with extremely low-speed flying characteristics. Stalling speed in still air: thirty-two miles per hour. Fixed undercarriage with long hydraulic spiral-sprung shock struts. Their exceptionally long oleo stroke made it possible to land from almost any altitude without rounding out and with the elevators fully actuated. In a slight head wind, the machine could land in less than fifty feet.

The 240-hp Argus AS 10C power plant chugged slowly but steadily along. Its robust and unbroken rhythm was reassuring. My pulse, which had been fast and irregular, settled down—took its cue from the engine's stolid sewing-machine beat. What if your guts have turned to ice water, Braack, the Argus seemed to say. Keep going like me. . . .

Fields pockmarked with craters, trees ripped and blasted by shellfire. The front line must be near. I crept even closer to the ground. There was no point in climbing. The Storch couldn't outclimb any sort of flak, however light, so the only answer was to fly at zero feet and rely on surprise.

Forest tracks and ranges of hills, piebald cows grazing,

*herons abruptly taking wing . . . A stream, a landing stage, a
rowboat rotting in the muddy shallows of a small lake. Then,
tanks.*

*I yanked on the stick despite myself, panic-stricken. There
were Soviet stars everywhere—on tarpaulins, vehicles, gun
shields. There it was, the barrier that lay between us fliers and
the forbidden land: the front line. Simultaneously, the
weather changed. Wisps of low cloud came snaking toward
me, gusts swirled about me.*

*There was the river, entangled in itself like a snarl of rope.
Wehrmann had given me a topographical clue: according to
him, Lenz had come down just beyond it.*

He had. His machine was lying there intact—no, sinking!

*The one-ninety had pancaked onto a meadow enclosed by
dense forest. The flat green expanse seemed to float like an island in the midst of a darker green sea. I put the Storch into
a steep turn and went down to twenty feet. What had given
me the impression that Lenz was sinking?*

*He was perched on the engine cowling with his orange
pilot's scarf fluttering in the wind.*

*Fact number one: he was alive. Fact number two: his
wings were awash with green slime. Fact number three: the
meadow wasn't a meadow, it was a swamp. Lenz was
stranded on a sinking ship. He hadn't managed to reach the
treelined shore.*

Fourth and last fact: I couldn't land.

*Grimly, doggedly, I orbited him at minimum speed. Had
he recognized me?*

*I slid open the side panel and waved. The Storch gave a
perilous downward lurch, rocking in the squalls.*

*Lenz, seated astride the cowling, had something black in
his hand: an automatic pistol.*

*Gusts hit me head-on. The storm front was bearing down
on me like a giant vortex.*

Turbulence made accurate flying impossible. The stick laid claim to a will of its own as I struggled to remain airborne, let alone fly some kind of controlled orbit. I soared above the treetops and skimmed the slimy green swamp in quick succession.

Slowly but steadily, the forest was being invaded. Heavy, tracked vehicles were converging on the swamp. The first of them had already entered the trees, though they wouldn't be able to open fire till they'd combed the entire area. The patch of swamp and its reluctant prisoner were visible only from the air.

Then a strange sensation flooded through me. It was like a blood transfusion administered under pressure. I felt brimful of energy and initiative, as though I'd spent months in idleness preparing for this very moment.

Within ten minutes at most, the first Russians would have reached the edge of the swamp and opened fire. I circled for another approach but was badly deflected. Fighting the gusts, I gauged the direction of the wind and tried to meet it head-on as I made a close approach.

Inky walls of cloud closed in, the ground seemed to rock and sway. Soupy green water was washing over the wings and elevators of the foundering one-ninety. The first time I hovered near Lenz at a bare thirty feet the wind veered abruptly and swept me sideways into the trees. Terrified, I heaved on the stick and found myself in darkness.

It was all over now. If I let-down blind I'd hit the treetops. A rending crash, a sheet of flame, and that would be that.

Tensely, I struggled to keep the turn-and-bank and vertical speed indicators on zero. Shreds of cloud were racing past, some paler than others. I headed for the paler ones. A trace of green, a vague glimpse of something solid, and down I went. Lower, lower still . . . At last I could see the ground again. I was skimming over a track through the woods. At the far end, steel mastodons were lumbering along with their trunks extended: Soviet tanks. I made a quick one-eighty, fighter fashion, and there was the swamp again with Lenz in the middle.

He watched me with desperate intensity, waving like mad, but his gestures conveyed no hope now, only fear. Above the drone of my Argus, he had evidently heard the grinding roar of engines, the rattle of tank tracks.

There was no escape. I couldn't land and Lenz couldn't leave his island. The swamp was neither land nor water. It was a sluggishly heaving mass, too deep to wade through, not solid enough to stand on, not liquid enough to swim through. I had no choice but to keep circling and see Lenz blown to bits or share his fate when the guns opened up.

Another approach. I cursed aloud each time I made an error.

Easy now, don't overcorrect! Show the bastards! Show these goddamn gradients and crosswinds. Get lost, you menagerie of meteorological monsters!

My predicament was quite as hopeless as it had ever been when I was attacking a box of Fortresses, but what vitality, what energy, what grim determination! I hardly knew myself.

Again I skidded past Lenz—he had a black smudge on his forehead, I noticed. A glance at the airspeed indicator: sixty miles an hour—much too fast. How slow could you fly a Storch? The figure thirty-two bobbed up in my mind like a life belt. I finally did what I should have done long ago: I lowered full flaps.

Another approach, another glance at the tanks. They were forging through the trees like giant saurians within scent of their prey. My latest approach told me precisely the course and throttle setting that would just keep the Storch in forward motion. The airspeed indicator was now reading forty. I edged slowly past Lenz at a walking pace. His figure danced into my port panel and out of it again. I juggled with the stick and throttle, kicked hard on the rudder, but it was useless. I'd overshot him.

Rain blurred the windshield as I went into another steep turn. The cloud base was getting steadily lower.

The tanks crawled nearer and nearer. Blue-gray smoke spurted from their exhaust vents and scudded away like startled bats.

The first shots rang out. A machine gun mounted on an armored scout car was pumping bursts of tracer in my direction. They vanished into the overcast. Tracer was a familiar sight —it held no terrors for me.

I now knew what to do. My next approach would have to be my last. . . .

BOOK ONE

I've taken off my decorations. I won't put them on again till the German Air Force pitches in and fights as it did in the old days, when I myself was highly decorated for doing just that. My orders are cut and dried, and I'm going to see they're carried out—ruthlessly. Our fighter pilots will fight to the last man. If they don't, they'll be transferred to the infantry. The German people don't give a damn how many fighters we lose.

Reichsmarschall Hermann Göring,
speaking at Hitler's Berchtesgaden
residence on 7 October 1943.

The day burst like a bomb—right in the middle of breakfast. Plates went flying, bowls of gruel and cups of non-ersatz coffee anointed the tables as a human tornado swept out of the pilots' mess. We sprinted for our machines.

Scramble!

All the loudspeakers on the base relayed the order. They hung from canteen walls and bunkhouse ceilings, from the lime trees bordering the main thoroughfare, and, of course, from posts on the edge of the airfield. A moment ago Evelyn Künnecke had been sexily intoning *"Sing, Nachtigall, sing"* above tar-papered roofs that had never seen or heard a nightingale and stank of carbolic. Then the announcer cut in:

Enemy aircraft heading north into the Katowice-Opole area. . . .

Next came the squawk and crackle of our public-address system: farsighted though Combat Control's plans for us might be, the voice that transmitted them had all the aesthetic appeal of a laryngitic crow.

Out we raced into the lustrous early autumn morning, scrambling into our flying suits, clipping on our parachutes with the ever-present help of the crew chiefs who boosted us into our cockpits.

Then Ketsch grabbed me by the elbow.

"Not you, Braack!"

My spurt of enthusiasm slumped like a fountain in a drought.

"I'm feeling fine."

"Sure, like a young god of war with a twin-row radial under his ass. I know all that, but you're still on sick leave till this time tomorrow."

"So?"

"So you won't park your butt in a one-ninety till I've put you through your paces—that's an order." Ketsch, our Staffel commander, glanced impatiently at the figures galloping past. "You've been gone ten days—I bet you've even forgotten where the stick is. This isn't a practice alert, man. No second chances, no raspberry juice—the blood's real. You're grounded till I'm back, is that clear?"

This was my cue to fix him with shining eyes and deliver a crisp little speech of protest, a few manly remarks on the subject of duty and self-sacrifice—the kind of photogenic guff so dear to the hearts of our war correspondents and newsreel cameramen. Instead, my baser self nipped all such utterances in the bud.

"Is that clear?" Ketsch insisted.

Baser self to all other components of my split personality:

"Yes, Herr Hauptmann."

My Staffel dissolved into the mists of approaching day.

It roared down the runway in company with the other Staffeln, hell for leather, enemy-bound. Several near collisions were only just avoided while the fighters assumed formation after takeoff. Sheer nerves made one pilot ready his guns too soon and inadvertently press the tit, loosing off a miniature firework display which must have filled his immediate neighbors with malign amusement.

Somebody failed to get airborne at all—his engine developed a minor intake fire while taxiing. A crewman rushed up with an extinguisher and kept it leveled as though blasting a whole squadron of Soviet tanks. No war for that pilot, not today.

I turned away from the field and strolled back down the road toward the main gate and my favorite hill, which gave a view of the whole base: Grojecko, operational headquarters of Jagdgeschwader JG 99, known as the "Tawny Eagle."

Lenz and I had christened our vantage point "Thyme Hill." Its slopes were thick with violet blossom in summer. Now, only the golden flowers of the thin-stemmed yellow centaury trembled in the morning air, which was cool and clear.

I listened to the airplanes' dying roar as if it held some whispered message. What did this morning, this takeoff, this mission hold in store for them?

The base lay spread out below me like a carelessly scrawled 5, bounded at its lower extremity by the main gate and guardhouse. Starting at the base of the 5, the airfield road swung boldly east and then west in a long unbroken curve. Enclosed by this curve were the principal buildings: mess hall, classrooms, bunkhouses, station headquarters. Beyond them the road ran due north, straight as an arrow, before describing a ninety-degree turn to the east and forming the horizontal arm of the 5. Beside this lay the airfield itself. The turf runway was angled slightly southwest-northeast. In an emergency like the one just now, however, fighters could take off from all parts of the field—from a standing start, so to speak—because they were dispersed at almost mathematically regular intervals.

Such was my world.

Or rather, such was the world that was only now becoming truly mine. Grojecko lay like an island in the fork of the Pilica, which discharged its placid waters into the Vistula somewhere northeast of here and north of Radom. From my elevated position, the Pilica looked like a broad stream with miniature sandbanks. Grojecko Island was surrounded by marshland and alder-infested water meadows, and its seemed to float on a rich broth of decay. The only link with the mainland, the outside world, was the approach road running past the guardhouse.

I drew up my knees and hugged them. Behind me, the railroad track meandered on to Piotrków. This was where I had jumped off the asthmatic little train three hours ago. Grojecko didn't boast a wayside halt, still less a proper station. Duffle bag and rucksack out first, then me. Why else had we spent weeks simulating parachute jumps, light landings, and forward rolls, if only with the crudely unrealistic aid of a practice tower and sandpit?

When I left here ten days earlier, the trees, grass, and roofs had been coated with leaden gray dust. The sun barely rose before it withdrew, appalled, into the haze that enshrouded the river valley.

Now, visibility was unlimited and the sky seemed an infinity of blue. The first day of autumn had dawned.

I drew a deep breath. In this sixth year of the war—total war, with women busy in munitions factories and fighter-control rooms, cripples and children serving at the front—I should really have reported back after four days' leave on the family estate. As it was, my mother had dropped a keg of molasses on my left foot—so effectively that our family doctor of thirty years' standing certified me unfit to travel.

Tired and depressed, I plucked at the grass and listened moodily for sounds in the sky. My belated return to base had driven a wedge between me and the rest of the Staffel. One week overdue and I felt like Rip Van Winkle.

My welcome from the sentry three hours ago:

"Papers, please."

I produced my paybook and held it out.

"Oberfähnrich Braack, 3 Staffel."

The little runt of a ground-crew noncom, his surly features potholed with acne, had ignored the paybook and stared at me curiously.

The old gang wasn't the same anymore—I sensed that after the first handshake, the first stale joke to travel from one tier of bunks to the next. And the sentry with his captured French rifle—the way he'd looked at me, like a licensed buffoon with a hunting permit! Had the base been smitten with plague and put in quarantine? No wonder I felt as I did after a whole night in a train full of warriors returning to the fray, with an air raid en route and plenty of detours because Warsaw was reportedly in Russian hands. We had been packed in like sardines, duffle bag to duffle bag, sweaty armpit to sweaty armpit, groping and fumbling in the darkened compartment. Her name was Monica. She'd smelled no better than a soldier or airman, but at least she'd smelled female.

My face felt grubby and sticky. So did my soul, for want of a better word. The eaglet had returned to its eyrie. I'd already spent four weeks in the training wing. Weapons instruction: the MK-108 aircraft cannon, the MG-51 machine gun, the armament of a Russian Yak 7. Gunnery instruction: acceleration, aiming off. Technical instruction: the BMW 801 twin-row radial engine . . . Home leave prior to combat duty. Now I was back, and Lenz had whispered to me, just before that breakfast with the built-in scramble, that everything—but everything—had changed.

Beyond the airfield, steppe and forest stretched to the horizon. And then, at first like an unheard vibration, something impinged on my senses—something that seemed to be approaching from out of the infinite morning radiance, alien but familiar. A one-ninety returning to base? Our FW 190A-8s had a range of more than five hundred miles and could remain airborne for over two hours. The Staffel wouldn't have turned back yet.

But there it was: the homing pigeon was a one-ninety, the machine whose awesome reputation had blighted my extra spell of leave and put me off my schnapps and smoked ham.

I jumped up and ran back to the airfield. The hum grew louder as I jogged past the stone-built canteen, classrooms, and officers' mess. The main lecture hall, a brick edifice, stood decorously back from the rest. Reeds sprouted from patches of marshy ground, sparse relics of a stream that had once flowed there but dried up—and no wonder, in the infernal dust and heat of a typical Polish summer. Not a sign of life in my own bunkhouse. The entire Staffel was somewhere far off in the burnished blue sky.

A whole army of blackbirds was singing in the poplars, the lime trees outside the mess, and the tousled-looking birches.

I saw it as soon as I reached the edge of the field.

The airplane was in a shallow turn from downwind and coming in to land. By now the sun had cleared the roofs and treetops. It hung there free and serene, the Polish sun, bathing Grojecko in golden light. A few belated skeins of mist slunk furtively along the river valley. Morning had come at last, a cloudless morning in September 1944.

I recognized the birch-tree emblem of our Staffel alongside the Geschwader's tawny eagle, an idea dreamed up by Ketsch, who came from Masuria, as did Lenz and I. The pilot was no slouch. His turn was steady and he seemed in perfect control as he leveled into the straightaway with a fighter pilot's panache, gear down, nose high.

A brief sidelong glance at the wind sock, limp and listless as a prick after a hard night.

Another five seconds at most and it would touch down, the one-ninety that haunted my dreams.

And then, at the very last moment, I saw why.

The leading edges of the wings, undercarriage fairings, and engine cowlings were riddled with more holes than my mother's best tea strainer. That would have been all right—the airplane was still flying and you could live with worse than that—but the wheels weren't locked and couldn't lock because the radius rods had been shot to pieces.

I dashed toward the landing area, waving frantically.

"Stick back!" I yelled.

The poor devil complied, but only—presumably—so as to round out into a smooth landing. It was a gentle touchdown but no smooth landing. His visual indicator didn't appear to be working and wings aren't made of Plexiglas—you can't see through them.

Metal grated against stone and the tormented airscrew bit into the turf. Clods went flying, fountains of sand whirled and eddied. Then, in slow motion, the tail reared up defiantly like the stumpy appendage of a belligerent terrier—up and over. There was a muffled crash as the fighter somersaulted and landed on its back. Terrible sounds of rending and splintering, then silence. Dead silence. A deathly, interminable hush.

A pall of dust rose. Fragments of metal fluttered, feather-like, to the ground. Then, better late than never, the cockpit canopy slid gently off into the grass.

I came to life with a jerk and started running. The turf was moist and spongy. Absurd questions raced through my mind. Where had all the dust come from? Was the pilot ferrying flour? Could the canopy be salvaged for reuse? I grimly suppressed the most important question of all.

Just as I reached the stricken airplane the pilot fell out of his straps and landed like a sack of potatoes. He lay there motionless beneath the wreck for one long, startled moment, then wriggled out from under, sprang to his feet, and dusted off his flying suit. *Pilots will preserve a smart appearance and correct military bearing at all times. . . .*

"Everything all right?"

It was Lenz. More on impulse than by design, we hugged each other. At long last, the fire truck came racing up. God created the world in six days—he never said anything about hurrying.

Lenz gave me a faintly shocked and glassy stare.

"Maybe now," he said, "I can finish my breakfast in peace."

Back to cured sausage, cookhouse bread, and crackers. The mess kitchen was standing by with a second dose of gruel laced with noodles.

I watched the survivors of the latest combat patrol drift in. Faces of every hue from insomniac gray to cadaver green. The only gap in the spectrum was the fresh dawn pink appropriate to stalwart young defenders of the Fatherland. My fellow pilots' lackluster eyes had retreated far into their sockets.

Being still in their flying suits, they also stank of sweat, but not just the glandular variety. Mingled with it was that excretion of the soul, the smell of fear.

Bread, molasses, and sausage—cement sausage, we called it. I pushed them across to Lenz while he rambled on, "Man, we've got it made in this outfit! Think how lucky we are, not having to tote a rifle around the countryside. Great, isn't it? No footslogging for us—no squatting over lousy field latrines."

"Come on, Martin, eat something."

Lenz got my portion of cheese as well. It crumbled under the knife like ill-mixed mortar left in the sun too long. In return he gave me some of his coffee, though the brew was so watered down it tasted like a substitute.

"And another thing. We don't have to march at attention when we salute—I mean, when raising the right hand smartly to the cap with fingers fully extended . . . Hey, Michael, remember the time we licked each other's blood? That makes us blood brothers."

"I know, it crossed my mind a few minutes ago."

"And I made you promise to become a pilot like me, just so we could spend the war together. You'd rather have stuck to your teacher-training course—that and your poems and diaries. You must be cursing me now."

"I'm as keen on flying as you are . . ."

I tried to conjure up a picture of us as earnest twelve-year-olds, exchanging vows beneath an oak tree, but I didn't get far. The siren wailed like a wood nymph being ravished by a cavalcade of satyrs.

Air alert, air alert!

Everyone rushed out again, fulminating.

Lenz thumped the table with his fist. Even the diluted molasses overflowed its banks.

"By God and St. Icarus, can't we ever have a quiet breakfast in this place?"

I followed him outside and headed for the field.

"Icarus wasn't a saint, he was a damn-fool pilot who caused the first air crash in Greece."

This witticism did nothing to dispel my awareness that I still had no machine and was grounded in any case.

"We won't be taking off either," Lenz said. "Taxi our crates into the dispersal pens, that's all we'll do. There must be some Russkis on the way."

We panted along side by side.

"And we don't tackle Russians, only Yankee bombers?"

"Affirmative. Where are you off to, anyway? Get down to the shelter."

"But that's crazy! Why trundle fifty machines into their pens for the sake of a few Russian hedgehoppers? We'd only have to scramble one Staffel and that'd be the end of them. It's what we trained for, isn't it?"

"That's not crazy, that's Steffen."

Steffen was our Geschwader-Kommodore. I'd already heard his name muttered more than once today: *It may be mad but it's methodical. Wherever there's method, there's Steffen. . . .*

And there were the Russians. Three fighters streaked toward the field at zero feet, skimming trees, cottages, and molehills. I hoped the bastards wouldn't prune my favorite clump of birches on the northeast perimeter. Letting ground-crew noncoms and cookhouse personnel precede me into the shelter, I savored the enthralling spectacle of three Russian fighters chasing forty-plus Focke-Wulfs into their dispersal pens. Forty pilots—men who had just done battle, more or less courageously, with U.S. bomber formations—turned tail and taxied their lumbering earthbound monsters along the tracks that led, four or five hundred yards away, to revetted enclosures surrounded by sheaves of rotting grain, fields of stubble, and tumbledown sheep pens.

Fountains of gray dust erupted from the field. Mikoyan-Gurevitch fighters, type MiG 3. The sound effects—a wild tattoo from the Russians' machine guns—followed an instant later. A vehicle went up in a mushroom of flame: the Volkswagen scout car parked outside the administration block. The fighters completed their first pass and went into a climbing turn. The light AA guns had started to yap. *Morning all, hope you slept well. . . .*

What would the Ivans and Gregors and Nicolais bag next time around? Why not half a dozen of our one-nineties, which were now tottering off down the farm and forest tracks like frightened chicks?

All they actually did was sew a seam of fiery stitches across the airfield without hitting a single machine. The quadruple pompoms in their concrete emplacement beside the control tower emitted another succession of barks, likewise without hitting anything. A second VW burst into flames, rising from the ground with all four wheels in the air before turning into a multicolored fireball and disintegrating into separate components. The Russians seemed to have it in for our poor old motorized bathtubs.

Pass number three, low enough to strip off the tar paper. The first one-nineties had reached their pens. This time an outbuilding went up in flames. There were sheep inside— who'd have thought it? Bleating, they skipped grotesquely between the one-nineties' wheels. The flak gunners couldn't fire as low as the Russians were flying—besides, they were scared of hitting our own machines. One MiG whistled past me, very close. I could clearly make out a dark, helmeted head through the Plexiglas. Some Cyrillic characters were stenciled just below the cockpit: ЗА РОДИНУ. I memorized them.

Then the trio disappeared unscathed over the eastern skyline, swallowed up by the birch trees and moorland and grassland. Peace and quiet returned.

So, very laboriously, did our one-nineties. I saw at a glance that at least five of them were damaged or immobilized, though not by gunfire. One had rammed a spruce with its port wing and others had buried their wheels in molehills. Another was standing on its nose, the airscrew a write-off. To that extent, the Russians had succeeded after all.

At one particular spot, just short of the firm turf of the runway, every machine paused and taxied in a circle, churning up the ground. The all-clear sounded. I ran over.

Somebody was lying there in an unnatural, contorted position. It was a noncom from the repair hangar. He'd stopped screaming. His eyes were wide and fixed, but so bright in the morning light that they might have been gazing up through the sky at a better world beyond.

My second home: Room 4, Hut 3. Walls painted drab green and stippled with the red remains of squashed bedbugs.

All the boys were safely back from their umpteenth patrol. Lenz's somersault was the only serious incident. The rest had barely made contact, as the saying went. Monica in the furlough train—that was contact for you, but this? No time for hairsplitting. Time must have galloped while I was away in Masuria. You couldn't turn the clock back.

The floorboards still creaked. When I opened my locker door, the whole thing swayed like a smokestack in a force ten gale. The feet of the two-tier bunks still stood in bowls of water on account of the bugs. This was my hut. These were the members of my Staffel. Sprawled on their beds or seated at the rickety table, they were digesting their lunch of fried egg on spinach and watery blancmange with synthetic caramel flavoring.

Welcome back.

They didn't sing it out, just muttered it in a kind of ironic undertone.

There they stood, lay or sat: Schwaneweber, Wehrmann and Wilk, Balzerat, Bächler and Rotsch, Illerts, Lenz and Lauritzen. Plus one newcomer.

"Where's Baltussen?" I asked, strapping up my rucksack and squeezing it into the space between my locker and Schwaneweber's. My eyes strayed uncertainly to the new boy standing in front of Baltussen's. "Something happen to him?"

"Right first time," said Rotsch, as if that explained everything.

Schwaneweber shuffled from one foot to the other. The hut's flimsy joists creaked in concert with the floorboards. I thought of the sentry. They were all giving me the same kind of look. Ten days away and I was a stranger. So where was Baltussen?

"Baltussen was shot down," said Illerts. "Killed."

"Killed?"

"Three missions, seven casualties." That was the newcomer. "The other Staffeln lost six between them. We only lost one. Baltussen. I'm his replacement. Krapinski."

"When you come down to it," Lenz amplified, "we ought to thank our lucky stars. Action at last, no more farting around. All the same . . ."

"Baltussen," I said dully. "And he started wearing long johns on September first, he was so scared of catching cold."

"Much good they did him," Lauritzen said in a low voice.

"Hey," I said, "what's your trouble?"

He hid his hands, but I'd seen them.

"Blisters," he said tersely.

The radio was putting out some mediocre swing by Willy Berking.

"Fire?"

But Lauritzen wasn't feeling communicative.

Illerts said, "If you're looking forward to some action and you think you're going to get a fair crack at the enemy, you're way off target."

"Way off," Schwaneweber chimed in morosely.

"It was a different story when I left," I said. "We couldn't wait to fly them into the ground."

Illerts grunted. "Into the ground is good."

Rotsch elaborated. "We don't have a snowball's chance in hell."

I scanned the faces that had grown so familiar over the past half year. Lauritzen's was the smallest and most delicate, Schwaneweber's the gentlest and most sensitive. I searched in vain for a trace of the girlishness that used to inhabit his features. Then Illerts and Bächler. Run-of-the-mill types—quite alike, but totally dissimilar as soon as they opened their mouths. You could cut Bächler's Hessian dialect with a knife. Illerts had a high-pitched, rather brittle voice and lisped whenever he lost his temper. Then there was Rotsch, a tall, blond, athletic youth to whom we happily conceded victory in every trial of strength or speed. Rotsch had been quick to gain his gold proficiency badge in the Hitler Youth, unlike Balzerat, our only Feldwebel. Bull-necked and broad-shouldered, he'd have been too lethargic to cut the noose if you'd strung him up and put a knife in his hand. Balzerat was thick as thieves with Wehrmann, an Oberfeldwebel and almost as powerfully built. Wehrmann had white-blond hair and a permanently puce complexion. He was also the only roommate I loathed. We came from the same town, and I'd hated him ever since we were dumped in the same playpen as three-year-olds.

Next, Lenz, my boyhood friend and blood brother. We two and Wehrmann were poles apart. Last of all, Wilk, a bright and chirpy youngster with a different girl for every day of the month. His only worry was how to keep them apart, legally and socially, after the war.

Lenz waited for me to complete my facial survey. Then, almost gingerly, he summarized the situation. "You've been gone ten days," he said. "We've had twenty-three full scrambles in that time, all against American bombers. Result—six force-landed, seven jumped, nine bought it. Confirmed kills, none—repeat, none."

"I've flown eighteen sorties," said Wehrmann. He grinned. "I'm an old hand already."

"We're all old hands," growled Schwaneweber. "Older than us you can't get."

"If the odds are so lousy, why do they send us up at all?"

"Send us up? Use us up, you mean!"

"So who's to blame?"

"Göring, the Geschwader—Steffen. Take your pick."

"It goes on forever." That was Bächler. "Tackle a swarm of Mustangs one day and they come back with three times as many Lightnings the next. Tackle the Lightnings today and tomorrow you'll find yourself up against Mustangs and Lightnings combined. It's hopeless."

I perched on the edge of my raw whitewood bunk. I'd always liked this vantage point. Sitting there and looking through the dirty, dust-filmed window of the hut I could see far out across the airfield, all the way to the horizon. And beyond the horizon lay all we'd ever dreamed of in our youthful naïveté. *Tomorrow the world will be ours. . . .* I'd always sung that version in the air cadets' branch of the Hitler Youth —substituting *gehört* for *da hört,* "belong" to us for "hear" us—because I'd genuinely wanted to conquer the world rather than sing about it. Not by force of arms, to be sure, but by the spirit of initiative and enterprise, the urge to explore. Sven Hedin, Mark Twain, and Jules Verne were the authors who'd kindled my imagination. *The very handsome and powerful paddle steamer* Quaker City *has been chartered for the expedition and will leave New York on the eighth of June. . . .* That was how I'd always conceived of my takeoffs.

"We haven't introduced ourselves properly."

Krapinski again. The newcomer was a callow-looking youth with pinched cheeks and a high forehead—twenty-one at most. Baltussen had been all of twenty-three. Nobody had known him well. Baltussen was laconic in the extreme, but not in the same league as Schwaneweber or myself. His frigid silences had been known to paralyze an entire bunkhouse.

"Michael Braack from Lötzen," I said.

"Günther Krapinski," he said. "Maybe I'd better tell you why I'm really here."

"You already did. Because of Baltussen."

"Wrong," said Krapinski.

"What do you mean, wrong? You're Baltussen's replacement."

"That's not strictly true," said Krapinski. "Count us."

I did so.

"The Staffel was up to strength without me," I said. "Baltussen's gone but I've balanced the books. All right, what *are* you doing here?"

"Standing by," he said. "For the next in line."

I reported to the administration block.

"You aren't due back till tomorrow morning." The Feldwebel clerk looked puzzled. He was a stranger to the joys of flying. "Right, I'll tell the Staffelkapitän you're here."

Ten minutes later I was face to face with Ketsch. At twenty-eight, he was the oldest of our Staffel commanders. All his nineteen kills save four had been gained on the Eastern Front, but he always insisted that they were equally well earned—that the Eastern Front fighter pilots were unfairly eclipsed by their glamour-boy rivals in the west. He was a fanatical flier who kept himself in peak physical condition, as his wiry frame betrayed. Ketsch had a reputation for being tough but fair, and toughest of all on himself. He never entrusted any dangerous mission to a less-experienced subordinate. His bony face creased in a broad grin when he saw me.

"What's up, Braack, flying-ants in the pants or girl trouble?" Ketsch was a flier through and through, not a stickler for military etiquette. "Take the weight off your feet."

I made myself at home in a sumptuous armchair looted from some Polish country mansion.

"All hell's broken loose here, I expect you've heard. Your pals are old hands. You'll soon be one too—far *too* soon, more's the pity." He idly shuffled an onyx paperweight to and fro on his desk. "It won't be long before you're up there feeling like a side of smoked ham, with a couple of hundred Yankee air gunners carving slices off you."

"The Russians are on our doorstep. I'd have thought we'd be more use operating against them."

"Thinking's for after the war—save it till then. We fight to order here. Repeat after me—*è così perché è così*—it's so because it's so."

"*È così perché è così.*"

"Never forget that, Braack. It'll help you take things in your stride. We don't want you going round the bend."

"I'll remember."

"And another thing. You'll be seeing plenty of horrors from now on—big ones, little ones, ones you'd never have dreamed of—but whatever kind of scrap you get into, fight fair. Someday I'd like people to think of our bunch as the last clean fighters in a dirty war, understand?"

"Yes, sir."

"Our Staffeln are down to nine or ten pilots apiece, as you know. Do your best to keep it at that. There aren't any more replacements."

"No keen young teen-agers itching to fly?"

"None capable of handling a one-ninety. Now here's the picture. The Yanks are extending their joyrides into Poland. They're overflying the whole of the Reich from west to east without collecting a scratch on the way. To put it politely, we're here to remind them of their limitations. Less politely, the situation stinks. I'd gladly give you a chance to meet the

enemy on level terms, one to one, but we all do what we have
to do. Any questions?"

"No questions, Herr Hauptmann."

*Lauritzen's blistered hands. Baltussen's ivory chessmen,
now taking the place of the cheap pocket set which Bächler
had always used for his marathons with Schwaneweber.*

"Good. I've got a brand-new A-8 for you. If there's no
alert this afternoon, take a good hour's familiarization flight.
Feel her right down to the stall and bone up on your local
landmarks. The Russians are getting pretty damned close."

"Any restrictions?"

"Yes, don't go within twenty miles of the front. Combat
Control will bring you up to date on that. And steer clear of
the opposition—that's an order. I'm aiming to take you under
my wing tomorrow and I need all the pilots I've got. Is that
clear, Braack?"

"Yes, sir."

2

I was standing in front of my factory-fresh A-8.

"She's a dream," said Rosenhain, my crew chief. "Everyone's itching to fly her."

The A-8 was the most heavily armed member of the FW 190 family. At last they'd produced a machine that could match the Americans. Two MG-131 machine guns above the engine and two MG-151 cannons in the wing roots, all four firing through the propeller arc. Another two pairs of MG-151s were housed in underslung pods which could also be fitted with the heavier thirty-millimeter MK-103 or MK-108 cannons.

"Fuel?" I asked, just for something to say.

"It's coming out of her ears," Rosenhain said. "They're like circular saws, these beauties."

"Meaning what?"

"Meaning they'll go through a bunch of Yankees like a knife through butter."

The A-8's armament interested me less than her other vital statistics. I circled her, inhaling the scent of fresh paint and rubber. She was camouflaged in my favorite colors: dark gray-green along the top of the fuselage shading to bluish-gray underneath, but dappled with gray-green flecks that looked as if they'd been applied with a shaving brush. The underside of the wings was pure sky-blue. The upper surfaces matched the fuselage, except that here the alternating colors were sharply defined instead of merging. Stenciled on either flank of the bulky engine cowling was the Geschwader's tawny eagle, and beside it our Staffel emblem, a Masurian birch tree. Its delicate silver shape looked incongruous on an aerial monster with such a devastating output of firepower, but why not? After all, there was an Edelweiss Geschwader.

Wehrmann materialized at my elbow, no less unwelcome than when he used to obtrude on my peaceful hours of play with Lenz beside the lake ten years before. *Remember the dead hoopoe you found, Martin? We solemnly interred its lifeless but colorful corpse between two poplar roots. Wehrmann observed our activities from a discreet distance, grinning, his mop of white-blond hair as conspicuous in the undergrowth as a giant cauliflower. Next morning the grave had been ransacked and the birch-twig cross savaged into the shape of a swastika, an emblem whose significance still escaped us. Out of the bird's body, which had been plucked clean, crawled a fat white maggot—white and stark like Wehrmann's hair. . . .*

"Just in case you didn't know, we all pull together in this outfit."

"Of course. What are you getting at?"

He interposed his bulging torso between me and the one-ninety.

"Anyone who doesn't toe the line is a threat to the whole unit."

"Out of my way, Kommodore," I said. "I want to do some flying."

"And I'm going to see you pull your weight. Yellow-bellies don't last long here. They get the chop."

"Sure, and don't forget to lower your wheels next time out. Sabotaging military equipment is a court-martial offense."

Wehrmann swallowed this allusion to one of his blunders

during training and sauntered off. He swung around after a few yards, menacingly.

"Remember what I said—they get the chop!"

My midriff tightened, constricted by a sneaking and irresistible sense of foreboding. I gulped despite myself.

Then, with Wehrmann's departure, the feeling passed and my initial euphoria returned.

The whole airplane—*my* airplane, identified by a white 8 —looked neat and trim. I gave her an affectionate pat on the massive engine cowling, beneath which slumbered the eighteen hundred horsepower of a BMW 801D-2 twin-row radial.

"What's her fuel load?"

"She'll do up to five hundred miles without a drop tank," Rosenhain said. "Her fuselage tanks have been enlarged. You've got a hundred and sixteen gallons plus twenty-five behind the radio bulkhead. The inboard tanks are self-sealing, of course, like before."

"Of course." I pulled out the retractable cockpit step. Self-sealing meant that the metal skin was hermetically sealed by a protective layer of crude rubber. Not a drop of fuel would escape if an enemy bullet punctured it.

"Give me a hand with these straps, would you?"

Crew chiefs were worth their weight in gold. Rosenhain helped me on with my shoulder straps and adjusted them like a mother plumping her baby's pillow. With all due deference to the V-1, crew chiefs were the war's only real secret weapon.

So there I was in my airplane. I was simply going to fly her, nothing more to begin with. First things first.

I fondled the stick with its finger-fitting grip of molded black plastic. I was simply going to fly—yes, but the gun buttons were also on the stick. I'd never had so much concentrated firepower at my fingertips before. Was that my reason for flying, to unleash it at other members of the human race?

Like the flaps, the guns were electrically actuated. There were two safety switches on the SZKK-4 console, number one for the guns in the fuselage and wing roots and number two for the outboard armament, but you had to watch your priorities with care. The wing guns couldn't be readied for at least three seconds after the others. Why? Because otherwise the battery would overload and fail to complete the first operation. Only when the fuselage guns were ready to fire did Madame Battery deign to service her next customer.

The two forms of armament were differentiated on the stick as well: A for inboard, B-1 for outboard. The visual indicator on the SZKK-4 told you how many rounds each gun had fired. Most productive of all were the MG-131s, for which four hundred rounds were supplied. The MG-151 cannons could manage only two-fifty, the underwing cannons a mere hundred and twenty-five.

The guns in the wing roots fired through the propeller arc, like the MG-131s mounted in the engine cowling. In other words, an interrupter gear checked them whenever one of the three whirling propeller blades entered their line of fire. This complicated arrangement was based on a brilliant invention devised and patented by the Hispano-Suiza company in, of all places, neutral Switzerland. Wasn't I scared, even so, of blasting my airscrew to bits when firing? No, not a bit, and I'd never heard of anyone who had. You couldn't beat the watchmaker's accuracy of Swiss precision engineering.

My reflector gunsight—a Revi 16B—weighed 1.76 pounds. It had a 21-watt, 24-volt bulb and a night filter officially listed as "Shade 71 (Dark Green)."

You set the flaps at twelve degrees for takeoff, though this figure wasn't recorded anywhere in the cockpit. The only settings given on the left-hand console were OUT, IN and TAKE-OFF. It was fun, operating the flaps by simply depressing a button. The same applied to the trim control on the right. Gentle forward pressure on the stabilizer trim switch gave you nose-down; backward, nose-up.

The exact position of the flaps could be checked from inside the cockpit by looking at the wings, which were fitted with a mechanical indicator calibrated from zero to sixty degrees. This had never been pointed out to us in training, any more than we knew that an oily windshield could be cleared by spraying it with fuel. Nobody had shown us the relevant switch—they'd simply forgotten.

A light northeasterly breeze was gently stirring the clumps of birch trees and sending fine grains of sand pattering against the wheel covers. I settled myself more comfortably in the cockpit. Overhead, fleecy clouds. Beneath me, the main fuel tanks—I was mounted on a dormant volcano. The seat itself was just a padded sheet of armor plate 0.30 inches thick— 0.50 inches behind the head and shoulders. At 1.8 inches, the windshield was strongest of all.

I could feel the pressure of the belt buckle against my stomach. This was it: the machine of machines—the answer to all my dreams. To fly her you had to know a host of things you'd forget as soon as the war was won. It wasn't a question of soaring through an azure sky pervaded by the buzzing of bees and the trilling of larks; the air was metalliferous with tracer from Lightnings and Mustangs. What, for example, were my chances against a North American P-51 Mustang? The two machines were almost equally matched, though my one-ninety climbed faster at any altitude. The Mustang 1-A's best climbing speed was ten mph slower than mine. What followed from that? It meant that whichever of us bounced the other from behind, my superiority would steadily increase the longer

we climbed. I also knew that my one-ninety handled better
but the Mustang's turning circle was smaller, that I could
accelerate far more rapidly out of low-speed flight, and that
the Mustang's best combat height lay between five and fifteen thousand feet. Once you lured it beyond those limits, it
was a dead duck.

All these things I'd absorbed at a time when I'd rather
have been training for a career in teaching. Others in my age
group had been granted longer exemption from military service. While they were studying the left-wing Hegelians or the
symptoms of decline in Beethoven's later work, I was learning
the best ammunition mix for the MG-131.

"Are you going, or what?" asked Rosenhain.

I returned to the present.

Right behind the stick and low down, the fuel and oil pressure, oil temperature and fuel contents gauges. Above them
the larger flying instruments: altimeter, airspeed indicator,
artificial horizon, vertical speed indicator, compass. On the
right, the supercharge pressure gauge and rev counter. At the
very top on the right, the outside air thermometer. Beside my
left hand, the chunky throttle lever.

It wasn't till my fingers closed around this lever that I really felt at one with the machine. Right hand controlling the
stick, left hand gripping the throttle: that was how you
harnessed eighteen hundred horsepower and made the world
your own. Feet on the rudder pedals, their metal soles and
heels perforated like a Swiss cheese to save weight. No problems. I was comfortably ensconced and concentrating on my
fighter pilot's helmet, a light mesh affair with heavy earphones. I fastened the throat mike, welcoming the gentle pressure of the twin diaphragms on my Adam's apple, and
checked my oxygen mask. I was now hooked up to my machine by straps, wires, pipes, and clips. I could feel my own

strength coursing the length and breadth of her. Like Icarus, I'd buckled on a pair of wings.

It was almost a climbing takeoff. I unstuck at excessive speed and pulled steeply away.

Yes, I still had the measure of her. She obeyed me as a spirited horse obeys an expert rider. A momentary attempt to yaw, but I quelled it at once with some rudder.

How light I felt—strapped into over four tons of machinery, yet light as a feather. A quick scan of the instruments: course, airspeed, rate of climb, boost, revs, oil temperature, and pressure—all fine. Slight turbulence at six thousand feet, caused by inversion. The fighter briefly trembled as though shaking off a tiresome insect, then quietened. Course steady, rate of climb constant.

Łódź swam into view on my left before receding into a blue haze like Atlantis engulfed by the sea. To one who felt as weightless as I, the war and terra firma had lost all meaning. I was flying due north and would hold that course until I sighted the Masurian Lakes near Osterode or Allenstein.

The altimeter was reading fourteen thousand. The cloud had almost gone.

Heiligelinde . . . The twin towers of the Baroque cathedral reared skyward, bright and luminous. I was over home ground.

There they were, the dense forests and dark lakes, the early autumn fields of grain and dull green tracts of pasture, the country lanes and water meadows of Masuria. Not a town without a lake of its own, not a village where fishing nets weren't drying in the wind.

And there was Sensburg, an expanse of rust-red roofs enclosed by no less than ten separate lakes. The narrow finger lakes that wound like rivers around hills and along valleys were the deepest of all—the abode of the legendary Topich. I had shunned them as a child for fear of the grisly water sprite who liked to drag little boys into the depths.

I curved around the cathedral and headed east toward Lötzen, simultaneously easing the stick back and cutting the throttle so as not to fly too quickly over this stretch of country-side between the Neman and the Vistula. Below me it was autumn. At this very moment, schoolchildren were gathering berries and mushrooms, wild bees droning around the tall-stemmed great mullein, storks congregating in the meadows.

The sky lent its color to the Mauersee, a deep azure flecked with dull red. Cranberries, bream and whitefish . . . I mouthed the words like an incantation as I cut the revs still further. The oil pressure wavered slightly. Up here in the cockpit it smelled of hot metal, down there of apples, honey and bonfire smoke.

There was my home town, Lötzen, flanked by the Mauersee and Spirdingsee, and there was the canal that linked them. The white steamer left there for Nikolaiken and Johannisburg at 2 P.M. And there were the beach huts! I'd stood there only yesterday, before making a dash for the jam-packed furlough train.

I rounded the castle and the Lutherschule, where I'd dreamed of flying for so many years. (*So you want to be a pilot, do you? Better turn in some decent math papers first. . . .*) The old drawbridge—you got a good view of the castle from there. The Löwentinsee . . . And there, at last, was the road that led to our estate. A pity my mother didn't know—I was only a couple of thousand feet away. Still standing in the yard were the two haywagons that had both sprung a rear axle the same day.

Carefully, I put the one-ninety into a shallow turn and nosed lower, heading for the big thatched roof. The fulfillment of a boyhood dream: I was piloting the fastest, handsomest fighter in the world on a flying visit to the family estate—to my mother. Anyone in sight? No, nothing was stirring except the smoke from the bonfires in the potato fields.

I circled once more, aimed the one-ninety at the avenue of birches, opened the throttle, and picked up speed. She tried to buck but I held her level, nose pointed straight at the group of lime trees beside the forecourt entrance as though I meant to fly in at the drawing-room windows and out through the attic.

Easing the stick back very gently, I climbed steeply into the unresisting blue sky and turned south. The fuel gauge was beckoning. Did it sadden me, not having seen my mother wave? Perhaps . . . I was invaded by mixed emotions. Pride and triumph coupled with regret at bidding farewell to a sheltered world which would never—this much I knew since reporting back to base—be wholly mine again. Forty-five minutes' flying time separated me from the day-trip steamers, the Masurian forests, the horse rides beside lake and lagoon.

I was leaving this world behind. Anyone who has ever viewed the world between the humming struts and stays of a Stieglitz biplane needs air between himself and the ground. Once in the cockpit, he alone is responsible for all he does; no one on the ground can usurp his place.

I opened the throttle and pulled back into a loop. Exhilaration overcame me. Masuria and its open spaces fell away, the horizon fell away—nothing now but dazzling sky. I seemed to be hovering at the summit of a Ferris wheel. Then the horizon, forests, and lakes rushed up to meet me. Throttle back, pull out, kick out the yaw with the rudder bar, open throttle. The earth was below me again.

Then into a stall turn, using the momentum of the loop.

Nose up, throttle back. The heavy machine hung there, poised on her tail, and then fell backward like a sack of coal on an almost vertical chute. Full left rudder. The nose swung left, and four tons of metal, fuel, and living tissue went hurtling on. I let the speed build up in the dive, pulled out, and opened the throttle again.

Now into a slow roll. Nose slightly above the horizon, stick left, right rudder. The horizon performed a neat one-eighty-degree turn, the whole world lay on its back. Gentle pressure on the stick to keep the nose above the horizon while inverted, then everything continued to rotate. No longer pinned against my straps, I felt the pressure of the seat return. Roll completed.

Slipstream noises, the roar of the engine, gusts of wind, sweat beneath my helmet, the stench of oil, needles fluttering . . .

I flew over Nikolaiken and the bridge adorned with a giant wooden smelt. We'd often tried our luck in the lake there, Lenz and I, only to end by buying a couple of grilled whitefish from the stall on the promenade. We knew every path between Lötzen and Nikolaiken, every spot that promised a rich harvest of mushrooms and berries, every breeding ground frequented by the black stork and white-tailed eagle.

It was mushroom time now, and suddenly, while adjusting the throttle, I thought I detected the earthy scent of a basketful: the fruity aroma of the *Boletus granulatus,* the spicy chanterelle, the club fungus which can be eaten only when young. And there was the woody smell of the landing stage when a ripple washed over it. . . .

The illusion vanished. All that now assailed my nostrils beneath the cockpit canopy was the engine's hot breath, its effluvium of oil and gasoline. (A monster reluctant to forgive even one mistake on the part of a young and inexperienced pilot fresh from his Arado 96 trainer, the machine had originally filled me with awe, not enthusiasm. Alarm and apprehension reigned during our conversion to the one-ninety at Zeltweg. Few weeks went by without our firing a farewell salute to one of our number in the little mountain cemetery. Too much throttle too quickly when overshooting, failure to oppose the torque of the powerful twin-row radial with your control surfaces, a half-roll, and into the ground you went. It was rage and defiance that had driven me to tame the brute. Thanks to its high nose-up attitude, the engine blotted out your forward vision when you approached, touched down or taxied. . . .)

I gave a start. My fuel was running low—a fighter pilot's occupational disease. The preflight calculations had been fine —wind, drift, and ground speed—but they hadn't allowed for aerobatics or visits home.

Adjusting the map board, I turned southwest over the Johannisburger Heide and away from the front line, which was said to be nudging Warsaw. I would have to refuel somewhere like Radom or Grójek, both of which I knew—I didn't want to fly back to Allenstein. No red warning light as yet.

Simple timber-built cottages, shingled or thatched with straw. Sandy soil, pines interspersed with birches and oaks. The deep pellucid waters of the Niedersee—sailboats beside the Königsinsel . . . And there was the Krutinna. Lenz and I had drifted down it in a skiff one summer vacation. Trees trailing their branches in the current, bobbing waterlilies and a crystalline view of the riverbed . . .

I tried to trace the Krutinna's innumerable twists and turns, caught sight of Rudczanny and Lake Guszin—and suddenly realized that I'd left East Prussia behind. There was a Staffel of Me 110s based at an airfield somewhere near Mława. I would be able to refuel there.

Then, beside the runway, I saw the signal square with its transverse stripe: landing prohibited, air raid in progress. I opened the throttle and climbed away. Now I was really in trouble. Regaining speed, I coughed nervously into my oxygen mask and strove to make out Warsaw in the haze on the eastern skyline. I quickly skirted the wedge-shaped salient and veered east again. The red light started winking. Only ten minutes' grace.

I was now heading doggedly eastward with a big city visible through the panel on my left. It had to be Warsaw. The dove-gray ribbon of a broad river . . . Any sandbanks?

Yes, sandbanks everywhere—it could only be the Vistula. I turned south above the river and glided almost silently down to fifteen hundred feet. It wouldn't be long before I hit Deblin, which boasted an airfield.

If I didn't find it in the next few minutes, there were only two alternatives: bail out or force-land.

My eyes strayed to the red emergency-release lever that jettisoned the canopy.

I touched down safely, but the engine died while I was taxiing. Deblin . . .

A sandy gray airfield, deserted except for a fuel tanker and its uniformed driver. Silence enveloped me like a shroud. Juniper shrubs and grassland, marshy subsoil, clumps of pines and birches. Beyond them lay the swamps and steppes of Russia, silent and menacing.

Just as I jumped down, a black grouse rose from the edge of the field, glided low over some hazel bushes and landed on the far side of a stream—the front line, for all I knew. Everything seemed infinitely peaceful, but appearances could be deceptive.

True to the traditions of a veteran noncom, the Obergefreiter in charge of the fuel tanker betrayed not a flicker of surprise.

"We don't have any fuel to spare," he began, casually but to the point.

I could see I was in for a rough ride.

"All I need is a hundred gallons."

"A hundred?" said the Obergefreiter. "You'll be lucky." He plucked a few withered blades of grass and started to chew them.

"How about eighty?"

"We don't have eighty either. There's no fuel left—there's nothing left. We're packing up and heading for home."

"Me too, but I won't get off the ground without some juice."

"I'm not authorized to issue any. Orders are orders. You can have twenty, but that's the best I can do."

"I've got my orders too. I've been ordered to Grojecko, and for that I need eighty."

"Forty, take it or leave it."

I knew forty would do the trick, but I also knew that my one-ninety would be the last German airplane out of Deblin. Half a dozen farm cottages and a schoolhouse were drowsing in the autumn sunlight. From the look of the place, the Russians were expected any moment.

"I doubt if forty'll get me back," I said. "Besides, it's ten to one they'll blow the whole base up before the day's out, and that includes your tanker."

"Maybe so," the Obergefreiter retorted mulishly, "but forty's all I can spare. Next time you drop in, be sure and bring enough gas with you."

Next time is rich, I thought.

I leaned against my machine, rapping out a march with my knuckles on her starboard wing tip. I knew that even twenty gallons would get her to Grojecko, but Ketsch would be pleased if I didn't land with a dry tank—I had to square him somehow for my unscheduled stop. Anyway, I was interested to see if I could beat this old sweat at his own game.

"Tell me something," I said. "Would it matter if they blew up forty gallons of gas more or less?"

"I wouldn't know," he said. "All I know is, orders are orders."

"Sure it'd matter," I sneered. "There's all the difference in the world between blowing up five thousand gallons and four thousand nine hundred and sixty—the demolition boys would spot it at once. Who cares if I run out of gas and ditch this machine in a forest full of partisans? That's far less important to the war effort."

"Fair enough," he said. "Eighty, but that's your lot."

I stared across the grassy plain while the man was running out his hose. Somewhere beyond the pinewoods and marshes were the Russians. Shots and detonations could be heard from time to time—the rolling thunder of enemy gunfire, the crisp, dry, scattered reports of our own.

A demolition squad was working its way through the cluster of buildings, laying fuses and charges all over the place. The villagers were huddled together beside the airfield like a flock of rain-sodden sheep, forbidden to return to their doomed homes—victims of our latest scorched-earth policy.

I might have been watching the scene from inside a sealed glass capsule. Thanks to my one-ninety, I was light-years away from what was going on here. In a couple of hours I'd be enjoying a beer or vodka in the mess at Grojecko.

I hunkered down beside the runway and looked on while the Obergefreiter busied himself with the hand pump. Filler cap unscrewed, dipstick withdrawn and wiped on dungarees. Reinserted, withdrawn again, held up for inspection . . .

I sat there in peace until the old schoolteacher appeared. You could tell at once he was no peasant in spite of the dust in his matted beard—his hands were too soft. His bare feet were stuffed into a pair of ancient shoes padded with yellowing newspaper.

"Will they leave our houses alone, Herr Leutnant?"

"I doubt it," I said. "You'd better get out while you can. They'll probably burn the whole place down in the next hour."

"But—my God, they mustn't do that!"

"What's so special about a few cottages?"

"Not the cottages, the Stainer. It's priceless, really priceless. There are innumerable fakes, but this one's genuine."

"What is?"

"My Stainer."

"A picture?"

"No, a violin. It's no fake—I identified it as a genuine Stainer right away. Shall I tell you how?"

"If you insist," I said.

The Obergefreiter was pumping away. In the background, some uniformed figures had almost finished loading a truck. If the tail wind held, I could make Grojecko in twenty minutes. I decided to fly there north of Radom.

"All Stainer violins have such convex bellies, you can see through the sound holes sideways on." The old man's face was transfigured. "Their convexity is greater than that of any other seventeenth-century violin. I acquired mine from a very reputable dealer, and I've absolutely no reason to doubt its authenticity. Do *you* think it's genuine, Herr Leutnant?"

"I'm not a Leutnant yet," I said. "If you say it's genuine, I'll take your word for it."

I watched the truck being loaded. The Obergefreiter had almost finished. He lifted the hose, hand over hand, and drained the surplus into the tank.

"You should see the varnish, Herr Leutnant—amber varnish! It brings out the full beauty of the glorious maple-wood back and the fine-grained belly. . . . If you tell those men it's a genuine Stainer—if you say it's my most treasured possession—won't they spare our homes and leave us in peace?"

"I don't think your Stainer would carry much weight with them," I said.

The old man's face crumpled as if he were crying somewhere inside.

"But I took years to learn to play it as it deserves to be played. The wood and varnish are very delicate—they'll crack if they're exposed to heat or excessive vibration. Please tell your comrades to stop."

"I doubt if they'd take any notice," I told him. A pillbox went up somewhere on the edge of the forest, causing an appreciable shockwave. Dust and debris spurted into the air. "Besides, they aren't my comrades." I shrugged helplessly. "I can't do anything for you, I'm afraid. Not a thing."

My machine was ready now, and just in time. Shells were beginning to burst on the outskirts of the forest. It looked as if the Russians meant to paste the airfield. I didn't want my joyride to land me in a different kind of war—I'd be sick of my own kind soon enough.

"I've wrapped it up carefully," the old man said. "Do you think the explosions will harm it?"

He wouldn't survive, I realized that. Nothing I said or did mattered. The whole village would be a smoking ruin by nightfall. Feeling sick at heart, I lied to give him a few minutes' peace of mind.

"No," I said, "I don't think they'll do any damage."

The old man smiled thankfully and shuffled off.

A shell whistled into the marshy ground only fifty yards away and burst with a muffled thud. There were few splinters, but an acrid smell of explosives drifted across the airfield.

When I looked up again, a girl had materialized beside me

like Aladdin's genie. She was wearing the blue-gray uniform of a Luftwaffe woman signaler.

"Glad you're enjoying the view," she said. "But you'd better get out of here fast or start learning Russian. We're all packed up and ready to go."

I didn't have a high opinion of female auxiliaries, but this one smiled in a way I wasn't used to. She was also good to look at in spite of her threadbare uniform. High forehead, blue-black hair, delicately arched eyebrows. Her gray eyes radiated a maturity and experience which suggested that she was two or three years older than I. She was lovely enough to banish the violence around us and conjure up things that hadn't crossed my mind in ages—for instance, the way my mother used to tune her cello in the old days, before embarking on a Beethoven sonata. It occurred to me that she hadn't touched the instrument for years. To be precise, not since my father had been posted to the Air Ministry in Berlin.

"Do you work in the signals center?" I asked, dusting off my trousers.

"Yes, and we're closing down in fifteen minutes. For good."

"Fine, that gives us all of ten minutes."

We sat down side by side in the grass.

A light breeze sprang up and blew her hair across her face. She brushed it away with two slender fingers. The firing had died down. No more shots, shell bursts, or explosions. Silence lay like a soothing hand on the runway, the grassy plain and distant fringe of trees.

"If you're wise, you'll take off at once."

I looked beyond her at the forest. The rays of the afternoon sun had dissolved it into an abstract interplay of light and shade. Silhouetted against it I could see the figure of the lonely old man, mercilessly exposed to a cold, alien, and incomprehensible world which was not his own and would soon destroy him. In the foreground, vibrant with life, a girl whose windswept hair smelled faintly of soap.

She spoke German with a strong Slavic accent. I asked if she came from the east.

"I'm a half-breed. Polish father, German mother. We lived in Luknainen for years. Then we moved to Landsberg."

Her name?

Maryla Brandys—a Russian name, really. Her grandparents had been of Russian descent.

"Maryla . . ." I repeated. "I know Luknainen well. I've often fished in the lake there."

"It always looked its best at sunset, when the swans came gliding in and the herons flew back to roost. The air was like cut glass—not a breath of wind. You could even hear nightingales singing in the alder bushes."

"Let's go there together as soon as we get time." I forced a laugh. "It shouldn't be long now."

"Only a few more lightning victories," she said gravely, "and we'll go there right away. Ever been up to Cranz?"

"Of course, for the weekend. Remember all the lake steamers and cafes and beer gardens? Crowds of people everywhere, laughing and singing . . ."

"It's what I've thought of most, stuck out here. White steamers, white tablecloths, white sails, sailors in white ducks. I've developed a real thing about white this summer, what with the dust and filth and noise."

"We'll make a trip to Cranz," I said. "Rossitten and Nidden, too. I'll show you the bird sanctuary and the Kurische Nehrung, and we'll rent a boat and sail into the wild blue yonder. You can take off your head scarf and stand with your back to the mast, waving at the gulls and the clouds and the east wind."

"I like the sound of that. Please hurry up and win the war. We'll go there as soon as it's over, right?"

"We'll tour the whole of East Prussia. The Rominter Heide, the Johannisburger Heide, Marienburg, Elbing, the Neman, Insterburg . . ."

"And you'll have to drive up to Königsberg every weekend."

"Is that where you'll be living?"

"No, studying, but you can take me out at weekends."

"Maybe we'll meet there anyway. I already spent a year at college, reading educational theory. I'd like to complete the course and take a teaching job."

"Sooner you than me. Personally, I fancy psychology and philosophy. Or the English dramatists—I'm crazy about Shakespeare. . . . But maybe they'll be extinct by then. The English dramatists, I mean."

"Why should they suddenly cease to exist when the war's over?"

"Because Europe will all be part of the Greater German Reich." She gave me a quizzical look. "There'll only be room for our own intellectual giants."

"Anyway," I said firmly, "I'll come for you every weekend."

"You'd better go now."

"Yes, I'd better."

We stood up. I held out my hand, but she'd already jumped to her feet unaided. She brushed the tousled hair out of her eyes again, listening to the gunfire. It seemed to have receded.

"Perhaps I'll have time to send you on your way with a radio bearing," she said. "Oh no, I was forgetting—you fighter boys don't carry radio operators. We had a group from Kampfgeschwader KG 52 based here till recently—Junkers

88s. Never mind, I'll have a quick word with you over the RT when you've taken off. What's your destination?"

"Grojecko. Where are you being transferred to?"

"Grojecko, eh? Much the same sort of dump as this." She paused. "Us? Not a clue where we're going. It's all top secret, meaning everybody's in the dark."

We were standing close together now. Birch leaves swirled in the autumn breeze like paper gliders, performing unexpected dives, climbing turns, crash landings.

"We'll meet up again, won't we?"

"Of course," she said. "Of course we will."

"I'll come for you—that's a promise."

"Of course," she repeated. The shell bursts sounded closer again. "It's time you went."

"May I give you a kiss—just a little one?"

"Just a little one."

I put my arms around her. She smoothed her skirt down first. The softness and warmth of her lips, the scent of her skin . . . Then it was over.

"See you soon, Maryla."

"After the war," she said.

I looked back as I walked over to my machine through the autumn leaves and dust. She didn't turn around.

I clambered into the cockpit. The tanker driver helped me with my straps, more dutifully than eagerly.

A whine from the self-starter and the engine fired at once.

I taxied off, trailing a cloud of dust which enveloped the Obergefreiter and coated him—little I cared—in millennial grime.

I opened the throttle wide and skimmed over the signals center, but I was too busy with my wheels and flaps to look out for a face behind the uncurtained windows.

I set the throttle at climbing revs, trimmed and switched on the radio.

"South Sea Island to Sauerkraut Seven, are you receiving me?"

"Receiving you loud and clear . . ." ("Maryla," I added softly.)

"Happy landings. No wasps, bees or bluebottles at three o'clock, just a good trip home."

"Message received and understood." I couldn't think of anything else to say. With my eye on the trembling magnetic compass I set a course for the evening sun, leaving the front line, the Russians, the Stainer violin, and Maryla far behind me. "I'll come and see you in Königsberg . . ."

Silence, then:

"Maryla?"

"South Sea Island to Sauerkraut Seven. Are you on course for home? No wasps, bees or bluebottles?"

"No problems."

"No problems here either. Repeat. No problems, no cause for concern. Over and out."

Over and out . . . I jabbed the buttons desperately but failed to raise it again, that voice from the lonely depths of the Polish plains.

A balmy Indian summer evening, the air like milk and honey, the river still patrolled by squadrons of mosquitoes. Lenz and I walked down to the mud flats after supper. Here, on a small eminence surrounded by stagnant pools, rotting piles, and marshy rivulets, a handful of birch trees stood clustered together like shipwrecked sailors on an island.

We stretched out on the grass beneath the trees, whose fallen bark scented the air. There were still some butterflies around—brimstones, cabbage whites, tortoiseshells. I wanted to tell Lenz about Deblin and Maryla.

"I flew over Lötzen this afternoon. You know the Mazeraths, down by the station? Their laundry waved my train good-bye yesterday evening, and it was still on the line today. It gave me a funny feeling, seeing it again."

I absently plucked the heads off some orange hawkweed. "But then came that refueling stop at Deblin. If only you could meet her, Martin . . ."

But Lenz hadn't been listening. His interruption jerked me brutally back into his world—my world too, from now on.

"The Geschwader lost seven pilots today—another seven on only three patrols. That makes—hang on—two-point-three recurring killed per patrol. Our Staffel has lost only one so far. In other words, we're showing a big fat deficit."

"Come off it, Martin. That's not mathematics, that's plain superstition. Why, it would mean we're all for the chop—you, me . . ."

Lenz nodded. "Exactly."

"Bullshit!"

Muddy brown clouds welled up from the bottom of a nearby pool and tiny volcanic craters seemed to spew black fire; the charcoal eyes of an orange-speckled toad glinted hungrily in the waning light. Lenz tossed a stone at the creature, which subsided in a flurry of alarm.

"Throw us to the wolves," he went on, "and we'd still have an outside chance. We could always shin up a tree, but in this outfit? Not a hope—we're out of our class."

"No wonder. They never took us up against a bomber formation all the time we were in training—they only taught us how to deal with stray Ratas or Shturmoviks. The whole set-up's absurd. The Russians aren't much more than a hundred miles away—they could be peeking around the end of our bunkhouse this time next month—and we're being wasted on the Yanks."

"It's Steffen," Lenz said curtly. "He's just about to give

birth to his Knight's Cross, but that's not good enough for him. He wants the Swords and Diamonds to go with it."

"And we're expected to deliver his abortion. I must say, it's the first time I've heard of midwives dying in childbirth."

"We could shoot the whole of the Russian front to pieces for the same price, but try telling that to our gallant Geschwader-Kommodore!"

"Is it all approved—up top, I mean?"

"If you're talking about Hitler, he'd begrudge us the dirt from under his nails."

"What about Göring?"

"Our Hermann? He's fallen out of love with his fighter pilots, you know that. We've failed, he says."

"He can talk! Remember what he said when the war started? 'If a single enemy airplane crosses the German border, you're welcome to call me Hermann Meyer.' Well, now his name's Meyer and he blames it on us."

"We may as well stop beefing, Michael, it won't change a thing."

Water beetles, leeches. We stared into the pool, which had cleared again. Some scorpionlike mandibles broke the surface. The predacious larva of a dragonfly shot out its prehensile labium and captured a beetle with brown and yellow stripes. Dragging its struggling prey into the shadow of some reeds, it proceeded to suck the dying creature dry.

"So we're really in trouble . . ."

"It's eat or be eaten. Like those things down there in the mud."

"But I don't want to be eaten," I said.

3

An airman's sky like something out of a picture book: aquamarine with narrow lanes of cloud, a light head wind, unlimited visibility.

A formation of Boeing B-17s had been broken up in the Breslau area and deflected northeast. A few crippled bombers were trying to sneak home via the Baltic, *sauve qui peut.*

I was acting as the Staffel commander's wingman, meaning that I flew on Ketsch's quarter and covered his rear. We had no definite orders to make contact. It was more an opportunity for the old hand to inure his green number two to the sight of triple tail guns and quadruple MGs.

I made an impeccable takeoff but had trouble holding formation from the start. Ketsch, in his superior machine, set such a cracking pace I could hardly keep up. Each of his course corrections left me lengths behind, as he promptly pointed out over the RT.

"You're waddling around like a pregnant duck!"

I tried to maintain a constant altitude, if nothing more, but found myself alternately below and above my leader. Another comment:

"Do you always play peekaboo like that?"

Over Piotrków we swung west and kept climbing to ten thousand feet. It wasn't long before I lost my bearings completely, I was so busy coping with turbulence and the vagaries of my ill-trimmed machine.

"Close up, Braack. Stick with me."

I closed up and stuck with him. My reward:

"Close up, I said—stick with me, damn you!"

Sweat trickled down my neck. I constantly overcorrected, certain that I'd slice through Ketsch's tail at any moment.

A quick downward glance: pale green fields, winding streams, roads veiled in long swaths of stratocumulus. Ahead and above: empty sky. I breathed a sigh of relief. How could anyone so preoccupied with formation flying ever find time to attack an enemy airplane? Another quick glance, this time at my instruments. If a bomber didn't appear in my gunsight soon, we wouldn't have the fuel to get us home.

"From now on, keep your trap shut and concentrate. Just hug my tail."

Ketsch was playing "I spy." Personally, I couldn't see a thing. We were climbing again, and he seemed to be trying to get the sun behind him.

My throat tightened. I was on the verge of my first tangle with the enemy. The next few minutes might spell the difference between life and death. I couldn't chicken out— that wasn't on, even if it meant dying. You could chicken out and cheat at aerobatics, low-level flying, target practice. You could pull out a fraction early as you hurtled toward the ground, fudge a steep climb when you were scared of losing too much speed. I'd often been afraid, but I forgot my fear as soon as I was safely down on the runway. Then I felt proud of belonging to an elite.

Suddenly I saw them.

They were heading north in a trio, betrayed by their contrails. One had lost altitude and was lagging behind, its plume of white vapor stained with black.

They were Fortress IIs.

I'd seen them in countless photographs, cross sections and silhouettes: the quarry I was paid to hunt. My whole life had been a rehearsal for this moment. Now it had come—now I had to act.

Were we still climbing? Yes, the altimeter needle was creeping past 12,700. Were we nearer the enemy? No, no nearer. Climbing had cut our speed, but we had to climb so as to bounce them from above with the sun behind us. Then it would be nose down and into the attack—except that the two leading bombers were too far ahead for us to overhaul them in a shallow dive.

The third and last ship was now emitting an unbroken plume of black smoke as it painfully limped along behind its companions. They took no notice—it couldn't keep up.

Sticks forward and down we went. Our target was unmistakable. The bomber assumed nightmare proportions in my windshield. Its port outer engine was smoking, the propeller feathered.

I could feel my mouth shaping words behind the oxygen mask. *No nearer—no nearer, for God's sake, we're going to ram! Why don't you open fire, Ketsch? Fire—no nearer, just fire!*

But Ketsch didn't fire—what's more, he told me after we landed that we'd have had to close the range by half to gain a favorable firing position. Instead, there was a sudden flash, a ball of flame, and the bomber exploded.

Ketsch hadn't fired a shot. Already damaged by other fighters or flak, the crippled giant had simply given up the ghost.

I thought I detected the shock wave of the explosion as we broke hard to starboard—as the bomber's port wing spun down like a sycamore pod and the first chutes opened and Ketsch started cursing.

"Bastard! Why couldn't he have waited till I got there? Now he's a goner."

We headed for home. Northeast of us, a sizable city drowsed in the haze. Łódź.

I'd forgotten to ready my guns and switch on my reflector sight, but that I failed to notice till it was all over.

K etsch speaking:

"Forget all you've ever been told about Yaks, Ratas, and LaGGs. We're up against a far tougher proposition—the U.S. Air Force." He pronounced it "Airrforrsch." "We'd have stood a fair chance against the Russians. Against the Americans we don't stand any at all, not even an unfair one, but we soldier on regardless. That's why we're here—you, me, the whole of Jagdgeschwader 99."

"The Russians are threatening East Prussia," I said mildly. "To be honest, I volunteered for fighters to defend my home."

"We defend our homes wherever we're sent." He didn't pursue the theme. "You'll have only two opponents to contend with from now on, so I want you to study their special characteristics whenever you can, day or night. They're the North American P-51 Mustang and the Boeing B-17G, commonly called the Fortress II."

"And the others? What about Stirlings and Lancasters and Liberators and Lightnings and Thunderbolts?"

"You'll bump into those from time to time, generally when they fly up from Italy. Against them you stand a genuine chance. You don't stand any against Mustangs and Fortress IIs, but you'll act as if you did, is that clear?"

"As daylight."

"The new B-17Gs are the real monsters of the old Boeing

brood. We'll discuss them during tactical instruction if we get time. Take a close look at your recognition and operational data leaflets. Keep studying the brutes, and if you spot a weak point, come and see me—barge straight in. I don't know of any . . ."

I duly took an interest in my new and fearsome foe:

"Boeing B-17G, Flying Fortress II. Maximum permitted bomb load, 17,600 pounds. Range, 1,850 miles. Shiny silver metal fuselage. Almost always operates in large formations. See also Liberator. Special characteristics: up to 17 (seventeen) gun positions. If several B-17s fly in close formation, there are no blind spots from which they can be attacked in absolute safety. . . ."

While engrossed in the firing arcs of gun positions A, B, and C, I recalled the press photos I'd seen of Flying Fortresses and their saturation raids. They were prize purveyors of death and destruction. Sample caption:

"On 29 October 1943, Flying Fortresses of the U.S. Eighth Air Force attempted to raid Bremen. Our heroic fighter pilots succeeded, as always, in inflicting heavy losses on these formations. Above: a pair of FW 190s swoop on their powerful foe and spoil the accuracy of his bombing."

Where Mustangs were concerned, 720 bombers had attacked aircraft factories in central Germany on 11 January 1944, escorted for the first time by a new long-range version. Escorting enemy fighters had previously suffered from lack of endurance and couldn't afford to engage in running battles with the Luftwaffe if they wanted to reach home. Mustangs were now equipped with long-range slipper tanks designed to be jettisoned on contact. They had a range of over three thousand miles and carried four or six cannons.

Five Mustangs and fifty-nine bombers had been shot down during the 11 January raid, though forty German fighters were also lost.

During the first large-scale daylight raid on Berlin on 6 March 1944, 630 Flying Fortresses dropped sixteen hundred tons of bombs. Sixty-eight of them and eleven Mustangs failed to return.

Sprawled on my bunk and studying the relevant literature, I was reminded of the essay I'd had to write for my fighter pilot's entrance exam: "Why I Want to Be a Fighter Pilot." I wanted to be a fighter pilot, I wrote with all the fervor of one who had just turned nineteen, because air raids sickened me. Having heard bombs whistling down on Danzig and seen the havoc they caused, I was eager to defend my native Masuria —and the homes of all who dwelled in the Greater German Reich—against onslaughts of such a criminal nature.

My effort had only just scraped a "Satisfactory," as I knew from a surreptitious glance at my personal file, perhaps because it suggested that I might view the dropping of German bombs on British cities with equal repugnance. The entry under "Character and Temperament" read:

"Sincere in his desire to obtain a wartime commission. Highly emotional, sometimes lacks drive. Popular with his comrades but enjoys being alone. Should try to develop a more get-up-and-go attitude."

After basic training at the end of 1943, I'd gone home to Lötzen on leave—home to a reunion with Braack, Sr., or B.S., as I called him.

My graying but still sprightly father had traveled east from Berlin, where he held down quite an important desk job at the Reich Air Ministry—something in Aircraft Procurement.

B.S. had entrusted the running of our estate to a bailiff early in the war. He'd always had itchy feet and was doubtless attracted by the prospect of a belated excursion into uniform.

Abruptly transported from the capital to Lötzen for a last precombat glimpse of his only son, he launched into some innocuous chatter about a recent visit to the celebrated Hotel Adlon.

"I hadn't been there for ages—not since '36. That was during the Berlin Olympics—the government's last attempt to give this country a cosmopolitan veneer. . . ."

Sitting on the terrace, over a bottle of schnapps, B.S. reminisced about the Adlon in its heyday. Everyone, but everyone, had patronized the place: King Boris of Bulgaria, the Duke of Hamilton, Mussolini's sons, Lord Vansittart, Prince Philipp of Hessen and his wife, Mafalda, the Swedish Crown Prince, Unity Mitford. Another of Lord Redesdale's five daughters, Nancy Mitford, was reputed to have made a name for herself as a writer. . . .

I sipped my schnapps, blinking in the glare of the late summer sunshine, and strove to recall what I'd been doing when war broke out between Britain and Germany. Homework, most likely.

"How's it looking now, the Adlon—I mean, after all the raids?"

B.S. gave me a long look. I suddenly sensed that there was something behind his verbal smoke screen—something on his mind. (Though when had he ever let his hair down—when had we ever talked seriously about anything? Each of us was as stubbornly East Prussian and uncommunicative as the other when things got personal.)

"The Adlon still holds its famous *jour fixe* even now, after five years of war. A pure charade, but the management keeps it up. Foreign diplomats meet there as usual every Wednesday —the Foreign Office insists on it. Everyone eats and drinks as

if the war had never happened. Waiters in tails, genuine
French cognac. It's an eerie farce, Michael. Berlin's in ruins
—the dome of the Hedwigskirche shattered, the Bristol and
the Kaiserhof gone, the Adlon walled up against blast—but
still the *jour fixe* goes on, still the cognac flows. Champagne
served with white gloves—now, in 1944, as if ration cards
didn't exist!"

"Was that why you went there, just to sample the menu?"

"Of course not. I had a luncheon engagement with Sintermann—you know, Sintermann of Focke-Wulf, one of their
top men. We've known each other for ten years or more. He
wanted a word with me off the record. The food was superb.
I saw Furtwängler among others, and Gründgens was sitting
at the next table with Elisabeth Flickenschild. They were only
there for a square meal and plenty of vintage burgundy, but
still—in 1944!"

"Did Sintermann take his head out of the trough long
enough to promise us some more front-line aircraft?"

B.S. sighed audibly and treated himself to another slug.

"He was singing the praises of his new fighter, the Tank Ta
152C. The logical development of your one-ninety."

"I've heard about it. A world-beater—or could be, if only
we'd mass-produce it."

"Precisely, that's why he wanted to see me. A last personal
initiative, so to speak, but you know the age-old problem.
Never mind if the Russians are knocking on our back door—
who cares if the Allies are in Normandy? Hitler still favors an
offensive bomber arm—he still opposes the use of fighters in a
purely defensive role. He hasn't abandoned his dreams of
bombing perfidious Albion to her knees."

"Is it true he's got a thing about fighter pilots? I've heard
he thinks we're a bunch of decadent elitists who fly the occasional patrol and spend the rest of our time holed up in Polish
mansions or French châteaus, swilling vodka and brandy."

"You've got to look at it in the light of his own combat experience, my boy. He spent the first war with his backside parked in a trench."

What was that, a defense of Hitler or stark contempt? How much did I really know about my father and the workings of his mind?

"We'd only have to mass-produce the Ta 152 to sweep the skies clean of Mustangs."

"I said as much to Sintermann, not that he needed telling. Those long-range Mustangs are the bane of our existence, I said. Over a thousand fighter pilots lost in the first four months of this year—each enemy raid is costing us up to fifty crews."

"And the Ta 152 could change all that. Maximum speed four-seventy mph, plus a fantastic radius of action—seven hundred and fifty miles!"

"Yes, but she'll do only four-fifty with water-methanol injection," said B.S., quelling my feverish enthusiasm. "Anyway, Sintermann was making a last desperate effort—no, that's wrong, I think he simply wanted to unburden himself to an old crony. The age of the jet fighter has dawned, Sintermann knows that as well as anyone. The Me 262 is here to stay. I told him so, but he argued that his Ta 152s' armament and maneuverability are superior. So they are, *and* it's a more reliable machine." B.S. gave a fatalistic grin. "What he didn't know is that even the Messerschmitt turbojet isn't destined to become *the* number-one fighter. Hitler plans to employ it as a high-speed bomber and assign the Ta 152 to an escort role."

"A fighter with a fighter escort?"

"Jets are extremely vulnerable and unmaneuverable on takeoff and landing. The Yanks are making joyrides to the Messerschmitts' operational bases and picking them off at their leisure."

"So at least we'll be mass-producing the Ta 152 on a modest scale, as an escort fighter?"

"Yes, that was the one crumb of comfort I could give old Sintermann. He swore at everything in sight. Damn Berlin, he said—damn having to spend every night in a cellar, damn not being able to buy anything but substitutes in the stores, et cetera. . . . When I remember how those radio commentators rhapsodized about the opening of the Olympic Games! The whole world has succumbed to the charms of Berlin, that was their theme song. And now? We're up the spout, my boy, but never mind. Tell me about your one-ninety. Are you pleased with it?"

"I hardly know one end from the other. First they skimp our training and now they expect us to tackle the Yanks, with all their superior experience and equipment."

"Listen, I'm going to tell you something not everyone knows. We flew a one-ninety experimentally against a captured Lightning. The one-ninety outclasses it up to eighteen thousand feet—remember that. From there on, the Lightning develops an edge of five or six miles an hour. Its rate of climb improves too."

"Our instructors at Zeltweg might have told us that, don't you think?"

"Your one-ninety's more maneuverable at all altitudes, and you'll always beat a Lightning in a dive. Make a mental note of that, and make a note of the only exception to the maneuverability rule—if a Lightning throttles back to one-forty, its smaller turning circle will leave you floundering, so remember —you'll always outdive it."

I could have gone on to ask about the Mustang and the Fortress and a thousand other things, but silence prevailed. With true East Prussian reserve, we both retired into our shells. To bridge the conversational gap, I said, "Is it true they're closing every theater and nightclub in Berlin from October first?"

"Yes. All our public entertainers are being drafted now—either that or sent to work in munitions factories. Goebbels has changed his tune. Any nation that abandons its art ceases to be civilized—that's what he said in the old days. . . ."

We confined ourselves to family topics until I left. Now, back in Grojecko, only one really personal remark lingered in my mind:

"You mustn't give up because you think it won't go on, because it will. On and on . . ."

Out of the blue, Maryla turned up.

Unexpected appearance of a noncom from the guardhouse: "There's a chick outside wanting to come in, but she can't. Says the Herr Oberfähnrich's expecting her."

The Herr Oberfähnrich wasn't, but he flung off his sweaty flying jacket and headed for the gate at a fast trot.

There she stood, her blue Luftwaffe uniform artfully civilianized with a scarf of her own, a suede belt, and a pair of suede shoes. No cap, long black hair worn loose.

I'd been having nightmares about Maryla. I saw her vainly trying to escape from Dęblin, hemmed in by swamps that plucked at her legs and sucked her down while Russians pursued her in monstrous great tanks. They trained their guns on the girl's solitary, struggling figure as she fled in slow motion. Now, surely *now* they'd open fire, but they didn't. They simply forged on and impaled her—transfixed her with their outsize gun barrels. Then Lenz slid down from the bunk above and shook me awake. . . .

"Well," she said, "here I am."

She must have given them the slip after all. Dreams could be deceptive.

"But where did you spring from?"

"My new unit's based at Konskie—that's only a few miles away. They say the Russians have already taken Deblin."

"I know Konskie," I said. "It's in the foothills of the Lysa Gora." Ketsch, ever insistent on the virtues of accurate navigation, had warned us that these hills could give trouble in poor visibility. "And now you're here."

"I felt I had to see if you'd made it back here safely after that sensational visit of yours."

"Sensational?"

"The tanker driver thought so. He went on and on about your barefaced cheek—the way you bullied him into giving you more fuel than you needed."

"What about the rest of it? Did they blow it sky-high?"

"Every last drop." She slipped her arm through mine. "Where are you taking me, Oberfähnrich?"

I'd have liked to take her somewhere chic. B.S. had so often sung the praises of Berlin, even after four or five years of war, but you couldn't meet for prawn cocktails at Kempinski's, not in the Polish backwoods. All they had to offer was birch trees and thyme-scented hills. I took her to my favorite spot. A rusty brown sun was floating in the buttermilk evening mist.

How had she contrived to get here?

"In the Oberfeldwebel's Volkswagen. He's here on duty—said he'd pick me up at the gate in two hours' time."

Two hours, almost the endurance of a one-ninety—an eternity!

"Maryla, I—I'm so glad . . ."

It couldn't have sounded lamer or less romantic. I reveled in the sight of her every movement, her soft shoulders, the curve of her full breasts when she turned to smile at me, her long legs and slender waist. I rested my hand there and felt the swelling hips beneath. . . . This, of course, was no way to reach the top of Thyme Hill.

At last we were lying side by side in the grass.

"By the way, your tanker driver sends his best regards."

"That obstinate son-of-a-bitch?"

"The same."

"And the old man with the Stainer violin, the schoolmaster —no news of him, I suppose?"

"What schoolmaster? I don't know who you mean."

"I'll tell you about him sometime."

A remnant of evening purple tinged the sky. The last damaged machines were being parked outside the repair hangar. A flight of wild geese whirred overhead.

"Michael, what exactly are you doing here?"

She lowered her dark lashes. What a question!

"I'm with Jagdgeschwader 99—you know that."

"Of course. I meant, what are you really doing here?"

Silence.

"I don't know, Maryla. I'm still trying to find out."

"When you do, will you tell me?"

"You'll be the first to know. Till then . . ."

"Till then, what?"

I put my arms around her. Her face was alive with a strange curiosity.

"We must do this more often, Maryla."

"That," she said, "will depend on transportation facilities, Herr Oberfähnrich."

Bunkhouse nocturne. Wehrmann was farting himself to sleep.

What a waste of breath, what an inept, inane conversation! Was that any way for a man to talk to the girl he loved? Yes, it was one way—my way.

"Maryla," I'd whispered eventually, "will you come again tomorrow?"

"Not a hope. Maybe at the weekend."

Only maybe? Never mind, at least the ice was broken. My parting words:

"Maryla, I think I'm falling for you."

"If you say so, Michael."

Maryla put an entirely different complexion on my brand-new career as a fighter pilot.

"You know what you're fighting for, don't you, Ober-fähnrich Braack?" When Steffen glared at me expectantly and, in default of the correct answer, supplied it himself—"For Führer and Fatherland!"—any mental image I might have had of the Führer and Fatherland was eclipsed by a vision of Maryla with her lips curled in a faint smile, gently shrugging as if to say "Don't let it get you down, Michael."

I didn't. Instead, I immersed myself in the specifications of my one-ninety. Being wedded to her for better or worse, I wanted to know her whole life story. Technical literature tended to sap my powers of concentration after a few pages, however, so I always kept some poetry handy—Eichendorff or Mörike, for choice.

My Focke-Wulf had first seen the light at the Ago Works on 8 March 1944. She was listed as an A-8/R1 or R2, depending on the armament she carried. One supplementary gun pod was slung beneath each wing, and each held two MG-151s. R2 pods were sometimes substituted for R1s, in which case a single MK-108 took the place of two MGs. MK was the technical abbreviation for machine cannon. In practice, any bomber hit by one of these weapons would be mangled—together with its occupants—by a thirty-millimeter shell.

Together with the guns mounted in the wing roots and fuselage, this gave a total armament of eight MGs or four MGs and two MKs—an arsenal that would have grossly overloaded the smaller, lighter Me 109 and almost pinned it to the ground. My one-ninety weighed 8,665 pounds without her wing guns and 9,452 pounds with them, though she could still produce a maximum speed of 412 mph fully laden. This made her the fastest and most heavily armed German fighter in mass production apart from the mysterious new Messerschmitt jet fighter. Mass production of the equally mysterious and newfangled Dornier Do 335, which had one engine mounted in the nose and another in the tail, seemed to have run into snags.

So far, so good. I leafed through page after page and made a lot of notes, eager to find out everything possible about the contraption I was going to live or die with.

Installation of the R1 armament had naturally entailed some changes inside the cockpit as well. On the left of the gunsight support were a safety switch, breechblock control lights, and selector switches, also rounds counters. Switches for the new wing guns had been added to the right-hand console.

Ought I, I wondered, to familiarize myself with the special characteristics of each type of weapon?

Ought I to note that the two MG-151/20s in the wing roots were carried on an St.L151/2 mounting? That the forward attachment was bolted to the front spar and the rear one to a bracket spanning ribs one and three? That the ammunition for these guns was stowed in the fuselage, in rear of the front spar? That the belt boxes were loaded from beneath and inserted into the fuselage? That the boxes were concealed by hinged doors?

I picked up my volume of Mörike. *He felt a joyous presentiment. When day came, he climbed down the rocks, and behold! There among the stones, little more than a hand's-breadth above the water, the discarded rose had taken root and was blooming most gloriously. . . .*

Back to work.

Ammunition for the two fuselage guns and the two MG-151s mounted in the wing roots is heated by the engine, though air cooling reduces the temperature to a tolerable level. The heat emitted by the engine is sufficient to preserve the ammunition from temperatures below minus 35 degrees centigrade. . . .

Like its forerunner, the Revi 12, the Revi 16B reflector gunsight projected an image of the range circle onto the windshield, hence the term "reflector sight." For zeroing purposes, a 7.9-millimeter collimator was housed in a tube in the port wing root. As further aids to zeroing, bench marks were affixed to the fuselage 470 millimeters apart.

To assist longitudinal adjustment, eyes have been installed beneath the fuselage, fore and aft, for the insertion of a plumb line . . .

> *How softly now the night wind strokes the leas*
> *and wafts its music through the budding trees!*
> *While day's rude voice has yet to blare,*
> *earth's forces can be heard, a murmurous throng*
> *whose soaring whispers mingle with the song*
> *that sweetly fills the upper air.*

Another of the one-ninety's vital statistics: her guns were connected to the armament switchboxes via an SZKK4 rounds counter.

Most wondrous are the voices borne to me
by warm and wanton breezes gently blowing.
Meantime, with threads of radiance faintly glowing,
the very sky appears to float away.

Although the servicing of the fuselage guns was really as irrelevant to an aspiring fighter pilot as the niceties of a virgin's toilette, I was interested to know what Rosenhain's job entailed.

Removal:

(1) Open the fuselage side panels and the fuselage armament cover.

(2) Withdraw the weapon-actuation cable from the EDSK-B1 distributor box and the firing cable from its socket.

(3) Pull out the forward-support locking pin and rotate it leftward to the stop.

(4) Pull the weapon rearward until its rear guide bushings are free of the rear-mount guide pins.

(5) Swing the rear of the weapon upward and withdraw it from the forward support.

Installation:

For installation, reverse the above sequence.

Even a swift perusal of this maze of technical intricacies banished any idea that killing a man was simple. If the earthbound preliminaries were as complex as this, the aerial procedures must be infinitely more so. It took a delicate conjunction of all available forces and resources to send even a single Mustang pilot to kingdom come. The knights of old had disposed of their enemies with far less difficulty.

That evening in the bunkhouse, Lenz and I poked fun at the stilted language of our instruction manuals. Official prose seemed to become even more bloodless than usual when its ultimate purpose was bloodshed.

"Withdraw the weapon actuation cable . . ."

"Pull the weapon rearward . . ."

"For installation, reverse the above sequence . . ."

Wehrmann, of course, was pursuing a different line of thought.

"You've left out the best part, you senile old monks. Listen to this. 'After the weapons have been serviced, the belt ejection cover is opened, the belt insertion strip introduced into the weapons, and the belt members'—I ask you, belt members!—'coupled up.'"

Lenz made a feeble attempt to nip this sexual innuendo in the bud.

"It ought to read 'belt members *are* coupled up.' As the sentence stands, 'members' is paired with a singular verb."

"Christ Almighty, what girl worries about your grammar when you shove your member up her!"

With Balzerat's assistance, Wehrmann proceeded to go through the whole section again. You had only to modify a few of the technical terms or stress the odd word and the result was pure obscenity.

Smirks, sniggers, and belly laughs all around. Bull session on a Greater German air base—enough to turn your stomach.

Lenz took a considerably less jaundiced view of things.

"Wehrmann and Balzerat are the only real smut merchants in our bunch. The rest just tag along."

He was right, but I had a dawning suspicion that sexuality and trigger-happiness might not be unrelated.

I was sitting in the cockpit of *my* one-ninety—my very own. I'd been in love with the airplane ever since my first familiarization flights in an SG 38 training glider at Reichenbach, near Schussenried. There was a monastery at Schussenried, carefully sandbagged against Allied bombs. I once squeezed through the antiblast walls to admire its frescoed ceilings and root around in the library, where I came across some illustrated accounts of a would-be eighteenth-century aviator—a flying priest. I was fascinated by the thought of this God-fearing man who had tried to fly for flying's sake. No need for him to justify his presence in the sky by aiming his guns at a Flying Fortress. . . .

So there she was, my one-ninety, and there was I in her vitals, in this airborne fuel tank, this winged projectile. Many pilots preferred the already legendary Me 109, but if the one-zero-nine was a pearl, the one-nine-zero was a diamond of the first water. A shame you couldn't do anything with her but kill. It should have been possible to fly such a gem of an airplane—just fly her for flying's sake.

Overhead, poor devils like me were already trying to clip the wings of our gum-chewing visitors from across the Atlantic. A hastily installed flak battery was peppering the heavens with explosive puffs of dirty black smoke. Friend and foe alike sailed straight through them. The men on the 88s were far too busy to worry about such trivia as the difference between ours and theirs. Sinister blossoms proliferated in the sky, turning it into a Beelzebub's garden.

It wouldn't be long before we heard the whistle of hot chunks of shrapnel. Sure enough, here they came! One fragment hit a waiting one-ninety from 1 Staffel, only three away from me, and went straight through the cockpit canopy. The figure beneath it slumped. It couldn't be true, but it was: a crimson fountain gushed against the underside of the Plexiglas cover. Within seconds it looked as if it had been doused with a spray gun. The man must be bleeding to death—wasn't anyone going to help him? Mahlke, the medical orderly, puttered up on his motorbike. He struggled vainly to unhitch the first-aid kit from his carrier, one arm raised in an instinctive but ineffectual attempt to ward off more shell fragments. Meanwhile, the whole cockpit was awash. I wondered how one man's veins could hold so much blood. Was there a sump in the cockpit floor—could you top up your tanks with it? Could the occupant of a one-ninety drown in his own gore? Mahlke and the pilot's crew chief were now trying to open the canopy. It had barely opened a crack when they were drenched like the victims of an elaborate practical joke.

In evident panic, Combat Control broadcast the order to take off. Self-starters whined and—blub-blub-blub—three dozen BMW 801D-2 engines sprang to life. I was retching. Slowly but surely, my stomach heaved beneath the clips of my parachute and safety harness.

Rosenhain was giving me the thumbs-up. I taxied off and had to make a detour around the dripping one-ninety. No single human being could have produced so much blood, surely —he must have had a girl friend tucked between his legs.

Throttle open, tail up, unstick. All that blood . . . It was just like forgetting to take your finger off the trigger at a gas station. . . .

The fighter shuddered and shook like a mad thing. She wasn't trimmed, wouldn't climb. What was the matter with her? Everything was vibrating—canopy, instruments, control column, me.

The revs weren't right, nor was the speed. The whole feel of the machine was wrong. . . .

Simple: I'd forgotten to retract my gear.

Wheels up. Revs fine, speed fine. My restive steed calmed down at once.

All that still felt wrong was Oberfähnrich Braack.

4

The gospel according to Ketsch:

"When you're told to take off you take off, on the button. Every minute's delay costs you three thousand feet, so no more leisurely cockpit checks as if you're straightening up the parlor for a tea party. Throttle open and away you go. Check your oxygen, set climbing revs, ready your guns."

Another precept:

"Never climb straight into the sun. If you have to head for it, tack at forty-five degrees. Pretend you're sneaking up on a bashful virgin."

And another:

"Never fly just above cloud—in other words, don't play submarines. Our so-called camouflage is useless anyway, but fly above cloud and you'll show up better than a coffee-colored cutie on white silk sheets."

And another:

"If you see an enemy machine on its own, always take it for granted there are three more in the offing. Enemy airplanes never fly alone on principle. If you can't see the others, they'll generally be breathing down your neck. Mustangs are like Spanish señoritas—Mama's always somewhere around."

And another:

"Blazing away is like braking on sheet ice. The longer you keep your foot down, the more you'll skid. Short, aimed bursts of two to three seconds only—you won't have an enemy in your gunsight for longer than that. Anything over a couple of seconds is a sheer waste of ammunition. It deserves to be punished like sabotage."

And another:

"One more thing. Anyone who dawdles along behind the formation doesn't just get home last—he doesn't get home at all. There's always some smart pilot waiting to bounce a straggler."

Although we strove to follow Ketsch's advice and instructions, our thoughts seldom transcended the basic problems of airmanship.

Each day and each attack was indistinguishable from the rest. We belonged to a touring company in which every member of the cast played every part. One was lucky, another bought it. One crash-landed, another came home flushed with victory. One jumped, another burned to death. Only the dead were exempt from further histrionics.

Someone proudly displayed a photo. It might have been captioned "The Youthful Hero and His Kill." A gloved hand on the Mustang's engine cowling, a beaming smile from behind the bent four-bladed propeller, the exposed mechanical entrails. He looked like a big-game hunter snapped beside his quarry.

Only our surroundings, our place of work, underwent a daily transformation. Sometimes the sky was smooth as polished alabaster, sometimes high-altitude turbulence whipped the contrails into an orgy of writhing limbs. Other reminders of these early autumn days: long strings of wild geese flying high in the pinkish haze of evening; the scent of potato greens smoldering in distant fields. . . .

At awkward moments, Ketsch's tactical instructions became the drowning man's straw that seemed to offer a chance of survival.

Aiming off, for instance: "When a fighter pilot engages a target traveling in a direction other than his own, he must fire at the spot where the enemy will be when his shots strike home. An ability to gauge the lead angle correctly is what turns a novice into an ace."

Steffen took a different line. You never heard our Geschwader-Kommodore talking about the Mustang D's six Browning MG-53 machine guns—he was more concerned with fighting for Führer and Fatherland, keeping a stiff upper lip, standing firm in the face of overwhelming odds.

When Steffen, a muscular man with slightly rounded shoulders, entered the lecture room, you could have heard a pin drop. A lock of dark hair kept flopping onto his forehead as he spoke, and he would brush it—no, swipe it—into place with a series of fierce staccato movements that helped to work him up into a lather of grim resolve.

"You all get the same chances in this outfit." Meaningful pause. "Well, I'm going to watch each of you in turn and see what you make of them."

Again that claustrophobic sensation—the one I'd felt during my skirmish with Wehrmann. Had the jaws of the trap already closed to the point where escape was impossible?

We'd assembled in the small lecture room after supper for the Kommodore's weekly pep talk, irreverently known as Steffen's sermon. I accosted Lenz in a whisper.

"What do you think he thinks of when he's shooting down a Fortress?"

"Nothing," said Lenz. "Neither then nor later."

"Ambitious bastard. He rides every one raw, including himself."

"You can't blame him for that. He's a well-oiled war machine—no complexes, no conscience."

We redevoted ourselves to Steffen's remarks.

"I'm aware that many of you think our fighters are hopelessly inferior to the enemy's. With the exception of the Me 262, of course. You all imagine you could outscore Mölders or Galland in a jet fighter. Well get this, gentlemen—every airplane is only as good as the man at the controls."

He paused for effect, leaned over the lectern, which had probably come from a political indoctrination center, and propped one elbow on it. Behind him stood a pair of giant blackboards inscribed with the names of every pilot in the Geschwader. Although the last two weeks' casualties could have been wiped off, they'd only been crossed out. Chalked in after them were their replacements, if any. I counted twenty-six deleted names on this crude roll of honor.

"There's something else. We've no right to regard ourselves as flying prima donnas. No right to expect the juiciest assignments. No right to chuck a job when we don't like it. We stand our ground wherever we're sent. All right, gentlemen, carry on."

Next morning the hunt continued. It was Sunday, and a pathetic jangle of church bells drifted across from Grojecko. They must be made of old tin cans, Lenz said, or they'd have been carted off to Germany long ago and melted down.

Our machines were already warming up. While we were trudging over to them, weighed down by our flying suits and parachutes, a party of cormorants flew past. They got caught in the propeller slipstreams, whirled into the air like specks of soot, and scudded out of sight beyond the birch trees.

The throb of exhausts punctuated the early morning stillness, dissecting such time as remained before victory or death into particles. . . .

The twin-row radials broke into a roar. We crept forward,

lumbering ponderously over the turf. Our bandy legs looked less elegant than the Me 109s' balletic knock-knees, but once we were airborne and tucked them away we became eagles, not frail blackbirds impudently mimicking birds of prey.

I took off late. Every time I started to open the throttle, someone else balked me. At last I was over the birches and climbing, but sluggishly. The machine felt reluctant and the engine bellowed like a wounded buffalo as it clawed the airplane into the sky in the wake of the assembling formation.

Forget about eagles—a crow was more my mark. I limped after the Staffel like a footsore recruit on an endurance march. Meanwhile, contrails were threading the sky with terrifying density.

Total destruction was on the march. There must have been sixty, eighty, a hundred bombers—no, well over a hundred. Above them, faithful to the classic pattern, cruised escorting fighters whose exhausts penned convoluted graffiti on the sky. The enemy formations climbed menacingly over the horizon like plesiosaurs emerging from a primordial sea. There was something prehistoric, something almost mythical, about this aerial battlefield.

Filaments of vapor trailed in all directions. Robot spiders were weaving the deadly web that would enshroud the doomed: the burned and blinded, the maimed and dismembered.

I was still watching the scene like a creature from another planet. From the isolation of my transparent canopy, I followed events as if they were being projected on a celestial movie screen. Alternative titles: *Ordeal by Fire* or *Death in the Sky.*

Dark blobs of flak. Through the massive barrage, brushing it aside like a curtain, came the Fortresses—whole boxes of them arrayed in vertical and horizontal echelon. Storming a castle on the summit of Fujiyama would have seemed easier.

Two or three plumes of smoke. The flak had scored some hits but failed to complete the job. Two bombers broke formation, struggled vainly to keep up with their companions, and slowly fell behind.

Now came the fighters' chance. Less like eagles than ravening wolves that lope along behind a herd, patiently waiting for a straggler to be abandoned by the rest, our Staffel jockeyed wildly for an attack on the crippled bombers.

I was already in position, flying wingman to Ketsch. I had it down pat now, the close-up and tag-along procedure. You had to be near enough to smell your leader's cold sweat, said Ketsch, then you knew the distance was right. . . .

Together, we pointed our noses at the slower of the crippled pair. Its two outer engines were streaming smoke and both propellers were feathered. We swooped on it, far ahead of the others. My vertical speed indicator was reading six thousand feet per minute. I was about to thumb the gun button, even before Ketsch, when a guardian angel yelled a warning over the RT:

"Six Mustangs right behind you. Break!"

I broke left and Ketsch went right, curling back like the petals of a flower. Brilliant streams of tracer flashed between us. One second had meant the difference between life and death. (It transpired later that our savior was Lenz, whose warning had landed him in a tight spot. Two of the Mustangs curved around and went for him, but he shook them off like a wet dog.)

Meantime, Ketsch and I had both steep-turned and met up again with the crippled bombers far below us. We now had four Mustangs on our tails. I powered the one-ninety into a dive, alone with two opponents who stubbornly refused to be shaken off. My first dogfight. . . . I hauled on the stick, trying to fly a tighter circle, and momentarily blacked out. Blinding daylight returned. Suddenly, a Mustang appeared in my gunsight. I fired but missed by a mile. Tracer streamed over-head: the second enemy pilot had tucked himself in behind me and was clinging like a limpet. The first, who had just eluded me, clawed around in an unsuccessful attempt to get on terms again, but I couldn't dislodge the second. He had me in his clutches.

Another two bursts skimmed the top of my canopy. I was in a blind alley with no way out. Dizziness, a constricted sen-sation in my stomach—naked terror.

My goggles were misted with sweat. I tore them off. My sleeve caught the throttle and wrenched it back. The sudden deceleration flung me against my straps. That was it—that could be the saving of me! I yanked at the stick and my speed dropped like a stone. Simultaneously, my pursuer flashed past with all his guns squirting metal into thin air.

I bullied the one-ninety into a stall turn. Bächler's White 5 appeared beside me. Was he still alive? Yes, we were both alive and flying—flying, as I suddenly became aware, with a whole flock of our own kind. They were all still there. I could see Rotsch's White 12, Schwaneweber's White 4. . . .

"Re-form heading west. We're going in again."

That must be Ketsch, who was usually so insistent on radio silence.

We turned back. Lenz turned too, slightly above the rest. He was lurking behind me all the time. I could guess his thoughts: *Poor old Braack, it's his first time out—not a bad show, considering. Mustn't let anything happen to him. That's more important than knocking down Fortresses. . . . Michael, you poor son-of-a-bitch, you don't know the half of it yet. Keep going!*

We all kept going. We wheeled in a body, and there they were again, looking as impregnable as ever. Full throttle and into them at Ketsch's heels.

"She's really got her legs open, that one," Wehrmann crowed, thinking aloud, and fired off everything he had.

Fired and kept on firing, then pulled back fast. Not a single hit, every one wide. "Shit!" Wehrmann bellowed over the RT. "Shit!"

"Can it!" snapped Ketsch.

He pulled back later, kept his thumb on the button an instant longer, and down it went, impregnable no longer, trailing a funeral streamer. Already, the first chutes were opening. His twentieth.

"Congratulations."

That could only be someone on the sidelines—someone who had cautiously lagged behind. The voice was unidentifiable. Rotsch? Illerts?

Now we turned away unbidden, as if Ketsch's single kill had let us all off the hook.

Suddenly I was gliding safely downward, homeward, with three other members of the Staffel. All that remained of the Mustangs were some contrails retreating north to the Gulf of Danzig while we swung south in a wide arc.

Friend and foe had been simultaneously stricken by that most merciful of ailments, shortage of fuel. . . .

I gave my imagination free rein. This wasn't a one-ninety, it was an unarmed sports plane—an Me 108 Taifun, say. I was a fabulously wealthy man, an East Prussian landowner with forests full of game, flying off to Monte Carlo to buy his ultradesirable mistress a bottle of French perfume the size of a demijohn.

Our yacht was bobbing off the Côte d'Azur. We were going to spend the whole of this glorious autumn cruising the Mediterranean. Fashionably dressed women and their white-flanneled escorts strolled along the palm-fringed promenade, exchanging friendly nods and smiles.

"Why Monte Carlo?" asked Lenz, when I told him my daydream that evening.

"No special reason. Just because it sounds exotic and far away, I suppose."

"Any other glamorous places on your itinerary?"

"Plenty. Samarkand, Inner Mongolia, the Mississippi Delta, the wilds of Kurdistan . . ."

"Don't tell me that's why you're in fighters, to see Tabriz and New Orleans."

I didn't answer. There was nothing to be said.

Piano, guitar, and drums. Evenings in the mess were enlivened by our own brand of jazz. Lenz, who was the founder of our group and kept us up to the mark, perched behind the piano like a terrier begging for sugar. His specialty was triplets in the top octave, a technique he claimed to have borrowed from somebody called Count Basie. Nobody but he and I had ever heard of Count Basie. We'd furtively listened to the BBC as schoolboys, and here at Grojecko we tuned in quite openly to the swing programs from London.

At four in the afternoon, when we weren't airborne and crossing swords with the swing fans from the other side, we made a point of catching the BBC's "Music While You Work" program. This featured various English dance bands. Lenz taught me to distinguish Jack Paine from Jack Hilton and Harry Roy from Joe Loss. Other regulars included Mantovani, Reg Pursglove, and a bandleader named Victor Sylvester, who stuck doggedly to the melody line and never improvised. He'd have gone down big in Germany, where improvisation was frowned on by the arbiters of state-approved music.

Lenz had done a lot to develop my feeling for jazz, and

Fieling had lately become a Staffel catchword. "My *Fieling* is, if I don't quit our Greater German airspace in double-quick time, I'll end up dead." Or: "If you want my *Fieling* on the subject, you're scared shitless." Lenz had also applied himself to my guitar playing. At home I'd used to tinkle away happily at sarabandes, minuets, or quadrilles by Carl Philipp Emanuel or Wolfgang Amadeus. Lenz taught me the rudiments of syncopation and the meaning of blue notes. For a while he made me play B flat instead of B and E flat instead of E on principle. *Bluhnohtz,* too, became a catchword. After a gruelling combat patrol, someone could be heard saying, "Christ, I've got a head full of *Bluhnohtz* and a mouth like a gorilla's armpit!"

I'd now mastered enough of the most common sevenths to wade through the least demanding standards, but I still couldn't manage more than a rhythm accompaniment to Lenz's extravaganzas on the piano. Our drummer, a noncom from 4 Staffel, was hot stuff. He egg-whisked the brushes and twirled the sticks with a demonic enthusiasm that would have made Beethoven turn in his grave and Himmler foam at the mouth. Although Himmler had given the German people leave to refresh their flagging spirits with light music in this fifth year of war—"light music" being his coy euphemism for jazz—one number from the Martin Lenz Group would have prompted him to cancel his gracious concession in a hurry.

One afternoon, Lenz heard the BBC put out what he described as a real sizzler—something called "In the Mood," played by Glenn somebody.

"I've forgotten the man's surname," he said as we were strumming away in the deserted mess. "Glenn . . . Glenn *Martin!*"

Braack, ever an attentive pupil during aircraft recognition classes in ground school, dredged his memory: "The Glenn Martin B-130 is a twin-engined midwing monoplane. Its gun positions are located as follows . . ." It later emerged that there weren't any Glenn Martin bombers in service with the Allies—they were used only by the Netherlands Air Force in the East Indies.

"No, not Martin—Müller."

"Glenn Müller?"

"Not Müller, Miller! *That's* it!"

And Lenz proceeded to whistle his sizzler aloud. Remarkable, the way he could hear a tune once and get it off pat. Before the notes could escape him, he jotted them down at top speed, using a numerical system running from one to seven.

"*Three*-five-one three-*five*-one three-five-*one* three-five-*one,* repeated. Then it switches to F major—*four*-six-one four-*six*-one four-six-*one* four-six-*one* . . ."

"You're right, Martin, it really is a sizzler—much hotter than 'Tiger Rag.' If Steffen hears *that!* He's got his beady eye on us as it is—our musical offerings are ripe for the chop."

"We'll have to keep an eye on the door, that's all. If he walks in, no matter where we've gotten to, switch to G major and go straight into 'Lili Marlene.' "

"I wouldn't announce it as 'In the Mood' either."

"Of course not. We'll call it 'In Stimmung' and pretend it's by Peter Igelhoff."

We explored the possibilities of "In the Mood" for some minutes, then lapsed into silence. I plucked soulfully at the strings, trying to work out my favorite song of the moment, *"Sing, Nachtigall, sing."* It wasn't the song, of course—it was Evelyn Künnecke who brought me out in such a rash with her husky boudoir voice. She must be quite a woman. I visualized her as a vamp in furs and silk with nothing on underneath. . . .

And from Evelyn my thoughts strayed east across the Polish plains to Maryla.

"What's that you're playing, Michael?"

"Nothing special."

"It sounds like a blues from the Virginia tobacco fields . . ."

"Roasting to death in my cockpit," Lauritzen confided one evening. "That's what really scares me."

We were strolling across a field of stubble. Nightingales were still singing in the hazel bushes. Didn't they ever fly south? If I were a nightingale . . . Lauritzen told me how he'd burned his hands.

"It was my second combat patrol. We hadn't made contact, not properly. Forty Mustangs were fending us off. They didn't fire a shot, just formed up between us and the bombers —you know, like 'Beware of the Dog!' They had the legs of us, and the height. We tried to get above them, but it was no use, so we gave up. The trouble was, I'd overcooked my engine. It started heating up, and suddenly I saw flames . . ."

The nightingales' song rose to a pitch of ecstasy, then ceased. Lauritzen gave an audible gulp. More birdsong.

"You don't say," I said, feeling awkward.

"I was in such a state I could hardly tell my throttle from my jettison lever. You know they say some animals dive straight into a forest fire instead of running in the opposite direction? Well, that was me—nothing functioned anymore. The blasted canopy wouldn't budge, so I had to sit tight and risk being cremated alive. I force-landed. For that you need to use your controls."

"Naturally."

A crested lark rose, trilling, above the last of the cornflowers. The sky was streaked with feathery wisps of cirrus.

"The stick was red hot, but I had to hang onto it if I wanted to get down. I did, and I made it."

That was all. Lauritzen said nothing more. Not a word about the story I'd heard from another source.

After his crash landing and discharge from the hospital, he'd been carpeted by Steffen. He'd proved beyond a shadow of a doubt, fumed Steffen, that he was incapable of setting a BMW 801 at regulation climbing speed: wrong revs, total disregard for boost pressure and oil temperature. His wanton destruction of Wehrmacht property was tantamount to sabotage—said Steffen.

The molten sun slid below the skyline and the lark, abruptly silenced, plummeted to earth. Would Lauritzen ever again be able to appreciate the romance of a sunset?

"Roasting to death in my cockpit," he repeated. "That's what really scares me."

5

A huge and unfamiliar airplane landed at our base, but not just any old relic of Lufthansa's prewar passenger fleet. This was a four-engined Focke-Wulf FW 200 Condor, registration CE + IB. We had been privileged to receive a flying visit from one of Adolf Hitler's personal aircraft—without him on board, naturally.

The Führer's personal pilot, Flugkapitän Baur, promptly disappeared into the mess for a snack, a jovial-looking man in a garrison cap and a fur-trimmed flying jacket that emphasized his girth.

Half the Geschwader crowded onto the airfield, sweet-talked their way around the sentries, and made a tour of the cabin.

"Is this the only one he's got?" Bächler asked a veteran noncom with a purple nose. "Adolf, I mean?"

The noncom enlightened him. Three Condors were reserved for the Führer's use: *Immelmann III*, CE + IB, and CE + IC, though the latter carried only guests and aides.

Curiosity centered on the legendary seat with the built-in parachute, which was the subject of many persistent rumors. Did the Führer always wear a chute? Could he eject himself in an emergency? According to Wehrmann, whose information about Hitler always painted him in rosy colors, our Leader had once declared that if Baur didn't wear a parachute, he wouldn't either. And why didn't Baur wear one? Because he'd been flying without one since World War One, said Wehrmann. Anyway, the bloody things were unreliable. A consoling thought . . .

I surveyed the cabin. Luxurious armchairs upholstered in a restrained chintz, the Führer's seat and table. Opposite, a daybed; beyond, two more chairs. A reading lamp was screwed to the exterior of the left-hand headrest. Not a parachute in sight.

The noncom, clearly proud of his superior knowledge, folded down the back of the Führer's seat with a flourish. There was a parachute behind it.

"But how do you get out of here?" asked Bächler, glancing at the rectangular curtained windows.

"Through the floor. The Führer sits with his feet on the trap."

The belly blister below, bristling with machine guns, had been specially shortened to leave the exit free. Bächler climbed out to check. He returned, looking as if he'd just inspected an enemy bomber, and reported his findings with a fighter pilot's love of detail.

"One MG-131 each in gun positions A and B, one MG-15 in position D, and you can see the door he'd drop through, plain as anything!"

Gone were the days when Hitler had been content to fly in a modest Ju 52, registration D-2600.

"But he'd never jump, the Führer wouldn't—not unless the other passengers stood an equal chance of getting out."

Wehrmann again. Truly noble of the Führer, that.

We were hardly outside when the sirens wailed. The Russians arrived a moment later—Yak 7 fighters. Baur raced out of the mess with a packet of cookies in his hand. His copilot, who'd spent the stopover in the cockpit, was already starting up. The Führer's precious airplane would have to make a run for it.

There was no time to scramble our one-nineties or taxi them into their blast bays. We took cover wherever we could —or couldn't. Heaven and earth had already become a single battlefield.

Tracer slammed into aircraft and hangar walls. Clouds of smoke enveloped huts and vehicles, light flak and quadruple pompoms pounded out an accompaniment to the Yaks' machine-gun fire, incandescent threads of tracer snaked over the canteen and runway, clods of earth and fragments of wood and metal filled the air.

And through it all lumbered the Führer's airplane. *Lousy dump,* Baur must be thinking, *let's get the hell out of here.*

Throttles wide open, the big ship gathered speed as she turned her back on the shooting and shouting and roar of engines and rattle of machine guns, the tiny human figures sprinting among fountains of earth and sheets of flame in blind rage or mortal terror. Bächler, lying beside me with his face buried deep in the coarse grass, made a sudden announcement:

"Christ, I could use a shit."

The Condor took off unscathed. It seemed crazy, flying into the teeth of a Russian fighter attack in a cumbersome four-engined transport, but Baur knew his business. He vanished almost as soon as he left the ground, down on the deck and low enough to fly through a barn door. No Russian would have dared to follow suit.

Flames were leaping from a gutted, engineless one-ninety. More fountains of earth sprang up. A long festoon of tracer, seemingly wafted by the wind, reached for a lone human figure running across the field. One moment the man was there; the next, nothing.

The fighters turned away. All clear. Final inventory: no appreciable damage, much ado about nothing. We also learned that Baur had made it safely back to the Wolf's Lair, Hitler's melodramatically named headquarters in East Prussia.

And the vaporized figure on the runway?

According to the Oberfeldwebel, he hadn't even belonged to our outfit. Some kind of semicivilian—a construction worker, probably.

Maryla had devised a novel and unconventional method of warning me when to expect her.

Her Luftwaffe base at Konskie was several hundred feet higher than Grojecko and several miles away. I couldn't see it even when I borrowed Schwaneweber's binoculars, but stationed there were a number of Russian prisoners who went off to work in the fields every day.

Maryla regularly slipped these Ivans a few loaves of cookhouse bread. In return, they raked potato greens together and set fire to them at prearranged times: six o'clock meant there was no chance of a rendezvous; five o'clock meant she was coming. I could easily make out these smoke signals through binoculars, wreathing the foothills of the Lysa Gora in distant promise or rejection.

Our communications system didn't work on misty days like today. When the mist closed in I went looking for her on the off-chance that I would see her. Goatsbeard heads displayed their seed clocks and spindle tree berries glowed red. Hundreds of swallows were resting on the wires of the makeshift telephone link between the air base and the outside world.

On our last date we'd come across a shack that must once have housed construction workers. I had to skirt a small lake on my way there—Cloud Lake, we'd christened it. The gray-green water was turbid with weeds and coated with water lilies, and clouds and withered sedge were wedded to their reflections on its leaden surface. I would be able to see from the lake whether there was a bicycle propped against the shack.

There was.

"We can always meet here," Maryla said a moment later. "If you like," she added softly.

We were inside the birthplace of my boyhood dreams. This shack was where Old Shatterhand had met Winnetou, where Robinson Crusoe sought shelter from tropical storms, where Tom Sawyer and Huckleberry Finn kept watch on the Missis-sippi. It also doubled as Ali Baba's cave and Uncle Tom's cabin. Sindbad the Sailor had passed this way, and so had Odysseus, but our private name for the shack was Shangri-La.

Shangri-La was overhung by huge holm oaks, and its rough-planed pinewood walls were thick with wild ivy on the outside. The low door was faced with birch logs, and the con-tinuous bench running around the interior consisted of similar logs bisected with their sawn faces uppermost. The floor had been left as nature intended: a carpet of moss inlaid with heather, all sere and brown for lack of sunlight.

I took her in my arms and kissed her. Her kiss was warm and affectionate but a little melancholy.

"Always, when it's foggy," I replied. At the nape of her neck, my fingers discovered a tiny whorl of hair that had defied the comb. "Good old Polish autumn mist—long may it last!"

A damp marshy scent drifted in through the unglazed win-dows. The rust-red tail of a squirrel darted behind a tree trunk and acorns pattered down through the leaves. Watery evening sunlight pierced the swaths of mist, turning Maryla's face the color of amber—the deep golden kind I'd found on vacation beside the Baltic. She had a minuscule birthmark on her throat.

I caressed her little ringlet, her neck, her breasts and thighs. I kissed her from head to foot. When the light had dwindled to a faint glow above the treetops, we stretched out on the bench. Her head brushed mine in one corner of the hut and we lay at right angles because the bench was too narrow to accommodate us side by side. We pillowed our heads on our clasped hands and stared up at the ceiling. There were cobwebs everywhere.

"I feel as if I'd known you for centuries," she said. "You can't imagine what Deblin was like. Soldiers retreating, evacuees milling around, utter chaos at headquarters. The officers carried off everything they could. Furniture, pictures —even a concert grand. Girls by the truckload, too. I actually saw some half-lame soldiers being ordered out of a truck because our headquarters staff insisted on taking their Polish girl friends along."

"Pure charity," I said. "If they'd fallen into Russian hands they'd have been slaughtered on the spot."

"That's one way of looking at it, but there wasn't even a bicycle to spare for the likes of me. I hadn't done what's expected of a girl signaler and been nice to the local officers and gentlemen, that's why. I was feeling pretty low, sitting in my hut beside the airfield. No, not even low—I didn't care anymore. Pack up and get out fast—I'd done it so many times before, and always we'd retreated to places that had to be abandoned in a matter of days or weeks. Then, all at once, I heard your one-ninety. I didn't even know we had any left. There'd been nothing but Russians over the field, day after day—Shturmoviks and LaGGs."

"Lucky I spent so long doing aerobatics over Masuria or I might have had enough fuel to get me back here."

"No, Michael, I'm being serious. To me, you were a creature from another planet." She gently stroked my cheek with fingers that carried a faint autumnal scent of herbs and mushrooms. "It may sound silly, but you appeared out of nowhere like a guardian angel. You put new heart into me. My instinct for survival came flooding back, stronger than ever. I stared after you for ages—long after the sunset had swallowed you up. Then I marched into the administration block and raised hell. There were four of us women auxiliaries all told, I said. What were we supposed to do, hang around while our gallant lords and masters hightailed it to the west—ostensibly to find us new quarters?"

"Still, it must have been a good fairy that made them pick on Konskie."

"Poland's shrinking so fast they didn't have much choice. Anyway, my mutiny did the trick. They squeezed us girls into a Volkswagen and away we went, heading straight in your direction."

We rolled over in search of each other and tumbled to the mossy floor. It was far softer and more comfortable than the bench. Why hadn't we thought of it sooner?

"Now all we need is another good fairy to keep us together," I said. A little brown beetle was crawling up her bare leg. I brushed it off.

She half sat up and looked at me intently.

"Listen, Michael. Even if you never lift a finger for the rest of this ghastly war, you'll still have done more for me by turning up at Deblin than a hundred fighter aces could ever do."

"I can't claim any credit for that," I said with a sigh. "It was pure chance—fate, if you like."

"Call it anything you want. The fact remains that you . . ."

Mosquitoes whined and a sleepless dragonfly whirred through the window. A distant rumble of antiaircraft fire.

"That I what, Maryla?"

"Saved my life. I'd given up, decided to stay put. I wanted to end it all."

The mist was thicker on the way back. Between the lake and the dispersal pens, the atmosphere had become transmuted into jungle-green soup, ghostly and featureless. I might have been groping my way through a malarial swamp beside the Amazon.

All at once some figures loomed up, apparently making for a bank of earth overgrown with chervil. Beyond it, a strange yet familiar shape jutted into the air like a newly erected monument. I recognized various members of the Geschwader: ground staff, airfield defense personnel, fellow pilots. Bächler was there. So was Schwaneweber—and Mahlke with his medic's motorbike. I identified the shape. It really was a monument of sorts: the tail section of a crashed one-ninety. The fin itself, adorned with a black and white swastika, was completely intact.

Nothing could be seen apart from the tail and a few feet of tapering fuselage. From there on, everything had gone—cockpit, wings, engine. There wasn't even a crater, just a shallow depression from which dim figures were retrieving objects and passing them down the line to Mahlke's sidecar.

"Here's an arm. . . . There, that could be a shoulder. . . . Careful, everything below the waist's in one piece!"

Waiting at the end of the human chain was a large sack. Mahlke stowed the remains inside and jounced them up and down to make room for more. Then, when the dark hollow yielded no more finds, he humped his salvage into the sidecar like a stevedore and roared off.

Schwaneweber was sitting on the bank with his hands over his face. I shook him.

"Who was it?"

Vile thoughts and fervent prayers took shape in my mind. If one of us had bought it, let it be . . .

"Nobody from our lot. Jankowskie of 1 Staffel. He'd been collecting a replacement from somewhere, found the field fogbound, and circled. When his fuel ran low he tried to land anyway. Bang went our new one-ninety!"

Had I at some stage, lying in Maryla's arms, heard a muffled crash? The sound of an engine, at least? No, nothing. My heart hadn't even missed a beat.

6

My one-ninety bore the serial number 16764 and had been built at the Focke-Wulf subsidiary works in Marienburg, East Prussia. Marienburg, St. Mary's Castle . . . It was a name that inspired romantic daydreams. My airplane was the fair daughter of a proud castellan—or, more realistically, the noble steed of a knight who rode forth daily to slay a dragon. More realistically still, a whole herd of dragons. This engine of war whose fate was so inextricably linked, for better or worse, with my own—who or what was it in reality?

I pored over operating and armament manuals in the hope of getting to know my steed better. After studying them, I often caught myself conducting imaginary inquisitions during dogfights and dives. *Turn tighter, damn you! Pull out, you bitch! What about your maximum reliability—what about all that pilot protection?*

And what did the operating instructions say about the one-ninety's vulnerability to a burst from quadruple machine guns mounted in the tail of a Flying Fortress? Which of her frail components would disintegrate first? The ailerons? The leading edges? The spars?

I was, however, informed that the first-aid kit could be found in a recess on the fuselage right side, and that access to it was provided by a hinged cover secured by quick-release fasteners.

That was an invaluable tip, to be sure—if only for members of a rescue team who wanted to take a trapped pilot's mind off his ruptured intestines and splintered bones by applying a farewell Band-Aid to his flattened nose. To actuate my one-ninety's undercarriage, which was hydraulically retracted inward into the wings and belly, the following sequence had to be observed: (*1*) *Flip up red safety cover over* UP *button.* (*2*) *Depress* UP *button.* So much technological ingenuity, so much effort and expense, and all for the sake of killing. . . .

My canopy could be opened and closed by means of a hand crank located on the right wall of the cockpit. This handle was spring-loaded and had to be kept pulled out during operation. If I wanted to jettison the canopy I had to apply vigorous pressure to the red jettison lever situated behind the hand crank.

At least once during every patrol I felt tempted to grab some fresh air this way—as if I were suffocating behind the mask, which was all that preserved me from asphyxia.

My fuel tank selector could be set as follows: ON, FORWARD TANK OFF, REAR TANK OFF, and OFF.

I had only to select OFF during a dogfight and it would all be over—the fighting, the fear, the war. I would wake from my nightmare and find myself back in Masuria, back in the midst of the Johannisburger Heide with my fishing line trailing in the placid waters of the Krutinna and a stork flapping slowly along its wooded banks.

All my one-ninety's secrets were embodied in an operating manual. *General Maintenance Instructions,* Section 7, referred to the cleaning of Plexiglas. It stated that dust and dirt should be removed with a damp sponge (water temperature 40–50 degrees centigrade) and the surface then buffed dry with a polishing cloth. Heavier dirt could be shifted with a dash of liquid soap or soda. Glasurit Aircraft Cleaner was also recommended, and Sangajol would remove varnish, grease, oil, or paint.

What about blood?

General Maintenance Instructions made no provision for the removal of blood.

But no air force was adequately served by an airplane that simply flew, however well. In an air force, particularly one entering the sixth year of a war whose cost in men and machines had been immense, no airplane could afford to be an end in itself. It could fulfill its proper function only by carrying weapons.

Consequently, and with flawless logical consistency, machine guns and machine cannons had been mounted in the nose and wings of my one-ninety. These were what I used to fire at that dehumanized target officially termed "the enemy," who in turn used his guns to fire at what his own superiors, in their undoubted wisdom, likewise referred to by the same designation. It clearly followed that there were no human beings left in this war, only enemies. The corollary of this was that I, too, had ceased to be a human being and was merely an enemy.

Once, when I suggested to Lenz that—according to this line of thought—I must be my own enemy, he mildly retorted that I thought too much. Thinking wasn't advisable in the sixth year of the war, he said. Fighting was the key word. Under certain circumstances, thinking could lead to a reduction in your life expectancy—not only in theory but from a purely practical point of view. These days, the thinking man was apt to die at least two weeks sooner than the dour nonthinker.

Very well. If I must think, better think about the guns that could prolong my own life expectancy at the expense of someone else's. Curiously enough, I was recurrently haunted by operating instructions—the technical and scientific trappings of death. SZKK stood for "Switch, Rounds Counter, and Control Unit," ZVK-FF for "Rounds Counter and Breechblock Control Unit for MG-FFs." And what was an ADSK 2-17? A "Firing and Cocking Switchbox for two MG-17s."

What could have been more important to a youthful student pressed into uniform before taking his finals than to know what ADSK 2-17 stood for? Shakespeare was of far less interest, being not only dead but English and, therefore, an enemy national.

And what of a youthful airman in the sixth year of World War Two? Were his activities limited to quoting passages from Shakespeare? Far from it. There were more essential objects of study at this stage in the conflict—the KG-14, for example.

The KG-14 was a one-ninety's control column grip. The firing lever mounted on it was normally set at REST—normally meaning "prior to the intention to fire."

Intention to fire . . . At night, midway between waking and sleeping, I often toyed with various alternatives: "My firing intention was to transfer Wehrmann from an altitude of fifteen thousand feet to a position six feet underground. . . ." Verbalized daydreams that lingered in the reality of the lecture room next morning, with its infernal stench of antibug spray. . . .

In this age of automated killing, guns cocked themselves and breechblocks were retained in the open position. Firing was electrically powered by the aircraft's twenty-four-volt system.

However hurried and slapdash our conversion to the one-ninety and its manifold opportunities for filling the air with metal, I'd never concentrated harder on learning anything than how to operate the MG-17 and MG-FF. In school at Lötzen we'd been treated to such politically enthralling topics as "The Significance of English Dandyism" and "The Military Value of the Island of Guam to the United States," but our lectures on the MG-17 and MG-FF beat them hands down.

I knew, therefore, that the MG-17's empty cartridge cases and belt links were ejected into space (unlike the pilot, who had to remain in his cockpit). I also knew that the belt employed was Disintegrating Belt No. 17/81. My guests at a convivial soirée twenty years hence might debate the symptoms of decline in Beethoven's later works, Goethe's theory of color, Lichtenberg's aphorisms, or Ernst Jünger's *Marmorklippen,* but my discourses would be limited to Disintegrating Belt No. 17/81.

The ground gave off a maternal warmth and wasps were belatedly buzzing through the autumn sunlight. I was hunkered down in front of my one-ninety, draped in cartridge belts and mixing a lethal cocktail.

Armorer Giesicke, whose job it really was, watched me patiently for the space of a smoke. Then he took the whole caboodle off my hands.

"I know how you want them. It hurts me to see you ruining those artistic fingers of yours. Better stick to playing jazz, like you did the other night."

"All right, how *do* I want them?"

"Two incendiaries, one H/E, one armor-piercing."

"If you say so." I'd blended the different types of ammunition without thinking, in a purely mechanical way. Some experts—the real professional killers—swore by two incendiaries and two H/E, others by two H/E and two armor-piercing. "I'd do a better job with candies," I said. "Two nougats, one caramel, one chocolate drop . . ."

"My God, nougat!" sighed Giesicke, deftly inserting a well-assorted succession of rounds in the belt feeder. "Remind me what it tastes like, would you?"

A crested lark soared into the humid air above the dispersal pens. A bell tolling in Grojecko announced that it was Sunday again. Two incendiaries, one H/E, one armor-piercing, and one tracer between each series of four.

Incendiaries were meant for fuel tanks, high explosive and armor-piercing for armor plate, but no shell could defy the laws of ballistics. If a human body happened to get between the muzzle of an MG and its target, the phosphorus intended for the fuel tank would burn out human viscera like a pest controller's flame gun. Similarly, a high explosive shell had no qualms about pulverizing a shoulder blade or cranium.

Two incendiaries, one H/E, one armor-piercing. Two charred rib cages, one mangled thigh, one shattered skull. And the bells of Grojecko were announcing that Sunday had come around again. . . .

Giesicke had only just finished rearming my machine when a standby alert was broadcast. Away went the chessboards, playing cards, and paperbacks.

"You and I in the moonlight . . ." A catchy tune, but more appropriate to a night fighter unit. "Holding hands and dreaming . . ." Maybe, but not now. Combat Control abruptly blighted this musical reverie:

Strong enemy formations approaching the Katowice-Cze-stochowa area, probably withdrawing north. Gruppen One, Two, and Three, cockpit alert!

No more time to set out chessmen, thumb through dog-eared novels, deal another hand.

"Darling, how lovely it was . . ."

My imagination went to work. This sentimental song might be my last-ever message from the land of the living. Just that, nothing less trivial?

"Sitting on the bench all alone . . ."

That wasn't even a reference to my pilot's seat. Fasten helmet under chin, check throat mike, main switches on: ready for takeoff.

The takeoff order came through a moment later. Green flares went up, Steffen's machine roared down the runway ahead of all the rest, looking pregnant with menace, and climbed steeply away. It was still Sunday morning, but I couldn't hear the bells any longer.

"Elephants at eighteen thousand feet."

I tagged onto Schwaneweber's tail. We were climbing through a thin layer of stratus.

"Quiet!" somebody said sternly over the RT, though none of us had uttered a sound.

I still hadn't snatched a downward glance. Schwaneweber's slipstream was buffeting me, but I stuck to him like glue. Company, that was my sole defense against fear. The altimeter needle continued to rotate: sixteen-five . . . eighteen . . . twenty . . . twenty-two . . . twenty-three thousand feet. There we stayed, and there *they* were—far, far below us. A perfect attacking position . . .

Gunsight on. Safety switch off.

Mustangs en masse, Fortresses en masse, contrails en masse. The whole sky looked as if it had been vandalized by a schizo with artistic pretensions.

"Attention all Hounds. Prepare to attack Elephants, ignore Wolves. Going in now!"

That was Steffen. But what if the Mustangs didn't ignore *us?* Did we press on regardless?

We were in among them now. No time to think. He who thinks, fires too late. *I fire, therefore I am.* Dirty brown smoke spewed from our exhausts as we dived.

Schwaneweber had vanished without trace. A fighter flashed across my line of vision—a Mustang, its eight cannon barrels jutting avidly. Had it been after me? No idea. Where was I diving to? Who was guiding me—what was guiding me?

Dead ahead, another Mustang traveling in the opposite direction. The same one? It gave a sudden lurch and rolled over on its back. A thin plume of smoke escaped from the cockpit, almost like a paper streamer. The liner was pulling away from the quay, smiles and tears, handkerchiefs fluttering, the strains of a brass band. . . . *Concentrate, Braack! Who fired at you just now? Had* someone fired at me?

Concentrate, Braack, or you're dead. A shape swam across my aiming ring. *Fire, Braack!* Before it dawned on me that he was an enemy, not a friend, he was long gone. I fired a burst into thin air for form's sake. The whole airplane shivered like a horse with colic.

Clouds of whitish glycol vapor hung in the sky, unfurled like a time-lapse sequence of cactus flowers, became tinged with red, then black. It came from Illerts' one-ninety. The canopy flew off. Was he getting out?

No, he wasn't.

"Jump, man! Get a move on!"

Illerts still didn't jump.

Only two days before, he'd said:

"If anything happens to me, forget I ever existed. Just forget."

While he was hurtling into limbo, his machine simply disintegrated: main planes, tail unit, exhaust stacks, wheels, fairings, rivets, screws. . . .

And Illerts the man?

Not a trace of him.

"Wake up, Braack! Three Wolves on your tail!"

Break and pull back, roll and loop, dive and climb. The wolves disappeared, like Illerts.

Mölders, himself long dead, was reported to have said, "The main thing is, don't let your first kill shock you—then you'll gain confidence." Apparently, he always felt happier when a defeated opponent managed to jump. . . .

None of our aces mentioned the holes in their own machines. How well would I cope with the shock of being shot down myself?

On with the fray, Illerts or no Illerts. . . .

The sky between Toruń and Grudziądz became a thundering, roaring, fulminating vortex. Anything that moved above the fleecy banks of cirrus was there to be attacked on sight. Wholesale slaughter was the order of the day. Each contested the other's claim to a single patch of sky, a single chance to soar there in freedom, for the sheer joy of flying.

Bursts of tracer streamed in all directions—into the Fortresses' gun ports, into tail gunners' turrets with their quadruple mountings, into cockpit canopies, engine cowlings, drop tanks, wheel doors and rudders, into the chests of Mustang pilots, into the eyes of navigators and bombardiers. Many Mustangs seemed to turn on the spot, belching flame like allegories of naked power, or brake almost to a standstill when slowed by the recoil of their eight heavy cannons.

One of our fighters failed to get in a single shot, keeled over, and spun earthward like a withered leaf. Throughout the sky, pilots took cover in their frail machines as if sheltering in concrete emplacements, yet one round of high explosive could reduce a whole cockpit to a shambles of steel, Plexiglas and aluminum bones, electrical and mechanical entrails.

A gargantuan Fortress, looming larger by the second, leveled its obese and obscene-looking rear turret straight at my head. A rapid succession of fat thirty-millimeter shells, pumped in foursomes at a wafer-thin human skull. . . . Airplanes were bursting all around me like overripe plums or deep-sea fish expiring in the shallows. . . . I had to get away. Twelve shells per second were streaking toward my poor fragile skull. I wrenched at the stick—flung the fighter away. Anywhere, just away.

Forced to lose height by layers of cloud at medium altitude and disheartened by our fruitless attacks on the impregnable Fortresses, we turned away from the last enemy formation and straggled back to Grojecko as best we could. Cirrostratus above us, altocumulus below. Between them, us, like the filling in a liverwurst sandwich.

My salt-encrusted eyes peered through the oil-streaked windshield. The fingers gripping my stick were numb with pressure, my skin and throat completely parched. No moisture at all, not even the cold sweat of fear. My teeth were coated with a sort of glue, like the tongue that desperately roamed along them.

I tried to salivate and swallow. No use. The breath rasped in my throat, which felt like ancient parchment, and my nostrils stung. Although the altimeter was reading seven thousand feet, I still had my mask on. Off with it! Delicious fresh air . . .

Not a whiff. Nothing but a stench of oil and gasoline, a miasma of hot rubber.

I'd been convinced I was going to die when we attacked. This had been a day for dying. It had all seemed so terribly logical and natural, somehow. I'd tossed and turned in my bunk for weeks, bereft of sleep. What form would my final moments take? How much would it hurt to die? My fear of death had been overpowering.

But, when the moment came at last, you accepted it as you accepted the fact that a theater was sold out. No more room on earth? Ah well, can't be helped, nothing to do but make a dignified exit. You fired a farewell burst—so we'd been told —and waved good-bye before plunging into the abyss. Over and out.

I'd always thought the fear of death would be more intense than any other emotion, yet I'd mastered it more easily than my resentment at the injustice of being given an undersized helping of beans. Three cheers for the system that had drilled us so admirably! Our whole existence in the Hitler Youth and armed forces had been geared to extinction. Discipline paid off. We were ready for an uncomplaining hero's death—that we could take, but not a watery cup of coffee before dying. *That* we found outrageous.

Dying per se was all right, as long as you didn't add any riders. Dying *for* something was another matter. That was where my problems began. Führer and Fatherland, the Greater German Reich . . . The very sound of those clichés provoked a resurgence of my will to live. Not for them—no, certainly not for *them!* To me, dying could only be the price I had to pay for flying. The choice had been ours and we'd made it. Now, death was standing at the turnstile with an outstretched hand. We had to keep our side of the bargain and pay up. With dignity.

We paraded in the cemetery at Grojecko and fired a farewell salute.

Slowly, the coffin containing Illerts' mortal remains sank into Polish soil. At the third volley, every bird in the nearby trees fled screaming.

His mortal remains? We all knew that the big pine coffin contained nothing but a tattered flying helmet. They hadn't even found his throat mike.

Forget I ever existed.

7

Y ou wouldn't have kicked a dog outdoors in such weather.

But Steffen did. He chivied his hounds of hell out and up to intercept some bombers reported in grid square Blue Six. *Strong enemy formations heading for Breslau and the whole Silesian area. . . .* Plus musical accompaniment. Ilse Werner flooded the airfield with song before the takeoff order came through. Thunderheads had been building up in the southwest. Now they towered there, rumbling and flickering. Steffen had only just ordered us into our cockpits when they fell on the base like a pack of wolves. The Staffel took off, overshadowed by the inky blue turrets and battlements of a huge celestial fortress. The runway turf steamed under the impact of raindrops that smote its sunbaked surface like bullets.

The air was charged with electricity. I sensed that almost as soon as my wheels were stowed, and it set my nerves on edge. The Staffel was trying to assemble behind a sulphurous yellow bastion of cloud from which lightning darted incessantly in all directions. When we'd finished formating and had time to look at the storm ahead, we found ourselves confronted by an immense wall daubed with vivid green streaks.

A breach appeared in the wall—a cavern into which we climbed with no idea of what awaited us, hidden treasure or some monstrous survivor from the age of the dinosaur. Solid-looking ramparts of cloud slid aside and dissolved, to be replaced by others. Flat expanses bunched themselves into fists, rounded domes became spearheads. There was an alternation of livid gray and vitriol green, earthy brown and batwing blue. The lightning's ice-cold fire snaked between our wings and festooned them like deadly paper chains.

We continued to climb regardless, huddling together with the tenacity of cattle on a rain-lashed hillside. The air was in turmoil, full of whirls and eddies. It was all we could do not to kiss wing tips when the gusts smote us like hammers. Suddenly I found myself in utter darkness. Panic gripped me. How did you fly blind? Feverishly, I switched on the artificial horizon. It took a while to right itself. Where were the others? Above, below, abeam—within spitting distance? Which way should I go to avoid them?

I rocketed upward, plummeted downward, rolled on my side. Hail rattled fearsomely against the bullet-resistant windshield. Tiny serpents of St. Elmo's fire played over the airscrew and pitot head.

Which way should I turn to avoid ramming my neighbors? I kicked hard on the port rudder and found it hard over already: I was in a steep turn to port and thought I was flying straight and level. The instruments toppled and shuddered. They told me no more than ancient Egyptian hieroglyphs. . . . Obedient to an intuitive feeling that the earth was below me and the sky above, I tried to keep the stick straight and the rudder central.

Lightning, cascades of it, and audible thunder. The engine was overspeeding. I hadn't touched the throttle, so why? A dive! I'd gone into a power dive, still under the impression that I was flying level. The needle of the airspeed indicator was climbing, the vertical speed indicator and altimeter unwinding.

Very well, the sooner I was out of this hell's kitchen the better. The ground had to show up sometime. I continued to accelerate, leveled my wings by feel, and kept watch below. . . .

Blue sky and dazzling sunlight broke through, directly beneath me. No ground beyond them, nothing but an infinity of sky and cloud. The earth had vanished.

Above me all was green and ocher, lines and intersections, patches of what looked like forest, aquamarine blobs resembling lakes. . . .

They *were* lakes: the ground was above me and the sky below. I'd been flying upside down—the cloud had given me vertigo. I performed a half-roll and restored heaven and earth to their proper places. The maneuver made me dizzy. There was nothing for it but to turn back and land. I'd no idea where the others had gone.

Not a single Staffel reached its patrol area. Every one had been overtaken by the storm and thrown into confusion. None of our pilots, not even the old hands, had any experience of flying blind through a thunderstorm of that magnitude.

Emergency landings, forced landings . . .

But it was Lenz who suffered the most preposterous fate of all and survived to tell a tale that passed into the annals of Jagdgeschwader 99.

Lenz, too, had taken a beating. He was seized by a giant thunderhead and brandished up and down for thousands of feet.

"At first I clung to my stick like a drowning man—then I grabbed at anything that offered a handhold."

He was flung around so violently that the straps bit into his shoulders. He showed them off that night, adorned with red weals that might have been inflicted with a rawhide whip.

"I chopped the throttle and lowered my gear, and still I went whistling down like a glider bound for the deck. Another time I tried fighting back with the throttle wide open, but it was no use. Down I went."

He entered the worst of the turbulence. Hail drummed against his spinner and leading edges, shovelfuls of sleet hit the windshield. Completely out of control, he was sucked into the maw of the storm, an inferno lit by darting, flickering, unceasing electrical discharges.

Then a huge fist knocked him flat on his back.

Panic-stricken, he put out his right hand and grabbed something. A bang, a blow in the face, and an icy blast tore his canopy off. He'd depressed the jettison lever. Now he was exposed to the full force of the elements.

The rudder and controls had ceased to respond. Every external surface was coated with ice. A wreck was hurtling through the fiery sky, airworthy no longer.

" 'Stay up!' I yelled. 'Stay up till I'm out, damn you!' And the bitch did just that."

He unclipped himself and struggled to his feet. He braced one heel against the stick and kicked it. No reaction. The elevators were iced up too. Suddenly he found himself falling.

"I must have been on my back already. . . ."

Once clear, he plunged into a void that seared him like a blowtorch. Cold, loss of pressure, and acceleration all conspired to torture him. His limbs froze, the lower part of his body became distended, the whole of his frame was racked by G forces and buffeted by conflicting currents of air.

At last the pain subsided. He fell as if disembodied, aware of nothing but a vague sense of chaos and dissolution. Parts of his brain seemed to be impinging on his eyeballs, vital organs compressing themselves against his pelvis.

He was falling through the sort of diffused glow cast by dying embers. There was neither height nor depth, beginning nor end to this indefinable region, but the light hurt him— made his eyes smart as if he were bathing them in a strong solution of seawater. Unable to shut them, he tried to scream but found he had forgotten how.

Something inside him was still capable of perception. He clung to it like a life raft, scrambled aboard it like a shipwrecked sailor. There was air around him—that he could feel. He was racked by shooting pains, rhythmical and gaining strength—those he could feel too. An inaudible groan escaped him. A turmoil of sensations and impressions overwhelmed him: noises like bursts of cannon fire, flashes of color like dagger thrusts. His body caught up with him as if the headlong descent of his inner self had slowed.

Lenz was back in his body again. "That's right, carry on," he told himself. "Fine, stick it out—good, good, excellent. You're conscious again. Not much longer now—you'll soon reach denser air. More oxygen, more pressure, less pain. Stick it out!"

He wrestled with a fiendish temptation to pull the rip cord.

"It would have been a damn-fool thing to do, I knew that. I didn't want to drift down slowly and freeze to death, did I?" He eyed us all in turn. We stared back, open-mouthed. "Keep falling, that was the only thought in my head—keep falling."

He finally pulled the rip cord because the thought of the ground rushing up to meet him became unendurable. As soon as he felt the pressure of the harness against his thighs, he knew he'd given in too soon—far too soon.

The turbulent heart of the storm closed around him.

Defenseless against the bellowing, coruscating inferno, he became a plaything of the elements. The raging up- and downdrafts were so powerful that they smashed into him like a succession of mighty breakers. Catapulted upward one moment, then hovering weightless the next before swooping into a ferment of cloud, dazzled by lightning and deafened by thunder, he spun, whirled, and somersaulted with helpless resignation.

"I felt like a bag of flesh and bones being bounced up and down on a concrete floor. . . ."

Bruised and bleeding, with lacerated fingers and swollen cheeks, he ended by fighting for his reason as well as his life. He was a prisoner running the gauntlet, a victim of torturers who squeezed him like a lemon one moment and strove to tear him limb from limb the next.

"I couldn't stop puking. . . ."

The peals of thunder did more than threaten to burst his eardrums; they seemed to be pulverizing every bone in his body, just as the glare of the lightning, visible even when he shut his eyes, seemed to cleave him like a broadsword.

He might have been a piece of driftwood shooting the rapids, the rain was so intense. He felt as if he were drowning, but that sensation paled beside another: the agony inflicted by sheets of driving hail which battered his ill-protected body like a mob stoning the target of their insensate fury.

Though subjected to the torments of the damned, Lenz endured the unendurable; though reduced to the status of a molecule in the meteorological system and divorced from all things human, he asserted his humanity by sheer willpower.

"I told myself, if you don't want to lose your mind, use it!"

He concentrated on his watch. He marveled that it was still intact and drew courage from the sight of his parachute, which was still in one piece.

"If that damned pocket handkerchief can take it, I thought, so can I."

At long last, the subsiding storm spat him out like a pip and dumped him in a marshy forest clearing. His landing and survival seemed of almost secondary importance. . . .

He trudged to the nearest army post. Some peasants threatened him with their pitchforks on the way, but they were too scared of SS reprisals to molest him. He contacted the local authorities in a backwoods town named Opoczno and was duly returned to us, complete with parachute.

Lenz reported back in time for supper. He toyed with his food in silence for a while, still a little on edge, but eventually dug in.

Whenever he wasn't actually flying or being shot down, Lenz could be found at the piano or in the mess, arranging books and sorting magazines. He had no inhibitions about displaying banned books as long as they came in gift parcels. After all, if his father hadn't owned the biggest bookstore in Lötzen he wouldn't have had a clue which authors were officially banned or approved. The result was that Adolf Hitler, Alfred Rosenberg and Baldur von Schirach rubbed shoulders on the shelves with such undesirables as Stefan Zweig, Erich Maria Remarque and Hermann Hesse.

As lovingly as he tended them, however, Lenz's books were seldom read. Few stray visitors to the library did more than skim through *Der Flieger, Kladderadatsch* and *Simplicissimus*—or, more rarely, *Das Reich* and *Das Schwarze Korps.*

It was here among the shelves, looted plush armchairs and garden tables supplied by a sympathetic quartermaster that I spent most of my precious leisure hours in undisturbed enjoyment.

I read, therefore I was.

I leafed, for example, through a magazine dated 21 September 1944. One double spread was devoted to a feature headed "11 ACES, 1,676 KILLS."

And there were the eleven heroes' faces—radiant, self-assured, confident of final victory. Hartmann, who led the field with 303 kills, had still been sitting on a school bench in 1940, like me. Next, Batz with 208 victories—a music student before he became a pilot and holder of the Knight's Cross with Oak Leaves. Next, Borchers with 118—his wife was Christel Cranz, the world skiing champion. Even the rising generation were proving their mettle: 64 kills for an unknown Leutnant R.

I carefully studied the captions. In addition to straightforward biographical particulars like those below the photo of Vönnekold ("Son of a Hamburg Harbor Master, Formerly a Motor Mechanic") there were brief comments such as "A Real Daredevil with Many Low-level Attacks to His Credit" (Leutnant Gratz, 116 kills) or "A Dogged Fighter and an Outstanding Organizer and Tactician—In Short, a Somebody!" (Oberstleutnant Hrabak, 126 kills).

All these eleven men belonged to a single Jagdgeschwader, JG 52, the most successful fighter unit in the Greater German Reich. I belonged to a less successful unit, JG 99. Our only record was one of failure. The fatal casualties in our component Gruppen far outnumbered the heroes who still survived in JG 52, though illustrated magazines did not, admittedly, publicize the names of its dead.

There followed a jubilant report from the Propaganda Company correspondent attached to the unit:

"Yesterday was a great day for us. All over the air base, one question was on everybody's lips: Would 'Sonny' Hartmann get his 300th—would he make it today?"

I slammed the magazine down on the table.

"Get out of bed on the wrong side?" asked Lenz, who was just unwrapping another parcel of books. They looked as if they'd been recovered from the library of a ship that had lain on the sea bed since 1890.

"My A-8 carries eight guns. Guess who I'd like to empty them into?"

"Well?"

"I'd rather not say."

"Never mind, I'll read you something." Lenz thumbed through a folder full of back issues of *Das Reich*. He opened one. Five columns of print. Top center: a reproduction of an 1828 engraving of the Odeonsplatz, Munich. Below it a poem by Hermann Stahl, very lyrical and quite unpolitical. Left-hand column: "EUROPE COMES TO WEIMAR. GERMAN LITER-ARY CONGRESS, 1941." Right-hand column: "The Reich and Ancient Greece," by Hans Rössner. Below and offset: "Ap-peal by Reichsleiter Rosenberg." Lenz grinned. "Like to hear how our small-town Nazi régime tried to boost its interna-tional standing in 1941? Listen to this:

"If there is one magical focus of European culture, it is Weimar. . . . Seated there, side by side, were all who enjoy renown in contemporary European literature. I was struck by Carossa's lucid and kindly expression, Svend Fleuron's noble bearing, Wilhelm Schäfer's look of profound spirituality, the handsome and distinctive features of Felix Timmermans, the magisterial intellect of the Frenchmen Chardonne and Bon-nard, the volatile enthusiasm of the Italians, led by Farinelli —what pen could do justice to this lineup of well-loved lit-erary figures? Like symbols of the spirit animating this congress, there also sat among them, stern-faced, the young German poets and authors who now wear field-gray: Zillich, Dwinger, Baumann, Bauer—an endless succession of the names we associate with Germany's creative powers. . . ."

"What was that again about the Frenchmen's intellect?"

"Magisterial, he called it."

"Very impressive. I can just picture all those well-groomed gentlemen with handsome and distinctive features, all contriving to look noble and Germanic at the same time. A pity their literary effusions don't contain some tips on how to fight off half a dozen Mustangs."

Lenz wagged his head.

"Honestly, Michael, I don't get you. A minute ago you were snarling at our war correspondents and their half-baked heroics. Now you're sinking your fangs into our leading exponents of the written word."

"The state-approved ones, yes. What happened to all the others?"

"You know that as well as I do. I was there that night in '33, when our local Nazis threw their own book-burning party. They staged a big torchlight procession and I tagged along as usual, loving every minute—I was only nine, don't forget. I didn't like the Communists. They had shawms in their street bands, squeaky old silver things. It sent a shiver down my spine whenever I heard them coming. In the Brownshirt bands everything shone like gold—trombones, kettledrums, drum majors' batons, glockenspiels . . ."

"Not the fifes—they were silver."

"Maybe, but that's not the point. They built an enormous bonfire and chucked everything onto it—books, musical instruments, you name it. Sometimes the people cavorted past so close I thought they'd end up in the fire themselves. My father wept."

"A bookseller would."

"I cried too. I didn't know why, of course."

"But you do now—we both do."

"I simply want to fly, Michael, that's all."

"So do I. I promised you that time under the oak tree, remember?"

"Yes, but you weren't as wholehearted as I was. One day—I don't know what you'll end up doing, not exactly, but . . ."

"All I want to do now is quit this place in one piece, and the sooner the better." I went back to leafing irritably through the pile of old magazines.

Lenz shrugged.

"It's like living on an island here, I grant you. How to shoot down a Fortress II, that's the only kind of problem we can conceive of anyone tackling."

"There are others," I said. "Take this article—'BENEFITS OF A MOUNTAIN CLIMATE. Changes Effected in the Blood at High Altitudes.' You see, somebody's expatiating on the virtues of weekend skiing, even in 1944. And we think ourselves lucky not to bleed to death at high altitudes—lucky to have some blood left at any altitude."

"You're like a rape victim who doesn't notice how much good it's done her till after the event. Unfair, I mean."

I was up in the control tower with the Old Man, otherwise known as Major Ohlshausen, our station commander.

The control tower wasn't a proper tower, just a big windowed corner room on the upper floor of the administration hut. The hut wasn't a hut either, but a really solid affair built of reddish railroad station brick. Every other station at home in Masuria looked much the same.

I Gruppe was airborne east of Wieluń, engaging some bombers and fighter escorts that had been deflected our way after a raid on Silesia.

Ohlshausen had spent three years in school with my father at Königsberg, so our relations were semipersonal. With the loudspeaker switched on, we were able to follow the RT traffic between the poor devils who were busy earning their flying pay and quarter pound of real coffee.

The room was warm despite the lateness of the season. Ohlshausen went to the window and opened it. A musty smell of damp leaves and mushrooms drifted in, accompanied by the shrill chatter of some jays. The airfield lay there silent and deserted. Beyond it, birches and alders drowsed in their autumn outfits of pastel yellow. The station commander had draped his uniform tunic over the back of a chair and was standing at the window in his shirt sleeves. Peace reigned outside.

Inside, we were hooked up to a radio spectacular straight from the disaster area. The excited, distorted voices of the combatants came through clearly:

"Watch it, White Three. Four Wolves above you at two o'clock!"

"Thanks, I'm off."

"*Achtung, Achtung!* White Ten, you've got a . . . Oh, damn, I've got one lined up myself . . ."

"I'm on fire! Bailing out now!"

Crackles and clicks. A distant voice:

"Get out of there quick, man—you aren't going to make it!"

Atmospherics, then other voices:

"Viktor, Viktor, we're in contact!"

"Me too. Boom-boom!"

Comment from Ohlshausen:

"That must be Strehlau—he was in night fighters. They always say 'boom-boom' when they're letting fly."

"One bull elephant gone!" said someone.

In clear: one four-engined bomber going down.

Another boyish voice:

"For God's sake jump, Rolf! You've left it too late!"

No reply, just the rustle of the airwaves. "Go on, jump!"

Nobody seemed to be jumping. . . .

Ohlshausen fell silent. So did the radio and I.

Then new voices and a new scenario:

"Help me, Kurt. There's one on my tail—I can't shake him off."

"I'm on my way. Don't worry, I'll fill his pipe for him."

A pause.

"Thanks, nice of you to light it as well. He's a goner."

Ohlshausen gave me a searching stare. "They all sound very bright and perky."

"Yes," I said, "very."

"I was a ground controller once, in Dakar. I often used to talk about my time there to your father—it took his mind off his own worries, one of which was you. You were still in school at Lötzen, and having trouble with your mathematics."

"I still do."

"I remember one evening in Dakar, standing out on the apron with my ears peeled for the sound of the plane from Recife. I was employed by the French at that time—my parents came from Alsace-Lorraine. We were hoping the weather over the coast would hold. Ground Control kept a blackboard with the names of the pilots chalked on it. One of them was Antoine de Saint-Exupéry. Ever heard of him?"

"Can't say I have."

"Your friend who's taken over the mess library—what's his name?"

"Lenz, Herr Major."

"That's right, Lenz. An admirable selection of books he's made—I thoroughly approve—but then, I gather his father's in the business. Anyway, he's got a book by Saint-Exupéry in the library—*Wind, Sand and Stars*. You ought to read it sometime, Braack. Saint-Exupéry isn't just a flier, he's a first-class writer."

"Is he still alive?"

"No idea. He may be serving with the RAF by now—flying a Lancaster or something."

"I'll get hold of the book, Herr Major."

The telephone rang. Simultaneously, the same plaintive, despairing voice issued from the loudspeaker:

"He didn't make it."

Outside, milky agglomerations of mist were drifting down the river like ships held clear of the surface by a ghostly hand. The clouds overhead were fringed with dirty foam.

The station commander was leaning over his desk, propped on one hand. His face turned pale and the arm supporting him tensed. I caught only scraps of what he said.

"No, no, out of the question . . . Yes, of course . . . No, naturally not . . ."

His Adam's apple danced like a Ping-Pong ball on a jet of water. I wondered what I was in for in the way of bad news about our returning units. Had two of our Staffel commanders collided on the return flight? Had a whole Gruppe been written off? Had a veteran Gruppe commander inadvertently shot down one of his own men?

Ohlshausen had hung up and was slowly coming to life again, but he looked shriveled—like a deflated balloon. He dropped into the nearest chair and sat there, dejection personified. Instead of confiding the worst at once, he made a detour.

"What were we talking about? Ah yes, Saint-Exupéry . . ." He absently stroked his brow. "Tell me, Braack. I hear you've got literary ambitions yourself. Is that true?"

An awkward topic. I merely shrugged, wondering what was behind the question.

"You should try your hand at writing sometime."

"About what, Major? Saint-Exupéry?"

"Forget Saint-Exupéry. I've just heard the latest on our jet fighters. The Me 262s—our only hope."

"Everyone says they're a great success."

"So they are, but their losses have been appalling. Twenty-seven out of thirty down in the last month."

8

Lenz had scored his first kill. No celebration—that he didn't want—but somehow it made me feel lonelier. He recorded his claim as follows:

> Oberfähnrich Lenz, Martin.
> Time: 1305 hours, 17 September 1944.
> Position: 1 mile west of Kaliscz.   .
> Altitude: 12,000 feet.
> Target: P-38 Lightning, USAF markings.
> Method: Fired from height advantage of 600 ft. while turning to starboard. Enemy aircraft caught fire and dived, trailing smoke. Seen to crash and explode on impact. Pilot failed to bail out.
> Ammunition expended: 100 rounds MG-151/20, 60 rounds MG-131, H/E incendiary and armor-piercing.

I felt as sluggish that evening as an obsolete Heinkel He 66 biplane. Was I really looking forward to our rendezvous at Shangri-La?

Maryla, studiously bright as usual, tried to cheer me up. Instead of responding, I nipped her attempts at resuscitation in the bud.

"Look what I came across today."

It was a snapshot of Lenz and me on a landing stage beside Lake Löwentin, taken eighteen months earlier on the day we reported to the Luftwaffe. Two virginal, immaculately boyish faces with cheeks like milk and roses, smooth as a baby's bottom.

Then I handed her my latest snap of Lenz—*The dashing fighter pilot pictured beside his powerful machine*—taken two weeks ago. His face was that of a forty-year-old with a lifetime of toil behind him. Lean leathery cheeks, dull eyes sunk deep in their sockets, innumerable wrinkles. Every dogfight had etched a memento into his skin. The helmet concealed prematurely balding patches, the once full lips had narrowed into a thin line, the chin and nose were sharper. Even Maryla was shocked by the contrast. She didn't say so, but I could tell she thought I'd aged the same way.

Rather than spend the rest of our precious time in mute consternation, I tried some black humor, Luftwaffe style. It was insipid stuff.

"At this rate, I'll be two hundred-plus by my thirtieth birthday."

She gnawed her lower lip.

"Don't let the war destroy you, Michael—you've got to fight back. Physically you can't do a thing, but mentally you can. Concentrate on something more important than killing."

"Like you?"

I kissed her. She fended me off, but not in earnest.

"I hardly know a thing about you, Maryla, do you know that?"

"There's nothing much to tell. My father was killed in the French campaign and my mother trained as a kindergarten teacher. I was in high school at Landsberg before they drafted me."

She rested her head against my shoulder. I stroked her soft hair, which had the bluish sheen of a raven's wing.

"What did your father do?"

"He was a dentist. He had beautiful hands—played the piano like a dream. Chopin was his great love. We lived beside the Kladow. That's a tiny little river which runs through the center of Landsberg before it joins the Warthe. He used to improvise or compose to the sound of the water."

She spoke quite dispassionately. As always on such occasions, I failed to come out with something appropriate, still less consoling.

"I had a little brother," she went on. "He's dead too."

"Dead?"

"Killed. We were on our way to Berlin to visit some relations. At Küstrin the train was strafed by British fighters. Typhoons, if you're interested in the technicalities. My mother was with us."

"If you mean Hawker Typhoons," I said in horror, "it can't have been long ago."

"It was this spring, before I was posted to Poland. They sawed him in half—literally sawed him in half. All that sound and fury, just to kill a little child. He was only six." Her voice was flat and expressionless, without a tremor. "He wasn't killed outright. He screamed, but not because he was in pain —at least, I don't think so. I think it was the sight of so much blood. Do you know what he screamed? 'Make me dead, Mummy, make me dead!' Just that, then it was over."

No tears. She was quite calm. Her outburst took time to mature.

"When this damnable war is over and we're at peace again, and if the generals and politicians get up on their hind legs and tell us we've got to rearm to prevent another war . . ." She lost her thread and began again. "I mean, if a new gang of political shysters claim that the next war really *will* be the war to end all wars, I'll be quite capable of exhuming my poor little brother and hurling his remains at anyone who dares to reach for a gun. At least *then* he won't have died in vain. . . ."

"Anyone who thinks the world's problems can be solved by force should be made to dig up a crashed one-ninety."

"And now let's drop the subject. What's done is done." She released herself and straightened up, shaking her hair into place. "Tell me about yourself. You read a lot, don't you? I always think it's important to know what a person reads."

I'd preserved a Trappist's silence about my own literary efforts.

"Well, I enjoy Tieck, Brentano, Eichendorff . . ."

"Eichendorff—yes, what a contrast! That's how flying could be—romantic and frivolous—but he's far too light-weight for these dark days. Tinkling fountains, marble mansions by moonlight, secret assignations in the castle grounds, forest glades, twittering birds and the strains of the posthorn . . . What a world! All very pretty-pretty, but it's straight out of dreamland."

"I find it helps," I said feebly.

Maryla rummaged in her shoulder bag and produced a slim leather-bound volume. "Here, if you must read the Romantics, read Novalis." She opened the book and wrote something on its faded flyleaf. "Go on, take it. Right now, you need it more than I do."

"Thank you."

"The microphone's monopolized by louder voices than his, these days. This is an age of blood and iron, Michael, but someday people will revere Novalis as a prophet. Then you'll come into your own, you fliers. Your journeys through the sky will take on a completely new meaning—they'll be transformed by a new kind of inner perception . . ."

"Goddammit, Maryla!" The words tumbled out like a stick of H/E leaving a Liberator's bomb bay. "Inner perception? They shit on inner perception, the powers-that-be—they always have and they always will. It'll never be any different. I'm not talking about your pathetic little Hitlers and Churchills and Roosevelts. I mean the really big boys in the background—the ones with the biggest clout and the biggest capital assets!"

Soft and melting all at once, she took my hand and drew me down beside her on the mossy floor.

"I love to hear you lose your temper, especially when you really think the same as I do. It's heaven."

And then began the fond half hour that preceded my return to the barrack-room jokes and beer sessions, the clangor of the workshops and the stench of the bunkhouse, the metallic insistence of the public-address system, the acrid smoke of Luftwaffe-issue cigarettes and the saccharine sweetness of Luftwaffe-issue chocolate.

And I marveled at her body, with its delicate limbs and soft curves, kissed her long slender thighs, buried my lips in the cool hollow of her neck.

Later, I read her dedication:

SOFT IS STRONGER THAN HARD, WATER THAN ROCK, LOVE THAN VIOLENCE.

After I'd waved until the figure on the bicycle had dwindled to a speck in the dusk, I made my way back to base. If it hadn't been for Lenz, I might have felt I was returning to a penal colony.

There were days that began with a spine-chilling scramble and ended in nothing more horrific than a joyride. The whole formation seemed to have been misdirected. Not a Fortress in sight, not a single contrail. Misdirected by whom—treacherous saboteurs or guardian angels?

On such days the wide expanse between the Elbe and Pilica, the Oder estuary and the High Tatra, lay sprawled there like an expectant mistress, pining for attention. Dark-eyed lakes, defiant mountains, pine-girt highlands, country houses set in splendid grounds, heathland scarred with sandy tracks and dotted with firs, meadows spangled with wild flowers, blue-tinged distances that might have been painted by Caspar David Friedrich: an amalgam of Stifter and Eichendorff, Fontanesi and Novalis, and all of it steeped in the music of Haydn and Bach, Handel and Frederick the Great. . . .

Amid Beethoven and Mozart, Tieck and Claudius, a small and insignificant token of our own activities: a tail plane jutting skyward like a rusty plowshare, fanned by the rose-petal breezes of Romanticism.

Occasionally, while strolling through the fields and pastures, we would come upon those who had been shot down.

Sometimes the impact had stripped off their skin like a leotard. Bumblebees and the sweet smell of putrescent flesh on a warm autumn day in 1944. Were there no vultures circling overhead—no vultures over Poland?

An assistant forester had, in fact, reported as much in the *Oberländer Volksblatt*. Rumors, rumors—numerous as the bombs on Königsberg.

Many of the dead had lost their ears. Borneo was renowned for its *koppesnellers*—its headhunters. Were there earhunters in the Government-General of Poland? What had the severed ears heard, back home in Kentucky or Massachusetts?

Had the dead airmen's ministers told them about hellfire, about the darkness of damnation, before they set off for Europe from Sparta, Illinois, or Bethlehem, Pennsylvania? Had they been regaled on the right liturgical formulas, mass-produced clichés, and otherworldly incantations?

There they lay, the boys from Babylon, Long Island, and

Frankfort, in a field of Polish grain. Had the last of the storks pecked their eyes out before moving on to more peaceful climes? Sometimes the white mass of brain beneath the almost neatly lopped cranium lay exposed like a succulent oyster. Sometimes, too, the faces had gone, leaving nothing but a clotted red mess. Where flak splinters had made a clean incision, ivory-colored nerve fibers hung from the flesh of the cheeks like intestinal worms.

The sky was our battlefield, but there were no shell-pitted moonscapes à la Verdun or ruined towns and cities like Dunkirk or Stalingrad. The air was riven by incendiary, high-explosive, and armor-piercing shells, but it recovered as soon as the tracer burned out. All that then bore witness to our battles was a fading blur of contrails.

There were no trenches or observation posts, no foxholes or bomb craters. We didn't burrow into the quaking earth, slink across forest clearings, and seek cover in ditches or behind tree trunks. Divorced from the ground, we inhabited a world of vapor, storms, and banks of cloud. Once the last contrail had dissolved, the sky resumed its timeless, featureless appearance. *Locate, attack, destroy* . . . Simple, straightforward formulas: open throttle, throttle back, climb, dive, pull out, port rudder, starboard rudder, keep going till the fur flies—if need be, jump. Operating instructions designed for the cool and calculating mind.

In practice, things looked and sounded different. Sometimes the barking of MGs and cannons was drowned by the shouts and screams in our earphones as bursts of tracer snaked around their victims like whiplashes. Sometimes I tried to memorize the expression of an enemy bomber pilot or air gunner: mortal terror or stark bloodlust. Sometimes I thought, *He looks like the man who cut my hair the other day* or *He reminds me of that boatman in Nikolaiken. . . .*

At other times our aerial corps de ballet whirled and spun

to no effect, as though the ballet master had taken a day off or the choreographer had run out of ideas. Nobody made a move, nobody fired a shot, nobody bailed out or was blown to bits. A peaceful morning's workout.

Until, quite suddenly, an invisible prompter gave the cue. Then the whole company came to life and milled around in blind fury as the scenario prescribed.

Once, just as I was about to let fly with everything I had, I clearly glimpsed a pair of glasses on the tail gunner's nose. My hand went limp. *The splinters,* I thought. *If his glasses get smashed his eyes will be a write-off.*

Sometimes when I sailed through the vaporous exhalations of the earth, girded about with steel and aluminum, I became a mythological bird. Earth, sky, and reality were extinguished. Why was I flying? Why did I exist? *Did* I exist? Did I exist to destroy others of my kind? Did this proof of my existence have a meaning?

Fate could have made things easier for me by leaving my victims unborn.

My victims were steel giants, hounds of hell, primeval Titans.

Some scenes recurred day after day. Glancing down in a steep turn, I would see villages with wind-warped hedges, escarped riverbanks picked out by the slanting evening sun, fields furrowed with miniature canyons, the river valley itself, dribbling gray mist in the comfortless wind of the steppes, churches and barracks, shacks and country mansions, prison camps and gabled town halls.

But above and amid all this, winged dragons, Flying Dutchmen, Flying Fortresses. Impregnable in the mass, but when one individual was crippled and broke formation, unable to keep up, it was at our mercy.

The bomber, hit in several places, was a hunted beast. It reared and stalled, reared again, and swooped still lower. With fire glowing in its entrails, it spiraled down as though trying to bite its own tail in mortal anguish, spewing smoke and oil and flames and fragments of metal and human bodies with the panic-stricken abandon of a doomed creature voiding its bowels.

Mellow autumn sunlight made the ground look as soft and yielding as a woman's body, to be gently entered or savaged at will.

The bomber exploded with a blinding flash. A poisonous black mushroom hovered above the point of impact for some time.

When it had been dispersed by the same balmy breeze that wafted a lingering scent of honey across the harvested fields of stubble, the noncom assigned to guard the wreck would gain an ever-clearer view of the tail plane jutting sadly, stiffly, into the September air, of bent propeller blades and blistered gun turrets. Perhaps, when he was dragged away from his game of cards and ordered to the scene of the crash, thin threads of smoke would still be curling from the cockpit and the sweetish smell of congealed blood slowly mingling with the resinous fragrance of sun-warmed pines.

Perhaps, if the noncom inadvertently blundered against the bomber's flank, fractured by the force of the crash, a contorted or heat-shriveled corpse would slither out and lie supine, blank eyes and mute lips proffered to the sky where their owner had so lately been king.

What of someone who met such a death in the sixth year of the war? Had he put his life to good use? Had he lived it to the full? Had he proved himself? For death he had been prepared, but what of life?

9

We spent hours on standby, lolling in deck chairs near our waiting machines. These weren't the worst times, especially when our friends in the other Staffeln were out at work. The air battles in progress far above, almost inaudible from where we sat, seemed doubly reminiscent of a martial ballet to the distant observer. The dancers turned and pirouetted and circled one another while we looked on from our front-row seats.

Sometimes, when the last of the Geschwader returned at sunset, the field would be wreathed in a haze like reddish brick dust. The fighters taxied to their dispersal pens and cut their engines. Then silence fell at last—until it was broken by the far-off titter of a tawny owl.

Supper in the mess could evoke an almost homey atmosphere. The coffee, genuine or ersatz, steamed invitingly and the "athlete's butter"—alias margarine—didn't seem to taste quite so strongly of tar. The other Staffeln often turned boisterous after supper. Compared to them, our own Staffel sounded like a deaf-mutes' convention.

One member of the Geschwader made his presence felt more than most. Wieschinsky recounted his feats of heroism night after night, but not flamboyantly. You could afford to act modest when you'd won the "tin necktie," or Knight's Cross, but Wieschinsky was still after the Oak Leaves and

Swords to go with it. He "squirted" everything in sight and "clobbered the oppo," he "filled the Yankees' pants for them" and "pumped shit" into any enemy airplane unwise enough to venture near him. He was also hoping to be "kicked upstairs" before long, and one day his dream of dreams came true: he was privileged to collect his coveted chestful of hardware from the Führer's own hands.

Wieschinsky returned from East Prussia cured of neckache, with the Big One dangling at his throat.

Night after night and slice after slice, he shared the rich cake of his personal experience with us. Ever since he had stood eyeball to eyeball with the Führer, Wieschinsky was a different—if not a happier—man.

From my point of view, his investiture had an unexpected by-product. Others might carve model airplanes or pore over chessboards, play skat or swap ancient cigarette cards in an attempt to make up for the boyhood they'd missed. I set out to record Wieschinsky's story in writing.

And Wieschinsky made it easy for me. His numerous repetitions of the tiniest details supplied me with plenty of copy, and so, as I sat in a deck chair beside my patiently waiting one-ninety, the first installment took shape.

Wieschinsky at the Wolf's Lair . . .

I was stuck before I'd started. How to kick off?

By enumerating his kills? If he hadn't made them the Führer wouldn't have sent for him. Nobody like me would ever stand face to face with the Supreme Commander at his East Prussian headquarters. You didn't get something for nothing, and Wieschinsky was a man of achievement—one of the most successful pilots in the Geschwader. Over 150 victories to his credit, plus a string of special missions for which he'd been decorated early on. He'd scored only twelve kills during his time with JG 99, but that was more than the whole of our Staffel.

So . . . No mass-produced slaughter, no visit to the Führer. I decided to skip all that and dive in at the deep end.

Wieschinsky had been summoned to present himself at Hitler's headquarters at 11 A.M. Four other highly decorated fliers were also to be even more highly decorated and would likewise receive their Oak Leaves and Swords from the Führer's hands. When he jumped out of the Fieseler Storch and landed on the damp grass at Rastenburg, however, Wieschinsky found no one there to meet him but an aide from headquarters.

The other gentlemen had been unable to leave Berlin on time, explained the aide, a youthful Leutnant with a glass eye. Their departure had been delayed by a heavy air raid, but the Führer would receive him all the same. The glass eye lent its sighted counterpart a curiously penetrating expression—as though he were being X-rayed, thought Wieschinsky. The bomb attack on Hitler was only a couple of months old. . . .

Rastenburg and the Wolf's Lair! To Wieschinsky, a mythical spot. This was the navel of the world, the place where every chain of command converged on one lone man who ruled the fate of nations. The town itself had been founded in 1330 by the Teutonic Knights and took its name from their castle. The proximity of the Führer's headquarters had made Rastenburg a household name. In autumn 1940, months before Russia was invaded, teams of engineers and laborers from the Todt Organization had embarked on the construction of a largely bombproof complex code-named the Ascania Chemical Works. Sited in the Görlitz, a forest east of the town, it outwardly resembled a health resort rather than a military installation.

Wieschinsky caught himself nervously recapitulating these facts during the drive there. For days now, he had been obsessed by the idea that Hitler would question him about them. The Führer's general knowledge was proverbial— everyone knew his capacity for broaching the most abstruse and irrelevant subjects. How long had he lived there? Ever since June 1941, and Wieschinsky experienced a sneaking sense of claustrophobia as he passed the outer checkpoint. What he saw, if only fleetingly, could have existed nowhere else in the world. He didn't know how Churchill, Roosevelt, or Stalin lived, but it was inconceivable that they'd been skulking below ground like moles for over three years.

Wieschinsky was a man whose composure remained unruffled by the tightest formation of Mitchells, but he was also a man who felt at home in the vastness of the sky and needed a panoramic view of the horizon as others need their daily bread. The farther he progressed into this labyrinth of flak towers, guard posts, and barbed-wire entanglements, the more he began to suffer from mental oxygen starvation.

There were warning signs in front of the fifty-yard-wide minefield. There were antitank ditches enclosing the whole complex like the moat of a medieval castle. There were barbed-wire fences between the various security zones: the one situated north of the railroad line to Angerburg, which accommodated Hitler and the senior members of his command staff; garrison headquarters and the communications center in the south zone; and Görlitz Station in Security Zone No. 3, where distinguished foreign visitors were welcomed.

While his glass-eyed companion explained the layout with robotlike indifference, Wieschinsky's eyes strayed repeatedly to the bunkers. They stood in the midst of glorious birch and oak woods like fossilized monsters—or, rather, like huge armadillos half buried in the ground.

My attempts to record the facts were often interrupted. For instance, by novel suggestions on how to deal with the bedbug plague.

"How about leaving a saucer outside the door of the hut, to lure them away? Blood and honey should do the trick."

"Why honey?"

"So they'll get stuck, the bastards."

"Where do we get the blood from? They're connoisseurs, bedbugs. They only go for human blood."

"One of us'll have to sacrifice a saucerful every night."

"I need all I've got, thanks. The bugs might as well do the job themselves."

"It wouldn't hurt if the medic drew it off with a hypo."

"No thanks, we have to do enough bleeding as it is."

After that kind of distraction, it always took me a while to find my way back into the world where holders of the Knight's Cross really came alive.

They were past the south checkpoint. On their right, flame-red autumn foliage was interrupted by the weather-worn gray concrete of the garrison officers' mess. Approaching the turn-pike of Security Zone No. 1, the Mercedes glided past the bathhouse, field post office, and garrison headquarters. These buildings screened the bunkers in Zone No. 2, where visitors and Wehrmacht Operations personnel were accommodated behind another barbed-wire barrier.

Into the holy of holies, thought Wieschinsky, as the car bumped over the railroad track and negotiated the final checkpoint.

"Even well-known generals have to submit to this proce-

*dure," the aide said consolingly, and transfixed him again
with his single eye.*

*Had Oberst von Stauffenberg made a similar entrance on
20 July? Wieschinsky knew next to nothing about the details of the assassination attempt. He knew only that divine
Providence had preserved the Führer and that Keitel had
promptly declared the Hitler salute obligatory for all members
of the armed forces.*

*There they were, the bunkers reserved for Göring, Keitel,
Jodl, and Bormann, for the Reich Security Service and Reich
Press Bureau. The Führer's bunker was situated on the north-
ernmost arc of the ring road—nowhere near the center, but
on the extreme periphery.*

*Strange, thought Wieschinsky. His sense of oppression be-
came almost stifling as the car drew up. These giant bunkers
possessed none of the dignity and grandeur of Greek temples.
He had toured the Acropolis while stationed in Greece. Every
fragment lying there retained its intrinsic perfection and in-
herent harmony of form. This was sheer gigantomania, stark
self-protection, petrifaction carried to extremes.*

*Wieschinsky had met Rudel, Mölders, and Galland and lis-
tened to their enthusiastic accounts of visits to the Wolf's Lair.
Mölders had positively rhapsodized about its yards-thick concrete walls. Odd, he reflected: there they were, but their effect
on him couldn't have been more different.*

*The aide leaned over and addressed him in an unex-
pectedly confidential tone. "You don't by any chance come
from East Prussia, do you, Herr Major?"*

*Wieschinsky shook his head. He'd hardly had an opportu-
nity to say a word. The aide had spent the whole of the brief
drive spouting information like a tourist guide.*

"No, Brandenburg."

"Good. The Führer doesn't like East Prussians, as you

probably know. The Masurian dialect gets on his nerves. His state of health . . ." He hesitated. They were now at the bunker entrance. "Well, it could be better. Few men have ever borne such a burden of responsibility."
Wieschinsky nodded curtly. "I understand."
Then they went in.

Lenz and I dodged the Führer whenever he made a radio appearance. We tuned into BBC London and dived for cover rather than be mowed down by his verbal fusillades, which we survived with the aid of British swing and American jazz.

It was pointless to try and follow what he said—we were in agreement on that score. You had only to hear those harsh consonants, those snarling vowels, that hoarse voice rising in an ecstatic crescendo of hatred . . .

Wieschinsky had, of course, realized that Hitler wouldn't measure up to the image presented by newsreels and newspapers, but the figure facing him bore no resemblance at all to that idealized picture: an elderly, bent, and bespectacled man with haggard features and a handshake whose firmness owed more to willpower than natural vigor.
The investiture was, however, succeeded by a conversation in which Hitler displayed much of the old mental agility and dynamism that had so often fascinated and enthralled those who knew him. Wieschinsky was staggered by his specialized knowledge of the one-ninety. Fighter pilots had evolved a new method of attacking bomber formations. One rocket-firing FW 190 would fly on ahead and break them up into separate aircraft, deprive them of cross-fire protection, and put them at the mercy of follow-up fighters armed with cannons.
Hitler knew the exact specifications of the rocket launchers

and the most effective mix of incendiary and high explosive. He could converse in equal detail about the firepower of the P-61 Black Widow and the spider of the same name—he knew, for example, that its underside was red. He lectured Wieschinsky with obvious relish for several minutes, leaning heavily on a huge table covered by a map of Eastern Europe. Although this made him look even more of an invalid, his expression progressively brightened. At last he put a genuine question:

"Well, Wieschinsky, how do you rate our chances against these American terror raids?"

Already pale, Wieschinsky turned paler still. The chill sterility and total isolation of the gigantic windowless bunker had almost incapacitated him. In the sky he was a king; here he felt as if he had been buried alive.

"We need more fighters, my Führer."

Why had he said it? Hadn't he been warned in advance? Anyone with experience of Hitler's moods knew he couldn't endure criticism. He was quite capable of cutting short an interview and storming out in a rage when told what he didn't wish to hear.

"Göring says it isn't the aircraft, it's the pilots. He says they're cowards. They don't press home their attacks—they sheer off without firing a shot."

Sure enough, there they were, the accentuated "r's" which he unleashed like rockets when something infuriated him. The fingers of his right hand drummed fiercely on the map, dislodging some of the colored pins that marked the latest situation on the Eastern Front. Warsaw was encircled, on the verge of capture.

Yes, Wieschinsky had been warned in advance. Greater men than he had battered their heads against a brick wall here. If big fish couldn't get anywhere, why should small fry like him fare any better?

Even so, he heard himself say:

"At our operational base, my Führer, there are days when we've a dozen more pilots than aircraft. We can't understand why the fighter construction program is still being neglected in favor of bombers."

Suddenly, Speer materialized behind him—a perfect entrance on cue. Wieschinsky knew that the munitions minister was all for building fighters as opposed to bombers and had recommended cutting back production of the He 177 and Ju 88. Hitler and Göring had jointly overruled him and called for a monthly output of four hundred He 177s and five hundred Ju 88s. Although Germany was turning into a sea of rubble, the Wolf's Lair authorities clung to their belief that more bombers were the key to victory.

Hitler's tone was fiercely dismissive.

"You don't look far enough ahead, Wieschinsky. We're in a tight spot. Our fighters can't cope with these indiscriminate bombing raids, I know, but that will pass. Then we'll need bombers to reduce England to ashes—then we'll teach the British a lesson they'll never forget!"

Speer still said nothing. Despite the chill atmosphere, Wieschinsky wiped the sweat from his brow. Moisture was streaming down the concrete walls. Buried alive, he thought again. All at once the situation struck him as symbolic. Blind as moles . . . These men were alive to details but blind to the overall picture. For that you had to leave the ground, not live in it. He yearned for his one-ninety—yearned to slam the throttle open and soar into the blue. Here he was out of his element.

"If only we had a fighter like the Mustang, my Führer! What a range, what firepower!" Again he was saying things he'd never meant to say, conscious of their futility. "We seldom get near the bombers themselves—the fighter escorts hold us at bay."

Hitler made no comment. Now it was up to Speer, who'd always backed the fighter arm until he, too, realized the futility of his efforts. Speer said:

"Aren't you looking on the dark side, Herr Major? After all, you've shot down plenty of Mustangs in your time, otherwise you wouldn't be here."

That was his cue to leave. He was being advised to eschew criticism, just take his medal and go.

As a child, in the days before Surrealism was banned, Wieschinsky had once seen a painting of a canary cage with a hand inside it. In the foreground: a pair of scales. Above: some screws and flying fish. The situation in the Führer's bunker seemed just as absurd and nonsensical—just as totally unfathomable. Were these men playing a part, and if so what? What did they really think? Who could guess what went on in their heads?

Another mental image: Sleeping Beauty. These troglodytes in the heart of East Prussia nursed unrealistic dreams of bombing England to blazes. The Russians weren't much more than a hundred miles away, yet they still planned to sink the British Isles with all hands. Göring had remained at his hunting lodge in the Rominter Heide till the very last minute. When partisans appeared, he'd moved to Goldap in a heavily guarded special train. Wieschinsky didn't know if the Luftwaffe chief had since decided to install himself here in his bunker. All he now knew was that no hard facts would be hard enough to jolt these subterranean visionaries awake. They even wanted to take a sensational innovation like the Me 262 jet fighter and use it as a bomber against England!

Hitler's parting handshake was almost ostentatiously limp. Speer shrugged. Had he caved in and conformed? Who could tell?

Wieschinsky surfaced with a sigh of relief. The aide had opened the door of the Mercedes and was standing beside it.

He could be back with the Geschwader in less than three hours.

He took another gulp of air and felt the blood course faster through his veins. The sky above the vivid autumn foliage was a dazzling aquamarine. A woodpecker fluttered past, tchick-tchicking to itself.

On impulse, Wieschinsky imitated the sound. He'd escaped from the underworld. The sky was beckoning.

BOOK TWO

"Between January and April 1944 our day-fighter force lost over one thousand pilots, including the pick of its Staffel, Gruppe, and Geschwader commanders. Each combat mission cost us roughly fifty crews. Our force is now on the verge of collapse."

From a report by Major General
Adolf Galland to his superiors

One fine day—panic all around—a Fieseler Storch landed at the base unbidden and unannounced. Out of it, plus aide, stepped Hermann Göring.

A squadron of Lightnings couldn't have thrown us into greater confusion. We dashed outside and formed up. When the biggest of the Nazi bigwigs appeared, some kind of parade had to be improvised for his delectation.

Few of us had ever seen Göring in the flesh, and most of us still openly or privately believed in his political integrity. Göring himself had commanded the famous Richthofen Geschwader. Although his Pour le Mérite had been won in the first war, how could any one-time fighter pilot fail to sympathize with the needs of his latter-day successors?

We'd heard rumors, of course. Rumors of the self-destructive vanity that impelled him to load his sumptuous uniforms with as much fancy hardware as they'd carry, of his displeasure at the fighter arm's achievements in the sixth year of the war, of his servile attempts to retain the Führer's favor by recommending our fighters for use as fighter bombers—rumors, yes, but who knew anything for sure?

There he was, anyway, having dropped in out of the blue in every sense (meteorologically speaking: visibility unlimited, wind light southerly, two to three). We would just have to wait and see.

In default of a Mercedes or staff car of any kind—thanks

to the latest Russian low-level attacks—the Storch taxied as close as it could to the repair hangar where our ragged ranks had been hastily drawn up. Out of it squeezed the figure so familiar to us from newsreel shots and press photos, wearing a heavy fur-trimmed greatcoat in spite of the mild autumn air. His ADC handed him the legendary marshal's baton.

"Heil Hitler, men!"

"Heil Hitler, Herr Reichsmarschall!"

We'd hardly taken it in because we were so preoccupied with our frantic attempts to dress off, but Geschwader-Kommodore Steffen had called us to attention and reported his unit present and correct in the regulation manner. Göring proceeded to inspect us while Steffen, hovering in the background like an attentive maître d'hôtel, tried to present the various Gruppe commanders. The Herr Reichsmarschall had taken only a few steps when it became blindingly obvious that he wasn't the Hermann of yore. He toted his massive body along like an overburdened, overage, cart horse. His bloated face looked infinitely old and weary.

I recalled something I'd heard from my father at the Air Ministry. The Reichsmarschall detested tours of inspection nowadays. He'd recently been shunning the limelight and didn't welcome visitors to his Karinhall estate or the Wolf's Lair. If so, why come to Grojecko?

He paused in front of Wehrmann, of all people.

"Any kills yet, Oberfeldwebel?"

"Not yet, Herr Reichsmarschall, but I'm working on it."

Only someone like Wehrmann would have risked such an answer.

Göring moved on, glowering, then halted again—expectantly.

"How many of you men have drawn blood?"

Numerous hands shot up in the other Staffeln, but Göring

happened to be standing in front of ours. Lenz, who was the only scorer to date, didn't move.

Ketsch leapt into the breach.

"This Staffel has only just been formed, Herr Reichsmarschall. They're the youngest and least experienced pilots in the unit."

"Then it's time they gained some experience, damn it!" Göring furiously stamped his foot. "There was a time when fighter pilots could afford to sit around swilling brandy and cuddling the girls, but those days are gone, gentlemen."

We felt sorry for Ketsch rather than stung by the injustice of Göring's snide remarks. Despite every official blunder and miscalculation, Ketsch still believed in "our Hermann," the father figure.

Was that all? Yes, except for one final incident—one which succeeding generations of fighter pilots, if there were any, would chew over for years to come.

Göring spotted, stacked against the hangar wall, some of the drop tanks that were slung beneath a one-ninety's fuselage to improve its range. As though to atone for his outburst, he observed:

"Very creditable. At least you drop a few bombs occasionally."

The whole Geschwader froze. Was it possible that the Commander in Chief of the Luftwaffe thought our long-range fuel tanks were bombs and credited us with bombing missions? It was. Later, the old pros claimed that it had been dark inside the repair hangar. Anyone might have made the same mistake, they argued. But not a Reichsmarschall, surely. If any man mistook drop tanks for bombs, whatever the lighting, no wonder he'd been rechristened Hermann Meyer!

They'd dug up a black Mercedes sedan after all—quicker than we took to intercept a bunch of Fortresses. Omniscience

Personified climbed in and purred off with his obedient minions, Ohlshausen and Steffen. A clutch of junior commanders followed in a second car.

The rest of the Geschwader stayed put, still stunned.

By nightfall the officers' mess was seething with rumors. It appeared that everyone on the base—except us pilots—knew precisely what had been discussed at the highest level. Verbatim reports were being circulated by storemen, orderlies, and mess waiters.

First, Steffen. Purely in theory, he'd earned himself a chestful of medals by insanely recommending the High Command to employ Polish-based fighters against enemy bombers deflected eastward from German territory. It was his bad luck that today's visit had shaken Göring's faith in the virtues of this idea. Steffen was particularly incensed because the query about kills had been directed at 3 Staffel, "that bunch of deadbeats."

"They couldn't very well dodge a question from the Commander in Chief," objected his second-in-command.

"Naturally not, but the Staffel commanders needn't have stood around like dummies. They could have shown some initiative. Some members of this outfit have scored a respectable number of victories. Veddersen of 1 Staffel, for instance—it won't be long before he collects his Swords and Diamonds from the Führer, if all goes well. The Reichsmarschall could have been steered in his direction—discreetly, of course—but no, he has to get stuck in front of a rabble like Number Three!"

"That's because he knows a rabble when he sees one, Herr Major, and a good thing too. Nobody wants a C. in C. who doesn't know the score."

"No, but he *would* have to pick on the intellectuals of Number Three—*that* shower of shit!"

Wehrmann couldn't stomach a downright insult of this magnitude, even when it was attributed to his commanding officer. He turned on the source of the information.

"Intellectuals, are we! If you don't button your lip, you and the rest of you rumormongers, I'll button it for you."

The fact remained that Steffen's initial delight at a visitation from on high had turned to dust and ashes. His shining armor had lost a little of its luster. He was further rumored to have uttered dire threats against us:

"Just you wait till I've finished with 3 Staffel—they won't know what hit them." And later, when he'd already had a drop too many: "They've only got two alternatives and they may as well know it—either they start scoring or I'll shoot them down myself. It's up to them."

But that, claimed Rotsch, was just as suspect an item of shithouse gossip as the one about the best-hated man in fighters, Adolf Galland. Likewise according to rumor, he was said to have insisted on a test of nerve when selecting pilots for a crack unit. Each candidate was required to perform a forward somersault over a gym horse standing one yard clear of the hangar wall. One hopeful failed to complete the movement in time and hit the wall headfirst, breaking his neck.

"Pity," was Galland's reported comment, "he'd have made a decent fighter pilot. Next!"

There was also a story that Galland used to send his underlings on ahead to soften up enemy bomber formations so that he could put in the last prestige-winning burst. This went the rounds of every Luftwaffe unit but had never been confirmed either.

While resentment at the latest buzz was still at its height in the mess, Lenz and I and a scratch rhythm section launched into "Tea for Two." For some reason, this innocuous choice drew a furious outburst from Wehrmann:

"Oh sure, you can play all right. It's your shooting that's the trouble!"

When Wehrmann threw down the gauntlet, that was it.

He scored his first kill the next day.

Scramble!

While Ketsch was taking off ahead of us and retracting his wheels and flaps, I found myself wondering desperately how he intended to lead his happy band against the enemy this time. At least I wasn't in his shoes. . . .

By the time I unstuck, Ketsch was orbiting the Staffel in a wide arc. He circled us with the assiduity of a sheepdog tending a young and inexperienced flock. Bächler's White 6 steered a shaky course from the start, dancing all over the place.

After a fair amount of chaos we all closed on Ketsch like children around a fireside storyteller and accompanied him west at thirteen thousand feet in a relatively civilized manner.

Slight inversion at five thousand, resulting in moderate turbulence. Fantastic visibility above the layer of haze—an ever-enthralling sight if only we had time to appreciate it. Everything below the haze looked milky blue: river valley, pastures, sandbanks. . . .

Ketsch called up Combat Control.

"Haybarn from Quixote Three. Are you receiving me?"

A haggard old fool tilting at windmills, or a solitary sage with his own peculiar notion of reality?

"Quixote Three from Haybarn, receiving you loud and clear. Elephants in Square Bertha Seven Ida Twelve, heading due east."

The Staffel stretched away behind and above me in echelon, an orderly formation armed with fifty-odd heavy machine guns and nine machine cannons.

Radio discipline: the alpha and omega of any fighter attack. Unnecessary chatter could alert an enemy and supply
him with clues to your position—even to your state of training. Experienced pilots didn't fill the air with a torrent of excited words, they attacked in businesslike silence.

The spider was somewhere above us in its vast ethereal
web, perhaps in the dazzling eye of the sun. One careless
radio message might set the threads vibrating and bring it
down on us from ambush with the concentrated power of a
dozen Lightnings.

"Quixote from Haybarn. Elephants still heading due east,
height eighteen thousand, badly mauled by flak. Party time
eight to ten minutes latest."

We climbed to twenty-three thousand for a high quarter attack. I hoped there wouldn't be any escorting fighters.
Equally, there was nothing I detested more than diving into
the inferno of cross fire from a score of multiturreted bombers
and nothing that relieved me more than the moment when
our engines of war dispersed for single combat. A duel on
equal terms: Don Quixote had yearned for that too, but what
did Ketsch's 3 Staffel know of aerial combat—how could his
flying schoolboys hope to compete with the superior guile of
veteran dogfight experts?

"There they are!" Not for the first time, somebody had
spilled his emotions into the RT. Rotsch? Wehrmann? The
technical requirements of combat reduced all verbal com-
munication to a single basic level. Individuality, humanity,
and personal initiative would revive once the war was over,
but it wasn't over yet—the contrails proved that. They came
from our quarry: two dozen four-engined bombers.
Fortresses, naturally.

Naturally, what else? Fortresses, Fortresses, and still more Fortresses. Above, among, and below them, Mustangs.

Battle was joined in a dove-gray sky.

Ketsch managed to get behind an enemy fighter with Bächler covering him. Short, crisp bursts, every one a winner. The Mustang's starboard wing disintegrated. It turned on its back and spun away. The pilot bailed out. The black speck with the still unopened chute trailing behind it looked like an outsize spermatozoon speeding earthward to fertilize an ovum.

Bächler's turn next. He put a short burst into another Mustang's tail and followed it up with a tempest of steel from every muzzle. Down went the Mustang, but this time nobody jumped. A mushroom of dense black oily smoke sprouted from the point of impact.

The Mustangs were into their stride at last. They seemed to shake themselves, doglike, as if they had dozed off during their long flight from the land of roast beef. *We* were for it now.

Six, seven—no, nine Mustangs pulled back abruptly and came thundering toward us from twelve o'clock. Were they trying to ram? We all broke hard to starboard, straight into the bursts of tracer that would otherwise have whizzed past. A deliberate ploy? Two of our fighters had already been clobbered, both from 1 Staffel. They screamed down as though in formation, simultaneously emitting plumes of smoke so pale that its origin puzzled me. A pair of chutes opened shortly before the two machines crashed, still in formation.

"See that?" somebody shouted over the RT, carried away by the heat of the moment. "They must be fairies!"

The Mustangs swung around like rearing stallions. I rolled on my side and pulled back into a series of steep turns. So far, I'd watched the scene with a sort of detached interest. Now I rolled, slipped, and yawed, kicked the rudders, pulled back on the stick, flung myself into aileron turns, blazed away with everything I had until the one-ninety bellowed, shook, and shuddered in every member.

No hits either way: in my book, total success.

But success was short-lived. The fight went on and we reformed loosely.

"Wolves closing eight o'clock!" somebody yelled. Nine Mustangs tore through us in a scorching dive.

"Let's get them!"

The Staffel broke up again. Each of us singled out an opponent or was singled out himself. Individual dogfights raged far and wide.

I kicked and poled through the sky, diving, turning, rolling on my back, plunging through contrails like insubstantial rivers of milk. Two airplanes swam into my gunsight and I blazed away at them wildly. The one-ninety gave another tooth-rattling shudder.

Missed—right between them. Just then, I myself was attacked by a Mustang coming in on my quarter. I broke to port in a steep turn that left me below and behind my opponent, who was spitting tracer into thin air. His instant's delay seemed to have bemused him. Now he couldn't shake me off. I stayed with him, turning tighter and tighter, then fired. Too high by a hairsbreadth.

Out-turned, the American rolled under and away. I went after him but was distracted by the sight of a fireball plunging past me, very close. Rotsch? Lenz?

No, definitely a Mustang. Its main planes, rudder, and bursting tires fluttered after it in forlorn isolation. No sign of a parachute.

A trio of Mustangs swooped on me from right ahead. I looked into their fire-breathing muzzles and poled forward with all my might. This was it—I was done for, finished. A momentary sense of finality. Then the Mustangs thundered overhead and I was still alive. I drew a deep breath. A tremor ran through my body.

Aircraft cannons hammering, windshields vibrating, puffs of cloud dissolving into amorphous jellyfish. Enemy bombers were exploding ahead of me. I made for the yellow flashes. Some parachutes blossomed into white flowers; others remained dark, compact, swiftly falling bolts of cloth—unopened buds of death.

Wehrmann's White 6 dived straight through a bunch of Fortresses, spewing flame from every muzzle. A wing tip broke off, and with it part of the starboard outer engine—a hit! The big ship, slightly above me and to port, began to spiral like a dog chasing its tail.

No fire visible.

Suddenly the Fortress straightened out and went into a shallow dive as though guided by an unseen hand. The pilot was fighting heroically to master his machine. Three times it swung, trying to run out like a reluctant steeplechaser, and each time he bullied it back on course.

Nobody bailed out. The whole crew must have been relying on their captain to make a forced landing. The Fortress disappeared below me and I was sucked back into the maelstrom of battle. Climbing rolls, dizzy dives, the rattle of guns, and—finally—the red light.

It was like a factory whistle signaling the end of a day's work.

About-face and head for home. In my earphones, the fight went on. A babble of voices, yells of triumph, staccato warnings, sometimes the sound of agonized breathing.

A whisper:

"I'm on fire—the whole damn cockpit's on fire. It—it won't budge. . . . Can't someone . . ."

But no one could. We were on our own, all of us.

Wehrmann's Fortress had come down only ten or twelve miles from Grojecko. It lay in an expanse of moorland dotted with marshy pools, low scrub, and stunted birches.

We drove as close as we could in a Volkswagen and worked our way laboriously toward the spot. The trees were veiled in leaden twilight, though streaks of red still lingered in the west. Shadows flitted through the vaporous atmosphere like spirits of the dead. A party of harsh-voiced nutcrackers whirred past. Sluggish currents of air stirred the undergrowth, laden with the odor of wet rags.

And then the Fortress loomed out of the evening mist like a ghost ship on the ocean bed.

There were three of us: Lenz, Wehrmann, and I. That was how we'd roamed the Johannisburger Heide in the old days, and Wehrmann had always been the spoilsport who shooed away storks, threw stones at shoals of fish, scoffed at our fanciful ideas—Wehrmann, the mighty hunter who showed off by drilling an empty cigarette pack with his air gun at ten paces.

Today he'd hit a Boeing B-17 at sixty yards, complete with crew.

A brace of army noncoms appeared. The rifles on their shoulders were the same as the ones we kept in our lockers at Grojecko, in case the airfield underwent a surprise attack and we had to play soldiers. They were 98-K carbines with captured French ammunition that didn't fit—pure show.

According to the sentries, who weren't overcommunicative, the bodies had been removed twenty minutes ago—removed "more or less," to quote the elder of the two, a gray-haired paterfamilias. His steel helmet was three sizes too big and grazed the bridge of his nose. Junior noncoms of forty-five and over were always family men. If they spoke at all, it was only a means to an end. Two minutes later you'd be admiring some faded, dog-eared photo of a plumpish, homely housewife and at least four offspring posed against a blurred background.

The fuselage might have drifted down into the ferns by parachute, it was so undamaged, but the wings had snapped off at the outer engines. The end of the port wing was lying thirty yards to the rear, where it had struck the base of a clump of birch trees. Before that, the Fortress must have shaved off the roof of a goatherd's shack. This had draped itself over the tail unit as though to shield the brilliant orange paintwork from the sun. The bomber had obviously attempted a landing.

Wehrmann shrugged. "A confirmed kill, that's the main thing."

Half hidden by tall ferns and low scrub, the fuselage looked almost like a derelict that had been lying there for months.

We gave Wehrmann right of way. He crawled through the nose, which was shattered, and disappeared inside. I invited Lenz to go first, but he found the prospect as spooky as I did and pushed me ahead of him.

Spanish galleons, submarines, or bombers—the interior of any wreck makes much the same impression. Except that this one still smelled of blood and excrement.

Absurdly buckled transverse frames, punctured pipes, frayed wires, tangled conduits, and partly disintegrated cladding. The barrels of the MGs in the forward gun position were bent backward as though in final, peaceful surrender.

The captain's rudder pedals were intact and unmarked. A felt flying boot was wedged in the left pedal with a fragment of leg inside it. The bone jutted up like the stalk of an immature flower. To the right of it, an equally unscarred, unmarked control pedestal painted rust-brown. There were cracks in the paint, which looked fresh.

Lenz jabbed me in the ribs. "Look, everything's gray on the left and brown on the right. Odd . . ."

The reason for the contrast became clear as soon as we reached the turret behind the cockpit. Its cupola was shattered too. The air gunner whose body had just been removed —more or less—must have hung there in his harness. Bits of him, none larger than an average fist, were still adhering to the shiny bluish metal of the turret superstructure.

This gunner had been manning a cannon. The breechblock had evidently sprung open when the Fortress crash-landed, and there behind the barrel lay an intact shell that had never been fired. It could only have been meant for Wehrmann, who had hurried on ahead. The belt holding the shell was the same color as the right-hand side of the cockpit—in fact, everything in the turret was coated in the same shade of rust.

Lenz said it aloud:

"The poor devil must have been liquidized."

We struggled on. The outwardly unscathed fuselage proved to be a frail bag of bones held together by skin alone. One nudge and whole sections of it collapsed in a cloud of dust and splinters as though eaten away by termites.

The waist gunners' positions displayed shreds of clothing and human skin, globules of molten metal, traces of oil, and scorch marks.

In the bomb bay hung an unborn child: a thousand-pound bomb which the Fortress had failed to deliver. It, too, bore scorch marks, but its destination was still legible, scrawled in chalk on the cylindrical steel casing: HELLO DRESDEN!

Wehrmann came and stood beside us. "Dirty bastards!"

For once, we were unanimous.

Right aft we found a chunk of the tail gunner's torso with the stump of an arm attached. The flesh was drained of blood and mildew-white, like mosses and lichens that never see the sun.

The only completely undamaged installation on board was the quartet of MGs in the tail. Metal was more resistant than the human frame.

The elder sentry walked up. "They forgot to take that."

He might have been apologizing for some slipshod housework.

Almost as one man, we turned and tottered away from the horrific scene like children emerging from a ghost train.

"Proud of yourself?" Lenz asked Wehrmann.

Wehrmann's lips tightened. "Didn't you read what it said on that bomb?"

2

Tiny Lauritzen had been dead since yesterday. He'd fallen, as the obits so aptly put it, for Führer and Fatherland.

Lenz and I escorted him to his last resting place—another apt description. We flew beside him until his death throes were over. Then he "fell" from a height of eighteen thousand feet.

Business had been as usual. First a trickle of morale-boosting music from the airfield loudspeakers, then: *Strong enemy formations heading for Silesia, probably intending withdraw east;* then: *Scramble!* And away we went again, into the celestial battle between the forces of good and evil, otherwise known as us and them.

We clawed our way up to twenty-five thousand and found ourselves facing more fighters than bombers. My engine was in a foul temper. It smelled bad from takeoff to touchdown and emitted sporadic puffs of dirty smoke. Nothing abnormal in other respects.

Ever since seeing Tiny's black deal coffin displayed in the chapel at Grojecko, I'd tried to conjure up a memory of his final minutes on earth. No, nothing out of the ordinary. All quiet on the Eastern Front.

He'd sprinted over to his machine. Had he shouted to me on the way—called out something profound or significant? Hinted at some prescience of his fate?

Nothing of the kind.

He'd merely slid his Galland canopy shut, like everyone else, and secured it. Had he cast a last glance at the surface of the planet on which he'd spent his twenty years? Yes, but so had the rest of us—no deeper meaning in that. No last words? Not unless you counted the usual formula: "Clear to start? Contact!"

Because we'd exchanged no word or glance, my farewell recollection of him dated back to the previous evening in the bunkhouse. Tiny had received a parcel from his elder brother, who was with a night fighter outfit at Twente in Holland. They were better off over there. His gift package of butter and bacon had also contained three tubes of real peacetime quality toothpaste (Chlorodont in the green, blue, and white pack) and a pair of genuine woolen underpants "for the Polish winter."

I couldn't stop thinking about these makeweights. All that trouble for the sake of teeth that were to shatter within hours against the flame-seared instrument panel of a doomed one-ninety. Woolen underpants in a blazing cockpit heated to five hundred degrees centigrade. . . .

We fought the good fight as usual.

Someone set a solitary Fortress on fire—a crippled straggler which would soon have crashed into the Baltic in any case. I saw flames gushing from the starboard outer engine.

Tiny Lauritzen must have seen them too. Did he guess that the next flamer would be his? Naturally not, or he'd have bailed out at once.

This Fortress—not a common or garden G, by the way, but a very rare E, obviously on some kind of special mission—was the only bomber Tiny or any of us got to see. Then we were up against fighters. Nothing but fighters of every description: Mustangs and Lightnings—even Airacobras, according to some observers—and all of them still equipped with that supreme luxury, a long-range fuel tank. As soon as they sighted us, the slender aluminum cylinders fell away like bombs.

Not a welcome sight from our point of view. Their movements were unhampered now. The prizefighters had stripped off their jackets and rolled up their sleeves. Now they could go to work.

Over sixty enemy fighters versus four Staffeln of one-nineties. Even Steffen saw the light. The RT crackled:

"Disengage and head east. Leave the Wolves to prowl on their own."

We all sheered off, including Tiny. Then we saw that he, and only he, had played Pied Piper to a gaggle of Mustangs. He was ahead of us. We tried to overhaul him and cut them off, but he, in terror, went to emergency boost to escape them. All he did was pull farther away from us. Steffen saw the danger, but our conscientious Kommodore had been the last to disengage and was even farther behind than we were.

"Four Wolves ganging up on White 3," he snarled over the RT. "Can't you bastards get stuck into them?"

But Tiny, instead of waiting for us to cover him, sped on at full throttle with the four Mustangs trailing behind him like a streamer advertising the U.S. aircraft industry.

Weather conditions: two eighths cloud, stratocumulus, visibility over Poland unlimited, wind light easterly.

Not a bolt-hole in sight.

We called Tiny and told him to take evasive action, give us a chance to catch up and take his pursuers from behind, but there must have been something wrong with his radio. Perhaps he'd fouled it up when pulling his mask on—it happened sometimes. We were out of touch.

If ever I went back to Poland or East Prussia—later on, as a civilian, when this senseless war had long been over—two eighths stratocumulus, a light easterly breeze, and unlimited visibility would always remind me of the minutes, the hours, it took for Tiny Lauritzen to die.

He roasted to death in slow motion.

The second Mustang got him in the port wing and engine. We hurled ourselves at his attackers and they allowed themselves to be driven off, but that didn't stop Tiny from floating on helplessly like a leaf in a gutter. Lenz flanked him to starboard, I to port.

Small and innocuous flames were licking over the wing. More small and innocuous flames issued from the engine cowlings. When they met, they were small and innocuous no longer.

And still Tiny sat there under his canopy like a diver protected from the waters of the deep.

I kept trying to persuade myself that the flames wouldn't harm him, but they slowly began to destroy his body. No, not his body—not right away. First to burn were his gloves, his flying suit, his helmet and safety harness.

Viewed from the security of my own cockpit, the individual flames resembled greedy, snapping beasts of prey—wolves, lions, darting cobras.

At last he was engulfed in smoke and flames like a fish baking in clay.

I assumed he was still alive. We knew from survivors that the airflow could fan flames in such a way that they attacked a pilot's clothing, skin, nose, and eyebrows without at first biting deeper. You could spend a long time dying in a doomed one-ninety.

For the first and last time, I wished my friend dead.

Flames are sadists—leisurely torturers. Was that a hand waving feebly in the red-hot heart of the cockpit? Was that an arm, already half incinerated?

Once, at the fighter pilots' school in Zeltweg, a one-ninety had crashed in flames on the runway. By the time we pulled the pilot clear his face was just a charred mask, blackened as though by a blowtorch. The only thing that moved was a trickle of unevaporated fluid from one eye socket. . . .

That was how Tiny Lauritzen died, trapped in a fireball of incandescent metal.

We buried him the way we'd buried all his predecessors and would bury those to come.

As the coffin was lowered into the mute soil of the Polish village churchyard, we yielded to the conventional illusion that in it lay a figure with hands folded and lifeless face upturned beneath the pinewood lid. Yet all the time we knew that the lid concealed nothing but a few shreds of cloth, the charred strap of a flying helmet, a fragment of felt flying boot or, at best, a stick plus a couple of fingers inseparably fused with the black plastic grip by intense heat.

On the other hand, they might simply have tossed in a few battered, shattered relics from the instrument panel: turn-and-back indicator, coolant temperature gauge, boost gauge, ignition switch, throttle button, rudder pedals. The personnel who filled these coffins were unsentimental types. They were reputed to have packed one coffin with useless scrap from the repair hangar.

The Geschwader-Kommodore's time-hallowed and unvarying words clove the misty autumn air:

"A loyal comrade and first-rate fighting man . . . example to us all . . . our duty to carry on the fight . . . did not die in vain . . . for Führer and Fatherland. . . . Fire!"

Did each of us imagine that he would be the next to lie down there, or did we all suppress this thought and see ourselves speeding through the sky like victorious and invulnerable Siegfrieds?

Tiny Lauritzen's mother was a frail-looking little woman. None of us saw her face because she kept it permanently hidden behind a heavy veil. When her son's coffin sank into the ground her black-enshrouded figure seemed to shrink as though part of her had gone with it. She'd made the long train journey from Hanover alone—terrifyingly alone. Those of her family who survived our blitzkrieg in the west had been wiped out by air raids. Her husband had been posted missing at Smolensk a year ago.

The echoes of the final volley died away. Silence returned and the startled crows flopped back into the grass of the surrounding steppe. The sky above Grojecko was dark with cloud. Sometimes, like a gesture of reconciliation, the northwest wind tore thin blue rents in the overcast.

We doubled back to base. The unaccustomed 98-K carbines were dumped at the back of our lockers, where they continued to rust away quietly. For how long? Till next Saturday? Till tomorrow? Whose carbine would stay put when its fellows were produced for another military burial?

We fighter pilots were the most heavily armed members of the Greater German Wehrmacht. Our arsenal comprised the following: one 98-K carbine with matching blank cartridges for ceremonial salutes and nonmatching live rounds captured from the Poles or French; one Walther automatic with which to defend ourselves against partisans if forced down; one flare gun; six to eight heavy machine guns and two to four machine cannons; and, last but not least, a gun platform propelled by nearly two thousand horsepower.

No one watching us jog back to base would have guessed this. We looked more like an ill-armed, defeated rabble. At the gate—III Gruppe had already been issued with a cockpit alert—we were greeted by the optimistic strains of a popular foxtrot.

Later, in the hut. Lenz's shock of fair hair appeared over the edge of the upper bunk.

"If we ever get out of this war in one piece, what do you plan to do?"

"Write about it."

"I aim to go on flying."

"In the Luftwaffe?"

"No, with Lufthansa. That's the only reason I took up flying, so I could become an airline pilot someday."

"I know, you used to talk about it in school."

"We promised each other we'd both learn to fly, and we have."

Silence. Memories invaded us both. A sentry tramped noisily past the bunkhouse. The tawny owl on duty in the lime tree outside the mess gave a muffled hoot.

"How do you see things turning out, Martin?"

"I'll tell you." Lenz's bunk creaked as he snuggled down again. "Another two years and the war'll be over. The Russians will surrender first, then the Americans. Once the fighting stops, Lufthansa will really go to town. I'll be captaining a Ju 52 by 1947."

"It'll be years out of date by then."

"I've heard they're designing a Ju 252 with a retractable undercarriage. Fantastic!"

"Where will you fly to?"

"In my postwar Lufthansa Ju 252?" Lenz thought for a while. "I'd like to be based in Berlin—Berlin'll be the center of Europe. From there I'll fly all over the world. Tripoli, Cairo, North Cape, Moscow, Velikie Luki, the Crimea . . ."

"What about America? Won't you be going there?"

"Sure, but not in a Ju 252. They'll improve the Ju 90 and enlarge it. I've even seen blueprints for a Ju 290. Fantastic, I tell you! That's what I'll be piloting to New York by 1950, if not sooner. Every country in the world will buy German. Junkers, Heinkel, and Messerschmitt will dominate the world market—Boeing and Vickers'll be floored by their technical innovations. Heinkel's already designed a 377, did you know?"

"I can see you taking off now. Berlin to New York direct in a four-engined He 377. A hundred-plus passengers instead of a bomb load."

"And the Yanks'll be grateful for the privilege of using our obsolete Ju 52s on their short-haul routes between Chicago and New Orleans, or wherever."

"But what if we . . ."

"What?"

"Nothing. Sleep well, Martin."

"You too."

Still later, by flashlight: essays in literary composition. I folded the big white intimidating sheets of paper in half to get them under the bedclothes and crouched there in my tent of blankets. The flashlight made it look more like a cavern. Mysterious recesses yawned and vanished as I moved.

Outside, far above, waves of RAF bombers droned past. They were the night fighters' baby, not ours. No air-raid warning? Yes, according to regulations the siren should have sounded by now, but good old Ohlshausen broke that rule on his own responsibility. How could we fly up to three combat missions a day and then spend the night in a shelter? When would we get any sleep? Anyway, past experience showed that these bombers had far more worthwhile targets to paste than a measly fighter base which would soon be overrun by the Russians.

During lulls in their relentless invasion of our airspace I could hear the snores, sighs, belches, nightmare murmurs, and farts of the sleepers around me. Whenever someone farted halfway up the scale and down again in rhythmical Morse-like bursts, it had to be Wehrmann.

Retreating into my cave and trying to write was my sole form of protest—the only way I could cope with my environment. *I write, therefore I am.* . . .

This nocturnal cave of blankets was a replica of my cramped cockpit. There too, with the whole airplane strapped to my back, I felt at home. I was charged with unsuspected energy by the steady breathing, the metabolic rhythms of my BMW twin-row radial. The stick in my hand imparted a sense of security. But once up there under the glaring sun, in the unrelenting nakedness of the sky, the big Galland canopy seemed to become a prism that collected all the enemy's lethal rays and focused them on my person. Then I longed for a curtain to hide behind and feel safe—invisible. . . .

I got this sensation at night in my cave. My Othello Brand Grade 2 pencil recalled the secure feel of the stick. Freshly sharpened, it emitted a faint scent of wood. Here I could feel at home, here I could live in peace.

All at once and for the first time ever, Maryla inspired me with genuine passion. Till now I'd simply felt we were drifting closer and allowed myself to drift, doing nothing to assist the process. But today on this sultry autumn evening, as greenfinches and chaffinches settled on the roof of Shangri-La, I suddenly began to assert myself with all the verbal exuberance of a twenty-year-old.

"Nothing's ever going to separate us again, Maryla. Nothing, no matter what."

"Well, well," she retorted dryly, "you've caught on at last. Why else do you think I got myself a bicycle?"

"No, I mean it. We'll make up for everything once the war's over."

"One night out on the town—one disgustingly extravagant dinner at a really swanky restaurant, that's what I'd like. In Berlin—yes, it'll have to be Berlin. Berlin'll be the capital of the world by then. Know any smart places there, Michael?"

Much I knew of the *beau monde* and swanky Berlin night spots! Still, I did recall my father's descriptions of the place whose name he always uttered with such reverence.

"The Hotel Adlon—we'll go to the *jour fixe* at the Hotel Adlon. It's every Wednesday. You needn't feel ashamed to be seen with me—after all, I'm an officer in the Greater German Luftwaffe. We'll be waited on by distinguished-looking old gentlemen in tails and white gloves."

"I want to find out what caviar tastes like."

"And French burgundy—only the best. Château something or other . . ."

"And *pâté de foie gras*. They say it's a dream."

"And we'll sit there surrounded by the cream of German society. They still go there now, my father says. Sauerbruch, Gründgens, Furtwängler . . ."

"I'd like to try some Armagnac too. Will you buy me one after dinner?"

"Why not two? We'll try the lot—framboise, Calvados, Madeira, port . . ."

She sighed and squeezed my hand. "What would the main course be?"

"Frogs' legs, you bet."

"Frogs' legs are only a starter, you sophisticated man-about-town."

"All right, how about *Kasseler Rippenspeer* in red wine sauce—something like that?"

"Sounds great, except you'll have to call it *Côte de porc fumée avec sauce vin rouge.*"

"Maybe they'd have a Masurian specialty on the Adlon menu. Whitefish in cream sauce, for instance—pardon me, *sauce à la crème.*"

"Fine, let's make it whitefish."

"My mother always puts in a knob of butter, one to two tablespoons of flour, and a pint of stock, plus salt, pepper, and chives. That's not counting the cream, of course. Still, it wouldn't do for the Adlon."

"Why not? My mouth's watering already."

"You've got to serve whitefish with potatoes boiled in their jackets—I ask you, unpeeled spuds at the Adlon!"

"Just call them *pommes à l'Adlon,* then it'll be all right."

"Our farmhands used to net crows, down by the lake."

"Well?"

"They killed them with their teeth—bit right through their soft little skulls."

"And sold them in the nearest town as partridges. I know, it's an old trick."

"Maybe that's what we'd get at the Adlon if we ordered partridge," I said with a grimace.

"Remember pigeons in sour-cream sauce? You soaked them overnight in a bowl of milk with a wineglass of vinegar added . . ."

"And juniper berries and sliced onion and bay leaves . . ."

"And a few birch leaves and a sprig of fir . . ."

She planted an affectionate peck on the tip of my nose. "Goodness, am I hungry! Nothing but stale cookhouse bread, cement sausage and coffee substitute, day after day, not to mention coal-tar margarine and a choice of molasses or four-fruit jam."

"All right, let's get back to the Adlon. We'll spend the night there, naturally. I can afford *one* night, even on my pay. We'll book a suite with a great big Second Empire bed."

"A what?"

"A Second Empire bed—that's what they sleep on in these suites. You'll have the most luxurious bath you've ever had, complete with expensive bath salts and bath oils and exotic soaps. And then . . ."

"Then what?"

"Then you'll put on a nightie—a really flimsy one."

"Aha! And then?"

"Made of this newfangled American stuff—pylon, something like that."

"Never heard of it."

"American parachutes aren't made of silk these days, they're synthetic. Nylon, that's it—*nylon*. And you'll reek of Guerlain or d'Orsay. *Madame sera très, très chic!*"

"Now you're trying to beat me at my own game. What's Guerlain?"

"A perfume. Anyway, this new American material—this nylon—they even make stockings and underwear out of it."

"You seem to know more about panties than five-course dinners. All right, what happens when I've got my nightie on?"

I toyed self-consciously with the lapels of her uniform tunic. A silver Luftwaffe eagle glinted on her left breast.

"For a start, I'll kiss you there"—I gently indicated where I meant—"and there won't be any stupid bird with a swastika in its beak to get in the way."

"*That* stuffed parrot? If that's all that's stopping you . . ."

Solving this problem took time. Outside in the deepening dusk, nutcrackers flitted among the branches. A tawny owl added its call to the evening chorus. Maryla sighed and sat up, brushing the hair out of her eyes.

"Hey, did I tell you what I found lying around in our communications center? A confiscated copy of something madly wicked—I must show it to you next time. Know anything about Kiev between the eleventh and thirteenth centuries?"

I drew her gently toward me. "Eight Ju 88s dropped in here to refuel the other day. They were on their way back from Kiev after bombing the city center—that's all I know about Kiev." I kissed her ivory throat. "Lenz would go on to tell you what he'll be doing in 1950, when he's captaining a Lufthansa Ju 290. There'll be several flights a day between Berlin and Kiev by then."

"It's a terrific book—black magic, sort of. Haven't you ever heard of the Novgorod Chronicle?"

"Never. By '53, Lenz says, we'll be flying the North Atlantic daily, the way we fly the Baltic now, in an improved version of the Focke-Wulf Condor. Seating room for at least fifty passengers, Lenz says. No competition, of course. The Yanks'll have lost the war, so they'll have to make do with our cast-off Junkers and Heinkels. If they behave themselves, we may throw in a few clapped-out Ju 90s."

"There's a Volhynian Chronicle as well. All about Prince Roman and Khan Otrok."

"Khan Otrok? I only know what an Fu G16 is."

"So you don't know the sermon on the Mosaic Law and the eulogy on Prince Vladimir by Metropolitan Hilarion of Kiev? Of course you don't—I'll bring them with me next time."

"You do that. And when the lean years are over, we'll be able to afford a house of our own and summer vacations in the Crimea, Finland, the Rhineland—you name it."

"Michael, you talk as if we're already . . ."

"Would you like that?"

We both fell silent. From outside came a whir of unseen wings.

"Yes, I think I'm in love with you."

There were eight hours at least till the next scramble.

3

The "Ten Commandments" were hanging in the latrine, coyly referred to as Meyer's front parlor. Newspaper being in short supply, some sacrilegious soul had collected all the spare memos and leaflets he could find, torn them into handy squares, and threaded them on the string provided.

I squatted there, separated from my next-door neighbor by a pithboard partition, and leisurely perused "The German Soldier's Ten Rules of Warfare."

(1) The German soldier fights chivalrously for the sake of national victory. Atrocities and pointless acts of destruction are unworthy of him.

(2) Every combatant must wear uniform or specially authorized and clearly visible insignia. Fighting in civilian clothes or without such insignia is prohibited.

(3) No enemy who surrenders must be killed. This also applies to irregular troops and spies, who will receive their just deserts from the courts.

(4) Prisoners of war are not to be abused or maltreated. Weapons, plans, and documents must be confiscated, but no personal belongings may be removed.

(5) Dumdum bullets are prohibited, nor must any ammunition be converted into the same.

(6) The Red Cross is inviolable. Wounded enemies are to be humanely treated. Medical personnel and military chaplains must not be prevented from carrying out their medical and pastoral duties.

(7) The civil population is inviolable. No member of the armed forces shall engage in looting or wanton destruction. Places of historical interest . . . divine worship . . . works of art . . . scientific and charitable institutions . . . merit special consideration. . . .

I tore the mutilated commandments off their string and put them to charitable use.

Rudi Schuricke and his Trio were painting a musical picture of a little white house beside a big blue sea. I'd only just made it back when they were rudely interrupted.

Cockpit alert, cockpit alert, cockpit alert!

I raced to my machine. Twenty or thirty twin-row radials whined, spat blue smoke, coughed, retched, roared into life. The first one-ninety was already rolling—Ketsch's, of course. Any Staffel commander worth his salt was quick off the mark.

Dust and shreds of heather whirled into the air, pebbles skittered along the runway, birches were lashed by the gale from our propellers. Ketsch and his wingman were already airborne. Flaps up, gear up, climbing revs. We were on our way.

I was one of the last to shake the dust off my heels. At least my pants weren't at half-mast. Some heroes had been known to take off in pajamas, they were so keen to die.

We assumed formation behind Ketsch. Ketsch would know for sure where the action was. Where else but up among the contrails?

Fortresses again. We prepared to bounce our umpteenth formation. No fighter escort? None to be seen. I didn't know which I detested more, the Boeings or their escorts. Boeings droned placidly along, content to be left in peace. Their crews aimed to be back in some English pub by nightfall, raising a glass to a successful mission, swapping drinks and repartee with the buddies they'd left behind. The Thunderbolts, Lightnings and Airacobras, the Mustangs and Mosquitoes—*they* didn't want a quiet life, *they* went looking for trouble. On the other hand, there was nothing more awe-inspiring than the cross fire from two dozen tail gunners in a close-knit bunch of Boeings.

"All Hounds from Quixote, close up, close up!"

An old, old song. We knew it by heart, thanks to postcombat pep talks. The only way to offset our definite inferiority in firepower was to concentrate it. Anyone who broke formation would be picked off by eight or ten enemy fighters roaming around with nothing better to do than wait for a straggler to commit suicide.

We closed up—tighter than I'd have thought possible.

Then everyone around me started going down fast. I dived too, only half aware of what was happening. I opened the throttle, built up speed, and headed for the enemy with the rest of the pack. There they were, the Fortresses, a shoal of silver fish looming larger and larger through the scud of their own contrails. So we were going to ram them. . . .

But we didn't. We didn't even open fire, just went on closing. It was all right, we still hadn't rammed them, but there were the dreaded cupolas, the MGs and multiple cannons.

I flipped my safety switches in turn. The reflector sight was already on.

I was blinded by contrails and rocked by turbulence—unable to aim. *Thank God,* I thought, *we'll have to break.* But nobody broke. We thundered on with Ketsch far enough in the lead to show how big a margin still existed between us and them. Now—*now* we'd have to break or we'd be in among them. . . . Still no move, still no tracer, still no lethal flicker from the enemy guns. Each side was holding its fire for an instant longer. Beware, professionals at work!

Professionals . . . Was *I* one? Yes, I was holding my fire like the rest. Another few moments of this armistice and we'd be through them—either that or dead and past caring. But we weren't through them yet. The tail gunners' Plexiglas turrets seemed to beckon like the gates of hell. *All hope abandon, ye who enter here.* . . . Then at last came release; then at last, three seconds from eternity, we all—friend and foe alike —let fly. A holocaust of tracer tore the sky to shreds. Tail gunners (in gray-green denims), churning airscrews, massive wings adorned with off-white stars (time they were repainted) . . . Break, *break,* BREAK!

I wrenched at the stick, pulled it hard into the pit of my stomach. The windshield filled with sky and there were no more Fortresses, only soothing, reassuring blue.

But the icy azure of this aerial battlefield was etched with chill white trails left by engines of war. The thing that flew and fought, swooped and fell to destruction here had nothing in common with the silver bird romanticized by those who pen the poetry of flight. Its menacing proboscis dripped death like that of a malarial mosquito. Nothing remained of it, when trampled underfoot by fate, but an unsightly little blob —a crushed carapace oozing blood and vital juices.

Mythical, primordial savagery ruled the war-torn Polish skies. There was nothing in them that recalled the dragonfly's balletic grace. Immured in the cockpit of a blazing airplane, the man who plunged to his death had time enough to learn the meaning of insanity. Those whom the gods would destroy, they first make mad—with terror.

We picked up formation again. The fight had barely begun—no, not even that. How many more times would we have to regroup like this? For how many more hours, weeks, months, years? Schoolboy soldiers had done the same before going over the top in World War One, and how many of them had returned to tell the tale?

Insanity powered the mental mechanism that impelled us to commit such acts of folly. Each cockpit canopy enclosed one body plus contents: bones, blood, lymph, marrow, brains, muscles, and the lust for life.

"All Hounds from Quixote. Drop tanks, break right, and form a defensive circle!"

We reefed around to starboard and formed an unbroken circle. A dozen or more Lightnings were orbiting above us, but Wehrmann, Lenz, Rotsch, and I were as safe in our own orbit as Lazarus in Abraham's bosom. This maneuver had been devised by a U.S. fighter ace of the first war and still bore his name: Lufbery. We circled, nose to tail, so that anyone who tried to break the ring would be exposed to the fire of the next in line. You could keep this up until one side ran short of fuel, which in our case meant the Americans, who had a longer return trip ahead of them.

All went well until Rotsch tightened the circle a fraction too much. The heavy one-ninety stalled and went into a spin. From my position on his tail, I thought at first he'd been hit.

Immediately, three Lightnings peeled off and gave chase. Rotsch pulled out three thousand feet below and emergency-boosted in a desperate effort to regain the protection of our Lufbery, but it was hopeless. The Lightnings hammered away with everything they had. Now was the time for someone to rap out an order and stop us breaking the magic circle. Too late: within moments the pattern had dissolved and we were streaking down to help Rotsch, outnumbered by more than three to one.

Fierce dogfights ensued. Above, a sky strewn with tracer and contrails; below, bathed in peaceful morning light, the fortress of Modlin on the Vistula.

Rotsch's one-ninety was past saving. The Lightnings shot it to pieces, but he managed to bail out. His chute opened safely and he landed without a scratch.

Things looked less healthy for the rest of us. We were all busy trying to shake off our opponents and sneak away. Only Wehrmann—who else?—managed to maneuver himself into a good attacking position and let fly. One of the Lightnings spun down out of control. Nobody bailed out this time.

Lenz had taken several hits in the wings and tail plane but was still flying. He escaped by making for the deck and crash-landed on a sandbank in the middle of the Vistula. His machine was a write-off, but he survived. He sat there with the waters of the historic river swirling around him, waving vainly at the distant and deserted banks. The autumn nor'easter pelted his unscathed but ill-used body with spray till midnight, when they finally picked him up, numb with cold and stiff as a cannon barrel.

As for me, I also dived for the deck and weaved my way along the wooded banks of the Vistula near Modlin, feeling genuinely protected by my camouflage for the first time ever. Its gray-green stippling harmonized well with the drab autumnal tints of the riverside poplars and water meadows. A trio of Lightnings chased me, lost me, and abandoned the hunt for lack of fuel. They climbed back to a comfortable cruising altitude and headed for home.

Arriving over Grojecko, I was treated to the spectacle of

Wehrmann making his approach just before me. He waggled his wings as if he'd just shot down a whole clutch of bombers. There'd be a celebration tonight, and the more I thought of this binge in Wehrmann's honor the wearier I felt. All else apart, it would be my duty to supply eyewitness confirmation of his latest kill.

But the defensive circle was no panacea against "lead poisoning," our jocular term for an enemy shell in the wrong place.

Steffen showed 3 Staffel how to break up a circle at will. The Geschwader had pinned down four Thunderbolts over the Pilica, near Piotrków, and the Americans promptly sought refuge in a Lufbery. While 3 Staffel orbited high above them, uncertain how to proceed, Steffen laid on a personal demonstration. He turned, circled in the opposite direction, selected one of the enemy, and dived at him head-on. One short burst and the Thunderbolt careened away, trailing smoke. Steffen regained height, picked out his next victim, dived, and fired again. A second Thunderbolt went down. . . .

His comment on this technique at the evening postmortem:

"The first fighter pilot to try it was Hans Joachim Marseille. He shot five Tomahawks out of a Lufbery over Libya on 6 June 1942. Attacking bombers is different, mind you. With them the old rule still applies: forget about tactics, close to point-blank range, and blow the shit out of them."

I saw Ketsch wince. The phrase must have offended his sense of chivalry.

Wehrmann duly threw his party—after all, two kills were a ticket to the Iron Cross Second Class. Champagne, vodka, and beer flowed like water, and no wonder. The quartermaster was a crony of his.

Lenz and I had been going for a stroll on Thyme Hill, but we turned up all the same. Wehrmann greeted us with a sardonic smirk.

"Well, well, if it isn't my dear old playmates from the Masurian backwoods. What an honor!"

A new U.S. Air Force term was going the rounds: "debriefing." Wehrmann explained its finer points.

"When the fat-assed Yankee bastards and the yellow-bellied Britishers and the stinking French Canadians get back from their terror raids, they celebrate their dirty work and call it 'debriefing.' One day we'll get the last of the swine, and that'll be the end of their 'debriefings.'"

Like every such binge in a Polish bunkhouse in autumn 1944, this one ended in a welter of obscenity. Every smutty story, couched in language of almost esoteric grossness, was rewarded with multitudinous bellows of raucous laughter.

"Say you've got crabs. How do you tell the difference between a male and a female?"

"Search me."

"Strain 'em through your teeth. The one that gets stuck is the daddy."

Paroxysms of mirth.

"Heard the latest?" Wehrmann deliberately turned to me. "Our girl signalers are being issued with new uniforms. They zip up the front to save time."

Lenz, who was beside me, muttered, "Come on, let's go."

"No," I said, quite casually, "we're staying."

"Don't play the hero," Lenz insisted. "Let's go."

"You go. I'm staying."

He stared at me uneasily.

Wehrmann came two steps nearer, looking inordinately amiable.

"Did I tell you about my last trip to Warsaw? I shared a compartment with two of our girls in blue. When I propositioned them at Breslau they told me to get lost. At Łódź they said I was a devil. By the time we reached Warsaw they were calling me a gorgeous brute." Very deliberately now, he took one final step. "Mark you, Michael, I'm not saying either of them was *your* bit of skirt . . ."

Half a pace toward him brought me well within range. I couldn't see his face any longer, just the cross wires in my gunsight with the target plumb center. Then I let go.

Lenz, who had seen the whole thing coming, said tersely, "Good shot."

I withdrew my throbbing hand. It was bleeding, unlike Wehrmann's mouth. My grazed knuckles were the only sign of injury. Wehrmann just smiled.

"Don't hold it against the lad," he enjoined the room at large. "He hasn't scored yet and he's scared—scared shitless of Steffen. It's preying on his mind."

He didn't so much as wipe his lips, let alone hit me back. There was no need. Lenz tugged a handkerchief out of his pocket and wound it around my hand.

4

Each day's routine was as unrelenting as the last. Morning, noon, and afternoon we took off, climbed, and searched the sky. *Locate, attack, destroy . . .* The formula never varied.

This morning the sky was a cool, pale shade of duck-egg blue. Streaks of mist drifted across the grassy steppe. The damp fuselages of our airplanes steamed and glinted in the early light, engines ticking over gently.

Ferry flights to Russia had been reported. The Americans were flying bombers, transports, and fighters to Russian airfields under the terms of a lend-lease agreement. Our task was to intercept them. How we did so was largely up to us, the one proviso being that we didn't disperse too widely.

I started by climbing to three thousand feet and trimmed out level. Beneath me were the dusty white roads that led to the Lysa Gora. I adjusted my revs, curved slightly to port, then starboard, and vaulted a few little stratocumuli. A small river joined the roads, twisting and turning in a series of convolutions so extreme that they almost overlapped. The outlying foothills of the Lysa Gora came into view, ridged and scaly as the backs of crocodiles sunning themselves on a sandbank.

Among the clumps of birches, goats showed up as tiny black dots. Beyond the first range of hills the ground fell away, giving the impression that I was climbing. Plains tufted with bullrushes, grazing cattle—white, speckled, or rust-red like the beechwoods to starboard. Villages clung to rocky escarpments like random blobs of mortar from a bricklayer's trowel. Plenty of dust still. The roofs, gardens, and belts of trees seemed half submerged in it.

The others were far above me by now. I opened the throttle and climbed.

The ground climbed too—range after range of hills interspersed with valleys full of overripe and rotting grain. Where were all the men who should have harvested it weeks ago?

I felt a sudden urge to swoop down on those fields and land, jump out and ask someone. I had a whole arsenal of questions stored up inside me—questions I was unable or unwilling to resolve in the river-girt seclusion of Grojecko, whose airfield was my only link with the world of man.

There they were! Two—no, three squadrons of Mustangs. No warning, no contrails, no bomber formations, just Mustangs on the prowl over Poland. Not a sign of the transports we'd been told about. We were all widely scattered when the joyriders bounced us out of the blue. Within seconds, tracer was flying and the RT had come to life.

"All Hounds from Quixote, close on me!"

A moment later:

"Hurry up, you're ambling along like a herd of pregnant cows!"

"Pregnant? Don't you mean in calf?"

"Save it, you aren't in agricultural college now."

To judge by what came over the air, my fellow fliers were a bunch of dashing, devil-may-care optimists. Actually, they were all scared stiff and yakking to keep their spirits up. *Get lost, said the flea to the elephant, or I'll squash you like a bug. . . .*

"Watch your tail, Braack!"

Someone had tucked himself in behind me. Panic! I pushed the stick hard over and then pulled it back against my belly, two-handed. Away I went into the steepest, tightest turn I'd ever attempted, a roaring, whining, hissing turn that sent vapor eddying from my wing tips like steam. My guts slithered into my flying boots. The sky and its fleecy puffs of cloud raced past until I felt I was riding a runaway carousel. The circle drew tighter and tighter, my body became heavier and heavier. I was now controlling my altitude with the rudder pedals. At little short of ninety degrees, the rudder acted as an elevator and the elevators as a rudder. A glance to port. The American was on my beam—I was looking straight at the top of his head. Like me, he was wearing leather gloves as a protection against fire. His legs were wider apart. He had the same build, the same set of the head.

He drew no nearer, I drew no farther away. He was an evenly matched opponent. Now he tilted his head a little to look at me. His face, to the extent that it was visible beneath the oxygen mask, resembled mine. I seemed to be looking at my double, my supra- or infra-ego.

Now he edged closer. I'd momentarily relaxed my pressure on the stick, so his turn tightened relative to mine. Back on the torturer's wheel I went, round and round. My brain was nudging the roof of my mouth, my hands were made of lead. Clouds whirled past and the sun seared my eyes, coming and going, coming and going. I was hurtling through space in a centrifuge. My anguished engine blared and shuddered, reeking of hot oil.

Another glance at the Gorgon's face. He wasn't gaining, he was falling back—flying backward, so it seemed. Then he drew level again. We would fly on forever like this, neither of us ever getting the other in his sights. . . . Now he was definitely falling back. I eased the stick forward, and at once he resumed his antipodean position. If I hauled on the stick with all my might, I would get him lined up for a burst. . . .

A sudden insane thrill of hope: if he realized that survival was my dearest wish—live and let live—would he call it quits? Would he sheer off and wish me happy landings? How could I convey that I meant him no harm, that self-preservation was my sole concern?

I raised my left hand, two fingers extended, and waved to him. My pressure on the stick relaxed again. At once, he dropped back until he was almost astern of me. A burst of tracer whipped past, well wide. Panic-stricken, I poled back with every ounce of strength I had left. The world went black and my stomach felt as if it had been catapulted into space through the soles of my boots.

Suddenly the whole machine shook from stem to stern, bucking like a goaded stallion. Then it flick-rolled to starboard, out of the racing, skidding turn. The human frame could withstand such treatment, but it was more than any airplane should have been asked to endure.

I was hurtling, yawing, plunging into the void. The instruments had gone crazy. What was the matter with them?

Nothing. I was spinning, that's all.

Should I jump for it—abandon ship?

I heaved at the stick. No effect.

Then I kicked a rudder against the spin as I'd once done in a tiny Bücker Jungmann biplane. It worked. The rotation ceased and I went into an accelerating dive. I cut the throttle and eased the stick back gently. The engine had overheated badly. The cockpit stank as if someone had tipped water all over some uninsulated terminals in a generating plant.

Pull back slowly, ease the throttle forward. We were flying again, the one-ninety and I. The whistling, roaring, and hissing had stopped. No tracer from over my shoulder?

No tracer. The Mustang had sheered off. Contrails were receding westward.

Mask down, deep breaths, wings level, cruising revs.

All limbs present and correct? Affirmative.

Vision restored? Black curtains drawn? Affirmative again.

Course? On course for home.

Half an hour in the life of a manual laborer working under high-risk conditions. Down tools and head for Grojecko, that wonderful, welcoming little patch of terra firma.

Four ounces of real coffee, a packet of cookies, and half a bar of Schoka-Kola, all well earned by honest toil.

"Congratulations," Lenz said eagerly when I'd landed. "I saw the whole thing from upstairs. I was just coming down to help you, but the way you shook him off with that fantastic roll-under . . . real class, I call that!"

I made no comment—wisely, as it turned out. Ketsch saw my exploit in quite a different light.

"The one-ninety can be a perfect bitch, aerodynamically speaking. You'd better get a couple of things straight . . ." He waved me informally into a chair. We were in his private quarters. There was a bottle of brandy on the coffee table—Hennessy, not that the name meant anything to me.

"When you're making these really steep turns, the outer wing—the upper one—travels through the air far faster than the lower one. That means you have to stay on the ball. Why? Because airflow conditions on the top surface become quite different from those on the lower, more stable half. That's why the vapor starts forming there first. Quite simply, the airflow at the outer, upper end breaks up. No more lift, in other words. The Americans have a term for that phenomenon—they call it a high-speed stall. Breakup of airflow caused by excessive speed. The air doesn't have time to exert any lift on the wing. Result—you flick-roll out toward the wing that's lost its lift, which is just what happened to you. They ought to have taught you that in basic training, but I don't suppose they have the time these days."

"It wouldn't have done me much good," I objected. "I didn't have any choice. If I hadn't kept reefing around till I went into one of these high-speed stalls, he'd have clobbered me."

"Exactly, Braack—there you have it. That's the one real problem with the one-ninety. From every other angle, it's the fastest fighter in general service."

"It certainly has the highest rate of roll," I said.

"There's only one answer when that happens—relax your pressure on the stick and throttle back. At your height you got away with it, but lower down—well, we've lost a lot of pilots that way."

"The Allies can't be sorry."

"Every airplane has its pros and cons. It pays to know your enemy's weak points."

"For instance?"

"Well, take the Lightning. Don't be misled by its size or twin engines. In the first place, twin-engined airplanes are a lot more complicated to maintain than single-engined. Secondly, they're just as much of a dead loss with one engine on fire as a single-engined fighter. They'll never get away unless you let them. A Lightning with one engine cut is slower than a constipated snail."

That night in my bunk, while enemy bombers droned eastward high above us, I had a recurrent vision of the face in the Mustang's cockpit—the one I'd half fancied was my own—and of the man I mistook for myself edging in behind me and opening fire. . . .

"Shit and derision!" growled Balzerat. "Where in hell are those goddamn night fighters?"

They'd come at last, the ferry formations, but they weren't our baby now. They were—or should have been—the responsibility of the night fighters: the Ju 88s, Do 217s, and He 219s equipped with Lichtenstein radars.

"Your feet stink," Rotsch retorted. "Now shut up and get some sleep."

Gala night in the mess. A number of Staffeln had been showered with Iron Crosses. Only ours was distinguished by its almost total lack of heroism. Wehrmann alone had a new kill to celebrate.

More than enough reason for us not to play, but we did—with a vengeance. Jazz was to Lenz what my diary under the bedclothes was to me: a form of protest.

We'd spent the afternoon rehearsing. . . . Lenz was nothing if not artful. After my last reunion with Maryla at Shangri-La I'd picked up my guitar and idly strummed a minor progression. He'd jotted the chords down, knocked my disjointed ideas into shape, added a melody line, and produced an arrangement behind my back. Now the new number—mine, according to him—was ready for a tryout. "It's great, Michael," he said approvingly. "We'll call it 'Blues for Maryla.'"

"The hell we will. I don't want her name bandied about by a roomful of drunken oafs like Wehrmann and Co."

"That's a point. We'll just call it 'Love Song.'"

"No, 'Song of the Steppes.' After all, that's where I met her."

"More evocative, eh—stronger associations?"

Lots of them, to be honest. A host of associations and memories, yearnings and cravings. Mawkish fancies, too, like "Heart's Desire from Light of Love, rendezvous Cloud Nine soonest . . ." Tawny eagles circling, birches bending in the breeze, autumn mists above the marshes . . .

"All right, we'll play it tonight, but it's your number. I'll only stick in a couple of improvisations."

"Let's leave the composer out of it, shall we?"

We rehearsed the latest BBC swing and AFN jazz for a full four hours. Lenz had picked up three new numbers from a British band led by someone called Geraldo—simply jotted them down in his numerical shorthand. He whistled the tunes aloud and we hummed, strummed, tooted, and tinkled them as best we could.

We were going into action at full strength tonight. In addition to the regulars, we'd acquired an alto saxophonist from 1 Staffel who claimed to have been a semipro—an Oberfeldwebel with a high opinion of himself but an enviable flair for improvisation. The other newcomer was a trombonist. Although his knowledge of swing was nil, he made up for it by copying whatever Lenz whistled, note for note.

Our session began at nine.

The mess hall had never been so full—jam-packed and buzzing with expectancy. Even before we started, tunes were being hummed and whistled in unison, titles called out and requests hurled at the stage. Pilot losses had reached an all-time high in the previous week, it was true, but so—discounting 3 Staffel—had the Geschwader's tally of kills, hence the general euphoria.

If anything blighted the atmosphere, it wouldn't be us.

We opened with a mild swing number by Helmut Zacharias entitled *"Gut gelaunt"*—a so-called *Augenöffner,* or "eye-opener," as Lenz, with his intimate knowledge of BBC London, would have termed it. This drew louder applause than on most mess nights. Rather than pull out all the stops at once, we inserted some solid German standards—Peter Igelhoff's *"Mein Herz hat heut Premiere,"* for example. By this time, however, Oberfeldwebel Krabusch of 1 Staffel had the bit between his teeth and was swinging his alto line with a zest that had the whole room spellbound.

Lenz, who took this as a personal challenge, switched to trumpet—something he seldom did so early in a session because his lips gave out too soon. We launched into a full-blooded rendering of a number that was really called "Aunt Hagar's Blues" and had been composed by the author of the banned but celebrated "St. Louis Blues," a black American named William Handy. Lenz Aryanized Aunt Hagar by introducing her as *"Meine Tante Helga,"* and she went down big.

Our drummer was flailing his skins like a maniac. Lenz, at the piano again, was better than ever. I was relieved to see him back there because it always made me uneasy when he reached for one of his other instruments. His playing was more Negroid than any dark-skinned denizen of the Deep South.

Next came "Studio 24," a swing number popularized by Fud Candrix. This had been broadcast by every radio station in Germany, but there was a difference between using it to impress foreigners in the hope that they'd listen to our news bulletins and playing it for pure enjoyment's sake. That was the way we played it now, and it finally coaxed me out of my private place of exile. With Django Reinhardt as my sacred inspiration, I picked up my guitar and really let rip.

We'd all had a few too many by this time—more than a few, where our audience was concerned. The big hall, which seemed to stretch away forever, rang with applause and glittered with officers' braid, and the loudest applause came from the most senior ranks present.

Our musical exertions didn't go unrewarded. We were lavishly plied with genuine East Prussian schnapps by the Oberfeldwebel of I Gruppe, a normally dour old sweat who now sat glued to his seat in the fourth row, clapping along with the rest.

Were we, slowly but steadily, blowing a gasket? It seemed so, because Lenz suddenly announced a number called *"In Stimmung."* I'd warned him time and again to avoid numbers which we could have heard *only* on the BBC, and his Germanization of Glenn Miller's "In the Mood" wouldn't have fooled a baby. Our alto sax star had to admit defeat, so I took over his part on the guitar, playing like a man inspired.

There followed tumultuous applause and scattered requests for *"Schwarzer Panther,"* which was simply a Teutonic version of "Tiger Rag." Shouts of "Barcelona!" could also be heard. Both titles were code words familiar to the jazz underground. Wherever these two protest numbers were played was home sweet home to all who still felt averse to dying a hero's death at this late stage in the war and preferred padding around on crepe soles to tramping around in jackboots. I knew, even then, that I'd never again wear boots if I survived and never trust anyone who wore them, however modishly civilianized. You couldn't dance in boots, certainly not to Glenn Miller. But then, nobody would *want* to wear boots once this holocaust had burned itself out. We'd have learned our lesson once and for all. . . .

To cool things down a little, we slipped in a thoroughbred German standard: *"Ich hab dich und du hast mich"*— another of Peter Igelhoff's. Fine, except that I was alarmed to see Lenz reach for his trumpet again. By the time he'd finished with the number, you could hardly recognize its German origins. It was all Virginia, South Carolina, chain gangs, Negro slaves, muted cries of anguish and protest. Did I say muted? Lenz used mutes that sounded bluer than Goebbels or Himmler could have dreamed of in their direst nightmares.

More shouts from the gloom at the back of the mess hall: *"Schwarzer Panther, Schwarzer Panther, Schwarzer Panther!"* So we played it. Or rather, we played something that progressively turned, chorus by chorus, into a pure and unadulterated rendering of "Tiger Rag." Krabusch valiantly stayed with us, even though he'd never listened to the BBC. It was our high spot. The applause went on and on. Cries of "Encore!" rang out from a whole row of seats, evidently occupied by fliers who'd been stationed in France.

Then, as the clapping died away, Lenz stepped into the glare of the footlights and announced the next number.

"And now we're going to play the 'St. Louis Blues,' based on a tune which American slaves used to hum during the tobacco harvest as an undercover protest against their own lack of freedom and their masters' delusions of grandeur."

Every stage has a trap door. Was I on top of it? I felt as if I were sinking through the floor—and glad to be—but I wasn't. I was still cradling my guitar and improvising, improvising, improvising as I'd never done before out of sheer admiration for Lenz's effrontery. It was the first time he'd refrained from introducing the "St. Louis Blues" as *"Heimweh nach dem Schwarzwald."* I couldn't bend a melody line the way he could, worse luck, but I did my best. Another storm of applause, one encore, and that was it. In nine hours at most we'd have to be ready to shoot down men from the country whose music had earned us our ovation.

We packed up our instruments while the hall emptied. At last we were standing there, all set to return to the cramped confines of the bunkhouse. All set for tomorrow's daily routine: *Locate, attack, destroy.* . . .

But the hall wasn't entirely deserted. Two men had stayed behind. Civilians in brown trenchcoats, hands in pockets. They sauntered slowly up to the stage.

"Tell me, which one of you's the maestro?"

Late-night bonhomie. I felt like stepping forward and taking the heat off Lenz, but it was too late.

"Enjoy the show?" he inquired—adding, although he'd guessed at once what the score was, "We're putting on another in three days' time."

"Great," chorused the two bland strangers. "Especially those transatlantic numbers," one of them went on. "They still know what rhythm means over there, eh? Do you like Glenn Miller?"

Lenz said nothing. I said nothing. Krabusch, who'd been on the point of leaving, jumped in with both feet.

"If you mean that new number he whistled to us—it's terrific."

The idiot! Hadn't anyone caught on except Lenz and me?

"He whistled it, did he?"

The ears of the two jovial strangers seemed to assume gigantic proportions, like caricatures on a national security poster. *Careless talk costs lives. . . .*

"Yes," said Lenz, "I whistled it."

The strangers let it rest for the moment. Almost abruptly, they changed the subject. A fine collection of instruments we had there. Personal property, or—ho-ho-ho!—borrowed from the local inhabitants? No, of course not. Probably purchased out of donations sent by the folks at home to our gallant lads at the front. Could they buy us a drink? Surely there was some kind of bar on the base?

Drink . . . They actually used the English word.

Lenz nearly lost his temper at that. We were still flushed with success and breathing fast. Our heads were buzzing with music. I could almost lip-read Lenz's unprintable retort.

Two minutes later we were sitting at the slop-stained bar counter. The canteen was deserted. It was late, and the first scramble might come at dawn. Krabusch, who'd suddenly cottoned to what was going on, disappeared without a word. They let him go, perhaps because they intended to question him separately.

"My son," began the taller and leaner of our two unwelcome visitors, "went to the Reich Bandleaders' School at Weimar. He plays the C trumpet. Incredibly talented lad, Günther—stick a score in front of him and he'll sight-read it straight off. You do that too, I suppose?"

Lenz hesitated.

"More or less . . ."

"I assume the scores you use are approved by the Ministry of Cultural Affairs?"

The smaller, fatter man gave Lenz a companionable nudge.

"Or did you get them from a friend on the Western Front —a brother, maybe? There's a lot of genuine American sheet music in Holland and France, I'm told. Nothing wrong with that."

I was getting sick of the whole business.

"We don't have any sheet music."

Braack, the subtle diplomat. Four eyebrows arched in genuine surprise.

"You mean you play everything by ear? Where do you get it from, the radio?"

"There are plenty of German swing bands to copy," Lenz said in an expressionless voice. "Take 'Bye-Bye Blues.' Heinz Wehner played it on his 4 P.M. program yesterday—that's where I lifted it from."

"Quite." A pause for liquid refreshment. The two men, still trenchcoated, raised their glasses to us. "So you pick up the arrangements by ear too, not just the tunes?"

"Yes."

"But Heinz Wehner's arrangement bears no resemblance to the one you played tonight. The same applies to some of your other numbers—'In the Mood,' for example. You may have heard that on Radio Bremen. Ernst van't Hoff plays it."

"Yes."

"The tune, though, not the arrangement. Your arrangements are noticeably different from the ones used by German bands."

"That's logical enough. We're only a small group—we have to adapt the numbers to suit our lineup."

"Naturally." The tall man gave his shorter colleague an inquiring glance. *That's it,* he seemed to be saying, *let's call it a day.*

The glance was far too ostentatious to be genuine. The shorter man stepped in at once.

"But I'm familiar with all your arrangements." He paused. We were there at last. "They're identical with the ones played by British and American dance bands. Would you mind showing us your radio?"

The trap swung shut with an almost audible click.

Over to the bunkhouse, pale-faced and gnawing our lips as we trudged there on leaden feet. We were streaming with sweat in spite of the cool night wind.

The others had already retired to their bunks. Our radio was standing in lonely but conspicuous isolation on the windowsill. Everyone stared as the tall man switched it on. ". . . concludes our programs for today," said an English voice. Then, just to put the lid on it, came a roll of drums and the strains of "God Save the King."

Three bars were enough for our visitors. Everyone sat bolt upright in bed.

"So that's where you get your music from," drawled the lanky man. "Do the pair of you accept full responsibility, or are your roommates equally implicated?" Then, once this point had been settled: "You realize it's a capital offense?"

That was all. The two genial gentlemen left the bunkhouse and the base in quick succession. We stood outside, staring after them. Lenz slumped against the trunk of an old lime tree and puked. His nausea was infectious. I felt asphyxiated, as if somebody had rolled me up in a rug.

"Give me the sky any day," said Lenz. "At least you can lose yourself up there. . . ."

All at once I experienced a strange thrill of triumph. Scared or not, I also felt vindicated. Till now I'd attributed my crass performance as a champion of the Third Reich to bad marksmanship and cowardice in the face of the enemy. Were there deeper reasons for this failure to acquit myself well? If so, I could only congratulate my subconscious on doing the right thing. *I* wasn't going to risk my neck for a Germany where listening to Glenn Miller was a capital offense.

We were still struggling with our rebellious stomachs when Ketsch came storming around the corner of the hut.

"What bloody fool let those men past the gate?"

"The guard commander, of course. They had special passes."

"Special passes be damned!" Normally so calm and composed, our Staffel commander was breathing fire. "They can stuff their special passes! Only one person on this base decides who goes in or out, and that's Major Ohlshausen. I already phoned him, and he doesn't know a thing about it. What the hell happened, exactly?"

Lenz mopped his mouth and delivered a brief résumé. Although I was feeling as sick as a dog, I tried to identify the real Ketsch. Was he taking our part because spies and informers were anathema to his old-fashioned sense of chivalry, or was he simply trying to save his own skin? We were

members of his Staffel, after all, and that made us grist to
Steffen's mill.

"All right, don't lose any sleep over it," Ketsch said sooth-
ingly, for his own benefit as well as ours. "I wasn't there tonight, nor was Ohlshausen. You know I'm no jazz lover, but
the station commander says what goes here, and he doesn't
have anything against your brand of music. So carry on playing, and if that means listening to the radio—well, how would
I know where you get your stuff from? They ought to print
more of it on our side of the fence."

"What about the death penalty?" asked Lenz.

"Death penalty? We're in the front line here. We risk our
necks every goddamn day, that's quite good enough. . . ." A
pensive glance at me. "Mind you, Braack, it's time you
started showing your paces. Nobody's going to lay a finger on
my pilots, not while I'm around, but they've got to produce
results. I try to be fair, though, so don't think I'm pressuring
you."

"That's fair all right," I said quietly. "One death penalty's
as good as another."

5

Today, airplanes came dropping out of the sky like over-ripe windfalls.

Seven Fortresses, four Lightnings, six Mustangs, nine one-nineties, and thirteen Me 109s belonging to a Silesian Jagdgeschwader—death shook all these out of the tree of life within a few miles of each other.

The Reichssender played down our losses and rejoiced. The BBC played down Allied losses and rejoiced. Listeners on both sides welcomed the absence of depressing news and re-joiced likewise.

I tried to imagine how it would be if thirty-nine civil air-craft had crashed on a single day in peacetime. I pictured the look on people's faces, their initial incredulity, their sheer hor-ror when the truth finally sank in:

"CIVIL AVIATION'S DARKEST HOUR. CHURCHILL, HITLER, STALIN, AND ROOSEVELT PROCLAIM INTERNATIONAL DAY OF MOURNING.

"A Lufthansa Ju 52 plowed into a residential suburb while coming in to land at Croydon Airport. An Air France Breguet crashed on takeoff at Copenhagen and a Junkers Ju 90 did the same at Palermo. Two Messerschmitt Taifun sports planes are reported missing in the Alps. A Russian Antonov airliner caught fire and plunged into the Pripet Marshes. A

Douglas DC-3 belonging to KLM came down in the Channel off Dover. . . ."

But it was wartime, and no amount of carnage could ever have quenched the worldwide thirst for other people's blood.

Wehrmacht Supreme Command broadcast a special bulletin, preceded by the customary fanfare, to the effect that seventeen enemy aircraft had been destroyed over the Government General of Poland. After hearing it, Lenz and I retired to Thyme Hill.

"I'm not one of these death-or-glory boys who drink themselves delirious after every kill," Lenz said mildly. "On the other hand, your kind of attitude won't wash either."

"Tell me one that will."

"I can't. I only know those bomber crews are killing our own people. As fighter pilots, we've a duty to stop them."

"You're always talking about symptoms, Martin. If something's poisoning you, you attack the seat of the infection."

"Bull! No poor shit of a fighter pilot is ever going to get near the seat of the infection, wherever that is, but one thing's for sure—anyone who refuses to fight the symptoms, as you call them, is guilty of helping to destroy our cities."

"Talking about guilt," I said, "I've remembered something."

"Well?"

It was another of my father's indiscretions during our last reunion—top-secret information restricted to a handful of senior officials at the Reich Air Ministry. B.S. hadn't balked at sharing such a sensational tidbit because he knew I'd keep my trap shut, just as I knew that Lenz, my blood brother, would keep mum too. Once he'd sworn not to breathe a word, I described an episode from the present war—one that couldn't be publicized until it was over.

"You remember that raid on Hamburg during the night of 24–25 July 1943? *We* know the facts, even if the general public doesn't. *We* know the RAF sent over seven hundred and ninety-one bombers and lost only twelve—twelve in all. So why did our air defenses take such a hammering? Why did Bomber Command turn Hamburg into a blazing inferno and lose only a dozen planes in the process?"

"An aunt of mine was killed in that raid," Lenz said quietly.

"But who was guilty? The bomber pilots? 'Bomber' Harris? Winston Churchill? Our own Hermann Meyer? People like me, who feel inhibited about shooting enemy fliers? The answer isn't as easy as you think."

"You tell me."

"Right, but first you'll have to imagine a change of time and place. The place was Aalborg in Denmark and the date was 9 May 1943, ten or eleven weeks before the Hamburg fire storms left thousands of corpses barbecued in molten asphalt."

"For God's sake, Michael!"

"I'm only setting the scene. Based at Aalborg were some Ju 88s which operated against enemy aircraft carrying strategic supplies to England from neutral Sweden. That meant they regularly patrolled the stretch between Aalborg and Kristiansand in Norway. Well, on 9 May 1943 one of these night fighters—registration Dora Five—landed at Kristiansand to refuel before flying back to Aalborg. The crew consisted of Leutnant Heinrich Schmitt and two noncoms, Oberfeldwebel Paul Rosenburger and Oberfeldwebel Erich Kantwill. At 1650, Dora Five took off on her return flight across the Skagerrak."

I could picture the whole sequence of events—one of the most dramatic and momentous in the present war. I saw Dora Five climb away from the Norwegian coast, heading for

Aalborg. Twenty minutes after takeoff she began to lose height. Beneath her lay the heaving, storm-tossed Skagerrak, lashed by spring gales. Kantwill, the radio operator, tapped out a distress signal: *Engine on fire, ditching . . . Engine on fire, ditching . . .*

Then silence.

I saw the airplane dip toward the foaming sea. Then, thirty feet above the waves, Leutnant Schmitt leveled off and turned west. Neither of his engines was on fire. Everything on board was fine.

"In other words, treason and desertion." Lenz gave a low whistle. "So they'd been planning to bolt for merrie England all the time. Still, you don't go waltzing up to the British coast in broad daylight, not in a Ju 88. They must have reckoned on being intercepted and shot down, surely?"

"My father suspects that Leutnant Schmitt had been working for the Allies since 1940. His father was on Foreign Minister Ribbentrop's staff. Schmitt may have contacted the British Secret Service through him, either in Switzerland or Portugal."

I omitted to mention something else my father had told me. "Michael," he'd said, "I'm not concerned with the bare facts. I just want you to know what people are capable of and what they can be induced to do, one way or the other, for better or worse. Never trust anyone, that's the moral."

Then began the ticklish, nerve-racking approach to the British coast. The Ju 88 made her landfall near the RAF base at Dyce, not far from Aberdeen. Had the Secret Intelligence Service been forewarned or not? Nobody on board knew.

Suddenly, some Spitfires appeared.

Schmitt lowered his undercarriage. In panic, or as a prearranged signal to the British fighters? Whatever the truth, the Spitfires' Brownings remained silent. The antiaircraft guns at

RAF Dyce blazed away when Dora Five made her approach, but she touched down safely. The crew were promplty detained and taken away for interrogation.

"And what's the connection between this saga and the raid on Hamburg?"

"I'll tell you. The very next day, a squadron leader flew up from Farnborough, took charge of Dora Five, and ferried her back to the south of England with a Beaufighter escort. First, though, he stripped her of a vital piece of equipment and sent it south by road for safety's sake."

"*Now* I'm beginning to see."

"Exactly. Dora Five had one of our first airborne radars installed in her nose—the FuG 202 Lichtenstein, a Telefunken gadget operating on four-eighty megacycles. We heard miraculous stories about it in training, remember?"

"Yes, and it helped our night fighters to pick off a lot of RAF bombers. Until then . . ."

Too true. With the FuG 202 in their possession, the British were able to experiment at leisure with methods of jamming and confusing it. Dora Five was given an RAF paint job and the registration PJ 876. In June, a Halifax bomber was used as a guinea pig for mock night-fighter attacks. The British had already been experimenting with a jamming system code-named Window, and tests carried out with the aid of their abducted Dora Five showed them to be on the right track. The trick consisted in releasing innumerable little strips of metal foil. The Lichtenstein proved allergic to them and registered so-called snowstorm echoes. Each of these echoes might have represented an enemy bomber; equally, it might not. The Lichtenstein's bafflement was so complete as to render it virtually useless.

"Then came 25 July and that appalling raid on Hamburg. The British were able to take off that evening with an easy mind. 'Window' confused the radar-controlled flak as well as the night fighters, which was why their scoring rate took such a disastrous nose dive."

"So much for the subject of guilt, eh? Tinfoil equals total confusion."

"People get confused too," I said, "not just radar sets."

Which, though true, sounded trivial.

I took Lenz along to meet Maryla—the only outsider I ever admitted to Shangri-La.

Maryla took to him at once. We sat down on the mossy ground with our backs against the wall of the shack while a milky sun percolated the treetops. Maryla, who'd managed to purloin half a bottle of brandy from somewhere, dealt out three paper cups.

Lenz was diffident and reticent. He stared as reverently at Maryla as if she were a Madonna—which to me she was. It must have been ages since he'd chatted informally with a member of the opposite sex. We both stayed put when our roommates made nocturnal forays to Grojecko, where a few Polish whores and fun-loving girl auxiliaries were always on the lookout for male companionship.

Conversation lagged badly. Maryla said she'd gathered from me that Lenz planned to carry on flying after the war.

"That's right."

"As an airline pilot?"

"Yes, with Lufthansa."

"They'll have an enormous network by then."

"Yes . . ."

"And good pilots will be at a premium. So many of them are getting killed."

Talking more to me than Maryla, Lenz gradually got into his stride. "I wonder if it'll be the same in civilian life—I mean, will everyone who's a household name have to earn his reputation at other people's expense?"

"No," I said firmly. "It'd be a dog's life if the same old rivalries persisted, the same—sorry, Maryla—the same ass-licking attitude. There'll be no more of this rank-conscious fawning on the mighty and trampling on lesser mortals."

I knew I could always galvanize Lenz with a pinch or two of idealism. Sure enough, he rose like a fish.

"Who says? The heroes of today will be back on top in two minutes flat, take it from me. It's human nature to kowtow to people with thicker skins and sharper elbows."

"But you'll be joining a civil airline. You won't have to jostle for medals and promotion in Lufthansa."

"You poor innocent! What do you think went on in the prewar Lufthansa setup? What about the big-time pioneers who opened up new routes or made trailblazing flights over deserts and mountains? They got the glory, but how many men did they elbow aside for the sake of the extra prestige?"

"But look," Maryla protested, "you can write off any form of personal achievement like that. You're dismissing the existence of heroism."

Lenz and I exchanged a glance. We thought alike there. Where we differed was a point I reverted to a moment later.

"Still, there won't be any more jockeying for position when the war's over. Everyone will get an even chance."

Lenz gave a sardonic grin but said nothing.

Maryla passed the bottle around. She was looking lovelier than ever today. Her eyes sparkled like dew at sunrise. She turned to Lenz.

"I tell you what. *You'll* make all the big pioneering flights for Lufthansa after the war, and *you*"—she patted my hand

—"you'll convert his pioneering achievements into great literature. If that isn't a fair division of labor between friends, I don't know what is."

"At least he'll be able to do his writing at a desk," said Lenz. "He won't have to sneak under the covers at night."

Maryla cocked an eyebrow at me. "Is that what you do?"

"Now and then."

"Sounds a bit uncomfortable, scribbling by flashlight in a cramped little tent of Wehrmacht-issue blankets." Then, when I didn't answer: "I know, Michael, real life's a lot less comfortable. It's your way of coping with it—your form of protest."

"Actually," I said, "I regard our music-making as a protest."

"That too, yes, though I've never heard you play together. Someday, when this is all behind us—safely behind us . . ."

"Stop it, Maryla. Nowadays they give people medals for sounding as optimistic as that."

"I'm only thinking of your future as a writer. One day the critics will say, 'He burst upon the literary scene out of nowhere. He emerged from the forests . . .' Not any old forests, mind you—no—'He emerged from the forests of his boyhood, from the mystical, magical depths of the Masurian backwoods!'"

Maryla was unusually lighthearted today. She refilled our cups with brandy, and the very act of pouring lent the atmosphere a touch of domesticity. In an age of surrogates, Shangri-La had become a substitute for my childhood. It represented security, warmth, young love.

I was five years old. Slipping out of bed, I padded barefoot to the front door, and there it was, hanging on the knocker: a white drawstring bag full of breakfast rolls. The whole bag seemed to glow with the warmth of the oven. I buried my damp little nose in the scent of fresh bread—of security. All was well with the world. . . .

Later, after Lenz had left, I told Maryla about our jam session and its aftermath. She turned pale.

"But, Michael, don't you realize what could happen to you?"

"What do you expect me to do about it?"

"Well, if you were one of the Staffel commander's blue-eyed boys like that—that Wehrmann creature you're always telling me about . . ."

"What then?"

"Well, I mean, if only you'd shot *something* down. Then you'd be sitting pretty. Couldn't you manage *one*—just an itty-bitty one?"

"Would you like me to?"

"Damn it, Michael, you're in real trouble. They'll court-martial you for listening to enemy broadcasts—that is, unless . . ."

"I said, would you like me to?"

"No! No, but I'm feeling scared all of a sudden."

6

Early morning. Gossamer threads of cloud were veiling the sky in delicate silver tissue.

I received a prebreakfast summons to the Staffel commander's quarters. Ketsch himself was already at the table. With the practiced eye of a junior pilot, I noted at once that he enjoyed better fare than we did in the mess: a brace of fried eggs, a double ration of cookies, white bread, a bowl of fruit, a pitcher of apple juice, plenty of real coffee. He was welcome to the lot. Anyone who had to answer to Steffen whenever 3 Staffel flew a combat mission had earned it in full.

Ketsch's genially unmilitary manner boded no good.

"Sit down. Coffee?"

He was lounging there in his blue Luftwaffe shirt. No tie, belt, or boots.

"Thank you, Herr Hauptmann."

Twice as strong as ours. The aroma alone was enough to drive you crazy. Real coffee . . . it had been worth joining the air force just for that.

He pushed his tray indifferently aside. One of his eggs was untouched and going cold.

"I've received a formal complaint about you from a senior fellow pilot of yours, Oberfeldwebel Wehrmann. Can you guess what it's about?"

"No, Herr Hauptmann."

Ketsch picked up a sheet of paper and scrutinized me over the top.

"It says here, 'Yesterday, while I was recording my third confirmed kill on my tail plane, I was approached by a roommate, Oberfähnrich Braack. He proceeded to make the following offensive remark . . .'" Ketsch decided to paraphrase the original text. "Apparently, you asked him why he was painting white lines on his tail plane when it would have been more appropriate, in his particular case, to substitute a—a certain portion of the female anatomy. Is that true?"

"Yes, Herr Hauptmann. It's all the same to Wehrmann whether he squirts a Mustang or screws a woman."

"The finest weapon a man possesses is the one he's born with. You may be young, Braack, but you ought to know that by now."

"In that case my remark wasn't offensive."

"If Wehrmann wants to equate Mustangs with women, let him. The main thing is, he shoots them down."

"Does that mean you're in favor of defiling our racial heritage, Herr Hauptmann?"

"Come again?"

"There are Negroes and Jews in the U.S. Air Force. Anyone who engages in sexual intercourse with persons of inferior racial stock is liable, under Himmler's decree dated . . ."

"I love your sense of humor sometimes, Braack, but it's macabre—*and* dangerous. I can't cover for you much longer. Wehrmann outranks you. I ought to report this to Steffen, by rights, and then you'd really be for it. The best thing you can do is chalk up a kill at last, for my sake as well as your own."

"And if I don't?"

"Then the softest number you can hope for is a transfer to a Sturmstaffel. A voluntary transfer, naturally."

That evening I skimmed through a Propaganda Company report on Sturmstaffeln in the magazine corner of the library. It was headed, "DEATH'S-HEAD FIGHTERS, THE LATEST ADDITION TO GERMANY'S AIR DEFENSES."

"Enemy fighters," the article proclaimed, "are now being shot down at point-blank range or—if all else fails—rammed."

I read on.

"During the lightning air battle over Oschersleben, in which these units were first engaged, two enemy bomber formations comprising fifty-four four-engined aircraft were totally destroyed. . . . Only ten Americans out of more than 540 managed to escape death. Ever since then, the recurrent question among enemy bomber crews has been: 'Will it be our turn next?' The enemy now calculate that two to three formations will be annihilated whenever the death's-head fighters appear. Like a shaft of lightning with its forked ends widely but purposefully extended, the Sturmstaffel pilots plow into bomber groups out of the blue and smash them to smithereens."

Farther down, I learned that the survivor of a successful ramming attack was entitled to record his kill in a special way: instead of painting the traditional line on his tail plane, he adorned it with a skull and crossbones.

What fun. I folded the August 1944 issue of *Der Flieger* and replaced it on the shelf. At least I knew what I was in for.

My throat tightened again. Knight's Cross or noose, that was the question.

Next morning I unexpectedly got into a dogfight with a Mustang and—more unexpectedly still—into a good firing position. The American pilot seemed young and inexperienced. He didn't have the first idea how to shake me off. Compared to him, I felt like an old hand. I was right behind him now. My opponent went into a shallow dive but maintained speed instead of accelerating. He might have been out for a Sunday spin.

I slowly closed in from behind. I could already calculate when my thumb ought to press the button and send the knucklehead spinning down through the autumn sky with his thoroughbred fighter shot to pieces.

The few seconds that separated me from my first kill seemed to crawl by. Quotations leapt into my mind: *I pulled on the stick with all my might, aimed off well ahead and waited for him to enter my cone of fire. Then I let fly with everything I had and cut him to ribbons. He just disintegrated. My eighteenth!*

The Mustang pilot took evasive action, but only half-heartedly. I was back on his tail in a flash, as if held there by an invisible towrope. He wouldn't hear the rattle of my four cannons. Perhaps he'd simply pitch forward into his straps, killed outright—perhaps his head would be pulverized by a twenty-millimeter shell.

The Vistula unwound beneath me. Sandbanks, belts of poplars, fallow fields, brandy-brown grazing land dotted with piebald cows. He would die within sight of this autumn landscape, and I would be his executioner. It wouldn't be long before the first snow fell in the Lysa Gora highlands, but the Mustang pilot would never see snow again.

He was flying along as impotently as I myself had flown a few weeks before.

Slowly, I eased the throttle back. The shape in my reflector sight dwindled and finally disappeared. I kicked hard on a rudder and reefed the one-ninety around in an unnecessarily

tight turn. Then I opened the throttle and headed for Grojecko.

I taxied up to the repair hangar after landing. There I
bumped into Steffen.

"No luck?"

"No luck, Herr Major."

"Sometimes," I said to Lenz, "I feel like running off and hiding in the woods. Or going sick."

"You couldn't do it." He jerked his head at the others, who
were out of earshot. "They're your comrades, like it or not.
You wouldn't run out on them."

"Know something else?" I said. "Sometimes I imagine the
war's over and people are sitting in a movie theater, watching
it all on the screen—dogfights, airplanes going down, men dying—and it doesn't shock one little bit. Playacting, that's all
it'll seem like to them."

"They'll be fascinated by the mechanics of killing—the
sheer technological brilliance of it. You can't blame them for
that."

"But we'll have to bring it home to them what it means
when a machine goes down in flames—when the pilot's still
conscious but trapped because his legs are shot to pieces."

"People will always get a kick out of guns and bangs and
high-performance airplanes shooting the hell out of each
other. You'll never cure them of that."

"What if one added a few subtitles like 'Cockpit Now
Smells of Roast Pork' or 'This Man's Body Was Crawling
with Maggots When They Dug Him Up'?"

"I've told you before, you think too much."

"I'd sooner think than shoot."

"Pity the enemy doesn't share your preference."

"That's what they say about us."

"Tell you what, Michael, let's compromise—you do my thinking for me and I'll do your shooting."

"Fine, but couldn't you manage a bit of thinking too?"

"In this place? It's against the rules."

Dense fog kept us loitering in the mess. You could tell it was Sunday—the station loudspeakers were churning out record requests. Operas and operettas, popular classics and movie hits.

"Come on, Martin," I said, "let's take a stroll up the hill."

Lenz followed me reluctantly, averse to such a lone-wolfish withdrawal from society.

Halfway up Thyme Hill the fog began to dissolve into thin skeins. All the trees around the base and beside the river had shed their leaves. The ground was soaking wet and redolent of iodine. There were mushrooms everywhere, mainly agarics and brown birch boletes. The leaves of the dead nettles bore pale spots resembling tiny caterpillars. Scores of corn buntings and yellow hammers were busy roaming the undergrowth.

Everything looked dark and dismal. The landscape conveyed a haunting sense of dejection, an almost palpable melancholy.

Suddenly, Lenz nudged me hard.

On the track below us stood a freight train. Somewhere out of sight, a signal must have been set at red. The train was not only stationary but silent as the grave. Even the locomotive seemed to be holding its breath.

Armed guards were pacing noiselessly up and down the track with their rifles slung. All the boxcar doors were shut.

"Looks important," I said. "Munitions, probably."

"No!" Lenz had spotted something. "Look back there!"

The train was some two hundred yards away, wreathed in

fog but visible enough. Two guards were opening the doors of the penultimate boxcar. They slid apart to reveal a dark mass of human figures so tightly packed that they almost spilled through the opening.

More guards stationed themselves in front of the doors and four men jumped out. They tumbled onto the grass verge and lay there for a moment as though injured before struggling painfully to their feet. Then they disappeared down the embankment. What they were doing in the dip, menaced by half a dozen rifles, we couldn't make out.

"Prisoners," Lenz said dispassionately.

"Yes," I said.

"Civilians," he said.

"That's right," I said.

"From a concentration camp," he said.

"Obviously," I said.

Three things—no, human beings—were tossed out of the boxcar. Involuntarily, we made our way down the slope at a crouch. As if aware that we were witnessing a forbidden spectacle, we crept closer through the fog that drifted past the train in streaks, uncovering one aspect of the scene as it blotted out another.

Compared to the faces that met our eyes, fighter pilots exhausted by months of combat looked positively well nourished, tanned, and glowing with health. We watched as three stiff, emaciated corpses in ragged clothing were toted down the embankment and buried by the squad of prisoners assigned to the task.

Or rather, not so much buried as unceremoniously bundled into the ground because the engineer had already blown his whistle: no delay could be countenanced for the sake of a few dead bodies. Rifle barrels motioned the burial party back into their boxcar. They were indistinguishable from the men they had buried, like puppet corpses operated by strings.

I would never forget the fog-borne screech and rattle of the heavy doors as they slid shut, never forget those ghostly, ghastly simulacra of eyes and cheeks and mouths that had once been animate. If living men could look more dead than the dead, I had just seen them.

"Come on," Lenz said in an undertone, like someone leaving a theater in midperformance. "Let's go."

We went. I said, "Listen, Martin . . ."

"No," he broke in, "don't start. Shut up for a change. These things exist—we've known that for ages. The Führer talks about them. *Der Stürmer* writes about them. Every administrative district in Germany has its own concentration camp with thousands of respectable citizens living on the doorstep. It's all down in black and white. Read *Mein Kampf,* read the *Völkischer Beobachter.* Everybody knows, so why make a song-and-dance?"

"It isn't that. You don't . . ."

"When new camps are opened they announce it in the dailies. Of course we know about them, every last one of us. If you always turn your back at the right moment you'll never see a thing, naturally, but you have to know when to turn."

"That's not the point. You don't know what I'm getting at."

"Well?"

The fog thickened on the way back. I tried to marshal my thoughts and define them clearly, but it was hopeless. Emotion got the better of me.

"I'll tell you why I'm so worked up, Martin. If we want to abolish the sort of human misery we've just seen—and you admit we all know it exists—we'll have to . . ."

"Have to what?"

"Well, end the war as soon as possible."

"Everyone wants that."

"Not the way I mean. We'll have to lose, otherwise these

things will go on forever—otherwise they'll really start in earnest."

"But . . . if we lose, the enemy'll take up where we left off. Personally, I'd sooner be on the winning side."

"That's all very logical, but I sometimes doubt the connection between logic and reality. Reality is what we always knew but never saw till just now."

"What about the fire storms in Hamburg and the piles of corpses in Dresden and Leipzig and Cologne? They're real enough too."

"You're just doing sums. A corpse for a corpse, is that what you want?"

"What do *you* want?"

"I wish I knew. I only know I'm nauseated by all this gambling with human lives, all this muscle-flexing and glorying in violence for its own sake—yes, and I'm nauseated by the Gallands and the Steinhoffs and the Speers who are doing their utmost to win this war. I mean, how unimaginative can you get! Don't you see, Martin? Every extra jet fighter and bomber we build helps to ensure that more human garbage will be tossed out of boxcars and dumped in a ditch. If they're so full of guts, these people, why don't they show it by getting rid of you-know-who? They've got their priorities wrong, if you ask me."

"For God's sake keep your mouth shut, Michael, or you'll be in trouble—if you aren't already. You'd better not let Galland or Steinhoff or Speer hear you talk like that. They'd never forgive you."

7

I was flying east under a matt-gray sky the color of aluminum.

In fifteen minutes at most I'd be crossing the front line. The Geschwader was strictly forbidden to venture within fifteen miles of it.

The airplane under the seat of my pants was a Fieseler Storch. I'd flown a Storch only once in my life and exactly a year ago. This one belonged to station headquarters. Ketsch had merely shrugged at my request.

"If you insist . . . I could forbid you to do such a damn-fool thing, but the whole idea's so crazy I needn't bother."

This piece of sophistry gave me carte blanche, so I pinched the headquarters runabout, skimmed through the operating manual, and took off. Just like that. I was fifty feet up before I'd decided whether to unstick. You simply couldn't keep a Storch on the ground.

Beneath me lay the serried foothills of the Lysa Gora. A range of clouds like frozen cascades echoed the conformation of the mountains.

We made a clumsy pair, the Storch and I. The map kept slipping off my knees. Whenever I bent to retrieve it the little machine bucked as though she'd abandoned flying in favor of seven-league boots.

The reason for my unusual mission was anything but a

joke. Lenz was missing—he'd crash-landed far behind the lines.

I hadn't heard the grim news until we touched down after our latest combat patrol, which had yielded little contact with the enemy but deflected us a long way east and into the forbidden zone. Only Wehrmann claimed to have seen Lenz pancake.

"It couldn't have been *that* far behind the lines," I snarled at him. "Didn't you even circle the spot and pinpoint it? Could you see if he was hurt or not?"

"I wasn't close enough for that." Wehrmann had just enough tact to keep a malicious smirk off his face, but he couldn't resist adding, "We'll have to write him off, I'm afraid. Too bad. That's the last we've seen of poor old Lenz."

Now I was hedgehopping over treetops, rooftops, and rivers in the hope of crossing the lines unscathed. The Lysa Gora looked mottled, like the coat of some mangy beast.

Smoke from autumn bonfires punctuated the landscape, which was lit by viscous smears of light from a hazy sun. The cloud lanes above me were as close-meshed as chain mail.

If Lenz had any chance at all, the Storch was it. Laboriously groping my way over the same stretch of countryside I had crossed at ten times the altitude and almost ten times the speed only an hour before, I scoured my mind for any lecture-room snippets that might have stuck.

The Fieseler Fi 156 Storch, a high-wing monoplane with extremely low-speed flying characteristics. Stalling speed in still air: thirty-two miles per hour. Fixed undercarriage with long hydraulic spiral-sprung shock struts. Their exceptionally long oleo stroke made it possible to land from almost any altitude without rounding out and with the elevators fully actuated. In a slight head wind, the machine could land in less than fifty feet.

The 240-hp Argus AS 10C power plant chugged slowly but

steadily along. Its robust and unbroken rhythm was reassuring. My pulse, which had been fast and irregular, settled down—took its cue from the engine's stolid sewing-machine beat. What if your guts *have* turned to ice water, Braack, the Argus seemed to say. Keep going like me. . . .

Fields pockmarked with craters, trees ripped and blasted by shellfire. The front line must be near. I crept even closer to the ground. There was no point in climbing. The Storch couldn't outclimb any sort of flak, however light, so the only answer was to fly at zero feet and rely on surprise.

Forest tracks and ranges of hills, piebald cows grazing, herons abruptly taking wing . . . A stream, a landing stage, a rowboat rotting in the muddy shallows of a small lake. Then, tanks.

I yanked on the stick despite myself, panic-stricken. There were Soviet stars everywhere—on tarpaulins, vehicles, gun shields. There it was, the barrier that lay between us fliers and the forbidden land: the front line. Simultaneously, the weather changed. Wisps of low cloud came snaking toward me, gusts swirled about me.

There was the river, entangled in itself like a snarl of rope. Wehrmann had given me a topographical clue: according to him, Lenz had come down just beyond it.

He had. His machine was lying there intact—no, sinking!

The one-ninety had pancaked onto a meadow enclosed by dense forest. The flat green expanse seemed to float like an island in the midst of a darker green sea. I put the Storch into a steep turn and went down to twenty feet. What had given me the impression that Lenz was sinking?

He was perched on the engine cowling with his orange pilot's scarf fluttering in the wind.

Fact number one: he was alive. Fact number two: his wings were awash with green slime. Fact number three: the meadow wasn't a meadow, it was a swamp. Lenz was stranded on a sinking ship. He hadn't managed to reach the treelined shore.

Fourth and last fact: I couldn't land.

Grimly, doggedly, I orbited him at minimum speed. Had he recognized me?

I slid open the side panel and waved. The Storch gave a perilous downward lurch, rocking in the squalls.

Lenz, seated astride the cowling, had something black in his hand: an automatic pistol.

Gusts hit me head-on. The storm front was bearing down on me like a giant vortex.

Turbulence made accurate flying impossible. The stick laid claim to a will of its own as I struggled to remain airborne, let alone fly some kind of controlled orbit. I soared above the treetops and skimmed the slimy green swamp in quick succession.

All at once, something strange happened. I was flooded with a sense of boundless self-assurance, a sort of *joie de vivre* that was wildly at odds with the hopelessness of the position. Why? Lenz was waving like a drowning man, and my only recourse would be to wave back until he and his machine were sucked under. Why *joie de vivre?*

It was an idiotic reversal of values. I found myself retching, retching continuously, but my next circuit compounded the horror of the situation. Slowly but steadily, the forest was being invaded. Heavy, tracked vehicles were converging on the swamp. The first of them had already entered the trees, though they wouldn't be able to open fire till they'd combed the entire area. The patch of swamp and its reluctant prisoner were visible only from the air.

Then the strange sensation flooded back again. It was like a blood transfusion administered under pressure. I felt brimful of energy and initiative, as though I'd spent months in idleness preparing for this very moment.

Within ten minutes at most, the first Russians would have reached the edge of the swamp and opened fire. I circled for another approach but was badly deflected. Fighting the gusts, I gauged the direction of the wind and tried to meet it head-on as I made a close approach.

Inky walls of cloud closed in, the ground seemed to rock and sway. Soupy green water was washing over the wings and elevators of the foundering one-ninety. The first time I hovered near Lenz at a bare thirty feet the wind veered abruptly and swept me sideways into the trees. Terrified, I heaved on the stick and found myself in darkness.

It was all over now. If I let-down blind I'd hit the treetops. A rending crash, a sheet of flame, and that would be that.

Tensely, I struggled to keep the turn-and-bank and vertical speed indicators on zero. Shreds of cloud were racing past, some paler than others. I headed for the paler ones. A trace of green, a vague glimpse of something solid, and down I went. Lower, lower still . . . At last I could see the ground again. I was skimming over a track through the woods. At the far end, steel mastodons were lumbering along with their trunks extended: Soviet tanks. I made a quick one-eighty, fighter fashion, and there was the swamp again with Lenz in the middle.

He watched me with desperate intensity, waving like mad, but his gestures conveyed no hope now, only fear. Above the drone of my Argus, he had evidently heard the grinding roar of engines, the rattle of tank tracks.

There was no escape. I couldn't land and Lenz couldn't leave his island. The swamp was neither land nor water. It was a sluggishly heaving mass, too deep to wade through, not solid enough to stand on, not liquid enough to swim through. I had no choice but to keep circling and see Lenz blown to bits or share his fate when the guns opened up.

Another approach. I cursed aloud each time I made an error.

Easy now, don't overcorrect! Show the bastards! Show these goddamn gradients and crosswinds. Get lost, you menagerie of meteorological monsters!

My predicament was quite as hopeless as it had ever been when I was attacking a box of Fortresses, but what vitality, what energy, what grim determination! I hardly knew myself.

Again I skidded past Lenz—he had a black smudge on his forehead, I noticed. A glance at the airspeed indicator: sixty miles an hour—much too fast. How slow could you fly a Storch? The figure thirty-two bobbed up in my mind like a life belt. I finally did what I should have done long ago: I lowered full flaps.

Another approach, another glance at the tanks. They were forging through the trees like giant saurians within scent of their prey. My latest approach told me precisely the course and throttle setting that would just keep the Storch in forward motion. The airspeed indicator was now reading forty. I edged slowly past Lenz at a walking pace. His figure danced into my port panel and out of it again. I juggled with the stick and throttle, kicked hard on the rudder, but it was useless. I'd overshot him.

Rain blurred the windshield as I went into another steep turn. The cloud base was getting steadily lower.

The tanks crawled nearer and nearer. Blue-gray smoke spurted from their exhaust vents and scudded away like startled bats.

The first shots rang out. A machine gun mounted on an armored scout car was pumping bursts of tracer in my direction. They vanished into the overcast. Tracer was a familiar sight —it held no terrors for me.

I now knew what to do. My next approach would have to be my last.

Lower, Braack! Slower, Braack!

I was abeam of my target to begin with, but I had to duck behind the edge of the wood to keep out of the tanks' range of vision and field of fire. Their antiaircraft machine guns had opened up now. I noticed for the first time that they were American-supplied armor, not T 34s. They mowed down trees and sent uprooted bushes whirling through the air as they pressed on, hell for leather.

Don't lose your nerve, Braack, not now!

Nothing had ever calmed me as effectively as these absurd self-exhortations. I clamped the thrashing stick between my knees and leaned back to open the door. The handle wouldn't budge at first, and my simultaneous struggle with the door, the stick, and the whole machine left me half drowned in sweat.

I had to go in now or risk a hail of fire on my final approach that would put out my light for good—mine and Lenz's both.

Down! Lower! Slower!

Lenz got the point at once. Though plastered shut by the slipstream, the unsecured door gave an occasional flap of invitation.

The fighter's engine cowling loomed ahead of me. The airscrew had buried itself so deep in the ooze that it was festooned with duckweed.

Watch your speed!

I gripped the throttle hard, easing it back and forth, opening and closing it just enough to keep from stalling. The gusts were bestial. They slammed into the bobbing, weaving Storch like charging rhinos. Thirty-five miles an hour—I had to try and hold the airspeed at that. Thirty-five would bring me slowly up to Lenz. . . . Three yards forward, two back—sometimes vice versa.

Lower, damn you!

Now I had Lenz in my windshield, dead center, dead ahead. Another two or three yards and my airscrew would smash his skull to pulp.

He'd scrambled out onto the wing by now and was standing there poised, with his arms extended. Nonsensically, his right hand still retained its hold on the pistol. Then a gust of wind bore me backward and upward—high enough to see along the forest track. It was too narrow in places to accommodate the tanks, but the ironclad colossi were relentlessly beating a path to our door.

Down again. I hovered there, making no headway at all. Were my wheels already awash? I crept another yard. One false move on Lenz's part and he'd be in the water; one false move on mine and I'd sweep him off the wing.

Another couple of feet. His face was hovering in the panel beside me. Now! He made his move—grabbed at the door handle with outstretched fingers. I jiggled the stick like a madman, but to no avail. I'd overshot him again.

Then another gust drove me backward like a leaf. Lenz reappeared, clinging hard to the one-ninety to avoid being blown off. . . . One more try . . . Either he'd make it, or I'd sandwich him between the Storch and the one-ninety. He had hold of the door now. Clinging to the handle, he kicked off and swung his legs over the sill. I opened the throttle and wrenched the stick to starboard with no thought but to clear the wreck and climb away fast. If he failed to hang on he'd be dead—killed by me.

He hung on, struggling aboard inch by inch, wriggling through the gap between the sill and the door, which was being forced against his body by the slipstream. There were the tanks, their machine guns spitting fire at the sky. . . .

And there were the clouds. Everything was blotted out, but not Lenz. Lenz was still there. He squeezed into the seat behind me and secured the door. We were too far gone even to exchange a smile.

We let-down quickly. The cloud base rose the farther west we flew, increasing our freedom of maneuver. By the time we reached the Lysa Gora, the sky was clear.

Like liquid honey, the late afternoon sunlight brought out every shade of gold and amber in the hills below us. I shouted over my shoulder.

"If we ever get out of this war alive, Martin . . ."

"Yes?"

"We'll take our first vacation down there, in the valleys of the Lysa Gora. Is it a deal?"

"You're on."

Lenz smiled at me for the first time. He had the map on his knee and his finger on the patch of forest we were flying over.

Had he given my shoulder a squeeze just now, when he climbed aboard? I could almost have sworn it.

There was a celebration in the bunkhouse that night.

Even Steffen popped his head in (*"Achtung! Der Herr Geschwader-Kommodore!"*) and slapped me on the back.

"Well, Braack, not a bad show—not bad at all. You may not have scored yet, but at least you've kept your Staffel up to strength."

This autumn can't bring itself to say good-bye. We might have had some snow by now, and the birds haven't even moved on."

We were sitting around a campfire outside Shangri-La. Maryla had gathered some kindling on the way, and there was plenty of wood around.

Without answering, I picked up my guitar, launched into a Handel minuet, lapsed into a bourrée, and lost my way in a gavotte. Maryla was sitting with her knees drawn up, hugging them. We could have sat there like that for hours—no, days.

"Are you still reading that old Russian history book of yours? You started to tell me about it once."

"Yes, I'm up to Hilarion now—you know, the Metropolitan of Kiev. It's the language and the prayers I like most. 'May God bestow his mercy on you and bless you in perpetuity, you and your wife and your daughter and all your house. You have done good and acted righteously. Amen.' That's just a routine salutation, believe it or not."

"Only goes to show how impoverished human speech has become. These days we're reduced to 'Heil Hitler.'"

"I've just been reading how the Germans attacked Pskov in the thirteenth century. They slaughtered two abbots and a lot of Dominican friars, not to mention women and children."

"When was that?"

"Twelve sixty-seven, or thereabouts. You see? There's always time to read if you really want to. My roommates at Konskie spend their evenings mooching around and bemoaning the state of the war, but where's the sense in that? It's pointless unless you're prepared to do something positive. Me, I'd sooner read and keep quiet."

"Yes, but there's enough blood flowing as it is. Why read about religious massacres in the thirteenth century?"

"Because it's comforting, Michael. It shows you the extent of human endurance—it makes you feel you're more than a helpless, defenseless little cog in a big machine."

"I got talking to an old Pole the other day—an ex-teacher who collects the garbage from our admin block twice a week.

He said much the same thing—something like 'Those who endure suffering are stronger than those who inflict it.' "

"The problem's beyond us, if you ask me. I doubt if we'll ever get to the bottom of it—maybe we aren't even meant to."

"The old man said something else. After the war, he said, people will look for entirely new ways of dealing with violence because they'll have learned that trials of strength only breed more violence, no matter who wins. After the war, they'll only elect politicians with enough—how did he put it?—enough . . ."

"Vision?"

"No, creative insight. With enough creative insight to combat armed force by spiritual means. There'll be no demand for politicians whose sole response to military threats is to rattle their own sabers. Any nation incapable of fighting spiritually, he said, will forfeit its claim to be civilized."

"What about Hitler? Do you think he'll dispense with *his* armed forces when this is over?"

"I wonder." I was absently strumming my guitar again. "Know what I'd like? I'd like you to cook me a really decent meal sometime."

"Wait till 1960 and I will. You'll emerge from your study, where you've been putting the finishing touches to your latest literary masterpiece, and I'll serve you up a great big dish of french fries. There's bound to be some proper lard in the shops by then."

"God, am I starving!"

"I've got an idea for next time. Could you rustle up a frying pan?"

"I might manage an old saucepan lid."

"That'll do. This place is knee-deep in mushrooms. We'll pick some and fry them over the fire."

"Great! I'll try and save up my margarine ration."
"I might even bring a knob of butter along."

They were blissful, those evenings with Maryla—quintessentially serene and secure. I wouldn't have swapped our shack for a country mansion. Its atmosphere of peace was unrivaled by any I'd known save possibly on Thyme Hill or down by the river in recent days—days so summery they might almost have slipped out of the calendar and been reinserted in the wrong place. . . .
"Well, you dreamer? Enjoying yourself?"
I'd laid the guitar aside.
"Yes, I'm in clover compared to a dogface in a foxhole. Soldier boys never get out of the front line. We're back on the ground again in two and a half hours maximum, one way or the other."
She threw her arms around my neck and kissed me.
"Make sure you always get back the right way."

8

Ketsch, well-meaning as ever, had sent for me again.

Ketsch: "I'm only thinking of your own good, Braack. You've no idea how much we all have your welfare at heart."

Braack: "And I still haven't scored yet—I know, Herr Hauptmann, it's ungrateful of me."

"If we were having a drink together in peacetime, Braack —and I look forward to that—I'm sure we'd get along like a house afire. Your verbal acrobatics genuinely amuse me sometimes, but there's a war on. Let's hope it doesn't last much longer."

"There's an ideal cure for that. I could get myself killed and the war'd be over in two minutes flat—for me, anyway."

He let that pass. "As I say, I can see us sitting in front of a roaring log fire on your family estate in Masuria with a bottle of real French brandy between us, laughing at our present, er —differences of opinion. But we've got to live that long, Braack, and you—I'm giving it to you straight—*you* won't make it unless you pull your socks up."

"I probably won't even if I do."

"Either way, the Geschwader-Kommodore's received an official complaint about you. You've been accused of undermining morale and listening to enemy broadcasts."

I forbore to ask why an entire country with an army that had overrun Poland, France, Belgium, and Holland, plus

most of Scandinavia and the Balkans and large tracts of the
Soviet Union, should feel menaced by Stan Kenton's "Big
Band Sound." Presumably, all crumbling political and social
structures were apt to blame their collapse on the behavior of
tiny cliques and minorities. As soon as a handful of people
went their own way, the state and society felt jeopardized.

"Your friend Lenz is in trouble too, but him we can get off
the hook. He's won his spurs, and we need every experienced
combat pilot we've got. I like you, Braack. For God's sake do
me a favor and shoot something down. One little kill would
solve all my problems. You don't think I'd enjoy sending you
to the gallows, do you?"

"But . . ."

"But what?"

"Surely it's quality that counts in war, not quantity."

"I don't follow."

"Well, it isn't a question of how many human beings you
kill, it's why you kill them that matters."

"For a start, Braack, we don't kill human beings in this
outfit, we destroy the enemy."

"All right, we destroy the enemy."

"That's just the trouble—*you* haven't destroyed a blind
one."

"That's still a purely quantitative problem, Herr Hauptmann. It doesn't have any bearing on the moral justification
for killing—I mean, destroying."

"Which is?"

"That all enemies are vermin by definition."

"And have to be destroyed—quite so."

"Yes, but what's more important is the quality factor. *Are*
they vermin?"

"Of course, or they wouldn't be our enemies."

"Exactly. You don't go around killing your friends. That's
why I say quality's the primary factor. The quantity factor—
how many you dispose of—is secondary."

"Primary, secondary! We won't win the war that way, Braack."

"Nor any other," I said quietly, "not now."

Ketsch stared at me sadly—almost infinitely so, I felt.

"I didn't hear you say that, Braack. But you—you hear this: unless you start scoring pretty damn soon, given the right opportunity, you're sunk. I won't be able to save you, nor will Steffen. As for splitting a bottle of brandy in front of the fire, we can both kiss that idea good-bye."

One evening Lenz handed me some old press clippings he'd found in the library. One of the passages he'd marked came from a speech delivered by Himmler to some SS generals at Posen on 4 October 1943:

"Whether other nations prosper or starve to death is of interest to me only insofar as we need them as slaves for our own civilization."

I handed the piece of paper back.

"That speech must be known to Galland, Steinhoff, Speer, and all the other advocates of a bigger and better Luftwaffe."

"Of course."

"So how can they want a man like Himmler to win the war?"

"We don't have any choice now we're in it. As for Himmler, he's a misbegotten product of total war. Nobody'll want anything to do with him once it's over."

It was a recurrent nightly shock to abandon the cool, clear air of the Polish steppes for the cramped interior of our hut, with its six pairs of superimposed bunks.

You almost caromed off the stench of rotten eggs, moldy urine-soaked blankets, congealed vomit, and dead rats.

Wilk, who accompanied me back from the latrine one night, had a theory about this phenomenon.

"They don't just have nightmares about dying—they piss the fear out of their systems as well."

I reverted to the subject next evening.

"That," I said, "is one good reason for giving us all the Knight's Cross in double-quick time. You don't stink once you've won your tin necktie."

"Sounds plausible. Why not?"

"Knight's Crossers suffer from another kind of fear—one that doesn't smell."

"What's that?"

"All they're afraid of is not getting their Oak Leaves and Swords on time."

Wilk grimaced. "War should be banned, if only because it concentrates so many foul-smelling men in one spot."

"We could always can the stench and send it home to their ever-loving wives. I bet they'd make sure no man did his patriotic duty for the next hundred years."

I was flying a straightforward circuit of the field to try out an undercarriage indicator that had just been repaired. All my ambitions were centered on a textbook approach and touchdown.

I eased the throttle back to 9.5 psi and brought the speed to 140 mph. Downwind I set the flaps at TAKEOFF, verifying their angle with the aid of the wing indicators. Then I selected landing gear DOWN and pulled the lever. I checked the wheels' descent by watching the visual indicators in the main planes and eased the throttle forward to offset resistance and hold her at 135 mph. Making my final turn, I selected full flaps, retrimmed, and set her down. I then retracted the flaps while taxiing.

Procedures like these were clearly defined. Following them carefully was my way of trying to conquer the imponderables of combat. It gave me confidence when something reacted just the way I wanted.

In my mind, I was already rehearsing my next conversation with Maryla—the one we'd have while frying mushrooms.

"Why is the world such a trite and trivial place in spite of all our fine phrases and high-flown ideas?"

"Because it's full of magic."

I simply put the words into Maryla's mouth. I'd dreamed them and awakened with them imprinted on my memory.

Their meaning escaped me. I belonged to a generation whose lack of broad-based impressions had kept it childish; on the other hand, war had scarred it in a way that far transcended the normal range of human experience.

Lenz could not only write me subtle guitar accompaniments that made a Peter Igelhoff number sound like the Hot Club de France. He also had an explanation of my dream phrase on tap:

"It's because ninety per cent of Western humanity are in favor of triviality. They don't want magic to gain the upper hand."

But the same could be said of Lenz himself. Considerations of this kind never prompted him to modify his behavior patterns or indulge in soul-searching. Lenz was a realist. There was a war on, so anything that didn't present an immediate threat to his existence had to be deferred. First things first.

Still, at least you could hold a normal conversation with him. Many of our fellow pilots were showing signs of extreme fatigue. Off duty, they vegetated in a deep and enduring state of depression. Hallucinations, nightmares, and claustrophobia were everyday phenomena. So were lapses of memory ("What's the name of that movie where Hans Moser plays a Viennese bellhop?"—"He never plays anything else, stupid!") and persecution mania. One of our number didn't dare visit the latrine after dark ("There's always someone standing there spying on me. I wrote my mother about it!") and duly joined the bed-wetting set.

I came across a reproduction of Dürer's *Apocalypse*. The four horsemen were entitled Pestilence, Famine, War, and Death.

"Silly of him," I said to Lenz. "He left out Fear."

Lenz had unearthed another Himmler quotation:

"Most of you must know what it's like to see a hundred corpses lying side by side, or five hundred, or a thousand. To have stuck it out and preserved our decency—discounting a few rare instances of human frailty—has toughened us. This is a glorious chapter in our history that has never been written and never will be."

Hadn't Lenz, the incorruptible, developed any kind of eccentricity? None at all?

He once said, "We aren't living, we're surviving. There's a world of difference between life and survival."

Another time I overheard him mutter something as he climbed into his cockpit. Just four words: "All aboard the Ark!"

Sometimes the evening sun seemed to bathe our wings in bloodstained sweat.

Despite the order to maintain radio silence, everyone let rip on the postcombat flights back to base.

"Heard about the guy who swallowed a rubber? He went to the latrine that night and his next-door neighbor caught sight of the result. Jesus, he said, look at that! A fart with skin on it!"

"Pardon me while I puke."

"I'm only trying to boost your morale. Some of us are tougher than others, sonny."

"Tougher? You'd go ouch if a butterfly landed on your pecker."

"Hey, you two, can't you keep off latrines and rubbers? We're supposed to be knights in shining armor, fighting for the survival of Western civilization."

"Anything's better than letting Europe go Bolshevik."

"And anything's better than a solid diet of turnips and horsemeat sausage. Sugar-beet molasses, synthetic honey, ersatz coffee—ugh! I even tried a toothpaste sandwich the other day, I was so hungry."

Touchdown. Supper. A mess dance, one female to fifteen males.

Lenz had another quotation ready. It was from Hanns Johst, the great national—i.e., National Socialist—playwright whose latest drama was touring the Wehrmacht theater circuit:

"Whenever I hear the word 'culture,'" it ran, "I flip my safety catch."

9

Cockpit alert. The pilots of 3 Staffel were already strapped in, the crew chiefs lounging under the wings.

I'd slid my canopy right back. It was late afternoon, and the air had a tang like Masurian schnapps.

A brimstone butterfly was hovering around the radio antenna. It settled on the wire, then fluttered off and disappeared into the scent of grass and herbs that still reached our nostrils, war and gunsmoke notwithstanding.

Cohorts of clouds were congregating overhead like mailed knights of old. They reared and fell, reared and regrouped continuously. Above them, agglomerations of finer vapor were almost imperceptibly drifting through the troposphere.

Could you smell clouds? Lenz claimed you could—he said you could smell ozone when flying very high and close to a thunderhead. He also said the earth looked concave at extreme altitudes, not flat or spherical.

More clouds were advancing, rusty as abandoned plows, with shreds of cirrus scudding above them like leaves in a gale.

A multitude of swifts soared past. As though remote-controlled, they all flapped their wings at once, then glided, flapped and glided, flapped and glided. . . .

By sitting bolt upright I could escape the long-familiar smells of the cockpit, the vomit left over from the last dogfight, the urine that had seeped from a body numb with fear. . . .

They'd fitted a new airspeed indicator—the old one had been smashed by a shell fragment from a Mustang. The scent of rubber and factory-fresh paint helped to counteract the other smells, almost like a breath of home in a hostile world.

These minutes of solitude in your own cockpit afforded time for reflection and recapitulation. I strove to recall the various cloud shapes and savor their beauty in retrospect like someone studying detailed photographs of a landscape swiftly glimpsed in passing.

Sometimes we flew over cloud lanes that might have consisted of coarse rubble. Leaden rivers of stratus oozed between them while fine wisps of cirrus drifted high above the Polish steppe like the dispersing remnants of a smoke signal from earth.

Wisps of cirrus swirling like autumn leaves, banks of vapor with a spongy, slimy, putrescent look, October clouds suspended in the heavens like washing hung out to dry, much of it moth-eaten. . . .

If each cloud had its own peculiar scent, cumulus would smell wantonly of musk, nimbus of seaweed, moss, and inshore waters, stratus of oven-fresh bread, cirrus—subtly and discreetly—of cinnamon and cloves.

Clouds could look like scarecrows or fish heads, lizards or caterpillars, stalactites, skulls and angels of death, mummies and carnival masks, hobgoblins and hounds of hell.

The light was all-important. It could irradiate a dome of cloud and then go out, leaving darkness to well up from within, or turn a scattering of cirrus dust on altocumulus to icing sugar.

Clouds were a motley crew of noblemen and serfs, knights and vagabonds, social climbers, dropouts and wallflowers, baroque braggarts and romantic ne'er-do-wells, chimeras and dragons. Many had an archaic simplicity, some a Dionysian exuberance, others an Apollonian severity or rococo frivolity.

Tobacco-brown shreds like mashed cigarette butts, early risers with unshaven, hung-over faces—clouds as lovely as Cleopatra herself.

I often devised names for clouds. Some I christened the Flying Dutchman or the Iron Chancellor, others merely Fatso, Beanpole, Garden Gnome, War Memorial, or Holy Grail.

The most beautiful cloud I ever saw was over Masuria. We'd been diverted northward and had to make a refueling stop before flying back to base. The cloud in question was hovering over a lake near Ortelsburg.

It was pregnant with moisture from the water below, and its skin was at first so ethereal that I could see the delicate ramifications inside it through an opaline film. The serene morning light played over its virginal crest. Before long, as I flew past some distance away, its contours took on greater solidity. It seemed to blossom like a white flower with fine-veined petals. The petals became swollen and distended, suffused by the early light with every shade from pale pink to deepest purple, and the crest broke into a veritable orgy of self-reproduction, piling mound upon mound until the whole edifice exploded in slow motion and dissolved into a shapeless mass.

My cloud had regained the delicacy of its youth, but it was a fragile delicacy. The light that had illumined it from within was extinguished. Looking carefully, I could see that its skin was growing wrinkled and leathery. I circled it once before it broke up. Then the west wind blew its remnants away.

Another visit to the control tower.

"Did your father ever tell you about Poltava?"

I shook my head. "I've only heard rumors, Herr Major."

"Only rumors?" The station commander irritably clicked his tongue. "I'm surprised Goebbels hasn't turned the story into a folk song and broadcast it."

For the first time, I learned the truth about Poltava.

On 21 June 1944, 1,373 Boeings and Liberators bombed Berlin and rendezvoused over Poland with twenty-six Mustang fighter groups. Why? Because, having raided the German capital, they were under orders to head for bases in the Soviet Union instead of flying back to England. The Mustangs, which were fitted with drop tanks, escorted them from Leszno onward. They'd been warned by their commander, Colonel Don Blakeslee, not to jettison these tanks until they'd sucked them dry. Every last drop would be needed because they were operating at maximum range.

"You have to take your hat off to the Yanks for completing the first part of their mission. Seven and a half hours' flying time to Russia—not far short of two thousand miles. Quite an achievement."

"But didn't any of our fighter units engage them—here in Poland at least?"

"Oh yes, twenty Me 109s intercepted them over Diedice."

"Twenty versus nearly two thousand. Pretty long odds, weren't they?"

"Long enough, Braack, but an accurate reflection of our current situation. Still, we did get a couple of them—one fighter and one bomber."

After disposing of this final attempt to thwart their historic flight, much as a giant might have swatted an importunate fly, the Americans landed in Russia according to plan: at Morgorod, Piryatin, and—last but not least—Poltava. The proven possibility of launching two-way air attacks on Germany by shuttling bombers between England and Russia not only packed a big strategic punch but was likely to pay dividends in morale and propaganda. No wonder the Americans were feted when they touched down on Soviet soil.

But now came the second and, from the American angle, less glorious part of the saga.

A Heinkel He 111 had shadowed the Americans and carefully noted the airfields where their armada now stood in serried ranks, as though drawn up on ceremonial parade. It was a typically American blunder. They felt perfectly safe—so safe that they saw no need to disperse and camouflage their machines, man observation posts, or maintain a state of readiness. They and the Russkies fraternized with the aid of liberal quantities of vodka.

It is fair to assume that not many American airmen were sober when the Luftwaffe attacked Poltava that night. The B-17s were still standing in midfield, parade-ground fashion, and the few Mustangs that did try to scramble had no chance at all.

"Nineteen forty-four has been a pretty bleak year so far, but that was one of our major successes."

"Were there any survivors?"

"Yes, a few pathetic oddments were ordered out of Russia in a panic and diverted to Italy—they even bombed a Polish oil refinery on the way. However, the Mustangs didn't feel at home in Italy. The dust played havoc with their engines and fuel lines because they hadn't been fitted with adequate filters."

My return from the control tower was slightly less glorious than our raid on Poltava. An Me 109 from a neighboring base had crashed into the mud flats near the river. I'd not long left the tower and set off on a short stroll when I bumped into the salvage party. They'd just hauled the airplane onto firm ground with a team of horses and opened the canopy.

The dead man had been dashed against the instrument

panel. Judging by the grotesquely distorted appearance of the lower part of his body, all his intestines were ruptured and every bone was broken. His arms hung limp like strings of sausages.

The top of his skull had been sliced off with surgical precision by a shell splinter which could still be seen buried in the fighter's side. The exposed brain floated there like a white cloud in a dusky red sky. (It would soon emulate a stranded jellyfish by shriveling into a gelatinous mass.)

Another splinter had gouged out the pilot's right collarbone. Muscle fibers, clusters of tendons, and one red lung could all be seen. The remains of his face were draped over the stove-in jaw like a soft rubber mask.

I took to my heels as if the devil incarnate were after me. To exorcise my horror, I flung wild accusations at an imaginary mob:

"But that's what you wanted! You were raring to go— itching to get your own back. You fought one world war, but that wasn't good enough for you—you had to have a second helping. Well, that's what it looks like, your godforsaken war. Take a damned good look so you never want another!"

Just when I thought I had the measure of my one-ninety, she played a dirty trick on me. The control unit failed as I was coming in to land.

The control unit was a gadget that automatically monitored and adjusted the relationship between boost pressure, engine revs, and propeller pitch. No pilot had time to check all three readings on the dials and adjust them separately. From that aspect our one-nineties were nice and automatic, but we were in trouble if the gadget malfunctioned. Because German fighter pilots possessed a certain value in their capacity as destroyers of the enemy, a second gadget ensured that we didn't fall out of the sky right away: the engine, likewise automatically, went to emergency boost. In my case, that meant I found myself unable to throttle back just before touchdown. The only way to lose speed was to switch off the ignition.

Anyone who mistakenly cut his engine sixty feet off the ground instead of three was asking for a quick ride down in the elevator followed by a burial with full military honors.

I got away with a few bruises.

Rotsch got away less lightly. He died next day, rammed by an enemy bomber that shot out of a layer of cloud, lifted him on its armor-plated nose, and then, like an infuriated bull, flung him down. The bomber exploded into a frightful black-fringed fireball and the one-ninety's wreckage vanished inside.

The bunkhouse was silent that night.

We roamed the woods, Maryla and I, like two young innocents on their first secret mushrooming tryst.

The countryside was thick with edible fungi which no one had bothered to pick—cepes, chanterelles, buttons, field mushrooms with enormous caps. You could have fed the whole base on them.

By the time we'd lit a small fire outside the shack and were cleaning our haul, we found we'd brought something else along. Ticks had rained down on every imaginable and unimaginable part of our bodies. We scratched ourselves liberally while peeling the mushrooms and arranging them in our makeshift pan. Maryla had produced some real butter—even a small strip of fat bacon. Bacon . . . so it still existed. I wondered where it had been hiding all these years.

I built up a good birchwood fire while Maryla finished preparing a gargantuan feast of mushrooms. Before long they were all sizzling beautifully over the flames. The tick bites itched like mad.

"*Ixodes ricinus*," I pontificated, "otherwise known as the wood tick, has only one ambition in life. It climbs onto a branch and lets go as soon as a living creature, preferably human, passes by—that's because it responds to skin odors. Then it buries itself in your flesh and lays its eggs there. The young hatch out and hurry off to the nearest tree, drop off, dig in, and lay some eggs of their own. And so on ad infinitum."

Maryla presented her back. "Scratch me there," she implored. "Really hard—ooh, that's heaven!"

The mushrooms hissed and sizzled and spurted water and fat. The firewood, which was damp in parts, crackled and gave off showers of sparks. Our most idyllic evening ever. . . .

"Maryla, do you love me?"

"First let's see what those mushrooms taste like."

"And then?"

"Then I'll show you."

Some of the mushrooms were a trifle on the black side and others underdone, but they all tasted delicious. It was the meal of a lifetime.

Torpid and replete, we went inside the shack. The fire had lapsed into smoldering silence.

Maryla sat up with a jerk.

"There's somebody out there!"

She was right. A shadowy figure was lurking near the window.

The brawny shoulders and beefy buttocks were unmistakable. As soon as Wehrmann saw I'd spotted him he gave a sheepish grin—yes, sheepish.

I'd never seen Wehrmann embarrassed before. There was something ominous about the way he backed off, still grinning, and retreated into the gloom.

BOOK THREE

"As you will have heard, Churchill told the British Parliament a few weeks ago that the whole of East Prussia and parts of Pomerania and Silesia are to be given to the Poles. Seven, ten, or eleven million Germans would then be evacuated. . . . This is pure theory. This is a ludicrous flight of fancy."

Adolf Hitler addressing his
generals on 28 December 1944

There's only one way to shoot down a Shturmovik," declared the eminent fighter pilot. "A stern attack from below. That's the only way to get at the oil cooler. The Shturmovik's oil cooler is its Achilles' heel—its one weak spot."

We were sitting in the Richthofen Saal, the biggest lecture room on the base. Our distinguished visitor had flown in straight from a forward airfield on the Eastern Front to share his wealth of experience with us. His current score was over 150 kills, and he was every girl-next-door's idea of what a Knight's Cross fighter ace should look like: young, blond, and dynamic, with well-chiseled features and lips set in a victorious smile.

"These goddamn chairs!" sighed Rebhan, massaging one cheek. "Anyone'd think we were a bunch of fakirs. . . ."

The blond ace went on:

"The Shturmovik is so heavily armored that the fuselage will shrug off a twenty-millimeter shell. It's the toughest airplane flying today, and I had to take a lot of punishment before I perfected my own method of attack. I'd advise any beginner to think twice before tackling a Shturmovik."

Lenz whispered, "Isn't anyone going to tell him he's got his wires crossed?"

"They can't have told him we're Anglo-American meat," I

whispered back. "Ilyushins and Ratas, that's all his outfit has to cope with."

"Another reason why it's so hard to knock down a Shturmovik," pursued the ace, "is that it flies low on principle. There's only one tactic that pays off—dive on it from astern and level off a few feet above the ground—then you can tuck yourself in below and behind. I've brought down over thirty Shturmoviks that way. There isn't any other."

"How do you bring a Fortress down?" whispered Rebhan. "That's what I'd like to know."

"Still more to the point, how do you get back in one piece even if you don't?"

Having delivered this rhetorical question, I surveyed the big room with interest. All four Gruppen were fully represented, and I could see that a lot of the men were hanging on every heroic word.

"Close to spitting distance before you fire, that's the whole secret. Better not press the tit at all than press it too soon—your tracer'll give the game away. Mind you, squirting at point-blank range does have its dangers. . . ." The much-bemedaled speaker stood looking down at us with that blend of nonchalance and athleticism which we all so admired and imitated. Fliers were fliers, after all, not footsloggers. . . . "You have to be careful not to collide with the enemy's wreckage. Fire and break hard!"

I carefully studied the tanned and weather-beaten features of this pilot who had received his Oak Leaves and Swords from the Führer's sacred hand. From sleek eyebrows to jutting chin, his whole face conveyed bold and undiluted optimism. He seemed quite devoid of any doubts about his own competence or the inevitability of final victory.

"My method of attack has four phases. One, look. Two, decide. Three, attack. Four, disengage or take a breather."

I scanned the lecture room again. It all seemed so unreal:

the pilots' radiant expressions, their unmistakable enthusiasm, the lecturer's infectious self-assurance. He had made them feel that everything depended on *them,* that all Germany was looking to *them* to tip the scales—now, with the Russians at the gates of Warsaw, less than a half hour's flying time from where they sat. Discounting the station commander, very few of those present were over thirty. So much youth, so much idealism, so much faith in final victory . . .

The successful fighter pilot paraphrased another successful pilot, Werner Mölders:

"For a novice, the most important thing is to gain his first victory without suffering too much of an emotional trauma."

Although Mölders was dead, a long and distinguished career in the air had intervened between his first victory and his death. Many of us had still to risk the trauma he'd spoken of, but the average interval between a pilot's first and last kills had shrunk year by year.

"I once shot down five LaGG 5 fighters in the course of four sorties. That was my best day's performance."

Rebhan whispered, "Yes, but a third of his Staffel got clobbered in the process. They made the running, he scooped the pool."

"Shut up," I said.

I recalled another lecture we'd listened to. It was devoted to one of the supermonsters of modern air warfare, the North American B-25 Mitchell.

The Mitchell was a killer—the war's most heavily armed aircraft. Though only twin-engined, the B-25 H carried sixteen machine guns and a seventy-five-millimeter cannon but could still deliver a bomb load of three thousand pounds. I visualized the diagram: the rotating twin-MG turrets, the concentrated firepower of the quadruple MGs in the nose. The Mitchells terrorized all who ventured into their field of fire. If these apocalyptic demons flew in tight formation—as they invariably did—there was no blind spot from which a frail little fighter could attack without running the gauntlet of their fire.

Our highly decorated visitor offered no hints on how to shoot down a Mitchell, still less on how to survive an attack on one, but that wasn't his fault. There'd been an administrative blunder. The poor man couldn't be expected to know that we tangled with Americans so near the Russian front, not Russians. It only went to show how the gap between the fronts had narrowed.

This evening's lecture was full of old-fashioned chivalry and fair play. No wonder Ketsch was listening with eyes aglow.

"War isn't a life insurance policy. . . ."

Another quotation from another heroic contributor to the history of air warfare, Oberst Hans Ulrich Rudel of Stuka fame.

Platitudes, I thought.

I'd once leafed through a top-secret file on my father's desk at the Air Ministry. It gave the true losses sustained as a result of Allied raids on Germany.

In 1943 the RAF had dropped 136,000 tons of bombs. By 1944 some British critics were opposing further raids as "uneconomic" on the grounds that many German towns had nothing worthwhile left to destroy. Despite this, a further 20,000 tons were dropped in March 1944 alone. The ruins of Cologne by then housed only 20,000 out of an original population of 800,000. In the same month, the RAF announced that its tally of bombs dropped on Berlin had almost reached the 45,000-ton mark.

These figures came as a shock to me. My knowledge of the war had previously been based on newsreels and Propaganda Company reports. "I closed in for the kill, blazed away, and gave him a bellyful of lead. He spun down trailing black smoke. I pulled out and went looking for the next one. . . ."

I read on. German figures for January and February 1944: 275 tons of bombs on London and 1,700 tons on the British Isles as a whole—one twenty-seventh of the enemy's total.

"Locate the enemy! Inquire his whereabouts, not his strength!" proclaimed the speaker. Loud applause from 1 and 2 Staffeln. "That," he went on abruptly, "is the Russian fighter pilot's motto."

Dead silence. Everyone froze. Lenz and I pricked up our ears. Could this lord of the Greater German heavens be a secret skeptic after all?

The Geschwader-Kommodore nervously straightened his chair.

"I know the Russians firsthand. Some people claim that their role in the air is that of subhuman imbeciles compared to the Western Allies' bomber fleets. If so, they're mistaken." Another gelid silence. "The Soviet aircraft industry has produced fighters which are superior to our Me 109 in many respects—many respects. . . . I've had comrades with over thirty victories to their credit, but it didn't stop them meeting Russians who were more than a match for them."

Just shows how wrong you can be, I told myself. I'd taken him for a stiff-upper-lipper, and he'd suddenly turned out to be a realist who weighed the odds. Good for him!

"On average," he went on, "Russian fighter aces have a higher kill rate than their allies in the West. That's worth bearing in mind."

"Bighead," muttered a pilot in 1 Staffel, rather loudly. "He's only plugging the Russians to make himself look better."

A complete about-face. The wind of public opinion had veered with a vengeance. How easily influenced youngsters of my age were, I reflected. 1914–1944 . . . it was doubtful if anything had changed in thirty years.

"Although we tend to regard the Anglo-American air offensive as our main focus of effort, the Russians have lost twice as many aircraft as the Western Allies."

More consternation.

"That man's good," Schwaneweber remarked suddenly.

Rebhan shrugged. "So he should be."

"Finally, let me give you an example of Russian fighting spirit. Near Orel a Russian fighter damaged an Me 109 flown by a pilot with over thirty kills. Our comrade had to force-land and managed to dump his machine just behind the Russian lines. The Russian orbited the spot and correctly gauged that his enemy stood a good chance of evading capture, so what did he do? He landed beside the Me 109, hurled himself on our comrade, and throttled him with his bare hands. Then he took off again. So much for the Russians' fighting spirit."

An embarrassed hush. What were we supposed to do, execrate the subhuman Mongol hordes or applaud them?

Geschwader-Kommodore Steffen stood up.

"My dear sir, none of us can have failed to derive fresh courage, strength, and determination from your inspiring . . ."

Lenz was absolutely hipped on the idea of becoming an airline pilot. He sometimes shouted to me when we scrambled that he was off to New York in his Focke-Wulf Condor: forty-eight passengers, thirty-two hours' flying time. He also kept pestering me for inside information about secret aircraft projects gleaned from my father. If all these esoteric schemes had come to fruition, we'd have won the war in a week.

In addition to secret military projects such as turbojet night fighters, six-engined long-range bombers, and twin-boom rocket-propelled interceptors, however, there were civil projects such as the Focke-Wulf 300, a four-engined pressurized airliner designed as a successor to the FW 200 Condor, with all passengers accommodated in individual cabins. There was also the eight-engined Tank Ta 400 long-range bomber with two auxiliary Jumo 004 turbojet power plants, which would surely lend itself to conversion for civil use. Or would it? Lenz liked to debate such points for hours. He was further titillated by my allusions to the Do 214, a Dornier flying boat with sixteen engines mounted in tandem. Crew of twelve, accommodation for forty passengers on two decks, saloon, dining room . . .

"Yessir, I wouldn't mind captaining a ship like that!"

To think that Lenz, the eternal dreamer, had the gall to accuse me of fantasizing! My father had violently opposed the last-named project at the Air Ministry back in 1942, on the grounds that it would squander precious labor on a utopian civil scheme at a time when insufficient manpower and resources were available to meet our combat requirements (and, ultimately, those of his son).

"Forget it, Martin. Even though Dorniers stressed the possibility of using the Do 214 as a flying depot ship for U-boats on long-range patrol, the Air Ministry terminated their contract last year."

Well then, how about the Junkers Ju 390, another big machine—crew of five and forty-eight passengers—designed with an eye to postwar air travel? No, that was out too. Most such schemes were stultified by the realities of the air war over Germany, and any that proved feasible were dogged by an acute shortage of suitable engines. However brilliant our designs for fighters, heavy interceptors, and bombers, they always got the power plants they needed too late and had to be fitted with obsolete and underpowered engines. Neither the Jumo 222 nor the Daimler-Benz DB range (603, 605, 606) was ever available on time and in sufficient quantities.

Lenz stuck to his guns. He still aspired to captain a Ju 390 on the Königsberg-Vladivostok run.

Despite the occasional rattle of aircraft cannons and the muffled thud of flak wafted to our ears from the east, Thyme Hill remained a common source of pleasure to Lenz and me.

One day up there I confided to him that, while flying, I sometimes fancied the surrounding air would bear my weight and felt an itch to go strolling along the pillow-white lanes of cloud. This urge was intensified by the sight of a mechanic's footprints on the wings—or, still more so, by bursts of tracer from a pursuing enemy. Then I simply wanted to climb out and run away, hide in a vaporous featherbed, burrow into it, fall asleep, and dream of a better world.

Lenz confessed to secret temptations of quite another order. He said he could understand the appeal of dropping bombs on the toy villages and towns we flew over. It must be fun to watch the little orange fountains spring up and see buildings collapse like a child's box of bricks.

"You wouldn't hear a thing," he pointed out. "There'd be no sound effects, no groans or death rattles. You wouldn't even see any people."

I stared at him with a mixture of horror and fascination.

"But the people would be down there, you know that damn well."

"I wouldn't think about them."

"I just don't believe you."

"If a real live man went for me with a knife, I'm not even

sure I'd defend myself. But an anthill four miles down? Totally abstract—nothing human about it."

"Of course there is. It's full of men, women, and children.
You'd know because your intellect told you so."

"Ah, but that's the big satanic temptation, Michael. Up
there you succumb to the sort of dizzy rapture that gets you
when you run short of oxygen." He smiled. "Anyway, come
down off your high horse. You've squirted enough hot lead
around the sky in your time. They're human beings too, those
little black ants behind their gunsights and multiple MGs."

"Yes," I said quietly. "They're human beings too. That's
the hell of it."

From Thyme Hill I could survey the whole sky from horizon
to horizon. It was good to sit there very early in the morning,
while the peace of God still reigned.

If I take the wings of the morning . . .

I'd rediscovered this line from the Psalms in the pocket
Bible that had once, unbeknown to the rest of us, reposed in
Lauritzen's locker. I'd filched it when his possessions were
unlovingly tipped into a blanket and removed by a beefy noncom. Theft? Tiny Lauritzen wouldn't have minded.

I liked to get up so early that even the earliest scramble
wouldn't take me by surprise. Sometimes the sky looked like
rock crystal, luminous but colorless. The light swathed the
morning like a robe, concealing and revealing by turns. I'd
never seen such light as here in the east. Steppe-light . . .

"Martin?"

"Yes?"

"I don't think I'm up to killing anyone."

"All right, but what about your conscience?" Not for the
first time, I wondered if he was being sarcastic. "You certainly
ought to feel a twinge or two."

"I do have a conscience—at least, I think so. That's the whole trouble."

"Not a bad one, though. If you don't kill enemy pilots they'll kill other people."

"Maybe they act on the same principle. It's insane."

Lenz sometimes behaved as if he never expected to become an airline pilot at all. "We've been robbed of our youth."

"By whom?"

"Fair question. By ourselves—the responsibility's ours, so don't let's ever try and palm it off on anyone else."

We'd swapped roles. He was speaking my lines.

"Look on the bright side," I said, deputizing for him. "We may never be asked to make such a supreme effort again—nor be prepared to do so."

"So what?"

"I can see us sitting on a park bench, two impotent, half-senile old codgers. 'Remember how we scaled the heights of heaven like a pair of young gods,' we'll say, 'wasn't *that* our finest hour?' "

"And our fears? Our dead contemporaries?"

"They'll be forgotten by then. Memory transfigures everything."

"You sound senile already."

Yes indeed, our lines were infinitely interchangeable.

We were living on an island whose span of existence was limited. The radio kept us only vaguely informed of front-line developments.

The Warsaw uprising had been launched on 1 August. The Russians were reported to have backed off and watched the city and its inhabitants being annihilated by our forces. They were also reported to have denied the use of their airfields to the RAF and USAF. Only three months earlier, seven hundred American aircraft had flown on to Russia to refuel after raiding East Prussia.

RAF transports attempted to reach Warsaw from the south and drop ammunition and supplies to the beleaguered rebels —an airlift which even the BBC described as extremely costly. These were the planes that sent us down to the shelters at night. Again according to the BBC, their efforts were discontinued after only six days. By that time Warsaw's destruction was complete. Our own news bulletins stressed that the Poles had been betrayed by the Russians.

The July issue of *Der Flieger* contained a report on the Allies' postwar plans for reorganizing civil air traffic. Among the points discussed:

"(1) Unhampered right of passage throughout the world.

(2) Unrestricted use of all airports on a reciprocal basis.

(3) Curbs on competition to be imposed by binding agreements."

The article read like a fairy tale.

Right of passage unhampered by fighters and flak. Unrestricted use of airports, not their destruction. As for curbs on competition, competing by means of reciprocal gunfire would be totally prohibited.

Bunkhouse alert. It was drizzling, but the layer of stratus was thin enough to reveal the sun behind it, melting like a pat of butter.

We were so dog-tired that the dank air hardly bothered us. We simply pulled the blankets over our heads and switched off. Sometimes an individual limb would get the postcombat shakes, a leg tense up, an arm jerk uncontrollably. Balzerat had developed the most glaring idiosyncrasy of all. He scuffed a tree or wall every ten or fifteen paces and simultaneously flicked one earlobe four or five times with his thumb.

Spasmodic blinks and tics were commonplace. Many knit their brows with mindless ferocity and others had trouble controlling the corners of their mouths. Wilk tilted his chin several times before launching into speech.

"Tell me," asked a visitor from 1 Staffel, "are we heroes, or aren't we?"

"That word gives me a nasty taste," retorted Rebhan. Nobody else uttered a word. They all relapsed into torpor, all feeling stupefied, all nursing headaches and stomach pains brought on by incessant dogfights and relentless exposure to G forces. Many got gooseflesh as soon as the music died in the station loudspeakers.

2

Over seventy assorted guns were aimed and fired at me today—over two thousand bullets and shells, each with its own designs on a single human life.

What joy to wake up sometime in the knowledge that my days as a target were over.

Steffen had scrambled the entire Geschwader. A swarm of gnats whined angrily across the sky toward the giant beasts whose juices they aspired to suck. I was an individual member of the insect community, a part obedient to the laws of the whole.

I mentally stripped us of the few millimeters of metal that encased us. There we were, gliding through the sky on parachute-upholstered seats of steel like strange proboscideans in a hostile element where air pressure and oxygen were halved and the outside temperature stood at minus twenty-three centigrade.

A feeling of unreality overcame me. Did my component body cells feel equally naked and insecure and incongruous up here above the earth? Was the earth still down there? What impelled our insect swarm to diverge, spin, circle, and dive? Whose puppets were we?

A minuscule structure of flesh, blood, bones, and vital organs, coated in skin, clad in fabric, and held in place by straps, was hurtling through the sky—a sky like a nonstop movie program illustrating the various forms of death that could be suffered and inflicted.

I imagined how it would be if my plane escaped the earth's field of gravity. I saw myself long dead, decayed and moldering in my cockpit. The one-ninety orbited on forever, and with it the machines of former friends and foes, Flying Dutchmen who would never find rest or a scorch-marked crater to fold their bones in a compassionate embrace. Wings and fuselage were encrusted, shiplike, with innumerable shells—sky barnacles, cloud algae, wind wrack. Nose and tail were steeped in chill, obnoxious colors by verdigris and rust from distant stars. Bombers' gun ports gaped like toothless mouths. Old machine guns swung to and fro, creaking in the breezes of eternity. Radio antennas fluttered like rotting clotheslines on a derelict housing estate.

We were living in a no-man's-land between life and death. The bridges behind us were burned to a cinder. Our future was as gunmetal gray as the steel projectiles that threatened to kill us.

It was autumn now. I wanted to take Maryla to the Baltic lagoons, stroll across the soft, yielding dunes, watch elks emerge from blue-green forests and amble down to the shore.

Instead, I signaled to Rosenhain to close my cockpit canopy, opened the throttle, and took off, flying wingman to Ketsch. Ketsch had told me it was time I earned my place in a one-ninety. Steffen kept needling him about me, he said, and he was getting sick of it.

Matters came rapidly to a head. The mastodons of the troposphere had reappeared, a whole herd of them. I dived on a Fortress from astern and overhauled it, unmolested.

The big ship was floating in my gunsight now, steady as a

rock. Range: at least three hundred yards. I seemed to hear a chorus of admonitory voices in my earphones: *Closer, Braack, closer—much, much closer!* I didn't fire. I eased the throttle forward and slowly closed the range. No enemy fighters behind, above, below, or ahead—nothing, not even a medal-hungry superior eager to snatch the juicy morsel from my grasp. The bomber spread its wings across the concentric circles projected on the windshield by my reflector sight. There was the rear turret with its quadruple guns, there the massive tail unit with its brilliant orange paintwork. . . . Still I didn't fire, still I crept closer with my thumb poised over the cannon button and my forefinger resting gingerly on the MG toggle switch. All was as it should be, nothing could go wrong now. *Close to spitting distance!* How could you spit into the wind without getting a faceful yourself? I wrenched my thoughts back to the business in hand. There it was, my windfall, my bonanza, my club membership card. It wouldn't escape me now, not now. *Closer, Braack! Better ram than fire a moment too soon!* The tail gunner was looking at me—I could see him quite clearly. Was he wearing glasses? Was there a human face behind that oxygen mask? This Fortress was *my* meat. Meat . . . The word conjured up visions of an emblem on the huge tail plane: a chicken on a spit. I was holding the spit. In another few seconds the chicken would be spitted on my bursts of gunfire. *Close to spitting distance.* . . . Now I understood: *that* kind of spitting distance!

Invisible forces buffeted my wings. The gargantuan bird was tossing me about in its slipstream. I fought to keep it centered in my gunsight, lurching through the sky like a drunk. Now was the time to fire—now, *now!*

I'd never fire, I knew that. The bomber punished my neglect by firing at me instead. Flame belched from every muzzle —from the tail, the mid-upper turret, the belly. I tore through a flickering fireworks display of tracer. It was almost like a cheerful salutation. Greetings from us to you.

We reassembled for another attack, rolling, yawing, banking, diving, climbing, spinning through the autumn sky.

Voices testified to the exhilaration of combat:

"I screwed the ass off that Yiddisher nigger, and what did he do? Kept on going, the fresh bastard!"

"Must be something wrong with your equipment."

"Ask the girls back home. They'll tell you different."

"Wham, there goes another! I wouldn't give a wet fart for *his* chances."

I threw the one-ninety into a scorching dive that set her wings vibrating. Meanwhile, my imagination went its own perverse way. With death in the air all around me, my earphones had started their tricks again. This time they were relaying hits from contemporary musicals. *One, two, three,* crooned Johannes Heesters, *love is pure sorceree* . . . A kill on the starboard beam: one Mustang spinning down riverward, no parachute. . . . Evelyn Künnecke melodiously inquired if I'd ever kissed a girl in the dark. *You know, if so, how lovely it can be* . . . Twelve rounds of incendiary, twenty of armor-piercing. *My heart lost its way one evening in May* . . . I was ready to lose anything, my heart included, as long as I could keep my life.

"Christ, that shot the fillings out of my teeth!"

"Help, I'm . . ."

The sky was a mass of pastel shades. Filtered by contrails, the sun shone down with mellow radiance. Below us, a serene Sunday afternoon. The angelus would soon be ringing out across the fields.

We were in among them again. I tore after Lenz, slightly in echelon. His slipstream rocked me violently, making it impossible to aim. Some Mustangs curved in behind us and opened fire. Serpentine tongues of incandescent tracer licked around a neighboring one-ninety. *Not Lenz—anyone but Lenz!*

A huge shape hurtled past in an even steeper dive than ours, intent on its own doom, not mine: one whole Fortress, bound for perdition with a complement of tiny figures struggling to extricate themselves from their plummeting sarcophagus. Those who were still alive would now be screaming, yelling, writhing, squeezing their burned and mutilated bodies through the gun ports, becoming entangled or dashing themselves to death against the tail planes. Arms, legs, torsos, blood and bunches of human grapes, bursting shells and eddies of flame, limbs and fragments of flesh almost lovingly dissected by a cosmic surgeon. . . .

I found myself back near Chelmno on the Vistula.

Somebody materialized beside me. I tried to escape—poled back hard and stall-turned away—but he stuck to me like glue. Suddenly he was with me in the cockpit, inside my headset.

"Braack, you cluck, it's me! See that Fortress at two o'clock? That's your first kill. I'll help you—I'll guide you in. All you've got to do is press the tit. When I say fire, give him a good long squirt!"

It was Ketsch in person.

Ketsch, who only wanted to help. Autumn 1944 . . . How did you help a young man in the sixth year of the war? You helped him by giving him a long-awaited chance to kill. His first and greatest achievement was at hand!

I tagged onto Ketsch, opened the throttle, and climbed back into the disaster area. Exploding wings, fireballs, plumes of oil and glycol, bursts of tracer. Ketsch pressed on regardless.

"There you are, Braack, go get him!"

Ahead of me was a Fortress G-7, above me a pair of Mustangs. Ketsch, now acting as my wingman, was holding the enemy fighters at bay.

"In you go, Braack. Concentrate on the forward section. Get in closer, but for God's sake don't fire yet. Closer, much closer . . . Wait for it . . ."

My opponent was even jumpier. He'd already started shooting. Long streams of tracer flew lazily toward my cockpit canopy, then whipped past. His aim was poor, far too high.

"Get in closer, Braack . . . Easy does it . . . You've got it made . . . Keep your eyes on the target, I'll hold the others off . . . Get ready . . ."

I was very close now—so close I thought I could see what I'd always dismissed as a literary fiction: the whites of the enemy's eyes.

The tail gunner blazed away madly, idiotically. The nearer I got the higher he seemed to fire. Was it only a mock attack? Animals reacted that way, and Americans—said Steffen— were little removed from the animal state. USAF bomber crews had to be enticed out of their trees and into their Fortresses—said Steffen—with bunches of ripe bananas.

"Now, Braack! *Now!* Fire, for Christ's sake!"

But he should have said that to the fool ahead of me. His guns had jammed. He threw one arm up over his face and cowered away, trying to be somewhere else.

"Fire, damn you!" I muttered. "Fire so I can fire back!"

But he didn't—he'd given up. I'd ram him if I didn't break at once.

I broke to port and Ketsch pulled back. Our paths diverged.

"You're an asshole, Braack, a complete asshole!" I reefed around onto a reciprocal course. "Why in God's name didn't you open fire? There's nothing to be done with you—nothing!"

So that was that. My next touchdown would be my last. I

felt tempted to rip off my oxygen mask and drift into sleep, slowly and painlessly.

The unexpected appearance of three squadrons of Lightnings brought Ketsch's tirade to an abrupt end.

"Lightnings at three o'clock. Let's go, boys, I don't think they're onto us yet!"

Moments later, half the Geschwader had wheeled to starboard and launched itself at the new enemy. The adrenaline of battle was really flowing today.

"If there's one thing I hate, it's those bastard Lightnings!"

"Hey, Wehrmann, did you get him?"

"You bet! With that much lead up his ass, he must have choked on his own shit."

My one-ninety was bucking, bucking all the time—I'd only just noticed. Had she gone on strike? Was she trying to demonstrate her loyalty and solidarity?

"Watch your RT discipline!"

Steffen's voice. Wehrmann seemed to have excelled himself today, but Steffen, punctilious as ever, was calling our hero to order.

All was confusion now, like an oriental bazaar. If it hadn't been for the Lightnings' twin booms, nobody could have told friend from foe.

I orbited, looking for Ketsch. Suddenly he was back in my earphones, sounding curt and surperhumanly well-disciplined.

"Shut up and close up! We'll go in once more, but not like last time. That last attack was an utter shambles. Wehrmann, keep your trap shut or you'll be up in front of the Kommodore—and fight fair. I saw you squirt those parachutes."

"But I got three kills, Herr Hauptmann—three minimum!"

"That's enough! Right, boys, let's polish 'em off, but only the ones that can still fight back."

A final attack from ahead. Eight bombers in the lead—

eight out of thirty-two, and each with a crew of ten or twelve. That made nearly a hundred human lives. During the first eight months of 1943 alone, the RAF had dropped forty-six thousand tons of bombs on Germany, eleven thousand of them on Hamburg. Statistics and people, people and statistics . . . *Vengeance is mine; I will repay, saith the Lord. Eye for eye, tooth for tooth . . .*

Don't think, shoot! Four radial engines waxed huge in my windshield. Now or never: court-martial or first-kill booze-up. The gall of the Yanks, not camouflaging their daylight raiders —what a nerve, painting their tails and wing tips bright orange! Suddenly everything swam before my eyes. The quartet of engines, the menacing turrets, friend and foe—all were obliterated by blinding, wavering streaks. I pulled back hard, then half-rolled off the top of the loop. Below me, now heading in the same direction, were the surviving bombers. Others were spinning down like autumn leaves.

Windfalls and leaves underfoot. Autumnal melancholy. Silence. What had happened—what was the matter?

My engine had seized, that was the matter.

More than that, my windshield was coated with oil—hence the streaks and blurring. My BMW 801D-2 twin-row radial had spewed up its guts like a queasy drunk. While I was blithely continuing the attack, it had died on me—succumbed to the first hit or ricochet from a Boeing's air gunner and shot its bolt.

Forced landing!

Forced landing? No forward vision, windshield as black as Tutankhamen's tomb. Would I ram the nearest bomber or plow into my friends? Afraid? No, not that. Training paid dividends. *Release straps, depress red jettison lever.* Sure enough, the canopy flew off. *Great, keep calm, Braack, everything's going fine.* A rushing sound, an icy blast. *Mask off, can't be more than ten thousand feet up. Tighten parachute harness*—yes, that too. Ice-cold. Ice-cold Braack was going to bail out. *Easy, take it nice and easy.* Left foot braced against the plastic grip of the control column. *All clear below? Affirmative.*

Kick the stick forward—right forward!

The one-ninety performed a deep obeisance like a courtier in the Kaiser's day. I flew off into space. *Never fear, Braack, never fear!* The whole procedure had been carefully worked out and laid down. Success was guaranteed. . . .

Why didn't my chute open? The ground was rushing up to meet me—couldn't anything slow its progress? My stomach rebelled as waves of nausea rippled through it. *Pull, Braack, why don't you pull the rip cord?* Twenty-two, twenty-three . . .

I pulled. Fine, as long as I'd started counting in time. If not, the guarantee became void.

Ploof, ploof! A two-edged sword sliced the inside of my thighs.

The leg harness . . . Straps had been known to break before now, but mine were tightly secured. Here came the ground. Already? Had my chute even opened yet?

A muffled thud. No attempt at the sort of roll we'd so often practiced in the sandpit, just hard and merciless contact with the ground. A stab of pain shot through me and the light went out.

"Hi there, buddy!"

Rings of fire swam before my eyes, superimposed on a plump smiling face and a bulky fur-lined leather jacket. The giant was supporting my head with his left hand and holding a flat bottle to my lips with his right. Whatever the bottle contained, it tasted strong and smoky.

From the lower branches of a birch tree in my field of vision, companionably entwined like laundry hung out to dry, dangled two parachutes. My surreptitious flirtation with the BBC paid off. At least in broad outline, I gathered that Joe was the pilot of a downed American bomber. I was unconcious when he landed beside me, and he'd spent the better part of an hour trying to bring me around, hoping in vain for a patrol to take him prisoner and convey me to a field hospital —a patrol which would, he surmised, consist of black-uniformed, black-helmeted myrmidons wearing the death's-head insignia.

"You know, those motherfuckers in the SS."

Joe came from the Middle West. His jaws were still busy with the gum he'd been chewing when he bailed out. The USAF had evidently refined its bailing-out procedure to such a pitch that half a bottle of whiskey came too. This particular beverage was called Bourbon. Since making its acquaintance, I'd begun to wonder if violent contact with mother earth was entirely responsible for the fiery circles roaming my eyeballs.

We'd landed in a clump of birch trees whose branches were a staging post for dozens of vociferous linnets. Joe, who was unhurt, examined the gash on my forehead with deep concern. He apologized for having no penicillin with him.

"No what?"

He explained what penicillin was.

"It helps when you've been with girls, too. Are they good-lookers, the girls around here?"

He had an open, ingenuous face. I tried to steer the conversation toward jazz—jazz and the latest sensation: Stan Kenton.

"You listen to Stan Kenton?" I asked.

Sure, sometimes. Joe came from the States and only listened to Kenton *sometimes?* The new dimensions he'd opened up—the white-hot, stratospheric blare of his trumpet section, the throbbing, elemental bass of his trombones . . .

"He just doesn't swing . . ."

Kenton didn't *swing?* Good God, what would Joe do if he heard our own swing bands, so-called? Bestow a pitying smile on our lack of cultural development, probably. With our kind of music, no wonder we'd never win the war.

Glenn Miller was another matter. Joe "dug" Glenn Miller.

I proudly reeled off a string of titles: "Chattanooga Choo-Choo," "Moonlight Serenade," "String of Pearls. . . ." Joe was unimpressed. He took it for granted that anyone would know them, Krauts included.

"Like another snort?"

He passed me the bottle. I could have lain there forever, chatting to Joe about Stan Kenton and Glenn Miller, but Joe was more interested in surrender. When would those "motherfucking SS men" turn up? He wanted to get it over and done with, torture and all.

"No SS, Joe. No torture. Whistle me a new American hit—something I haven't heard yet."

Joe whistled something. With difficulty, I identified it as the chorus of "My Blue Heaven."

"Okay?"

"No, not okay. That's as old as the hills."

"Oh yeah?" He tried a snatch of "Rhapsody in Blue." "Better?"

"But Joe, that's Gershwin. He died in 1937!"

"You don't say."

"What did you learn to fly in?"

"A Piper."

"Good machine?"

"Too goddamn good-natured. You can treat it like shit, not like the types we moved on to. They converted us too fast."

I caught sight of three Polish peasants advancing on our copse across a field of rotting grain. Their manner became threatening as soon as they saw the American. I jumped up, swaying like the drunk I was.

The Poles eyed Joe with redoubled menace when they saw

me. It was a topsy-turvy situation. Had even Polish peasants been so thoroughly conditioned that they spat on their American liberators for fear of us Germans?

The infuriated trio brandished their pitchforks. I drew my automatic and warned them off. Less than two hours ago I'd been pointing eight machine guns at a planeload of men like Joe. Now I escorted him to safety at the army post in the next village, guided there by the dilapidated church whose red-brick tower stood out against the green of the surrounding trees.

On the outskirts of the village, Joe smilingly handed me his own automatic. I'd forgotten to disarm him and remove his paybook. Before we came to the first sentry he slipped me the Bourbon bottle too, grinning all over his face.

"Here, buddy, you need it more'n I do. My war's over."

Late that afternoon I told Lenz what had happened. He frowned and shook his head.

"Honestly, Michael, I give up. You don't know if it's Christmas or Easter. I bet you wouldn't even unload a bomb if you had to, right?"

"Maybe not."

"So what about the swine who are bombing our country to blazes?"

"Listen, Martin, I want to whistle you something. It's called 'Intermission Riff'—Kenton's latest. Wait till we try it out—it'll bring the house down."

"You might at least be as hard on the other side as you are on yourself. That's fair, isn't it?"

"Listen—G, G sharp, over and over. That's all, but you should hear what he makes out of it."

"You're hopeless, honestly."

"I know, we're having the time of our young lives. Flying, killing, swilling—oh yes, and occasionally getting killed ourselves. That's only to be expected after five years of war."

"Talk about bitter! If they wrung you out and poured the result into Churchill's brandy he'd drop dead. What would you prefer to be, a pirate or something?"

"Ah, pirates—if only we were! Freebooters of the celestial seas. If only we were fighting for treasure—gold ducats or bars of silver—but all we're offered is a tin necktie. Some incentive!"

"Carry on this way and you won't be around to bellyache."

"You're right. If I were captaining an airliner, nobody'd want to fly with me. I reek of failure. This is a meritocracy. We're geared to producing things—like corpses—and I'm nonproductive."

"For God's sake give it a rest, Michael. To change the subject, why aren't the others back? They can't have more than a few minutes' fuel left."

We were lying among the hemlock stalks on the edge of the runway. Our eyes had often scanned the sky in the past half hour. Ketsch had rounded up a small patrol and gone a-hunting on Steffen's orders. No enemy activity had been reported, but you never could tell.

"I can hear something!"

It was the characteristic deep-throated hum of a BMW 801D—almost inaudible as yet, like a vibration that barely flutters the eardrums or sends ripples across a pool. The hum grew steadily louder and more polyphonic.

"There they are!" cried Lenz.

High time too. Twilight was closing in with the speed of a gathering storm.

To judge by the way they hurriedly lowered their flaps and gear and came in to land, the red light must have been on in every cockpit. One undercarriage failed to drop.

"Rebhan," said Lenz.

Rebhan made a wheels-up landing. He slithered along the runway with a screech of metal, sending up dust and clods of earth, and came to a stop just short of Combat Control. Canopy back, a quick exit, and there he was, safe and sound.

Lenz spotted Bächler's White 6 with part of the radiator cowling gone and the upper section of the rudder assembly torn and fluttering in the slipstream. He'd just made an immaculate landing when someone from 1 Staffel fouled him. The newcomer swooped in at an angle and slammed into the side and rear of Bächler's fuselage. They were both safely down, at least, but the two fighters stood there in midfield, interlocked like a pair of mating bugs.

Wehrmann had to overshoot and started to go around again. Just then his fuel ran out. Undaunted, he skillfully deposited his White 8 on the riverbank, only yards short of a clump of birch trees. You had to hand it to him.

Wilk, with a beard of off-white smoke trailing behind him, came in low—far too low. He leapt the hangar roofs like a stag, and then, with all the grace of a full-grown elephant, flopped onto the field. His machine ground to an almost immediate halt. No sign of fire. Off with his canopy and out in a flash. Terra firma had reclaimed him.

At last they were all down unscathed, Ketsch included.

While he was taxiing, an adult roebuck cantered straight across his front. Ketsch braked like mad and stood his machine on its nose. The airscrew was a write-off.

Skintight cockpits and boundless skies.

Our operational base in the marshy embrace of the Pilica was as isolated as a lone aircraft carrier. To attain the infinity of heaven we had, like cell-bound monks, to immure ourselves in cockpits. Our instruments spoke a cold, clear, unequivocal language. The air around was diffused and full of mystery—a grandiose spectacle for those strapped into Plexiglas cocoons. Skintight cockpits and boundless skies: quite a contrast. I wanted to write about it in my bunk at night. While writing, I was taking up arms against the whole rotten world and its inhumanity. While sharpening my pencil, I was honing a spearhead with vengeance in mind. My diary and my attempts at poetry were a protest, but I had no idea if I would be able to write once the war in the air was over. I tried to pretend that it was. I reached for my pen with a sigh of relief, only to find a void inside me. Nothing but silence . . . How many years would have to pass before I could write about this autumn—two, three, ten, twenty?

Whenever I was exposed to centrifugal force in a dogfight, my legs threatened to burst under the fivefold weight of my body; whenever I tried to describe the terrors of this period, I felt as if my brain would explode under the pressure of recollection.

Today had been marked by the simultaneous arrival of three letters from unknown girls. Presumably, some kind of welfare organization had distributed our names to the whole of the German Girls' League. Motto: write to our brave young boys at the front, who are doing their duty so far from home. . . .

All three letters bore an alarming resemblance. The lines could have been interchanged at random:

"At night, when the bombers fly overhead, I shall think of you, my dear brave pilot. . . . At this very moment—for all I know—you may be shooting down the last plane that stands between you and your Knight's Cross. . . . My heart melts when I think of you, my unknown hero, fighting for us so far away. . . . Three of the boys in our town have already won the Knight's Cross. Will you be the fourth, and will you pay me a visit? I can picture you standing there before me, all naked and big and strong, with the Knight's Cross glinting at your throat. . . ."

"These girls," Wehrmann declared that night in the bunkhouse. "They're Knight's Cross crazy. You won't get a finger up for less, believe me. There isn't one that'd open her legs for an Iron Cross First Class."

Wehrmann himself had received a letter, plus photo. As might have been expected, it showed a naked girl lying back with her thighs splayed. The inscription on the back, penned in a neat copybook hand, read, "You can always see me like this, but only if you turn up wearing a Knight's Cross!"

None of us could boast a similar enclosure. How did Wehrmann manage it? Had his very name given off a whiff of lechery perceptible at three or four hundred miles?

Military letter forms and more military letter forms, all made of ash-gray paper flecked with slivers of wood fiber. Many of them had made a circuitous journey from Lötzen via Berlin, Brandenburg, Dresden, or Katowice. Warsaw, it was rumored, had finally fallen to the Russians.

Had Warsaw still been part of the German postal network, the drab little letters wouldn't have taken so long to arrive. It didn't matter anyway, because they were not only timeless but identical in tone.

First, Edeltraut, a pretty girl from down the road. I'd been fourteen the last time I held her in my arms ("Go on, then. Kiss me, silly!): "Your mother tells me you're a fighter pilot now. Terrific! How many kills have you scored?"

Rosemarie, then seventeen, had ridden past with a come-hither look in her eye. I pulled her down off her horse and kissed her hard ("Leave go of me, you devil!"): "Can I congratulate you on your Knight's Cross yet? Fighter pilots are the bravest of the brave. Be a credit to us!"

Gertrud at twelve. Three of us had tried to pull her panties down. She screamed, so we let her go ("I'll tell if you

don't!'') Now she wrote: "Stick at it, Michael—the Fatherland needs all the heroes it can get. Mind you don't come
back to me without the German Cross in Gold!"

Gudrun the gamekeeper's daughter, a randy and preco-
cious little brunette who used to pounce on us in the woods.
She'd later become a big noise in the Nikolaiken branch of
the German Girls' League. "Write me when you shoot down
your hundredth Allied terrorist, then I'll come and see you. A
hundred kills entitles you to a hundred you-know-whats!"

Lenz and I were squatting side by side in the latrine. The
last few scraps of gray paper fluttered into the mustard-brown
mess beneath my bare behind.

"When this lousy war's over," I said, "if they ever put the
losers on trial, you won't see a solitary man in the dock, only
women."

3

When the last engine fell silent at nightfall, the whole base subsided into lethargy. Even the knots of figures heading for the mess seemed to move more sluggishly, as if they had all switched off a cardiac supercharger that kept their muscles and senses taut throughout the daylight hours. Despite their human presence, everything looked eerie and deserted. The wisps of smoke curling from the chimneys were as melancholy as the strains of the guitar which someone was invariably strumming. Was this how the hermits of old had dwelled in their cells and troglodytic villages?

On evenings like these, my reunions with Maryla could never come soon enough.

"Give me a hug first." (Yes, I was still alive, neither hanged by parachute shrouds nor drawn by a shell splinter nor quartered by a tail gunner's multiple cannons. I hadn't even somersaulted on landing and burst into flames.) "That's not a proper kiss. Here, I'll show you." (I belonged to a generation better schooled in marksmanship than osculation.) "And here, don't forget to take this with you when you go. Real Westphalian ham!" (Anyone would have thought I was only out for what I could get.) "Right, let's see if you still feel like a bag of bones."

When at last we released each other, it was usually a signal for the first nutcracker to utter its rasping cry. Sometimes I brought my guitar along and played some old pieces—a sarabande by Friedemann Bach, an allegretto by Telemann, a largo by Vivaldi. Sometimes Maryla would sing while I picked out chord accompaniments to her repertoire of traditional Polish and Russian folk songs. Her voice sounded deeper than usual when she sang these melancholy refrains, and her fine dark eyebrows rose and fell in time to the music.

It was the perfect hour.

Every color was muted and the last evening clouds sailed past like ships bound for harbor. The first owl glided from its perch among the gnarled branches.

Make-believe: I'd just come home from teaching school in Lötzen with a pile of exercise books to correct, but they could wait till Sunday night. The weekend lay ahead. Tomorrow we'd drive to the Baltic lagoons or take a lake trip to Nikolaiken in a handsome white steamer full of gaily clad people, laughing and waving. Now, though, supper was on the table: a steaming bowl of Kasubian cabbage soup. . . .

Maryla sat up and peered through the window. Half obscured by intervening trees, a log fire was burning in the dusk. I recognized a few members of my own Staffel—Lenz, Rebhan, and Schwaneweber—but the rest were outsiders. They didn't see us. Lenz had probably forgotten about my date tonight.

They clustered around the roaring fire. One of them had also brought a guitar. When Maryla and I turned to look between kisses, the window framed a romantic picture: a campfire surrounded by dark figures singing in the night—the epitome of my boyhood dreams.

The air around Shangri-La was alive with fluttering bats, the calls of sleepless quail, the flame-cast shadows of the distant fire, but brighter than the firelight was the full moon shining through the branches. The whole wood became a chiaroscuro of dancing shapes. Above it could be seen a narrow segment of sky. The heavens arched above us, majestic and illimitable, like a glass dome inverted for the protection of our own private world.

Night scents pervaded the hut with sudden intensity while we kissed, as if stirred into motion by the activity outside. Thyme, mushrooms, rotting wood, freshly turned soil, the smoky scent of baked potatoes . . .

All at once the dome above us seemed to crack, and there it was again: stark and imminent reality.

Now that he had several kills to his credit, Lenz was a different person. Had he finally succumbed to the thrill of the chase?

He took half a dozen cigarettes and laid them out at regular intervals to represent six fighters chasing each other's tails in a defensive circle.

The fighter pilot's first commandment: one eye watching your front and at least one other watching your rear. The fighter pilot's mortal sin: watching a defeated enemy spin down to perdition. A fascinating sight, but one of his pals could swoop in from astern and avenge him while you were flushed with success and savoring your superior skill.

Fighters flying in a defensive circle had no need to fear a surprise attack. Each pilot kept an eye on the one in front and was simultaneously watched and warned by the one behind. No attacker could infiltrate such a circle without being spotted, but victory naturally went to the side with most fuel to spare. If a Lufbery had to be abandoned for lack of fuel, its separate components became easy meat for a patient enemy prowling overhead. During the Battle of Britain it had been the Germans whose fuel ran low first. Over Poland the advantage was ours.

And now, here was Lenz playing games with cigarettes.

"It's utter nonsense," he said. "The defensive circle's pure bluff. It's only ever worked because none of our pilots came up with the right idea." He fished a uniform button out of his pocket. "Here, this is a lone one-ninety. It dives on one of the enemy, gives him a squirt, and climbs back again."

"You'd have to be a real expert to do that, *and* pretty reckless."

On the radio, Willy Berking's band was playing a number with an intriguing trombone solo. Personally, I'd have preferred to discuss the soloist's approach to improvisation, but Lenz was well away.

"The attacking fighter can't be seen by its target in the circle—it's above and behind, right?"

"Right. Hey, just listen to that bass line!"

"The fighters behind the target see the attacker only at the last moment, right?"

"Sure, and they give him all they've got."

"That's just where you're wrong. They can't open fire or they'd hit the man in front. The whole thing's pure bluff, I tell you."

"Christ, Martin, you sound like Newton when the apple fell on his head."

"All that counts is, in quick, a couple of short bursts, and up again. Then in again."

"Why in again?"

"Because if the enemy see you're all on your lonesome they'll break formation and clobber you. You want them to think they're being attacked by half a Staffel, that's why speed's so essential."

His face was radiant. Willy Berking had moved on to "Piano Dreams," with a lot of Gershwin. Not bad either.

I tapped out the rhythm on the edge of the table, silently studying the features I knew so well. Lenz had a small scar on his right temple, not that anyone else would have noticed. We'd been playing cowboys and Indians beside the Krutinna. He was Winnetou and I was Old Shatterhand, and he'd slipped and fallen ten feet down the bank. There was a rock at the bottom.

(Two days after this conversation, while in the mess library, I came across an article on Hans-Joachim Marseille, the so-called Star of Africa, who'd shot down 158 British aircraft in his Me 109 before coming to grief on his 482nd patrol—not in combat, ironically enough, but because of an engine fire. Marseille had to bail out but failed to fall clear and smashed his spine on the Messerschmitt's rudder. Reading on, I discovered that he'd anticipated Lenz's tactical device and used it to shoot down half a dozen Tomahawks in eleven minutes.)

"But Martin," I could have told him, "this is Poland after five years of war. There aren't any sluggish old Tomahawks around, not these days, and defensive circles are out. Mustangs can manage without them better than we can . . ."

As it was, I said nothing and listened to the end of "Piano Dreams." Very nice too.

"Steffen called me a quitter today. He said I had a yellow streak a mile wide."

"And what did you say?"

"Nothing."

Lenz and I were taking our ease on Thyme Hill. Dozens of storks were high-stepping through the stubble fields and water meadows in search of mice, frogs, and beetles—their last square meal before the long flight south. Storks from Masuria had already passed high over Grojecko, together with swallows, lapwings, and marsh harriers. Departure was in the air.

Rumors of a move to the west were going the rounds of the base as well. The Russians were drawing nearer.

"And what did you feel like saying?"

"I'm a coward in your kind of world, Herr Major, but not in mine."

"Anything else?"

"Yes. In your world, Herr Major, courage is persistently equated with a reckless disregard for human life."

"There's a war on, Michael. That's how it is in wartime."

"But is bravery unique to wartime? What's left of it when the shooting stops? Look at our top-scoring aces with their Oak Leaves and Swords. What'll they amount to when the war's over?"

"Figures of fun, I'm afraid, with a little collection of scrap metal neatly mounted in a velvet-lined case on the mantelpiece." Four or five swans flew past, their wings whistling in the autumn breeze. We stared after them, entranced by the sheer beauty of flight. "All the same, Michael, you're wrong. Take unfair advantage of what little freedom you have now and you'll throw away your chance of a really free future."

"End up in jail, you mean?"

"If you're lucky. Anyway, Steffen isn't the only one who's muddled. You equate freedom with plain pigheadedness."

"All right, tell me what I'm doing wrong."

"You're pushing your luck. From their angle, Ketsch and Steffen don't have any choice. They'll have to dump you unless you conform. Stop bucking the system. After all, you volunteered to join it."

"In other words, score your first kill and get it over."

"Yes, then we'll all breathe easier. Steffen, Ketsch, me, the whole bunkhouse—the whole outfit."

"Why not the whole of the Greater German Reich? The Führer will look up from his map table with a sigh of relief.

Braack's done it at last, he'll say—I always knew he had it in him! As for Fatso Göring, he'll wipe away a manly tear. Surreptitiously, of course." I irritably dislodged some turf with my heel, kneaded the divot into a ball, and flung it at some starlings cavorting in the undergrowth below us, already wearing their speckled winter plumage. "You bring a lump to my throat, you and your altruistic concern for my personal welfare! I'll tell you something, Martin—I shit on freedom if someone else has to die for it, whether it's my own little pinch of freedom or the freedom of the Western world. If killing's the only way to get it, you can keep it."

Lenz didn't reply at first, just watched my laborious efforts to drive off the starlings with a trace of amusement.

"Tough talk," he said eventually. "This is the ideal place to practice public speaking—no one can hear you."

He jumped up and aimed a furious kick at the nearest tree trunk. It was his turn now.

"But what'll you do when you're behind bars? Who's going to dig you out then? Nobody!"

There were nights when, just before dropping off to sleep, I saw an armada of Thunderbolts, Airacobras, and Mitchells, and myself heading straight for them. Nobody fired a shot. We circled like dogs exchanging friendly sniffs. Each pilot recognized the other as a kindred spirit; each was proud to be a flier and none had any other thought in mind. By common consent, we joined forces against the mighty of the earth, who had perverted its finest profession into mutual slaughter.

Assuming formation at random—flying alongside, above, below, or astern of each other—we reveled in the beauties of the upper air, clouds and sunsets, landscapes wreathed in purple haze. We sang blithely into our microphones, the RAF of green English meadows and bleak Scottish highlands, the Aviation Française of the mysteries of the Latin Quarter and the lonely moors of Les Baux, the Red Air Force of wooden churches mirrored in the quiet Don, the USAF of stern-wheelers on the Mississippi and Missouri, the Luftwaffe of the lakes of Masuria, the valleys of the Rhine and Moselle, the somber depths of the Thuringian Forest.

Our airplanes were fully laden, but with roses, not bombs. The French dropped theirs on the extinct craters of the Eifel range, the British on Berlin, now restored to the Olympic splendor it had known in 1936. The Germans flew to Coventry and released whole bomb bays of moss roses over the ruins. The Americans showered Heidelberg and Munich, and the Russians—with rapturous enthusiasm—dispensed their fragrant cargoes far and wide.

Our mission completed, we soared in waves through the ether, wing to wing like dancers holding hands.

We climbed to fifteen thousand feet in three finger-fours and practiced controlled dives at Steffen's behest. His prior comment on our existing standard of performance:

"They can't fly straight, they can't shoot straight. All they can do is screw."

Only last week, in fact, the Geschwader had lost two replacement pilots who'd failed to pull out soon enough. Diving a one-ninety was a ticklish business. Although we dived in the course of every mission, we were now about to learn the perfect dive like grown men being taught to walk after decades on their feet.

The tyro's usual mistake when diving—an instinctive one—was to decelerate by chopping the throttle because a plummeting one-ninety could build up an alarming turn of speed. But cutting the throttle, it was now impressed on us, was a cardinal error. Starved of fuel, the engine's cooling system became inadequate. An engine was cooled not only by the outside airflow but internally as well, by the fuel in the mixture. Deprived of sufficient internal cooling, an engine developed piston seizure. (And to think we'd always attributed engine failure to enemy gunfire.)

Steffen, winding up his lecture:

"The BMW 801D-2 is a superb example of German precision engineering. If I catch anyone else chewing up his engine, I'll have him court-martialed for sabotage!"

After this lucid introduction to the relevant problems, we climbed to our allotted altitude and took it in turns to dive, pull out, and rejoin the rest. Steffen stationed himself on the landing tee and supervised our activities.

This kind of flying was fun. I dived and dived again, intoxicated by the sensation, happy to be assigned an aerial task that caused me no misgivings. I almost enjoyed blacking out when I heaved on the stick and clawed my way back.

Others seemed to dive with even greater panache. One of our number pulled out so late that his tail wheel flicked a treetop.

When we landed, Steffen personally and ostentatiously removed a fir twig from the offender's tail unit.

"Been looking for a Christmas tree already, have you?"

Our heavy one-nineties dropped so fast that we had to start thinking about pulling out at three thousand feet, no lower.

Someone from IV Gruppe, who was the last to dive, staged an impressive finale: he didn't pull out at all. His machine flashed into the ground at such lightning speed that it seemed an age before the dust flew. It was almost as if mother earth had been taken so utterly by surprise that she'd forgotten to react.

Lenz later claimed to have seen shreds of skin drifting down five minutes afterward. I accused him of gross exaggeration. The entire fighter had been compressed into a handy block of scrap metal five feet long. The fusion of man and machine was complete.

Obergefreiter Brummelkamp turned up from the staff office with news that the Herr Geschwader-Kommodore wanted a word with me at once. It was true. Steffen had decided to give me some private coaching: "How to shoot down a Fortress within seven days."

He didn't relish the thought of one of his pilots being court-martialed for cowardice in the face of the enemy—it would make a bad impression on Hermann. Philanthropy didn't come into it.

"And now, length of bursts . . ." Steffen had been bending my ear for a good half hour. I was an apt pupil, silent and attentive. "There are some bloody fools who think you can't overdo a good thing—they keep on squirting for six or seven seconds. "Well, they ought to be court-martialed for wasting ammunition."

I eyed him gratefully. A court-martial was just what his private coaching session was designed to spare me. Behind his head hung a photo-portrait of the Führer. On the shelf below it, reading from left to right, stood a bottle of genuine French brandy; a bottle of Tokay, likewise genuine; an omnibus edition of *Der Flieger* dated 1943; a deer sculpture by Renée Sintenis; Alfred Rosenberg's *Myth of the 20th Century;* and Volume II of Plato's complete works. Sandwiched between

Rosenberg and Plato was a king-size pack of Blue Seal rubbers in their drab wartime wrapper. That was genuine too.

"Yes, Herr Major."

"Two seconds a burst—three at most. That's the way to gain maximum results for minimum expenditure. We have to think in economic terms, Braack. Live enemy bomber crews cost us money, but so do dead ones. Assume your fire has been accurate. Debris flies off the enemy. He emits a plume of smoke and starts losing altitude. What do you do then?"

"Disengage and look for another target, Herr Major."

"Wrong, absolutely wrong! Boeings and Mustangs are as tough as old boots. Circle for another pass and you'll see they're still flying. In you go again. Give them some more short bursts, like Morse. Aerial shorthand, Braack, that's the rule. And another thing. When a Yank goes down, don't hang around congratulating yourself. Always make sure the sky's clear behind you, otherwise one of his pals will get mad and squirt you up the ass."

"Yes, Herr Major."

"Very well, Braack, remember what I've told you. Carry on."

I leapt to my feet. Lessons were over for today. My head was a beehive buzzing with useful tips. *If you hide in cloud with someone on your tail, never plow straight on, always make a ninety-degree turn. Never fly just above cloud. Anyone who plays submarines has only himself to blame. . . .*

"Thank you, Herr Major."

"I'll be keeping an eye on you, Braack."

Poor eye, I thought, and performed a reasonably smart about-face.

I was hardly back in the bunkhouse when a standby alert was issued, hardly in my deck chair when we were scrambled, hardly in the air when we made contact. Thirty-two Fortress G-7s were toiling northwestward in some disarray. The flak must have thinned their ranks.

Thirty-two? Just that, no more.

There were over forty of us. No enemy fighters? None to be seen. They'd probably run low on fuel after becoming embroiled in dogfights with our colleagues over Silesia.

Here it was at last, an even chance.

We charged them with every muzzle blazing. The dance of death had begun again.

We attacked in three finger-fours, using the well-tried leg-over tactic that had lately been nicknamed "Steffen's Switch." Into their midst we went, delivered at last from the threat of Mustangs and Lightnings. The first bomber spun helplessly down. A second yawed, veered off course, and collided with a third. Locked in a tight embrace, they plunged earthward. Tons of metal, canvas, plywood, and living tissue were blown to bits by the mighty explosion that signaled their arrival.

I was speeding straight at a Boeing's tail. I caught a split-second glimpse of a cruciform shape in the rear turret. A man was hanging there with his arms spread-eagled: the tail gunner, dead. There was a shell hole near his head, and the surrounding Plexiglas had splintered into reflecting facets. Then I swept past without firing a shot. Were corpses fair game?

We reassembled. The RT rang with excited voices. Wehrmann's was easily recognizable.

"Man, are we tearing the ass out of *this* bunch!"

Hatred bubbled up inside me. Hatred for Wehrmann, not the Boeings. Ten years ago his sadistic and destructive impulses had been aimed at me. Today they were centered on these bombers. Could I really play Wehrmann's accomplice?

A second attack. During the crossover, a view of the gaps torn by the first. The formation was trying to plug them by closing up like cellular tissue regenerating—joining forces to repel an invasion by foreign bodies.

The second attack was untidier than the first. Bloodlust had flared up at this first-ever chance to atone for our endless succession of aerial Waterloos. Gigantic shattered tail units, wings spinning down like amputated limbs, fireballs, flamers, plumes of oily smoke, exploding fuel tanks, and below them a flowery white meadow of blossoming parachutes. Death was reaping its autumn harvest.

Into the middle of the bunch. I almost rammed the severed tail section of a bomber as it sailed down complete with occupants. Eyes stared at me, dilated with terror. Through the inferno and out again, only to re-form once more. How many left? Twenty at most—no, fifteen or less.

At last we were the butchers, not the butchered, and again it was Wehrmann who spurred the others on:

"Get in there, boys, in, in, in! If you're out of ammo, fill 'em full of shit!"

No attempt to regroup now, no disciplined formation flying or orderly crossover. It was take what you could get and each for himself. *In, in, in* . . . Ketsch had lost control of us. Where was he, anyway? Steep-turning, I noticed some gaps in our own ranks too.

Wehrmann again:

"Kill the swine! Give 'em hell!"

A third attack, this time head-on. The nose of the nearest Fortress became grotesquely distorted as the range closed fast. It had lost sections of its port wing and elevator. There was a gaping hole in the port side just behind the wing root, and in it hung a mangled body.

We flashed past. Had I fired? No idea, but I certainly hadn't hit anything.

4

Ketsch had sent for me again. This time I couldn't think why.

He was pacing angrily to and fro when I entered. Up top he was in full regalia, Iron Cross First Class and all. Down below he wore his officer's breeches but no boots, just a pair of homemade felt slippers. They somehow inbued the Staffel commander's majestic exterior with a human touch—another of Lenz's BBC catch phrases, locally pronounced *Juhmen Tatsch*. (It occurred to me afterward that Ketsch might have donned the slippers for my benefit, to help me state my case.)

"Oberfähnrich Braack?"

"Herr Hauptmann?"

"At ease! Don't stand there like a graven image, goddammit, or you'll never get a word out in your own defense. You're going to find it hard enough as it is."

"Yes, Herr Hauptmann."

"Yes, Herr Hauptmann, yes, Herr Hauptmann! Stop saying yes when the right answer's no!"

"No, Herr Hauptmann."

"What do you mean, no? Are you contradicting me? You're through, Braack. I'm going to have to report you to the Geschwader-Kommodore."

So I was through—all washed up at the ripe old age of

twenty. Callow I might be, but I was mature enough for a court-martial. The same old problem: no kill. I could have said, "I request the Herr Hauptmann's permission to express regret at my continuing failure to score." But I didn't. Ketsch narrowed his eyes and gave me a sustained burst.

"Honestly, Braack, this is a clear case of sabotage. Willful destruction of Wehrmacht property."

Destruction of Wehrmacht property? Had I inadvertently shot down one of our own machines—Wehrmann's, maybe?

Ketsch opened a locker, removed something, and slammed it down on the floor in front of me. It was a half-open parachute with shrouds and folds of silk escaping from its gray-green pack. The bits of moss and birch twigs entangled in them made it easier to identify.

"Is this object yours?"

"Yes, Herr Hauptmann."

"And it was in this state when you handed it in to the parachute packer after your last patrol?"

"Yes, but I squared things with Feldwebel Öhlert by giving him a bottle of vodka. My last."

"Feldwebel Öhlert submitted a written report just the same —it was his duty to. There's nothing in regulations about neglecting your duty in return for a bottle of vodka. Feldwebel Öhlert is a very conscientious man—as a pilot, you ought to be grateful. He handed your bottle to me, unopened. Now you can have it back." Ketsch produced the bottle from a drawer and held it out. "It isn't even Russian, incidentally, it's Polish."

"Feldwebel Öhlert should have kept it for going to the trouble of submitting a written report. If I'm any judge, he speaks German better than he writes it."

"There you go again, Braack. That's what I like about you —halfway to a court-martial and still you come up smiling. However, a sense of humor won't save you now. Nothing

will! I don't suppose you bailed out during your last patrol
and forgot to report the fact?"

"No, Herr Hauptmann."

"No, he says. Then why in God's name did you turn in a
half-open parachute? Did you pull the cord by mistake after
landing? Combat fatigue, is that the explanation?"

"Yes, sir, I was pretty tired."

"Don't give me that, Braack! You didn't pull it when you
left your machine, you took it and headed for the woods.
Shall I tell you how I know? There's heather and moss on
that chute, not to mention hawkweed and musk—I checked
in the *Nature-Lover's Guide*. But that's not all." Ketsch
thrust his bare feet deeper into his slippers and shuffled
menacingly toward me. "Musk and hawkweed I can take,
and strands of long black female hair don't worry me, but
semen stains! Honestly, Braack, *semen* stains!"

I could have sunk through the floor with shame—through
the floor and into the gulf that would always exist between us
from now on because, for all his good intentions, I would
never be able to forgive him for demeaning us both.

Just to ram the point home, he went on, "Sexual intercourse on state-owned parachute silk! You really think the
Führer would approve?"

Ketsch wouldn't report me, of course. He was one of those superiors whose hearts are made of gold and situated in the
right place, who only mean well and treat their men like kid
brothers—our war correspondents' articles were full of them.
Little by little, though, I was growing sick of people who
meant me well. I was also growing sick of a world where people like me were able and privileged to exist only by courtesy
of protectors who kept their hearts of gold in the correct loca-
tion.

The whole of Eastern Europe was an aerial battlefield to-day. More than six hundred enemy bombers were reported over Germany's eastern territories, and the total number of hostile intruders exceeded thirteen hundred. In retrospect, iso-lated images, scenes, and details, inarticulate cries and snippets of speech combined to produce an infernal kaleidoscope that might have originated in the mind of Hieronymus Bosch.

Takeoff, attack, touchdown, refuel, rearm, takeoff . . . Sometimes we got entangled with other units composed of heavy long-range fighters—Me 110s or Me 410s.

One badly damaged Me 410 crash-landed on our field and cartwheeled twice, end over end. Its crew of two were ex-tricated from the wreckage, alive but unconscious. I peered into the two-man cabin and regretted my curiosity at once. It smelled worse than the washroom in a noncoms' brothel. The panic-stricken pair must have let fly fore and aft when they hit the deck. Wehrmann, who was craning over my shoulder, said, "Give me a dead rat any day!"

One of our pilots dozed off every time he refueled. His for-mation leader sprinted across and shook him. "Wake up, you lazy slob. Dig the sleep out of your peepers and be a hero!"

Less than ten minutes after his sixth takeoff, the slumberer's one-ninety came spiraling down in flames. A parachute de-tached itself from the burning machine and drifted gently into a neighboring meadow, but nothing stirred. An ambulance ferried the motionless figure to the nearest field hospital. A medical enigma: no sign of injury. Subsequent diagnosis: overcome by fatigue, probably on the way down.

"A Mustang shattered my canopy," Schwaneweber confided. "I cowered down and doubled up like an embryo. Dear God, I yelled, dear God, I'll never be bad again. I went on yelling at the Almighty—couldn't help myself. The next burst was lower—it caught the top of the instrument panel. Dear God, I shouted, I'll do anything you say! Then the tracer lifted and the lid flew off. The sky looked nice and blue and friendly again. I don't know what happened to the Mustang, but it just wasn't there anymore. . . ."

A memorably awful day—one long succession of losses and abortive attacks. Eight members of the Geschwader were still unaccounted for at six that evening. Steffen and his junior commanders sat glued to the phones in the staff office. Occasionally some obscure military police post would call. Were we a pilot short? They'd found one in a grain field. He looked pretty sick but he might pull through. . . .

That evening I fled to the clump of birches in the fork of the river. Lying back with my head pillowed on my folded arms, I stared into the waning glow of the sunset. The hum of belated bumblebees and the chirp of crickets mingled with the swelling roar of a BMW 801 as one of our pilots made it back to base after picking up fuel elsewhere. Toads croaked and crows cawed. The air smelled of warm sandy soil and smoldering potato greens, damp fungi and stagnant water, pine resin and rotting straw.

For a week now, the mutilated tail of a one-ninety had been protruding from my favorite field, till lately red with poppies and blue with cornflowers. A I Gruppe pilot had dived into the ground from six thousand-plus. They didn't bother to dig him up, just took a carton and filled it, like blackberry pickers, with gobbets of flesh no bigger than a fingertip. The earth had charitably closed over the rest of him.

As a makeweight, a copy of the New Testament (Armed Forces' Edition) was tossed into the coffin. This had been found in the dead man's locker. What I alone knew was that Obergefreiter Klabund, who performed such chores frequently—and expertly—as a punishment for returning to base after hours, had inserted a pack of rubbers between the pages of St. Mark's Gospel. In Obergefreiter Klabund's considered opinion, the deceased had had little enough fun in this life, so he might as well live it up in the world hereafter.

Looking across the tousled grain fields from where I lay, I could still see the jutting tail fin adorned with swastika and single brush stroke. The dead man had scored only one kill before succumbing himself. One minus one made zero.

More dogfights, nose dives, blackouts. Lead in our legs and guts, brains drained of blood, sight quenched and restored by G forces, hour after hour, day after day.

Back at the base, Schwaneweber was still tense after a long day's fighting, still puce and feverish with excitement.

He had to get it off his chest as soon as he touched down. He tumbled out of his machine and tottered straight into the hut, where he threw himself on his bunk, trembling in every limb. We'd already heard the gist of his story. A Lightning had shot his tail to pieces.

"Twenty-five thousand! I was nearly twenty-five thousand feet up—then the stick locked solid. . . ."

He blurted out the disjointed words as if spewing up morsels of undigested food.

"I cut the throttle and she started spinning."

"Why not lie down?" I said—superfluously, because he was already in his bunk, but writhing like someone with stomach cramps.

"I was sure I was going to die."

"Nobody dies that easy."

"I was sure, I tell you! I could hear myself whimpering. I couldn't pull out—everything was jammed—control column, rudders, everything—and the ground was spinning like a top, getting nearer and nearer. I could actually see the spot where I'd crash."

"But you didn't crash."

"Yes I did, I crashed a dozen times on the way down."

"Come on, pull yourself together. You're alive."

"I'm going to die—that's what I thought, over and over— I'm going to die!"

He tossed and turned on the hard straw mattress. Bile-green slime started trickling from the corner of his mouth. I ran to my locker for a bottle of vodka and poured some into him.

Instantly, he vomited. A jet of bile, saliva, and yellow gastric juices arched high into the air and splashed all over his bedclothes.

"Congratulations," Wehrmann snarled at me. "You should've been a nurse."

The performance continued. All Schwaneweber's sphincteric muscles failed, top and bottom. He was soon immersed in a pool of excrement that stank like liquid pig manure. By now, his wits had completely deserted him. He lay there with a stupid smile on his face, both hands convulsively paddling in vomit, urine, and diarrhea.

"Can't somebody fetch a medic?" I shouted.

Wehrmann thrust his grinning face into mine. "What would he do, pump it back inside him? Clean him up yourself, you and your finicky friends!"

Lenz got there first. He punched our old schoolmate so hard that he caromed into the wall and brought down enough dust from the ceiling to blanket the entire room.

Then the three of us set to work—Lenz, Rebhan, and I.

We dumped Schwaneweber in the bathtub and chucked his bedclothes outside. Rebhan couldn't resist a dig at official propaganda.

"Here you see some of our heroic young fighter pilots after another victorious day in the air. Even when the going gets tough, there's always time for some youthful horseplay."

At last he was back in his bunk, all cleaned up and sleeping peacefully, Schwaneweber of the girlish complexion and delicate sensibilities.

The day before he died, Schwaneweber said:

"We're like preying mantises, eating our mates in mid-copulation. We're destroying everything that could make life pleasant and worthwhile."

"Hurrah for a college education," said Wilk. "Any more biological marvels for us?"

"Yes, ever heard of leucospids? They attach themselves to wasps and bees and devour them alive. They puncture the skin and suck them dry, little by little."

"There you are, then. We're no worse than the rest of creation."

"And afterward, when the bodies are drained but still alive, they're left to mummify so they remain edible down to the last mouthful. Like dried cod."

"Eat or be eaten, eh?"

"The Gnostics were right about God being dead. His place has been taken by the Great Usurper."

Wilk raised his eyebrows. "The great *who?*"

"The personification of evil—the Lord of Darkness, if you like." No amount of sarcasm could shake Schwaneweber's composure on the eve of his death. "This daily carnage in the sky—it's just a diabolical, technological surrender to the law of the jungle. We've turned into mummified insects—we've lost our humanity."

Our humanity . . .

The words recurred unbidden when I saw him lying dead. Schwaneweber, the person who'd been closer to me than anyone but Lenz.

Schwaneweber had taken off with the rest of the Staffel. My own engine caught fire when I started up and was towed to the repair hangar.

How, I often asked myself, had the sky looked the day he died? We were passing through another succession of golden autumn days. Fallen leaves stuck to our tires and the winter gulls had arrived. Already half bare, the trees were veiled in a shimmering bronze mist through which thin fingers of sunlight tentatively probed the ground.

Schwaneweber took off into this honey-colored radiance and soared above the open plain. When the Staffel made contact, Wilk told me, Ketsch ordered a diving attack on a squadron of Lightnings. Just as Schwaneweber's finger-four was going in, it was balked by a pair of Me 410s and had to take avoiding action. Schwaneweber was rammed by one of the interlopers and forced to bail out.

"He had masses of time," Wilk said. "I just don't get it."

Schwaneweber fell clear but didn't release his chute. He continued his free fall until he hit the ground. Everyone was mystified. Why hadn't he pulled the rip cord? Had he been fatally injured?

Wilk shook his head. "Why didn't he pull the goddamn thing?"

Nobody would ever know. It was idle to speculate.

Worst of all, he actually survived the long descent—just.

He landed in a tree-fringed marsh, where his fall was broken by twigs and branches. They must have smashed every bone and ruptured every nerve tract in his body, but he could still groan. His vocabulary was reduced to the infantile syllables "oh" and "ah." He was dead by the time I got there.

We've lost our humanity. . . . No point in dwelling on that.

Milky light muted the colors and blurred the outlines of his broken body.

One day I saw Steffen emerging from Combat Control. He politely held the door open for a companion, then straightened up and sauntered off with one arm extended. He was walking a dog on a leash.

He spoke to the animal. "Come on, Wolf, be a good dog." He stooped to pick up a stone and threw it. "Fetch—that's right, fetch!"

I watched Steffen playing with his Alsatian for some time, keeping well in the lee of some hazel bushes. Steffen wouldn't have appreciated an audience.

There wasn't any dog.

He'd written over a dozen letters of condolence in the past week.

Early morning, two days later.

I was standing at the window of the bunkhouse, unable to sleep. Dawn light oozed across the steppe like maple syrup. Outside, less than ten yards away, stood a pilot from I Gruppe—I recognized him by his flaming red hair. He'd celebrated his fourth kill, a Lightning, the day before yesterday.

The man was standing there like a sleepwalker, wearing a nightshirt and flying boots. As I watched, he stamped on something with desperate ferocity. An adder? A rat?

His face became contorted. He leapt in the air and landed with both feet together. I pressed my face against the glass and could hear his labored breathing. Something on the ground had obviously scared him.

"You bastard, I'll teach you to sneak into my bunk at night!"

He pounded the turf again, but there was nothing there.

"I clobbered you fair and square. You're dead, do you hear —dead as cold mutton! Don't ever show your face here again, not ever!"

The disguising of reality by authorized means:

I went on another mushrooming expedition with Maryla. The mushrooms had never sprouted as luxuriantly as they had this autumn, perhaps because the skies had never manured them so richly.

We roamed the banks and water meadows of the Pilica, startling bitterns, whinchats, and buntings. Fly agaric grew as big as an officer's cap here, but edible fungi were also abundant.

One was the scarlet-capped *Russula emetica,* which loses its poison when cooked. In my native Masuria it was gathered and cooked in company with chestnut boletes and the sourish but palatable ringed variety. We also found field mushrooms and peppery milk caps, lawyers' wigs with salmon-pink gills, yellow-cracked boletes, devil's boletes and sulphur tufts— both to be carefully avoided—and great big edible cepes like vagabonds' hats with broad felt brims.

Maryla darted from one find to the next, gathering an ample harvest, and gaily promised to clean and prepare the mushrooms in time for our next rendezvous.

"I'll bring a pan and some margarine. We'll light a fire and fry them—no, this time we'll stew them!"

The autumnal hush of a Polish wood in 1944 . . . I felt I'd never know such peace again, however long I lived. By to-morrow I'd be back in my cockpit, throttle wide open, eight guns raping the virgin morning air. Was that how it would be, day after day, month after month, year after year?

On the outskirts of the wood, stunted birches protruded from an expanse of yellow bracken like writhing limbs. Before us, under a canopy of silver cloud, lay the open steppe.

Maryla tripped and went sprawling in the ferns, scrambled to her feet and flopped down again, helpless with laughter.

Then a strange thing happened.

Immediately to our front was an abandoned field over-grown with thistles.

Something in that pale violet sea was stirring, straining to reach the surface like a mythological beast of the underworld —a giant mole.

It was no mole.

Maryla clutched my hand. The ground ahead of us bulged and cracked. Fragments of topsoil flew into the air.

I started digging like a madman. Maryla had covered her face. I scraped away layer after layer, bare-handed, till I met resistance. There was another subterranean convulsion and the soil parted to reveal what I had been expecting all the time.

Folds of wet fabric undulated before my eyes, steeped in slime. Membranous bubbles swelled and burst with a dull plop. Straining cloth, swelling bubbles, then a glimpse of something white. . . .

"Michael, what is it?"

Maryla's face was frozen with horror. I wanted to stop digging, take her hand and run, but not before I'd made sure.

It was the cockpit of a one-ninety. The wingless fuselage had knifed into the ground with such force that the soil had closed over it, much as a carnivorous flower opens briefly to admit its prey and then snaps shut.

I rummaged around as though groping for a prize in a grab bag. The contents of the cockpit resisted my touch, heaving, belching corruption, grunting obscenely. I felt something hard and went on burrowing with the grim determination of an exorcist intent on laying bare the ultimate horror.

At last the skull grinned up at me. The eye sockets were empty, but shreds of decaying flesh still adhered to the shattered lower jaw.

The head was embedded in a balloon—an inflated cushion which almost entirely enclosed it. I unearthed only the uppermost portion of this balloon. Then I took to my heels with Maryla in tow, vomiting as I ran.

The pilot had been imprisoned in his cockpit like an ill-canned ham. Gases had inflated his body until the topsoil yielded under immense pressure and his stomach burst, voiding the intestines and allowing them to force their way outward and upward. The rest of him, swollen to three times its original volume, was too tightly encased to find an outlet. . . .

Maryla and I went on running.

Distant, diffused sounds from the airfield were carried to our ears by a westerly breeze: radio music, aero engines being started up and run on the chocks.

Who was seeking refuge from what and with whom?

We ran toward those familiar sounds like children lured by the seductive clamor of a fairground.

5

Why Zimmermann, of all people? He knew the drill, so why? Did I think it was fate? Lenz asked. It sounded almost like a reproach, as though the wheel of fortune was my personal responsibility.

Rosenhain had run my one-ninety on the chocks and checked the magnetos. No problems. The airscrew was idling and the spiral on the spinner coiling leisurely like a black and white serpent.

It was 5 P.M.—almost time to knock off. A chill white mist from the Pilica marshes was creeping across the airfield. (Is that relevant? Yes, because Zimmermann died looking at it.) I lay sprawled in the damp grass, relaxing. Jupiter, the evening star, was rising above the swaths of mist. The shrill "kewick" of a tawny owl momentarily drowned the engine's steady monotone.

Zimmermann walked up with a letter for Rosenhain, who was tinkering with the one-ninety's rudder before it was manhandled, tail first, into its dispersal pen. Zimmermann brandished the envelope and walked on, heading straight for the nose. Instead of halting just short of the airscrew, he went on walking—headless now, and flailing his arms like a speed skater. A red fountain gushed vertically from where his head had been. If he didn't stop soon he'd fall into the ditch at the rear of the pen and hurt himself. Careful, Zimmermann, I started to shout—mind the ditch!

He tumbled into it before his head, which was still spinning across the grass, came to rest. Exit Zimmermann.

I had another hearty puke. Not a promising start to the evening. Only an hour to go before my train left for Konskie, where Maryla would join it. For once we had something really special planned: a night out in Radom, miles away to the northeast.

I could still see Zimmermann's headless figure teetering along as I withdrew the pants of my best uniform from under the mattress. Had he been smiling as he strolled so nonchalantly into the airscrew? Always fond of macabre jokes, he had staged a macabre departure from this life. I could picture him hovering over his decapitated corpse, chuckling to himself. The river mist made it only too easy to imagine an ethereal Zimmermann whose troubles were finally over. I concentrated on my pants. We had all persuaded the workshops to supply us with plywood templates. These we inserted in the legs, which were a pretty tight fit, to simulate an elegant cut. We moistened the creases, slid the templates inside, placed the whole shebang between mattress and bunkboards, and slept on it for at least a night. The weight and warmth of our bodies produced quite a respectable crease—two or three creases, more often than not, and not always in the right place.

Around my neck went a pilot's orange scarf. Other Luftwaffe personnel were strictly forbidden such forms of personal adornment. We fighter pilots enjoyed the exclusive right to crease our pants and bedizen ourselves. Gray knitted scarves were all the clothing store issued, but enough fabric could be cut off one arm of a wind tee to provide enough scarves for several Staffeln.

I made the railroad embankment with less than a minute to spare. The little train came hissing and clanking toward

me. The engineer merely slowed, I broke into a trot, grabbed
a door handle, and hauled myself aboard.

Somewhere on the deserted airfield a light was flitting
around in defiance of blackout regulations. They were carting
Zimmermann away. I swallowed hard—a symbolic act performed in the hope that it would banish all potential threats
to the rest of the evening.

At Konskie my car was coupled to the front-line furlough
train for Radom and Maryla got in. She was wearing a spot-
less white silk scarf. We hugged each other on the cold, cold
platform until the troops hanging out of the windows started
making lewd remarks. Red Cross helpers were distributing
steaming mugs of ersatz coffee. Although we were bent on
pleasure, not bound for the front, we took one too. Inscribed
on the locomotive's tender was the hackneyed message
WHEELS MUST TURN FOR VICTORY.

Next day I received a surprise visit from my father. Our
correspondence wasn't notable for its volume—I never knew
what to write—but I felt closer to him than to my mother,
whose view of the war was colored by her literary coffee par-
ties. These she threw weekly for the local vet, a clutch of
schoolmarms, the dentist's wife, and our late fire chief's
socially ambitious widow. Readings and discussions were devoted to such authors as Hans Carossa and Rudolf G. Binding. Mother's last food parcel had included a box of expensive
cigars—"so you can offer one to your commanding officer
now and then. It'll be bound to do you some good!"

And now, here was Braack Sr., fresh from a visit to the
Führer's headquarters. He should really have gone straight
back to the Air Ministry.

"But I had to change at Toruń, and there, standing at the

very next platform, was a train to Łódź and Cracow. It was too good a chance to miss, my boy."

B.S. had disobeyed his marching orders and gone absent without leave, in effect, but that didn't worry him. He was a somebody, after all—he'd just been in conclave with the Führer.

We discussed his visit to the Wolf's Lair as soon as I'd summarized my own situation. That didn't take long, and anyway, B.S. knew more about our operations than I did because he followed them all from Berlin. He talked a mile a minute. Top-secret stuff, of course, but that didn't worry him either. Blood was thicker than Air Ministry ink.

We were sitting in the mess over Luftwaffe beer and a brace of rollmops. He'd brought the pickled herrings along, neatly wrapped in greaseproof paper, to sustain him on the journey back to Berlin. Pickled herrings! I didn't know they still existed, not in November 1944.

B.S. was bubbling over with the urge to communicate, presumably because he felt lonely at the Air Ministry. (Solitude seemed inseparable from the Braackian way of life.) His account of yesterday's meeting at the Führer's headquarters was studded with enthusiastic references to our new jet fighters.

"Every pilot who converts to them has to do ten hours in an Me 110 first, to get the feel of a twin-engined airplane. Then there's the nosewheel. It must be a novel sensation, taxiing horizontally instead of down by the tail. The important thing is, keep your revs as high as possible when you make your approach. Jet engines don't like accelerating fast from low revs—the sudden injection of liquid fuel makes them choke and puts the flame out. You have to be doing six thousand revs before it's safe to open up and go around again."

I'd sooner have been jailed than transfer to jets, but I refrained from saying so. B.S. had enough on his mind, even if he did have connections too. Despite myself, I felt a surge of professional interest.

"How do you take off in a machine like that?"

"You hold her on the brakes and slowly open up to eight thousand revs. When she's at full throttle, you let her rip."

"How about dogfights?"

"Hm, she isn't really designed for those. You can use her to shoot down bombers, but not fighters. She also has some rather eccentric diving characteristics. At very high speeds the control column becomes immovable and you can only pull out by carefully applying your trim tabs."

"You mean she isn't fully aerobatic?"

"Only up to a point. The other thing you can't do is attack head-on. The closing speed of an Me 262 and a bomber formation wouldn't give you time to aim and fire. These jet pilots are having to employ some entirely novel methods of attack, like breaking up an enemy formation with their new R-4M rockets. First they fire a salvo of R-4Ms, right into the middle of them. Then the other fighters can go to work." B.S. paused. "Do you know what 'rat catching' is?"

"Can't say I do."

"It's the Allies' name for their technique of shooting down our jets when they come in to land—the only time they can catch them. They pinpoint a jet base and mount a standing patrol over it, usually with some of their new Hawker Tempest Vs."

I was enthralled by such dissertations on the refinements of air warfare, but only until I had a sudden vision of maimed bodies in flying coffins and remembered what lay beneath the glamorous technological veneer. Lenz was aware of it too, and Tiny Lauritzen had also known. Why not everyone?

"And apart from that, Father?"

"Apart from that? Mm, yes . . . well . . ."

So much for his assessment of the general situation. Thereafter we confined ourselves to family matters and hometown gossip ("Old Matzeck—you remember him, ran the grocery store near the station—he stopped a bullet too. In Italy.") Our parting words:

"See you soon, B.S."

"See you soon, my boy."

I stood waving as his train receded into the darkness. What lingered with me was an urge to record that part of his story which had fascinated me most of all: his visit to Hitler's headquarters.

I got down to it that night.

Hermann Braack had contrived to be present at the Wolf's Lair on 6 November 1944, when Hitler was briefed on the events of 2 November, the blackest-ever day in the annals of our daylight fighter force. Early that morning, two huge task forces drawn from the U.S. Eighth Air Force had crossed the Dutch-German border. One, consisting of 325 four-engined bombers, was targeted on the fuel installations at Castrop-Rauxel and Gelsenkirchen; the remaining 683 aircraft headed for the Leuna Works south of Merseburg. Their fighter escort, which was exceptionally strong, comprised six hundred Mustangs and a hundred-odd Lightnings from the Eighth and Ninth Air Forces respectively.

Even before the Me 109s of Jagdgeschwader 300 could take off from their base at Borkheide, forty or so were destroyed or damaged on the ground by Mustangs. Another five hundred German fighters prepared to take off. Conditions were far from ideal: nine tenths cloud over Saxony and a deep depression in the Rhine-Main area. Owing to the bad weather, only three hundred of our five hundred fighters made contact with the enemy, or their losses would have been even heavier. The U.S. 55th Fighter Group under Major

Ryan reported shooting down nineteen German fighters for the loss of only one Mustang. Total losses: 134 German fighters as against eight Mustangs. Although the suicidal Sturmgruppen of JG 3 and JG 4 destroyed thirty four-engined bombers, their sixty-one armored FW 190A-8s sustained an equal number of losses.

What Mustang pilots and Fortress air gunners failed to do, the elements did for them. Many German fighters collided while taking off, formating, or landing. As B.S. quickly ascertained, no fighters based at Grojecko came to grief because of the weather. Our pilot losses amounted to three each from 1 and 2 Staffeln and none from 3 Staffel.

B.S. never uttered a word the whole time. The only speakers apart from Hitler himself were Major Büchs, aide to the Chief of Wehrmacht Operations Staff, and Generalmajor Christian, Chief of the Luftwaffe Operations Staff.

Hitler's gray complexion matched the walls of the bunker in which he was living. (Living? B.S. thought truculently. Lurking, more like—no, skulking!)

"I've just reviewed the matter," Hitler said. "I don't know if it's been reported to Reichsmarschall Göring, but I've carried out a reappraisal of the whole sorry affair. According to my calculations, eighty enemy aircraft were destroyed the other day."

"Eighty-two," said Büchs.

(German figures, thought B.S. The Americans put their losses far lower. After all that's happened in Germany since '39, I'd sooner trust their figures than ours.)

"Of the eighty," Hitler went on, "fifty were brought down by fighters and thirty by flak. Discount those thirty for the moment. Four hundred and ninety of our fighters engaged the enemy . . ."

"Three hundred and five," Büchs amended.

Hitler argued the point. Much to my father's admiration, Büchs stuck to his guns.

(What abysmal German the Führer speaks, *mused B.S. Quite unlike his public speeches. . . . He didn't tune in again properly for some time. By then, Hitler was summing up.*)

"*A thoroughly unsatisfactory result.*"

Christian essayed a feeble protest but was cut short.

"*Isn't there anyone on your staff who sifts these reports in a methodical manner? The Reichsmarschall is completely in the dark. Why, when he turned up here the other day, he still had no idea that our losses are even heavier than they seem because these so-called nonlanding returns distort the whole picture!*"

Christian objected that Göring was briefed daily.

"*I want those figures,*" *Hitler snapped.* "*They're proof positive, either that our pilots are useless, or that their aircraft are no good. One can't blame the pilots merely because they're getting shot down, so it must be the aircraft. You Luftwaffe people tell me otherwise—you say the aircraft are all right. It's a ludicrous state of affairs. Whichever way I add up the figures, the result is catastrophic!*"

My father's thoughts strayed off again. When had he last believed that politics was the distillation of wisdom or that the ship of state was steered by men of knowledge and ability? From the bottom up, everyone seemed to be muddling along. Intrigue and infighting were the order of the day. And Hitler himself? What he'd been saying sounded puerile and absurd. He was dependent on the information he received from his generals, each of whom was solely interested in feathering his own nest and putting his colleagues down.

B.S. forced himself to concentrate on the matter at hand. They were now wrangling over discrepancies in casualty re-

ports and claims of losses inflicted. Nothing added up—there were always remainders, double entries, or straightforward omissions. These men were juggling with figures, not names, not human beings made of flesh and blood. But his son was made of flesh and blood. Somewhere in this deadly game he represented a digit, an asset or liability, a plus or minus. The perfectionism of the German war machine . . . What a laugh! All they were doing was fudging figures, cooking the books, playing with a marked deck. Faites vos jeux . . .

"*A pathetic performance!*" Hitler was saying. "*I put up five hundred fighters and shoot fifty down. If I put up two thousand I'd shoot down two hundred, so with our existing aircraft I can never hope to . . .*" *He left the obvious truth unspoken.* "*Yet they're still being churned out day and night. It's a sheer waste of manpower and resources.*"

Despite his mounting agitation, Hitler was progressively wilting. His body became more and more bent as though trying to resume its embryonic position.

Christian cleared his throat. "*The real reason, my Führer, is simply that our boys hadn't done any flying for ten days.*"

"*I've heard your excuses before, General!*"

"*But it was bound to affect their performance, my Führer. The Geschwader that took off in the west landed without loss because it operates every day, even in bad weather. These things tell—it's only natural.*"

(Was Michael an expert all-weather flier? B.S. doubted it.)

"*I'm not criticizing our airmen,*" Hitler retorted, "*just their scoring rate. Nothing can alter that. With two thousand fighters I might—might—shoot down two hundred Allied aircraft. In other words, there isn't a hope of obliterating the Allied air forces by deploying fighters on a massive scale. That means it's crazy to go on producing them, just so that the Luftwaffe can operate with statistics.*"

There it was again, Hitler's ingrained aversion to the

*fighter in a defensive role. Even now, he was dreaming of a
bomber offensive. A whole succession of fighters had been
converted into fighter-bombers by the addition of bomb racks.*

*This was my father's cue to step in—the sole reason for his
presence. He itched to demonstrate the irrationality of Hitler's
policy, stress the shortage of fighter pilots and aircraft, rebut
the proposal that the Me 262 jet fighter—the scourge of every
enemy bomber and fighter formation—should be converted
into a flat-footed fighter-bomber, and complain that the jet-
propelled Arado 234 was already in production and launching pointless hit-and-run raids on England when our own cities
were being pulverized because there weren't enough fighters
to defend them.*

Be damned to it, B.S. told himself. *He was suddenly overcome by a feeling of infinite weariness and resignation. He'd
watched the dog-eat-dog power struggles inside the Air Ministry for years, but now that his long-awaited chance had come
he ducked it. He didn't say a word. The situation was hopeless.*

6

I glanced at the November sky, a bat-gray quilt with wisps of kapok protruding from it.

We took off and climbed steeply. Enemy aircraft were up to their tricks in the far north, according to today's reports, but the first tricks we encountered were meteorological. The air seemed to consist of pure electricity. As soon as I was through the first thin layer of cloud, St. Elmo's fire enveloped me like a thousand-tongued hydra.

Sparklers showered the windshield. The airscrew churned in an aura of bluish flame. More flames snaked from the gun muzzles, almost as if they held kerosene-soaked wicks, and rivet heads turned phosphorescent. Behind me streamed a comet's tail.

My earphones crackled incessantly. Electrical discharges flickered over the control column and worms of fire licked my fingertips. There was a stench of sulphur and ozone.

The dim shape of Lenz's machine loomed up beside me. Flames danced along its fuselage like luminous ticker tape spelling out MENE, MENE, TEKEL, UPHARSIN.

Then we emerged into a realm of absolute whiteness. Not a flaw or shadow marred its glassy, mirror-smooth surface. The machines below and ahead of me crawled across it like black insects. Even their contrails looked dark against the snow-white infinity beneath. The dazzling light afforded no horizon, no aid to orientation.

The Mustangs soon put that right. They appeared in a flash. From one moment to the next, we were in the thick of an aerial free-for-all. Ketsch, who had been preoccupied with navigational problems, just had time to shout a warning.

"Watch yourselves! We're in a high-altitude storm here— it's carrying us nor'nor'east, fast!"

More and more often now, I caught myself going through the motions of combat mechanically and without any real awareness of doing so. Afterward, my memory failed me. I hadn't the faintest recollection of what had happened. Instead, my mind—or my subconscious—fabricated complete scenarios which bore no relation to the course of the fighting.

They were flying on every side, their murky shapes gliding through the nocturnal sea like giant fish—all the crashed, maimed, shattered aircraft of the war. Around me, in a vast procession of the dead, cruised the Dornier Do 217s of London, the Focke-Wulf Condors of the North Atlantic, the Stukas of Dunkirk, the Henschel Hs 129 tank busters of the Eastern Front, the Messerschmitt Me 109s of the North African theater, the Heinkel He 111s of the Black Sea, the He 219 night fighters of Berlin. Fighters, bombers, interceptors, transport and reconnaissance planes—all roamed with me through the cosmic gloom. Below them swam their victims, the dead of Coventry, the buried of Bristol, the mutilated tank crews, the Ratas, Liberators, and Dewoitines. Below them, too, swam the earth they had ravaged, the charred forests of the Ardennes, the shattered streets of Manchester and Liverpool, the ruined churches of Odessa and the rubble of the Warsaw ghetto, the bomb-blasted villages around Bialystok and the crater-strewn moors of Belgium, the bridges of Rotterdam and the cave dwellings of Crete.

Mutely this cortège glided through the silence of the night, with noseless, eyeless faces, rib cages reduced to bloody pulp, burst lungs, crushed genitals. I myself accompanied it on dark wings of fear. The air was fetid with decay and viscous with blood. I struggled wildly like a wasp in a jam jar. I was being stifled by the fruits of our lethal handiwork. There was no escape.

I came to with a start.

A beam attack from port. Stick forward, nose down, open throttle, reef around hard for another pass.

The big wide sky, filigreed with contrails, was suddenly empty. Not a friend or foe in sight. I'd left them all behind.

Unusual noises. My engine was spitting—genuinely spitting, coating the windshield with oily vomit. No forward vision, but I could tell that the power plant had been hit and set on fire from the black smoke whipping past my right shoulder. I cut the throttle and switched off.

A benign hush, broken only by the whistle of the slipstream.

Altitude: eight thousand feet.

Decision: a dead-stick landing.

For the first time ever, I saw my airscrew motionless while high above the ground. It looked like a shiny metallic vee. The third blade was obscured by the engine.

The smoke dwindled and became transparent, as though a robot had finally bled to death.

Instead, flames.

Little tongues of fire appeared on either side of the cockpit canopy, then overhead, then between my legs, darting from the instrument panel, reaching for the control column. High-explosive shells had evidently breached the fireproof engine bulkhead.

One exceptionally venturesome flame snaked through the

cockpit and started to gnaw at the canopy rails, my flying boots, the jettison lever.

Revised decision: bail out.

I groped for the crescent-shaped handle of the emergency release and wrenched at it. The canopy opened, but only a crack. It was jammed. The flames became bolder and more brutal. They licked the instruments and attacked the rudder pedals. I hurriedly withdrew my feet. Could rudder pedals burn?

Braack to Braack: *Keep cool, everything's fine.*

I was breathless now. Smoke in my nose, throat, lungs. My eyes were watering, and what was the matter with my feet? They were on fire. Burning boots—the latest fashion.

Repeat order: *Keep cool, everything's fine.*

Then: *Off straps.*

I unclipped my safety harness.

Goddammit, mind you don't shed your parachute harness by mistake—you'll be needing that!

Don't worry, there's a locking bar, nothing can go wrong.

If you say so.

I raised myself in the seat and braced my head against the canopy. No point—it had to be slid back, not forced off. Flames were running up the control column, metal components glowing with heat, gauges illegible. The cockpit was full of smoke.

Roasting to death in my cockpit—that's what really scares me. . . .

Then jump, you fool!

The canopy gave, slid back, and flew off. Flames roared and smoke swirled in the sudden rush of air. Breathless and mortally afraid, I kicked the stick forward. Nose down, pilot out, success guaranteed.

I sailed through space in a wide arc, vulnerable and unsupported. With jarring abruptness, the chute snapped open and floated above me. Snow-white, white as thistledown and innocence.

I wasn't alone in space. A scorched and blackened wing spiraled down, ripped off my one-ninety by an unheard explosion.

The ground, olive-brown, olive-green. Bushes and streams. A sudden jolt.

I hit the harness release and my chute scudded away, trailing its shrouds like the legs of a waterfowl taking wing. Then I sank back with a sigh of relief.

Alder bushes and a marshy expanse of riverbank. My body had left a skid mark thirty yards long. I must have been dreaming when I thought I'd hit the release the instant I landed. My shoulders, buttocks, and calves were on fire.

I propped myself against a rotten stump and tried to think. I was soon ankle-deep in a pool of stagnant water, the ground was so marshy. The fighting must have carried me a long way north. Hadn't I caught a fleeting glimpse of the Baltic or one of its lagoons?

I sniffed the air. The wind smelled damp and salty. The northwest face of every tree in sight was thick with moss and encrusted with lichen.

I was still alive—a vivid sensation.

The sensation would be over for good if some Polish partisans appeared. I straightened up and felt myself all over. Nothing broken, just painful cuts and bruises and an egg-sized lump on the top of my head.

I unzipped my flying suit. The regulation prismatic compass and tin box of vitamin tablets were intact. I couldn't run out on life, so I might as well get going.

Did I realize what I was taking on? Had I known what lay in store for me during this trek through the desolate wastes of East Prussia, would I have set off as I did then? My boots were gone, reduced to charred scraps of felt. I'd often roamed the deserted Johannisburger Heide as a boy, but somewhere in the gloomy woods there'd always been a farmhouse or gamekeeper's cottage. Here there was nothing. I might even have been in Latvia or Lithuania.

Though thick, my flying socks were scant protection against the myriad torments inflicted by the inhospitable subsoil. It was soft beneath its covering of ferns, but infested with half-hidden roots, sharp twigs, and hard crusts of sand. I trudged painfully along, keeping to the low ground. Although visibility was almost nil, the alder bushes and brambles higher up would have been impassable.

I stumbled into potholes full of lukewarm slime. My socks imbibed it greedily and clasped my swollen feet in a leaden embrace. I glanced at my wristwatch. It said 2 P.M. Swarms of gnats and iridescent green mosquitoes whined around my head. I dared not stop to rest or they would close over me like a cheese cover.

The sky was dotted with miniature clouds. I tried to head northwest, but that was just where the wilderness seemed most impenetrable. My one hope was to reach the coast, with its fishing villages and centers of human habitation. I was bound to get there sometime—today, tomorrow, the day after. . . .

It took me only half an hour to realize that I'd be lucky to keep going till tomorrow, let alone the day after. My strength had been sapped by the long air battle and the exertions of bailing out. Every bush barred my path like a man-trap, and every obstacle was neatly camouflaged with rotting ferns or layers of soggy leaves. I blundered into knee-deep craters and tripped over decaying branches as thick as my leg.

Only the sky was clearly visible. The feather-edged clouds resembled birds flying south.

In less than an hour I was stuck. The undergrowth had thickened and the ground was becoming more and more waterlogged. I couldn't go on. All my efforts had been wasted. I would have to turn back.

At once the mosquitoes descended on me. Not a breath of wind now. I toiled past marshy pools, black as open sewers. The air smelled of resin and rotting vegetation. Croaking sounds issued from unseen pockets of water.

Then came an unexpected chance to break through to the northwest. Charred stumps and tree trunks marked the passage of a fire that had transformed the wilderness into relatively open country. Fresh shoots were sprouting from the blackened wood. Here the going was easier.

Before long I came to another obstacle: a lake almost big enough to be mistaken for the Baltic and surrounded by a belt of reeds which cruelly enlarged its circumference. I turned west because the western route seemed less of a detour, but I was only just abreast of the lake an hour and a half later. The pathlike alleyways between the reeds and rushes were so boggy that I often sank in up to my ankles. When my strength gave out, I flopped down in the undergrowth. A bittern took off, booming indignantly.

I extracted the vitamin tablets with trembling fingers and ate one. A light breeze had sprung up, but its salty tang gave me a violent thirst. The breath rasped irregularly in my burning throat.

I issued myself with new orders:

Get moving, Braack. If you lie here much longer this black slime will suck you in like a sponge.

I was aching all over, probably as a result of my collision with the ground, and my feet were smarting. My face and hands were a mass of scratches, and the twigs that stung my cheeks were almost as much of a torment as the insects.

Once past the lake I was confronted by another wilderness of reeds, thistles, and sedge. The ground became firmer again. I made some headway, faithfully escorted by a pair of circling black kites.

Just before 5 P.M., with no end in sight, I gave up and lay down beneath a clump of stunted willows. No sound of human activity, not even the distant barking of a dog.

The sun sank into a crimson haze. Everything became blurred and seemed to hover in midair: bushes, the labyrinth of reeds, the treetops. I could no longer feel the pressure of my body against its bed of twigs.

I was hovering too, like an incorporeal spirit.

Wasn't that a man in front of me? Yes, unmistakably—a bearded giant like an ogre in a children's storybook. When I floated toward him, he retreated.

A hallucination. Any minute now I'd see the dreaded Masurian water sprite, risen from some murky lake to claim me as its prey. Before that could happen, I closed my eyes and drifted off at once into a deep, dreamless sleep.

A view of the starry sky with the Triangle low over the horizon, the Pleiades and Taurus. I slept on.

Next morning I awoke in a flash. Filled with an instinctive certainty that I was being watched, I slowly turned my head. An elk was peering at me through the willow branches, motionless, with its huge palmed antlers slightly inclined. We stared at one another. Time stood still. Not a sound—I even forgot to breathe.

Abruptly, the beast shook its proud head as though dismissing some unspoken question, turned majestically, and trotted off with a flick of its snug-fitting scut.

Every limb protested as I scrambled to my feet. My throat was parched and my lips had split in several places. There was at least something to be said for the salt breeze that stung my nose and throat. It galvanized me—spurred me on.

The gently rising ground became more densely and variously wooded. As in Masuria, junipers made a sudden appearance among the oaks and larches, pines and maples. At last I came upon some berries. Juniper berries and blackberries—almost the makings of a full-blown meal.

I plucked greedily at the clusters of fruit and mashed them between my smarting lips to make the most of the juice. Then I struggled on in a state of feverish euphoria. I was going to survive—I had to. Sooner or later I would come to the sea and its fringe of fishing villages.

But that was when the dark wall rose ahead of me.

It was the nearest thing to a jungle I'd ever seen, even in Masuria. The ground bristled with ferns the height of a man, and above them hung a close-knit entanglement of branches and creepers, ivy and wild vines. There was no way through the barrier and no means of outflanking it. My slender reserves of strength and determination ran out. I cowered down among the fern fronds, hugging my knees. A cloud of stinging insects closed in. My feet were oozing blood.

Buzzing ears and aching lungs, senses reeling. No thoughts, no memories, no misgivings. I would simply let go and drift away. Dying was as easy as that.

It was a long time before I opened my eyes and looked up at the sky. Heavy leaden-gray clouds were chasing each other across it. I raised one hand and studied the lines on my palm. Shreds of skin were hanging loose, torn by their passage over tree trunks and rocks.

Above me, a snail was leaving a slimy trail on the stem of a horsetail.

Then my eyes focused on something strange and shiny beyond the creature's shell. Instantly, everything within me became active—brain, nerves, muscles. At the same time, I regained my awareness of pain. Life flooded back into my numbed limbs.

Scrabbling at the ferns, I hauled myself along until the tip of my nose was almost touching the foreign body.

Suspended in the undergrowth was a transparent, rectangular object. A sheet of glass—no, Plexiglas—with splintered edges.

The sight of it drove me to my feet like an explosion. It was a panel from an aircraft cabin. I quickly scanned the surrounding sea of ferns. Other objects caught my eye: a circular metal capsule, an aluminum strip, a metal rib. I pounced on each new find. Larger pieces of wreckage came to light, some in Luftwaffe camouflage, together with fragments of rubber and battered mechanical parts. Now I stood, panting, beneath the outermost branches of the impenetrable forest.

Some of the branches were snapped and scarred. A few feet overhead, the main stems had been lopped off. With a final burst of energy, I struggled through the outlying trees and found myself confronted by a clearing as wide as a highway running through the heart of what I'd thought was solid vegetation. It wasn't a natural phenomenon. It had been carved out by the wings of an aircraft.

Thirty feet up and fifty yards on, the starboard wing had lodged in a clump of firs that looked as if they'd been hit by a tornado. It belonged to a Junkers Ju 88 medium bomber.

The black and white cross was weather-worn but recognizable. Oil and gasoline had seeped from the fractured wing tanks and discolored the soil beneath.

The bulk of the airplane had come to rest another two or three hundred yards away. The tail unit and rudder assembly were intact but lying at a broken-backed forty-five degrees to the fuselage. Both engines had come adrift and buried their propeller bosses deep in the ground.

I approached the wreck from behind. My steps became slower and more hesitant the nearer I got. I dreaded the thought of investigating the cockpit, which also seemed to be intact. The gunner's MG was still pointing rearward and the antenna rods over the radio operator's position were only slightly bent. I made a wide detour around the port wing and port engine.

Then I looked straight into the clear-view cockpit.

At first I could see nothing but jungle-green reflections. Creepers had wormed their way through cracks and fissures in the Plexiglas and continued to proliferate inside. The massive control column was coated with moss and lichen. Red ants were marching in a dark and endless stream across the upper part of the canopy.

I concentrated on these details with desperate intensity, terrified of what I might see in the farther recesses of the cabin.

They were still in their straps, but only two of them: the pilot and his navigator. The radio operator and air gunner must have bailed out.

Although the straps had almost rotted away, they had little enough to hold in place. They lay loosely, almost caressingly, over the bare skeletons of the two remaining occupants. The bones were picked clean and soapy white, hence the interminable column of ants. Had it not been for the frightful skulls with their gaping eye sockets and the disarticulated, seemingly over-life-size hands, one of which still grasped the stick, the sight would have been almost endurable.

As it was, I vomited—retched until I sank to the ground with my heaving stomach on fire.

Then something in me rebelled. The sight of the skeletons drove me to my feet again. I couldn't give up, not like this, not here. I had to survive.

I climbed into the cabin from above. The stench of decay, of rank vegetation and moldering fabric infested with beetles, worms, and maggots, almost took my breath away. I removed the dead men's dog-tags, lifting them over their skulls as gingerly as an archaeologist in a Pharaoh's tomb.

A rat sprang at me with bared teeth from the rear of the cockpit. I lashed out, and it scuttled into the bomb bay, squeaking shrilly.

I survived the ordeal, turned my back on the abode of death, and stood there filling my lungs with air.

It was then I first heard it: a strange, monotonous sound like wind blowing steadily through treetops—no, more like the distant roar of the sea.

The sea . . . It not only sounded like the sea, it *was* the sea! Only twenty yards from the wreck the forest thinned. The ground became mossy and looked as if it had once been cleared. Quantities of blackish-purple russula were growing there. Despite my certainty that the sea was near, I threw myself on the mushrooms, crumbled their caps, and crammed them into my mouth. We'd often eaten them raw as children in the Johannisburger Heide, and their faint hazelnut flavor made them seem like manna from heaven.

Now that my body was bracing itself for a final effort, exhaustion brought me out in a welter of sweat. After crouching over the mushrooms, it was all I could do to struggle to my feet and stagger down to the shore.

It was a coastal lagoon, not the open sea itself. I just had time to take this in. Then flocks of sable-winged birds soared down and darkened my senses.

Early morning. I must have slept the afternoon and the night away.

I awoke in an instant, feeling stronger and fresher but parched with thirst. Then came a spectacle that banished every other thought.

Preceded by a whirring, whistling, humming sound from the marshy thickets of reeds and willows, clouds of birds sailed up into the glow of dawn—birds of every hue from earth-brown and mouse-gray to raven-black. A vast armada of migrants took wing in time to avoid the east winds that would spring up on this, the morning that had restored me to life.

A flight of gray geese, hundreds of siskins swirling like sulphurous smoke, innumerable goldfinches with vivid scarlet faces, flocks of hoopoes . . . A dozen swans took off, then threw up scintillating showers of spray as they splashed back into the lagoon, which was black with waterfowl.

The virgin air was filled with the sounds, songs, and warning notes of crested larks and warblers. Taking advantage of the early morning thermals, a whole squadron of buzzards and red kites circled above ocher dunes populated by curlews and restless wheatears.

Some gray herons milled around in confusion before heading south—young and ungainly birds that had left their nests too late. Their bright plumage seemed to wave farewell before disappearing from view. Swarms of corn buntings, chaffinches, and ortolans followed, swooped on by peregrines and pursued by sparrow hawks. Far above the melee soared a pair of white-tailed eagles.

Bustle, tumult, movement. I had been transported into another world and permitted to share in the mysterious rhythms that governed its existence. My heart beat in time to the cry of the wild goose, to the sudden twists and turns of the startled snipe. All that had conspired to bring me here was forgotten.

Flock after flock wheeled high into the air and departed, but the woods and marshy hollows along the shore remained alive with chirping, trilling, cackling, complaining colonies of plovers, reed warblers, goldcrests, ducks, goosanders, and great crested grebes.

The show was over. I leaned against a tree, sighing like a theatergoer who emerges into the street still dazed by the dramatic impact of what he has seen.

Then I caught sight of two fishermen walking toward me and knew that I was safe.

7

I returned to Grojecko unscathed apart from a multitude of cuts, bruises, and abrasions. Barely enough, these days, to keep anyone in the sick bay for longer than forty-eight hours —"time to lick your wounds," as Ketsch put it. I was puzzled. The poor man seemed delighted to have me back. Most people would have been delighted to get rid of a prize failure so neatly.

I must have been wandering around in the Deime delta near Labiau, if not farther north toward Elchwerder. Twenty-five or thirty miles northeast of Königsberg, this desolate region bordered the Kurisches Haff and faced Rossitten, site of the famous bird sanctuary. The great migration I'd witnessed there had started more than two months late.

I was put on a train to Königsberg and picked up at the airfield by a twin-engined Siebel 204 from station headquarters. It was piloted by two young probationers who were making their first major cross-country flight. Although it was all they could do to keep the Siebel flying straight and level, my trip in the radio operator's seat seemed as luxurious as a royal tour by special train.

Whenever the two youngsters weren't arguing over whether "that place down there" was Preussisch Eylau, Bartenstein, or Domnau, I pumped them for information. It appeared that a forester had seen the remains of my one-ninety nose dive into a marsh. All that survived of it was the tail unit bearing the registration mark.

Despite blizzards, icing-up, and unresolved questions such as whether we'd strayed across the Alle or the Neide, we made Grojecko in one piece. The base was almost unrecognizable. Overdue since October, the first snow had finally fallen.

Lenz threw a party in my honor when I emerged from the sick bay. Apart from coaxing a bottle of real French cognac and three of vodka out of the quartermaster, he'd produced a phonograph plus a box of spare needles and a pile of sensational new records. These had been lent for the occasion by Major Ohlshausen, who claimed—tongue in cheek—that they came from the station record library. I was genuinely touched.

The music that mingled with the fumes of vodka, cognac, Luftwaffe beer, and wartime rotgut was new to me. It was played by Stan Brenders and the Grosses Tanzorchester von Radio Brüssel. Lenz said I'd often heard them on the radio, but I couldn't remember. I was still bemused by my trek through the wastes of East Prussia, and anyway, what I wanted most of all was to be with Maryla. I'd had no news of her, nor she of me.

The discs were ordinary Telefunken recordings of outwardly innocuous titles from screen musicals. What made the music so sensational was the way Brenders played it. Ohlshausen had also slipped in one or two records which the omniscient Lenz said were for export and banned from sale in Germany. They included American numbers like "Well All Right," "Fascination," and "Moonglow."

"Well All Right" was a terrific piece of work—we played it over and over. Lenz bemused me still further with esoteric items of information. He knew, for example, that two of the trumpeters were called Raymond Chantrain and Eugene van Derborgh.

How did anyone come by such pearls of wisdom on a dilapidated Polish airfield in November 1944?

Lenz's reply was succinct:

"No blinkers, that's the secret. Take an interest in everything—keep your mind ticking over, never switch off."

Before long, serious conversation became impossible. Vodka and rotgut were having the required effect. We played "Well All Right" for the umpteenth time, pounding out the rhythm and heaping curses on the Reich Chamber of Music for daring to deny us such aesthetic delights. Wehrmann was alone in calling for the "Badenweiler," our Führer's favorite march. His scathing verdict on "Well All Right":

"That nigger jazz of yours sounds worse than a gorilla in heat!"

Then, in the middle of a really hot alto solo, Steffen appeared.

As room senior, Wehrmann called us to attention.

"Beg to report Room Four celebrating the safe return of Oberfähnrich Braack, Herr Geschwader-Kommodore!"

"Carry on," said Steffen. The alto continued to wail. He beckoned to Lenz and me. "You two, come with me."

We came. Stan Brenders faded as the door closed behind us.

"I've received some, er—some charge sheets from the standing court-martial at Königsberg. No, not Königsberg." Steffen nervously consulted a sheaf of papers. "Bromberg, not that it makes any difference—the whole thing's out of my hands, I'm afraid. I warned you often enough. Now you've been formally indicted. The hearings are scheduled for December fifteenth. Your movement orders have already been made out—collect them from my office in due course." He peered again at the papers. "That's right, Bromberg . . ."

"What sort of hearings?" asked Lenz. "Indicted for what?"

"Don't worry, nothing much'll happen to *you*. You're charged with undermining morale, that's all."

"Undermining it how?"

"By listening to enemy broadcasts, of course. In Oberfähnrich Braack's case, the charges go further."

"How much further?"

"He's accused of undermining morale and cowardice in the face of the enemy. Cowardice . . . That could be serious at this stage in the war, when our country's waging such a heroic fight for survival."

Lenz broke in. "Who charged Oberfähnrich Braack with cowardice in the face of the enemy?"

"I did, naturally." Steffen drew himself up. "It was my duty as a German officer—as a German, period."

"Very well," Lenz said curtly. "December fifteenth it is."

"You've nothing to fear. I've given you a first-class report. After all, you've scored several kills—how many is it now?"

"If you don't know," said Lenz, "I certainly don't."

"I could have sent for you, but I came myself," said Steffen. "I knew you were celebrating."

"Yes," said Lenz.

"A lot of things will become clearer to you later on," said Steffen.

"Yes," said Lenz.

"I had no option," said Steffen.

"No," said Lenz.

"I mean, take what happened just now. I walk into the bunkhouse, and what do I hear? Banned American nigger jazz!"

"That so-called nigger jazz," said Lenz, "was recorded by

Belgian musicians in German-occupied territory. The band belongs to Radio Brussels, which is under German control. The discs were manufactured by Telefunken, a German recording company."

"Never mind all that, you know what I'm driving at. For God's sake come to your senses and give this sort of thing a rest. You know damn well . . ."

"What you're driving at? Yes, I do."

Steffen turned on his heel. He hadn't addressed a word to me—hadn't even deigned to notice me.

"That was a bit below the belt," I said as we returned to the bunkhouse. " 'Well All Right' really *is* banned."

"He couldn't tell Bach from Basie. There'll always be know-alls like Steffen, win or lose."

We went back inside. The atmosphere had changed. Popular music of approved quality was oozing from the radio, interspersed with uplifting messages delivered by an announcer with a metallic voice.

"What happened to Stan Brenders?" Lenz said dryly.

The others hemmed and hawed. I suddenly felt lonelier than ever before. I barely knew the latest additions by name, not that they interested me very much. Schwaneweber, Tiny Lauritzen, Illerts, Rotsch, Bächler—all dead. The sole survivors of our Zeltweg training course were Lenz and Wehrmann.

"Listen . . ." Wilk had taken the floor. "You're making waves, the two of you, and we're getting the backwash. Seems to me the odd man out is Braack. I'm not saying he doesn't have a point, I'm only saying he's wrong to step out of line *now*. A person's got to judge when it's fair to buck the system. Sometimes it's right and sometimes it's wrong—not objectively, I mean, but depending on circumstances."

"Oh yes, and how do our circumstances look to *you*?"

Lenz didn't have to wait for our roommates to enlighten

him. The Greater German Broadcasting Service answered for them:

"There are some who glibly respond to the demands of our age by arguing that the government would call on their services if it needed them. Rest assured, their wish will soon be granted. . . ."

The metallic voice made way for Beethoven's Fifth. Almost immediately, Beethoven was dislodged by some background color from the fighting fronts:

"Take a lesson from our heroes of the air. Look, for example, at Major Dahl, a one-time Hitler Youth leader and music student. Yes, listeners, Major Dahl used to be a music student. Today he knows only one kind of music—the ratatat of his aircraft cannons. Today, at twenty-eight, he has emerged victorious from over seventy hard-fought air battles and now commands a Geschwader of death's-head fighters!"

Wilk again:

"Listen, Braack, we don't give a damn what you think in private, but your way of thinking doesn't jibe with ours. We don't want to think at all—we want to destroy the swine who are bombing our country. There'll always be loners like you, but they just aren't typical, understand? We don't propose to accept you as our spokesman, let alone help you carry the can. Where the hell would *that* leave us when we've won the war?"

"So the swine are bombing our country," Lenz said. "Haven't you ever stopped to wonder why?"

"Because Western capitalism wants to dominate the world, that's why! As fighter pilots, it's our job to save Germany from international Jewry and the plutocratic imperialists of America."

"Come on, Martin," I said eventually. "I'm just not typical. Better give up."

Steffen had lost every last member of his family. This only came out by degrees, over the grapevine.

His wife, children, parents, and grandparents had all been evacuated to the relative safety of Stolp, on the Baltic coast of Pomerania. There they were blown to bits by night-flying British Lancasters—not American daylight raiders. Steffen was now a lonely man.

All personnel turned out for the weekly parade. Steffen's bearing was courageous, admirable—stalwart as a German oak. He said, among other things:

"They may destroy our country. They may destroy our loved ones. They may even, though God forbid, win the war. One thing they will never do, men, and that is deprive us of our honor!"

I consciously studied his hands for the first time. Until then I'd always focused on his mouth, the fountainhead of so many senseless, nonsensical orders. Now I looked at his hands. They were the hands of a tired old man, with bulging veins, bluish fingertips, and pallid, wrinkled skin.

All at once I knew: I was stronger by far than this shadow of a mighty man.

Balzerat was the next to go. We'd never been close, but still.

He bought it during a scramble—veered off the runway just before leaving the ground and streaked toward a heavy truck parked on the apron. He poled back hard, grazed the top of the cab and pancaked, then skidded to a halt.

The one-ninety had crumpled like a smashed egg. What

seeped from it was a gooey mixture of oil, hydraulic fluid, and blood.

Balzerat's harness must have snapped, catapulting him through a mass of torn metal that flayed every square inch of his skin. His body was nothing but raw, exposed flesh when they extricated it.

It arched itself once and gave a single animal scream, or so I was told.

And still new faces kept appearing—replacements I couldn't even put a name to. They'd ceased to interest me. Their ideals, their fears, their hopes, their pathetic little dirty jokes all left me cold.

Although their eyes shone when they told of their prowess in the air ("I've only done thirteen hours in a one-ninety, but I've never screwed up a landing yet!"), their innocence no longer touched me. More and more, I fell back on Lenz's company and my own. It was the only way I could survive.

Rumors had been rife since my return.

East Prussia was being evacuated, it seemed. At the same time, everyone resident in the Warthegau, which lay much farther west, had been forbidden to leave. The man in charge there was Gauleiter Greiser, whose additional titles were Reich Governor and General of the SS. I thought of Maryla and Landsberg an der Warthe. Of East Prussia I seldom thought at all. I just couldn't picture my mother climbing aboard a hay wagon and trekking west.

There was recurrent talk of the D-9, a new version of the one-ninety powered by a Junkers Jumo 213A-1 engine. Unless one opted for jets, it was the most advanced fighter in service.

After recuperating, I too was given a Dora Nine.

Compared with this new diva of the air, my A-8 seemed like a clumsy old matron. Her longer and more slender nose housed the new Jumo 213, an in-line engine which greatly enhanced her speed and rate of climb. A large air intake on the port side of the nose betrayed the presence of the turbo supercharger that improved her performance, especially at high altitudes. She was reputedly capable of climbing to a height of seven and a half miles.

My new airplane bore the number 15 and came from the Cottbus Works. Jagdgeschwader 54 was the first unit to have been equipped with D-9s, we were told, but only for escort duty with jet fighters. Rumor had it that we too would soon be transferred west on a similar assignment.

I sweated blood during the first few circuits. The long nose gave quite a different feel, particularly on takeoff and landing, and visibility while taxiing was even worse than in the good old A-8. The D-9 felt nose-heavy by comparison. I took a while to master this characteristic when touching down, scared more than once by the thought of landing on my airscrew.

Later I realized that the D-9 was a racehorse compared to the stolid A-8. She was more sensitive, more of a thoroughbred. She was tougher on pilot errors too, but once you had her in hand—boy, did she give you a sense of power! Lenz fell in love with her even sooner than I did.

Having landed after half a dozen circuits, we waited for the order to practice formation flying and gunnery at higher altitudes.

But days went by and nothing happened. Gales and violent rainstorms alternated with calm spells quite suitable for practice flying, and still nothing happened. No alerts, no scrambles; we simply vegetated. Rumors continued to fly thick and fast: our fuel reserves had run out, the Russians would overrun us in the next three days, Hitler had offered the Western Allies an armistice on condition they joined forces with us against the Red hordes, and so on and so forth. Steffen kept mum and Ketsch kept out of sight. We were told to hold ourselves in readiness to quit the base at a moment's notice and fly west.

At last, on a clear and frosty November day, the monotony was broken.

Strolling back to the bunkhouse after lunch, we were transfixed by an unfamiliar sound. We all stopped dead and pricked up our ears, then sprinted for the field.

A peculiar hissing roar was approaching from the direction of the forest. It sounded like an asthmatic locomotive venting steam, except that the pitch and intensity varied continually. The whining overtone triggered an association of ideas in my mind: a siren song—yes, that was it.

Still nothing to be seen. We were gripped by an almost eerie expectancy that seemed to transform the appearance of the marshy landscape and the crystalline sky overhead. What was bearing down on us? Why hadn't we been scrambled? Had the Russians launched a secret weapon? Would it come bursting through the trees like some prehistoric monster?

A strange sensation of déjà vu. It was when the Graf Zeppelin flew over Lötzen on its way to Königsberg, and we'd all run outside when we heard the unfamiliar whir of its propellers. The gliding progress of the long silvery cigar had seemed like a mythological occurrence.

But now came the roar of an approaching typhoon—a tornado. The ground quaked beneath our feet. It was the end of the world. We ducked as a dark shape flashed past.

"It must be!" shouted Lenz. "It is!"

Yes, there it was, the legendary Me 262, our new jet

fighter. It curved to port and lowered its flaps and undercarriage, twin turbojets emitting long streaks of brown smoke. It came in low—even lower than us—and touched down, then settled onto its nosewheel and taxied toward the main buildings.

Most of our runway surface whirled into the air in the wake of its heavy, pregnant-looking engine nacelles as it taxied to the hangar. We cupped our hands over our ears, half afraid to go nearer. No visible means of propulsion . . . An uncanny sight.

That's one machine you'll never fly, I told myself. The roar died away. It was only then, as silence flooded back into the vacuum, that I realized how loud it had been.

The canopy slid open and the pilot climbed out. Our duty motorcyclist gave him a lift to Combat Control while sightseers converged on the latest sensation from all sides.

It wasn't until that evening in the mess that we got near the man of the moment, who'd been driven off course during a ferry flight by air raids and bad weather. He'd originally intended to refuel at Radom.

"Except that the Russians are already there, more likely than not. . . ."

We bombarded him with questions for hours on end. He answered them patiently.

"Acceleration? Piss-poor—she won't pick up speed. If you want to pull out, for God's sake don't yank the stick too hard. Go easy, as the hedgehog said to his girl friend. Two degrees angle of attack, otherwise you build up so much drag you lose all the speed you've gained. And there's another point worth remembering—hands off at extreme altitudes. No coarse rudder, no dives in excess of five-forty mph, no coarse throttle adjustments—not unless you want to risk your engines exploding. They don't take kindly to excessive fuel injection."

To loosen our jet pilot's tongue still further, we plied him with tumblers of carefully hoarded Polish vodka.

He wasn't used to vodka. He belonged to the famed Nowotny Geschwader and was stationed at Hesepe, where the most they got was Luftwaffe beer and diluted schnapps.

"Our new reflector sights need a lot more development," he told us. "Being gyro sights, they're supposed to compute the lead angle automatically. All you do is line up a target and fire—except that it doesn't work out like that. The image does a dancing dervish act all over your windshield, sometimes. . . ." He took another pull at his glass. "Tackle the Boeings from below, that's the best way. You've plenty of speed and power in hand." (He actually said *"Spiet"* and *"Pauer."* Anglicisms were becoming more and more fashionable in the Luftwaffe.) "You can't dive on them flat out. Once you're doing over five-forty, funny things start happening—like stick reversal. Pole back and she goes down steeper, ease the stick forward and up comes her nose. There aren't any dive brakes, either."

It was heady stuff. We all felt like prospective jet pilots listening to their introductory lecture.

"Thirty-millimeter cannons, we carry. I've cut through a Boeing's tail like tar paper before now."

Aeronautically, I was enthralled.

Politically, I'd forgotten something. I was due to be court-martialed at Bromberg in ten days' time.

8

We'd landed. We crawled out of our cockpits and were toting our parachute packs and weary bones across the apron when Wehrmann roared home late and put on a show for us. He buzzed the field, pulled up at zero feet, rolled over, pulled through, and repeated the performance in reverse, waggling his wings all the time.

"Bloody fool," Lenz growled as he trudged along beside me. "He'll scare our cows. If they panic, it'll be sour milk for breakfast."

Wehrmann might almost have heard. He abandoned his latest act and went into the next—cut his throttle, dropped his flaps, and swooped low over the woods. There was a flash of tracer followed by the muffled ratatat of his MK-108.

I dumped my chute on Lenz and started running. I knew, with piercing and absolute certainty, what had happened.

Two short bursts only, then Wehrmann lowered his gear. One brief yaw, a giant California sideslip, and he was safely down on the turf. Neat, very neat . . .

Lenz just shrugged and trudged on into the bunkhouse while I headed for the woods in my sweaty flying suit, panting hard. Twenty minutes' agonized jogging brought me to my dreaded destination. There was Shangri-La, or what remained of it.

No sign of fire. Wehrmann would never have been so

crudely unprofessional as to alert our fire-fighting team by setting the shack or the woods ablaze—they might have arrived in time to save something. Being the expert he was, he'd used armor-piercing. Two short bursts had reduced the shack to matchwood, and shell fragments had lopped branches off the surrounding trees like giant ax strokes. All that remained was a jumble of splintered wood, clods of earth, lumps of moss, fallen birds' nests, leaves and fragments of birch bark.

Shangri-La, my private paradise . . .

Birch bark was still drifting down. It had caught in the treetops and was now being dislodged by the evening breeze.

I felt unutterably tired. Wehrmann was a swine, but did I clench my fists and swear vengeance? No, I just sat there like an updated version of Dürer's *Melancholia.* . . .

A pair of soft arms stole around me from behind. A pair of soft lips kissed me on the ear, the cheek, the mouth. It was Maryla, who'd been visiting the local army post. She'd borrowed a bike and hurried to the scene after hearing gunfire and seeing a fountain of debris. Her first thought—heaven alone knew why—was that I'd returned from patrol with a Lightning on my tail and been bounced while coming in to land.

Now she rejoiced aloud and clung to me tightly, beside herself with relief.

She was glad—overjoyed at the sight of Shangri-La in ruins.

"Only the hut! My God, I thought it might be . . ."

Later she sat down alongside and looked me gravely in the eye.

"I see," she murmured. "So it wasn't a Lightning or a Mustang or a Shturmovik. The man who did this wasn't an American or an Englishman or a Russian. He was a German, Michael, and don't you ever forget it."

The noose around my neck drew tighter and tighter. With the destruction of Shangri-La, my hopes that all might yet end well had melted like the first winter snow.

I hit the bottle. It didn't make me more aggressive, strangely enough, just more depressed.

"The man's a romantic," Wehrmann sneered, apropos of some remark I'd made. "Fart in his face and he'd swear it was incense!"

Now that Shangri-La was no more, I steered clear of him as much as possible. No, I didn't walk up and beat him to a pulp. Yes, I deliberately avoided him. No, he didn't avoid me. On the contrary, he did his utmost to needle me.

I was a coward.

"You're a coward," Lenz told me.

"I know, I think too much."

"About what, you gutless wonder? Want me to bust him on the nose for you?"

"Why? It wouldn't bring back Shangri-La."

"But his sort always end up on top, no matter what they do. It'll all be the same in a hundred years' time, thanks to *your* sort."

"What if I did beat him up? Shangri-La would still be a thing of the past."

"Maybe, but you're handing him a license to keep up the good work."

"Suppose I followed your advice. Would it make him a better person?"

Lenz realized that he wasn't getting anywhere.

"No, I guess not. Wehrmann's all Saul and no Paul."

I shrugged. "You flatter him."

Strong enemy formations reported heading for . . .

We doubled to our machines and started up.

While taking off, I saw Wehrmann cut in on Lenz so recklessly that he was left with only two choices: to abort or steep-turn as soon as he was airborne.

Lenz steep-turned, and for one brief moment I thought he was going to hit the trees.

I saw red. My immediate inclination was to ram Wehrmann—give him an aerodynamic kick in the pants—but I had enough on my hands as it was. I'd sunk at least three large vodkas in an effort to dispel my fear, rage, and despair. In recent days I'd felt I couldn't endure the world for another twenty-four hours. Shangri-La had been my last resort, my last island refuge in a hostile sea.

I glued myself to Wehrmann's tail while we were climbing, with Lenz beside me and slightly in echelon. Our machines rocked and swayed in unison. The altimeter needle rotated steadily. Breathing in my mask seemed harder than usual— the medics always said that altitude magnified the effects of alcohol. Twelve thousand, thirteen-five, fifteen thousand feet . . .

Still no contact. The gentle turbulence, the vibration of the airframe, the roar of the engine, and the reek of hot metal and paint combined to induce a strange dreamy state in which everything around me seemed unreal.

My feelings and perceptions had dimmed. I registered the scene as if it were an aerial ballet whose meaning eluded me. I was part of a greater whole, as deprived of individuality as a bee in a swarm. Our movements were remote-controlled by some invisible and superior being.

But the slightest break in the rhythm was enough to jerk me back into my body, back to full awareness of my everyday surroundings, with a sensation akin to physical pain. And with that sensation came a resurgence of anger.

Nineteen thousand feet. If we went on climbing too long, we wouldn't have much fuel left to play with.

We sighted the Americans at the last minute. The Staffel winged two without knocking them down. The crippled machines limped after their companions, who turned north in an attempt to sneak home across the Baltic.

Somewhere these bombers must have done their bloody work—somewhere a town or city had gone up in flames. Terror was being visited on Germany. We gave little thought to the source or root cause of that terror. Had it been conjured into being by Hitler, by us, by Hitler working through us, by our refusal to negotiate? Now that it was there, we fought fear with fear, violence with violence. Was Hitler right to strike such a drastic balance of terror?

I felt myself drifting off again and angrily pulled myself together. Three shots of vodka couldn't knock out a seasoned fighter pilot, however unsuccessful. I saw Lenz squirt a bomber and reef around for another pass. Then Wehrmann streaked in at an angle. Already crippled by Lenz, the Fortress took Wehrmann's burst full in the gut, exploded amidships, and disintegrated into several sections which fluttered earthward as gently as leaves in the fall. Lenz straightened out of his steep turn, saw that Wehrmann had beaten him to the punch, and had to break hard to avoid a collision.

My bowels churned with fury.

I tore after Wehrmann, my urge to ram him reawakened. Suddenly, in the flames from the cartwheeling wreckage, I saw the shape of Shangri-La. . . . We were in the midst of a witches' sabbath of parachutes, contrails, bursts of tracer, puffs of smoke, white stars, black crosses, Plexiglas canopies, radial engines, stub exhausts, gun ports flashing like bared fangs.

I missed an American chute by inches. Nine or ten men were floating down through the blazing debris and wheeling airplanes. The glassy light made the sky look like a huge aquarium full of jellyfish, silvery scales and fins, lumbering turtles.

Wehrmann was ahead of me again. He chopped his throttle so hard I had to cut my own or break fast. Mysteriously, he even lowered his flaps and went into a gentle glide. Then I saw the enemy pilot hanging from his snow-white canopy and knew what Wehrmann had in mind—Wehrmann, who'd already been reprimanded for firing at defenseless opponents.

The sequence of events was almost too fast to follow. Wehrmann aimed his nose at the solitary figure, which dangled in its harness like a wooden doll, and opened fire. He fired bursts, not from his pair of fuselage-mounted MGs, not from the guns in his wings or pods, but from all of them at once. All light barrels opened up on the lone man suspended from his parachute.

I was past him in a flash, but I just had time to glimpse a dangling torso and two dilated eyes staring vacantly into space. Everything below the hips was gone, carried away by Wehrmann's shells. The spurting blood was wafted upward and spattered the underside of the chute with crimson. Then the remains of the body slid from its harness and spun down, flailing its arms like a drowning man.

Now I really saw red. My eyes, my windshield and gunsight were tinged the color of blood. Wehrmann's starboard wing swam into view. I thumbed the button and metal flew from the wing tip. I'd hit him—my first success—but Wehrmann seemed to shake off this minor inconvenience and curved to port. A moment later, six streams of tracer converged on him. They weren't mine. Two Mustangs roared overhead, but Wehrmann flew on and gave them the slip. My anger had ebbed like the fuel in our tanks. It was time to return to base.

Wehrmann was ahead of me again when I circled the field

before landing. Although his machine had taken several hits, he kept it manfully under control and made a normal approach. I was abeam of him and flying in the opposite direction when he prepared to touch down. Just then a flight of geese rose from the outskirts of the field and enveloped him like a cloud. The next time I saw his one-ninety it had pancaked and was lying belly down with its gear in ruins—a picture to cherish.

They admitted Wehrmann to the field hospital at Konskie two hours later. He'd sprained his back but was otherwise uninjured. It must have hurt quite a bit when they hauled him out of the cockpit. He couldn't move because his canopy had been shattered by a gray goose, Latin name *Anser anser,* which was lying dead on his lap with its neck broken. He later insisted that his cockpit cover had been riddled by bursts of Mustang cannonfire, like his starboard wing. Using every trick in the book, he'd managed to nurse his machine back to base and deposit it on the runway. His pancake landing had been due to loss of maneuverability at low speed. Geese? He hadn't seen any.

Nobody cared to argue with him.

The attack on Wehrmann dissipated my aggressive impulses but left me melancholy and depressed. In a world where all that counted was force of arms and derring-do, there were enough heroes already.

I did, however, feel a glow of secret satisfaction at the accuracy of my shooting. During gunnery instruction in the days before we were expected to fire at live targets, I'd been one of the top scorers.

Lenz had heard a story about a Geschwader of heavy long-range fighters based in Silesia. One crew belonging to this unit had apparently been arrested on the spot for talking to survivors from a crashed American bomber and offering them cigarettes.

"Relatively speaking, our local lords and masters are models of toleration. They're even allowing us to play at the Christmas Eve party."

Our Yuletide festivities were being moved forward because nobody knew if the Geschwader would still be in existence on 24 December. According to the latest scuttlebutt, we were all going to be split up and transferred to a wide variety of units. Some of us would escort jet fighters and others convert to jets themselves.

Grojecko had been lashed by severe gales for days.

Hailstorms and blizzards sent flurries of white through the rocking, groaning, straining rows of anchored fighters. The headquarters Storch broke loose from its moorings, reared up, and flipped over on its back, writing off the tail plane and airscrew.

No sooner had a gap appeared in the overcast than some of us were sent on patrol. I detected universal signs of fatigue and reluctance. Anyone who had survived this long wanted to be in one piece when the time came to pack up and move west —or "shorten our front," to quote the official euphemism.

My Dora Nine did me a good turn: her engine went on strike.

The rest of the Staffel took off, yawing and bucking in a way that made me doubly glad I wasn't with them. None of us had experience of formating in winds of this strength.

There followed the worst single disaster in the whole of the Geschwader's history.

The aircraft assembled over the field. Many of them went too far downwind and had to claw their way back against the gale, throttles wide open, to rejoin the rest. Everyone milled around like peas on a drum.

Then it happened.

Someone from 8 Staffel—a Green 4—slid out of a climbing turn. Immediately below him was Wilk's White 6, flanked by Rebhan, who was lurching around the windswept sky like a mad thing.

Perched on the wing of my immobilized machine, I watched the drama in close-up through some binoculars lent me by Rosenhain.

The Green 4 came crashing down—silently from where I sat but doubtless with a frightful metallic crunch—onto Wilk's White 6. I distinctly saw the cockpit canopy splinter as the Green 4's belly descended on it.

Rebhan reacted with lightning speed. He flung his machine into a steep turn, but too late. The raised starboard wing scythed straight into the entangled wrecks and buckled like cardboard. Rebhan spun down with his engine racing. I whipped the binoculars away from my eyes just in time to see smoke and debris erupt beyond the administration block.

The two doomed fighters sailed on through the storm like mating dragonflies. One showed signs of life. The 8 Staffel pilot jettisoned his canopy and jumped, but he was only a few hundred feet up. Although his parachute opened, he hit the ground a split second later—he couldn't have survived. The machines went into a steep turn, still locked together, and crashed into the base of a copse. Another fountain of debris but—incredibly enough—no fire.

We raced across the field. The pilot who'd bailed out had come down just beyond the landing tee.

He was lying flat on his back. Released by some unaccountable means, the parachute had fluttered away through the turbulent air and lodged in a clump of poplars.

His eyes were wide open. He was still alive, though every bone in his body must have been broken. His limbs had all the resilience of a rag doll. Even his skull had smashed like an eggshell and was only prevented from falling apart by skin and gristle.

He was dead when they lifted him onto the stretcher. Someone said his name was Petermann, but that was as far as our immediate information went.

Meanwhile, Steffen had scrubbed the patrol. We were still busy removing the body from the landing tee when the first machines came in to land. The wind was so strong that some of them seemed to hang motionless over the runway. There were pancake landings, wrecked undercarriages, and one total write-off from which the pilot walked away unhurt. I hardly bothered to watch anymore. The spectacle ceased to interest me once Lenz touched down, safe and sound but in a precariously stalled condition.

End of patrol.

Attempts to exhume the interlocked one-nineties were swiftly abandoned. The simplest volumetric calculation made it clear that little more than an oxygen maskful of Wilk could have been recovered. His bunk and Rebhan's were claimed by replacements even before "they" were buried with full military honors. The newcomers' names failed to register with me, as they so often did these days. I felt permanently stupefied.

All I wanted now, for myself and Lenz, was simple survival.

A chill wind swept across the open graves and whistled through our ranks during the funeral parade in Grojecko cemetery two days later.

It was a couple of weeks since we'd been ordered to surrender our Luftwaffe greatcoats in response to a special appeal.

Fighter pilots didn't need greatcoats to fly in, said the authorities, whereas our earthbound army comrades were grateful for any form of protective clothing. Apparently, supplies from home had been held up.

So there we stood, blue-lipped and shivering with cold.

It hadn't occurred to anyone that German fighter pilots had a duty to bury their dead in icy winter weather.

"Comrades," the Oberfeldwebel told us one morning in semi-official, semiconfidential tones, "the Geschwader party was originally fixed for Christmas Eve. We won't be here then, but we do have the funds, the schnapps, and the girls. In view of this, Christmas Eve will now be December tenth. All ranks will parade to celebrate the occasion at 1900 hours sharp!"

The plan was that we should provide dance music during the second and less formal part of the proceedings. The mess was lavishly bedecked with sprigs of fir and spruce gathered in the surrounding woods by members of the ground staff. Everyone, including them, was guaranteed a taste of the Polish geese that had also been procured, along with vodka and—so it was said—real French cognac.

We turned out to do our Christmas duty at seven on the dot.

All was in readiness. The ration noncoms and their minions had laid the trestle tables with loving care. Each place sported a cardboard plate laden with rye cookies, Luftwaffe-issue chocolate, and various edible oddments. The scene was festively illuminated by smoking tallow candles, and Handel's *Water Music* cascaded from a phonograph as we filed in. It should have been Beethoven's Ninth, but the Oberfeldwebel had inadvertently dropped a stack of records and smashed the lot.

That afternoon the wind had veered from the east to the southwest. Most of the snow had melted and rain was bucketing down. It was quite apparent that Steffen, whose task it was to deliver the grand Christmas pep talk, had been compelled to rethink his speech. He'd probably planned to cite the glacial and pernicious east wind as a symbol of hostile malevolence—of advancing Mongol hordes. Now he'd had to trim his sails to a steady and undramatic downpour.

"Men, comrades! Officers and other ranks!"

I couldn't even follow his opening remarks in peace because Lenz started humming some new ideas which he'd culled from the BBC that morning and tailored to suit our slender resources.

"Our nation is fighting for its very existence!"

Lenz drowned out most of this by launching into some melodic snippets borrowed from Lew Stone and his band. He was determined to give them a public airing before we finally quit Poland.

"We'd far better stick to Albert Vossen's stuff," I said. "We're in enough trouble as it is."

"Exactly," he retorted. "We're in so deep we can't get any deeper, not with a court-martial coming up in five days' time."

"Given that the individual's survival or extinction depends on the outcome of this struggle," Steffen was saying, "he and all his energies must be committed to the task of winning it. The logic of war demands such a commitment. Anyone who fails to grasp this fact is completely deficient in team spirit and can be induced to fulfill his duty to the Fatherland only by legal sanctions and the threat of punishment."

"Peace on earth!" I muttered.

"Know what?" said Lenz. "Nat Gonella made a guest appearance with Lew Stone this morning. He was great. Listen to this . . ." He hummed a phrase or two. "I'll be playing it later, so watch your chording and don't go too easy on the sevenths."

Steffen again:

"Wartime duties of the kind we all perform daily must be clearly defined. Any time left for activities of a voluntary nature can then be filled with a clear conscience. There are some who glibly respond to the demands of our age by arguing that the government would call on their services if it needed them. Rest assured, their wish will soon be granted."

"That sounds familiar," I said.

"He's quoting Goebbels," said Lenz, the mess librarian. "It's out of his 'total war' speech."

"Yes, but why quote that? I thought we were celebrating. . . . What *are* we celebrating, anyway?"

"The birth of Christ."

"On the tenth of December?"

"God's a broad-minded type. Time's his personal property. He's not going to quibble about a few days here or there."

"If you must play something by Nat Gonella, make it 'Mister Rhythm Man'—I can manage that pretty well. What shall we call it? *'Herr Rhythmusmann'?"*

"Rhythm's a subversive word in German, didn't you know?"

"I still think we'd be wiser to stick to Albert Vossen . . ."

"Men, comrades!" said Steffen. "Officers and other ranks! On this day, more than any other day of the year, the nation's thoughts turn to those who stand, as we do, in the forefront of the fighting." Somewhere, a cork popped out of turn. "Similarly, our own thoughts and those of our comrades turn to our dear ones at home, so near and yet so far. We're all alive to the deep significance of Christmas. The appearance of the Star in the gloom of a winter's night, long ago, bears a profound symbolic relationship to the battle that we, the champions of light, are waging against the demonic servants of darkness. On that note, a victorious Christmas to you all!"

Steffen's pithy salutation triggered off a cannonade from every bottle in sight. Beer and schnapps flowed in torrents. Gaps appeared at the tables as groups began to form. Voices were raised in song, though carols took second place to bawdy epics such as "The Landlady's Daughter." Lenz and I sat there feeling faintly forlorn. The human tide around us had receded, as it did from the silent, despairing drinkers who'd recently lost their wives, children, or parents in some bomb-blasted German city.

Imperceptibly, by slow but steady degrees, our table became a jungle of half-empty beer bottles, brimming ashtrays, plates of broken cookies, and puddles of schnapps.

An hour or so later we were playing fit to bust.

It was a Herculean task, making ourselves heard above the din. Jazz was out tonight, we realized that at once. For all their coarse jokes and rowdy behavior, the men were in a seasonal mood. Even if they didn't favor carol singing, they wanted to be attuned to their premature Christmas Eve by some undemanding and ultra-German standards.

We duly fell back on Albert Vossen & Co. or played numbers so heavily Germanized that no one could have detected their decadent plutocratic-Jewish origins—*Ich hab im Herzen nur Musik* (I've Got a Pocketful of Dreams), for instance, or *Nur ein Viertelstündchen* (Liza).

Wehrmann, freshly discharged from the hospital and more or less drunk, staggered onto the platform and tried to embrace us both in turn.

"I can't stand either of you, you shits, but you're all right just the same. Listen . . . later on, when I'm Gauleiter of the

Greater"—he hiccupped—"Greater Ukraine, I'll roll up in a big black Merc—the kind our Führer uses—and you two jerks can change the tires for me. Don't worry, I'll slip you a nice fat tip."

"And I'll tug my foreskin to you," said Lenz. "Sorry, I mean forelock."

"When I think . . ." I stared pensively after Wehrmann as he tripped and fell headlong down the steps. "I can see them all after the war, riding around in their Mercedes limousines. Miniature Hitlers, that's what they'll feel like. Personally, I'll settle for a Volkswagen."

"That's no better," Lenz retorted. "The VW's just a sop to the masses—a pocket Merc for the Greater German man in the street. The sensation's the same."

"Never mind," I said, "we'll own the world after the war— well, half of it." I wasn't really joking. "We'll be able to afford cosmopolitan tastes, even in Germany. We'll drive Citroëns and Fiats—maybe even Fords from the Reich Protectorate of Canada."

Lenz looked dubious. "*Is* Detroit in Canada?"

Neither of us could remember.

We simply gave up and called it a day. The only sober object on the base was the lime tree outside the mess. Even the tables were swaying gently, and no wonder, considering the amount of liquor they'd absorbed.

"Come on," Lenz said as we tottered outside. He sounded at peace with the world. "We've taken enough on board to refuel a one-ninety."

The rain, which was still pelting down, had turned the whole base into a morass. It was only a hundred yards to the bunkhouse, but we stumbled over enough inert bodies to cast a thriller set in the Everglades. Other unfortunates were writhing around, puking, pissing, and groaning.

Lenz had inexplicably vanished. Just outside the bunkhouse I came face to face with a gypsy woman. I wondered vaguely how she'd slipped past the sentries.

"Well, young gentleman, why are you staring like that?"

She had copper earrings, eyes as black as crows' wings, and a dark-brown complexion that conjured up my mother's childhood threats: "If you don't behave, the gypsies will come and get you. . . ." Everyone knew what gypsies did to naughty little children. They trussed them up and roasted them over a slow fire, or—a lesser penalty—trained them to dance like performing bears. One boy who'd refused to eat his supper had been turned into a parrot. A talking parrot, but still . . .

"What do you want?"

"Give me your hand, young gentleman." She had a Masurian accent. "Let me read it for you."

I opened the door of the deserted bunkhouse and ushered her inside. She bent over my palm and brushed it with the back of her hand as if wiping away the dust of the steppes. Then she peered at it more closely and blew on it through chapped and wrinkled lips. I felt the moist warmth of her breath on my skin.

"Well?" I said.

She cut short her inspection and looked up.

"This way won't do. You're an airman, aren't you? I must find out if you're going to be wounded."

"All right, get on with it."

"Give me a mark first." She called the coin by its dialect name.

"This isn't Masuria, Granny, you'll have to make do with zlotys." I fished in my pocket and produced a couple of greasy bills. "Here."

"I'm going to run my hand over your body. Wherever it stops, that's where you'll be hit."

She proceeded to feel me all over with her leathery hand. I could hardly detect its pressure, her touch was so light. For some reason, she started at my ankles and worked her way upward. Calves and buttocks, then up the spine to the base of the neck. Nothing. Then down the front. Forehead, face, throat. Just below my left collarbone the hand hesitated and circled briefly before coming to rest, hot and heavy.

"There, that's the place . . ."

I flew into a sudden rage.

"Get out, you old witch! Go on, beat it!"

9

I flew back to Grojecko for the last time, from my last patrol, and came in to land through a powdering of snow. Gunmetal gray since early afternoon, the sky didn't clear until I was down.

I filled my unscathed lungs with air and felt the blood throbbing in my unscathed temples. No ricochet had pierced an artery, no high-explosive shell had shattered a limb.

Time to quit. Work was over for the day.

An hour later I was squelching along muddy moorland paths on my way to Maryla. She and her unit were also supposed to be moving west in the next few days. Our hopes of spending Christmas together had been dashed, certainly where Poland was concerned. Sometimes, when the wind was in the right quarter, a distant rumble of gunfire could just be heard.

The air was crisp and clear, and the birchwood where we met was dusted with snow. We strolled along arm in arm in the gathering dusk, saying little. The snow crunched gently under our feet.

The last time we'd held each other beside the ruins of Shangri-La, I'd given her a detailed account of my wanderings in the wilderness. Now we confined ourselves to a brief exchange of information.

"They've postponed our court-martial hearing."

"Till when?"

"It's been transferred to Brandenburg. The authorities there will fix a new date."

"You're lucky they didn't arrest you right away, really."

"In case we deserted? Where would we run to? Besides, pilots are in short supply. They can't afford to lock us up."

"They may once they've tried you."

"Lenz thinks we'll be questioned by a court of inquiry first —he thinks Steffen's bluffing. Then they'll decide whether or not to court-martial us."

"Still, that's bad enough." She paused and looked up. "See how bright it is."

Abruptly, the pellucid winter sky split open like an oyster shell. Thrusting the darkness aside, the aurora borealis draped a shimmering curtain of light across the stars. Even Orion seemed to vanish beneath a coat of whitewash.

We leaned against a tree, holding each other close, and watched the spectacle unfold in all its grandeur.

The patches of sky that had been obliterated began to phosphoresce, gathered themselves into luminous clouds, and drifted above the horizon as though propelled by a high-altitude wind. Naked branches stood out against them like suppliant arms raised to heaven.

A ball woven of light rolled across the sky, leaving a tenuous trail. The trail reared into an arch. The arch collapsed and disintegrated into fragments, each of which became another arch, and the component arches overlapped and reared and turned and merged and separated again. Arcades of light spanned the steppe, then crumbled into particles and rained down into the pools of shadow that floated in the midst of the brightness.

"I'll wait for you," Maryla whispered. "No matter where they send you."

The glow behind the treetops took on a theatrical quality.

Fingers of light groped across the celestial stage as though seeking out the star of the show. And there she was! A lambent purple flame began to dance above the steppe, flexing and twisting its sinuous body. The white intensity of the footlights faded to a soft blue in which hints of green could also be discerned. A flash of orange came and went. Then the whole performance ended as if someone had thrown a switch.

"Don't worry, I'll find you."

"If things don't work out," she said, "go to Landsberg. I'll be waiting for you in front of the Marienkirche."

"That's a date. We'll meet there as soon as the war's over, if not sooner."

"And if I'm not there first, sit on the edge of the fountain and wait for me. Don't give up, though—I'll make it."

We strolled back to where her bicycle was leaning forlornly against a stunted birch. Its pedals caught the light of the rising moon. I couldn't believe this was our last time together in Poland.

"But we'll try and make it again on Sunday."

"Yes. Sunday, if we're still here."

"Take care, Maryla."

"And you, Michael."

"So it's back to the Reich," I said to Lenz. "The betrayed generation is finally heading for home."

"The betrayed generation?" He shook his head and grinned. "You've been thinking again. Cosmically speaking, this war's just a fart in a bathtub."

"So why take part in it?"

"Anthills exist, but so does the Milky Way. Can *you* spot the connection? What does the Milky Way mean to an ant? What does an ant mean to the universe? Ants are creatures of limited vision—they can't even see to the top of their nest. They do what instinct tells them. You expect them to think as well?"

Lenz was leaving Grojecko two days ahead of me. He'd been posted straight to Magdeburg, whereas I was to fly there by a roundabout route. Ketsch had promised to brief me in due course.

For the last time, we perched together on our hard but familiar bunks. Lenz had already packed his gear.

"Now the Ardennes," he said. "Hitler's last throw. It had to come sooner or later. The war can't go on—this'll clinch it one way or the other."

"What happens then?"

"What they're always telling us on the radio—victory or defeat."

"I sometimes wonder if that's relevant. What matters is how we come out of the war. We've learned more in our twenty-odd years than the older generation has in forty."

"Maybe, maybe not. I know this much—we'll take our picks and shovels, clear away the rubble, and start rebuilding."

"But that's just what we shouldn't do. We should sit on the mess and do some soul-searching—make up our minds who really destroyed our country."

"You're asking too much, Michael. Who did it? The wicked Allies, of course. And just so they never do it again, we'll have to grow an even bigger and better set of military muscles, double-quick."

"Wrong. There won't be any uniforms or medals or guns after this. Any self-confessed veteran will be put in the stocks and pelted with rotten eggs by an infuriated mob. Remember how they burned the books in '33? When this show's over, people will round up all the uniforms and medals and military toys they can find and chuck them on a bonfire. No child will ever point a popgun again. That's how it started in the Hitler Youth, with air rifles."

Some Russian POWs were trudging along the edge of the airfield, bound for the Reich like everyone else. I wondered how often and how far we'd already marched them westward from their native land. The men and women were almost indistinguishable in their tattered greatcoats and shapeless boots—uniformly gray and wretched-looking. The floor of the bunkhouse vibrated as they tramped across the concrete apron.

"They'll ban jackboots, too. Bloody things! Think of all the close-ups we've seen of them marching into Holland and France and Denmark and Russia. Boots give me the creeps—they always will . . ."

"You're exaggerating again. Even women would be wearing boots if we had the leather to spare. Not jackboots, maybe, but . . ."

"No, never again. Boots are the thin end of the wedge—boots and shooting galleries and rifle clubs and model T 34 tanks in the nursery and . . ."

"Hey, there goes our heavy gear! Let's hope your guitar and my trumpet get there safely."

The Siebel 204 had started up. Its green ducted spinners revolved slowly in the wind. It taxied into position and took off a few moments later, leaving miniature tornadoes of snow in its wake. The harsh, high-pitched blare of its engines was swallowed up by the morning breeze.

Lenz took off too. He vanished in a dazzling, whirling cloud of powder snow, just like that. I felt almost reproachful—one way of combating despair. Our time in Grojecko was up, so what was I doing there?

The movement control officer, Leutnant König, enlightened me a few hours later.

"You'll fly your D-9 to Danzig, where you'll swap it for an A-8—they'll have it all ready for you. Then you'll ferry the A-8 to Magdeburg and report to Geschwader headquarters. At Magdeburg you'll be re-equipped with a Tank Ta 152. Any questions?"

"No questions."

Absurdity had become the norm. The restoration of logic and sanity, if it ever came, would be an alarming and traumatic phenomenon.

I made a farewell tour of the base. There was Thyme Hill, there the river valley with flocks of black-headed gulls wheeling above it, there the mess and Lenz's library. Who would read all those books in time to come? The rats and bugs that alone would survive our departure?

The bunkhouses were deserted and half cleared of furniture. I'd never felt lonelier in my life. Nature seemed to be lying in wait, chill and silent, ready to fall on these works of man and engulf them in mud and vegetation.

Who, in ten years' time, would still remember the roar of BMW engines, the dull rumble of wheels on turf, the distant, disembodied rattle of aerial gunfire?

"Dig in," the canteen cook exhorted me. "There's plenty of everything. You won't eat better anywhere, not while the war lasts."

But my appetite had gone.

I pushed aside the eggs and white bread, the real butter, real coffee, and real cognac, hurried to my machine and took off.

The D-9 soared above the shell-scarred clearing where Shangri-La had stood. I orbited Grojecko cemetery once and waggled my wings in farewell to Schwaneweber, Rotsch,

Bächler, Illerts, Wilk, Rebhan, Balzerat, and Tiny Lauritzen.
Then I turned north.

I landed safely at Danzig Airport and found myself in another world. I'd been buried in the seclusion of the Polish steppes and forests for four whole months. Air battles apart, even the sky there had seemed wider, higher, and more solitary.

Here in Danzig, urban bustle prevailed. You were chivied by everyone from the met officer to the noncom in air traffic control. Speed was all. While deft fingers were sorting out your papers, their owner's mind was already on his next customer. The queue behind me included a Ju 188 crew routed to Northern Italy, an Me 109 pilot bound for Leipzig, and a Do 217 crew with orders to proceed to Mengen on the Danube.

I signed for a familiar old A-8. The procedure might be mad, but there was method in it. If only when it came to the unfathomable idiocy of swapping airplanes around, the notoriously orderly German mind was still in full working order. As I strolled out onto the tarmac and across to my new machine, the airport's hectic hubbub enveloped me like the noise of a fairground. Nobody seemed to know or care who landed, took off, orbited, overshot, and—occasionally—crashed there.

A Focke-Wulf Weihe glided silently in. Behind and above it, an impetuous Me 110 pilot realized too late that he was faster and couldn't land on its heels, so he went around as best he could. But the Weihe had to go around too because a Taifun ahead of it failed to get in the groove and blocked its approach. And because the Weihe didn't see the Me 110, it almost rammed the long-range fighter from below. The Me

110 pilot flung his machine into a steep turn and, for his part, almost collided with an inoffensive old auntie of a Junkers 87 which was plodding around the circuit in a placid regulation manner.

It was fascinating—I could have stood and watched for hours.

The Me 109 pilot who'd been next in the queue appeared at my elbow. His tone was confidential.

"Where are you headed, comrade?"

I swallowed my detestation of this form of address.

"Magdeburg," I said. "I'm on a joyride, more or less."

"I'm bound for Tutow—that's near Anklam in Pomerania. We could fly together for a stretch."

The loner in me promptly bristled.

"Sorry," I snapped. "I've still got some errands to do."

He grinned. Scornfully, because he'd seen through my lie? Acquiescently, because anything was possible in a world where illogicality reigned supreme?

His grinning face reminded me of a death's-head. It looked stiff and bony. The scalp showed through his close-cropped hair, suggesting the skull beneath, and his cheekbones projected beyond his temples. The cadaverous impression was heightened by deep, shadowy eye sockets and waxen skin like bleached leather.

"Be thankful you're off to the west, comrade."

"I've spent long enough in the east."

"The Eastern Front's falling apart. They're breaking through everywhere, the Russians. I wouldn't hang around here too long, comrade, or you won't get out at all."

There it was, the mysterious something I'd smelled and tasted ever since landing here—the intangible and indefinable smack of fear, nemesis, and defeat, but especially fear.

If there was anything I'd come to know in recent months, this was it. Here I was meeting it in the novel guise of a mass psychosis that colored every scrap of conversation my ears picked up—in the weather room, the hangar, the latrine. "The Russians . . . overwhelming odds . . . falling back . . . refugees . . ."

The subject of refugees cropped up again and again. It was said that they'd been on the move for months now, from Latvia, Lithuania, and Estonia; that the East Prussian roads were choked with them; that their cattle were freezing to death on the icy plains and their unmilked cows dying in droves with swollen bellies and stiffly extended legs.

And now, quite suddenly, all these rumors had crystallized into half a dozen monosyllables uttered by a stranger.

"What do you mean? Why won't I get out at all?"

"Because the show's over, comrade. We're finished, washed up, through."

Hadn't I known that myself? Hadn't I suppressed the thought until someone else came out with it, here at Danzig Airport on 23 December 1944? I'd always felt so alert and perceptive, and now it turned out I was neither. By refusing to accept what I knew, I'd shouldered a burden of guilt which would not be easily shed unless I joined the ranks of those who compromised on principle. Not wishing to do that, I must logically favor guilt and atonement. But was it a genuine impulse? Anything seemed better than joining the eternal conformists, but wasn't that just another form of escapism?

While I was still racking my brains for some way of blinding myself to the obvious, a mechanic walked up and reported my companion's machine ready for takeoff. Superficial as our conversation had been, I could have pursued it to a meaningful conclusion. Instead, I sought refuge in technicalities.

"I see you've got a 109K. Still on the secret list, isn't she?"

"That's right. She's a 109K-8 high-altitude interceptor—pressurized cabin and all." He pulled on his flying gloves. "So long, comrade."

I limply raised one hand. There was no reappearance of the skeletal grin, no change of expression in the dead face. He walked off like a puppet, with scarcely a gesture.

His canopy slid shut and the engine started up. Blue-gray smoke eddied in the wind.

I climbed into my own machine and taxied after him. No scramble this time, just a straightforward milk run to Magdeburg.

The 109K reached the end of the runway and turned into the snow-laden wind. Absently, I followed the sequence of events: open throttle, pick up speed, unstick . . .

Unstick? I braked to a halt and stared.

"Unstick!" I yelled.

But he didn't. He trundled on, fast but not fast enough. A hangar loomed up, and still he failed to lift off. Were his wheels clogged with frozen slush? If he couldn't pick up speed, why didn't he abort?

The hangar. The 109K. The man who'd insisted on calling me comrade. A ball of flame. An explosion, initially silent.

I gunned my engine and it roared, drowning the bang.

Some words ran through my desensitized mind as I accelerated, took off, stowed my gear and flaps:

Pity about that. A peach of a machine, the 109K. . . .

I didn't head southwest for Magdeburg, Pomerania, or Berlin. I turned east—homeward.

The Geschwader had adopted a new catchphrase in December: *the hell of it is . . .*

"The hell of it is, they're butchering us for no good reason."

"The hell of it is, the top brass gorge themselves on ham while we make do with cement sausage."

"The hell of it is, you can never screw as many pieces of tail as want to be screwed." (Wehrmann)

The hell of it was, I had orders to fly west and my mother was stranded in Lötzen.

So I flew east. I had to find out what was going on there. Fuel presented no problem—even my drop tank was full. How long had it been since I cadged enough aviation spirit to get me back to Grojecko from Deblin? How long was it since I really believed we'd never abandon Masuria to the Russians?

Elbing was below me now, and the frozen expanse of the Nogat stretched away over my right shoulder. The Frisches Haff looked like a solid sheet of ice. The Passarge came into view, also frozen. I flew over the Autobahn to Königsberg. A memory surfaced in my mind.

Lenz: "Know something, Michael? The much-vaunted German Autobahn wasn't invented by Hitler or Speer or anyone else in Germany. The Dutch opened an expressway from The Hague to Leyden back in 1934. That's where we cribbed the idea from."

Braack: "One day we'll be adult enough to admit it, Martin, but maybe not till the 1950s. By then we won't feel the need to steal other people's thunder."

Lenz: "The 1950s? You incurable optimist!"

My rev counter was reading 2,300 and my boost gauge 26.5 psi. The Alle showed up. Ahead of me lay Rastenburg and the Wolf's Lair. I gave the Führer's command headquarters a wide berth. If our observer corps network identified and tracked me, I'd be in handcuffs before I taxied to a halt at Magdeburg.

I climbed and climbed without thinking. Suddenly I saw the altimeter reading 8,200. I'd meant to feast my eyes on the Masurian landscape, so why? A wintry haze stretched below me. The sky overhead was as pale as death. No, if I were going to look at all, better do so while flying back west. I was afraid of panicking at what I'd see. I mustn't give up now. That would mean flying on eastward until the wintry light faded, climbing steadily, putting on my mask . . .

Frozen morainal lakes, snow-covered tracts of moor and grassland. There was Steinort on the Mauersee! I'd strayed too far north. Steer one-thirty—that would bring me to Lötzen.

And still I felt tempted to don my mask and go on climbing, go on flying east above the steppes and marshes and primeval forests, then simply remove my mask and go to sleep. Death from oxygen starvation at thirty-five thousand feet: an undramatic, untheatrical way to go. . . .

I pulled myself together and made a starboard turn, descending rapidly. A castle, a monastery, a labyrinth of lakes. I put on speed and curved south in a wide arc until I saw the eastern shore of Lake Löwentin.

Down to 1,500. Yes, there was Lötzen, the canal, the lake, the highway, the hill. There was my home!

I throttled back, lowered my flaps, and went down to three hundred feet. The pond where I'd caught my first tadpoles, the stables where I'd sought consolation with the horses after a rough day at school, the lime trees in front of the house . . . Not a sign of life. I had an urge to land and offer my mother a lift—*Hop in, I'm on my way to Magdeburg*—but there was no one to be seen.

I went on circling. Still no sign of life.

What had happened?

No idea. I only knew I'd have to head west if I wanted to reach Magdeburg before dusk. I headed west.

Then I saw them, the choked roads and snowy fields sprinkled with hundreds of black dots—cattle out to pasture in December. Here at last was the rumored exodus of refugees from the Baltic States to which my mother had only vaguely alluded in her letters, as if frightened of divulging a state secret: hundreds upon hundreds of tiny black figures, some resting by the roadside in their horse-drawn wagons while others toiled on westward.

Wagons, horses, and cattle were crowding along a river valley in total confusion. I skimmed over the changed face of the countryside whose farms and villages I had last seen bathed in the radiance of a glorious autumn day. Although I'd never been a son of the soil, it took little imagination to picture how the Masurians' leisurely way of life had been disrupted by this influx of jostling refugees, human and animal; how their fences had been broken up for firewood, their hedges stripped bare, and their snowy pastures trampled by cows with bursting or withered udders.

Horror, grief, and panic overcame me. For months I'd lived in the seclusion of an outpost. Now, all the rumors and conjectures circulating there had become stark reality. Now, with the Grojecko episode behind me, I faltered like a high-performance engine that can be flogged for just so long before blowing up.

Hedges, neglected gardens half obscured by snow, overcrowded farmyards, roadsides littered with abandoned vehicles. Tanks, artillery units, and columns of infantry were moving east. Wherever they encountered knots of oncoming refugees, the roads were jammed solid. Trees, cottages, fields —I soared over them all with a feeling of detachment which persisted until it occurred to me that one of the anonymous black dots thronging the roads might be my mother.

Rastenburg and the Wolf's Lair lay far away to starboard. I kept well south and steered for Heiligelinde Monastery, the landmark I'd picked up in September. Here, too, the highways and byways were clogged with people and obstructed by carts abandoned in the mud and slush.

I soared westward, sensing that I would never again see this land as it had been in my boyhood. Names flitted through my mind—names that summoned up the sights and sounds of home. I remembered all the dailies my mother and her friends had subscribed to—I could even see them lying on the crocheted tablecloths: the *Ermländische Zeitung*, the *Ostpreussisches Tageblatt*, the *Königsberger Hartungsche Zeitung*, the *Bote am Mauersee*, the *Lycker Zeitung*, the *Allensteiner Volksblatt*. I even recalled, with startling clarity, the intermediate stops on the Cranz-Königsberg railroad that had taken me on so many weekend excursions: Ellerkrug, Powunden, Karmitten, Bollgehnen, Kanten-Fritzen, Gross Raum. I let the names dissolve on my tongue like candy while the A-8 droned along, and with the names came mental images.

Coats of arms took shape in my mind, just as they'd appeared on the cigarette cards we used to swap as boys: the crossed axes of Bartenstein, the eagle's talons of Domnau, Heilsberg's lamb and crosier, Pillkallen's crenellated turret surmounted by a trio of windmills, Nikolaiken's crowned fish, Landsberg's fox with a goose in its jaws.

Landsberg . . . But Landsberg in East Prussia wasn't the same as Landsberg an der Warthe, and that—it came to me quite suddenly—was where I wanted to go.

I pulled on the stick and soared away from Masuria—away from all the memories that were beckoning me back to the dark forests and deep lakes of my homeland. With the Nogat ahead of me and Marienburg to the northwest, I set a course for the Vistula. My machine was enveloped in a film of cloud as soft and white as a gauze dressing on an open wound.

I was very tired. The refugee columns were far behind me now, and every outline had dissolved in the slanting rays of the sun. The Warthe came into view, a dull silver ribbon of molten lead pointing the way to Landsberg, Maryla's home. I somehow felt she'd be there already, waving a welcome outside the Marienkirche or seated on the edge of the fountain she'd described so often—the one in Marktplatz. I had only to land beside it and all would be well for evermore.

But everything was becoming unreal. My A-8 hung motionless in the haze like an insect trapped in amber.

Sweat bathed my hands and forehead and trickled down my back. My temples were hammering, my ribs pulsating with every heartbeat.

There was the wasteland in the fork of the Netze and Warthe. Bare trees jutted from the quarry Maryla had mentioned, each one crowned with a stork's nest. I was on course with fuel to spare, yet I felt as if I'd never see Magdeburg—as if I never wanted to. All my energies were centered on reaching Landsberg.

She'll be standing there in a white dress. We'll have a night out to celebrate. If there isn't a decent play or concert on, we'll go to a movie. . . .

I sat up and squared my shoulders. What was the matter with me—why did I feel so utterly exhausted? Was I sick, or something?

German boys are never sick!

There was the Netze, there was the Warthe, and there was the Schneidemühl. Had I already registered that, and if so when? How long had I been airborne? Once I'd landed, how long would it be before I had to take off again—take off and climb and wheel and fight the whole winter through, just as I'd taken off and climbed and wheeled and fought throughout the autumn? And when winter was past, spring would come, and even then the process would continue, irresistible as the seasons themselves.

I've had enough!

Someone in the cockpit was shouting and yelling like a lunatic. Not me—I was a mute spectator. My limbs, muscles, and nerves had rebelled and taken on a life of their own. My arms twitched spasmodically in a kind of St. Vitus' dance—so much so that my hand decided to release its hold on the stick.

Now my guts began to churn. My stomach erupted, projecting bile and bits of half-digested food into my mouth. I swallowed hard, but it was no use. Everything I'd suppressed for so many months came gushing up in a noisy, sour-smelling stream.

Warthe, Netze, wasteland . . . How could I pull myself together when something was tearing me limb from limb?

Black specks dancing before my eyes, black specks growing steadily larger . . .

Marauders, Havocs, Black Widows, Liberators, Manchesters, Lancasters, Fortresses, Superfortresses, Super Superfortresses, Thunderbolts, Spitfires, Hurricanes, Mustangs, Lightnings . . .

That was it, Lightnings!

They were streaking toward me from Landsberg, out of the setting sun. Twin-boomed, slim and graceful, they sliced the sky with tail planes as pointed as sharks' fins, as keen as a surgeon's scalpel. Twin-boomed death was approaching with silent elegance, cold and clinical. . . .

I saw the gypsy woman in my gunsight, one finger ominously leveled at my chest.

I went to emergency boost and yanked at the stick. The engine screamed like a beast in pain. I did everything wrong, kicked port rudder instead of starboard, poled forward when I should have pulled back, rolled when I should have dived. . . . They were everywhere now—above, below, astern, ahead. I spun and sideslipped and yawed and rolled through a dozen bursts of tracer. Upside down, with the ground overhead and the sun in my aiming ring, I spewed it all out of my system: incendiary, high explosive, sweat, vomit, urine. . . .

A roaring, blaring, rattling, hammering torrent of sound engulfed me. The A-8 quaked and shuddered. My thumb was locked on the button, my forefinger on the toggle switch. Eight rivers of tracer flowed toward the sun. The airplane reared, my body reared, the sun reared and whirled through the void, my body whirled through the void, the void whirled through my gunsight. . . .

The rivers of fire flowed on. I still had ammunition left. I was still alive, still afraid. When the ammunition gauges read zero, everything—life and fear—would be over. A Lightning was on my tail and blazing away. Its gun ports flickered in my rearview mirror. Tracer flashed overhead, but the blare of my engine drowned the rattle of gunfire. I zoomed into a stall and my speed dropped like a stone—the one-ninety dropped like a stone. I started spinning. The airstream howled and whistled over the control surfaces. The fighter gave a shrill scream of protest. She was full of life, unwilling to die—she fought me with her engine snarling defiance, shook herself, and leveled out.

The nacelle guns were empty. Something in me coolly checked my ammunition status on the instrument panel. The cannons had given up. Only the inboard MGs were still in business. *When every gun falls silent, good-bye war.* . . .

Climb and dive, Immelmann and turn. A half-roll. All the pints of filth I'd excreted—all the sweat, vomit, and urine— cascaded onto the underside of the canopy. I'd been full of stinking excrement. Now I was empty. Now the magazines were empty and I was inhaling my own waste matter through my oxygen mask.

No blood? Not a drop.

A momentary lull. All the Lightnings were after me now.

The next few seconds would settle everything. Creation, in the person of Oberfähnrich Michael Braack, held its breath. This was, would be, had to be the moment that banished war forever and restored the peace of the world—the death to end all deaths. . . .

A new stench penetrated my mask. I was wallowing in my own ordure—the cockpit seemed full of it. Why didn't they open fire and end it all, the fighting and the dying and the voiding of bowels?

There, that's the place. . . . No, not that, not my chest. They were firing now, but I didn't want my chest blown to bits. I pulled back hard.

A flash from behind me, a sledgehammer blow.

The one-ninety swerved like a shying horse. Through a dark haze, I saw the spire of the Marienkirche, the brickyard on the riverbank, the stone bridge, the paddle steamers. . . .

My engine had cut. The propeller blades were motionless and there were red lights glowing on the instrument panel. No sound now but the gentle whine of the wind. Frozen pools and snowy fields swam into view. My hand was still on the stick. I could feel a stabbing pain in the small of my back, but my chest was untouched. Thanks to the gypsy, I'd pulled back in time.

I leveled out. A flight of wild geese rose to meet me; then I landed with a rending crash. The Lightnings sped past, waggling their wings exultantly.

I'd come to rest with the red-brick tower of the Marienkirche centered in my windshield.

Get out quick!

I was already out. Something had blown off my canopy and deposited me gently on a frozen expanse of marsh. The ice held. I felt infinitely light, and no wonder. I'd puked, pissed, and pumped myself empty of excrement. My ammunition gauges were finally and irrevocably reading zero.

I leapt, bounded, floated over the ground. Maryla would be waiting outside the Marienkirche. We would soar above the rooftops together, circle the town in a fond embrace without benefit of BMW 801 or oxygen mask. I was really flying now, winging my way silently across the river to the town. My view of infinity was untrammeled by the cross wires of a gunsight. Around me flew a host of winged figures—birds like myself. I was a big white bird, climbing in company with the rest. When I neared the fountain in the square, it was wreathed in mist. A tall white figure barred my path.

It gestured imperiously downward. I had no desire to return to earth, but the figure emitted more power than all the guns and aero engines in the world. Infinite, impotent rage overcame me. I ached to join Maryla but couldn't—I felt duped and deceived. Down I drifted, slowly but steadily. It grew dark. My sense of weightlessness diminished. I could feel my legs and feet again, dragging me down at an ever-increasing speed.

I won't!

Nobody, not even I, heard the cry.

Dim shapes and pools of shadow. Was I back in my one-ninety, preparing for yet another dogfight?

I hit the ground with a sudden jolt.

"You're a lucky son-of-a-bitch!"

Y ou're a lucky son-of-a-bitch!" said the figure in the white coat.

A feeling of immeasurable sorrow flooded over me. My limbs were growing heavier and heavier.

"Why lucky?"

"Take it easy, don't get excited. Why lucky? Because you nearly bled to death through that hole in your back. I don't

even know how you managed to climb out of the wreckage—
you hardly had enough blood left to fill an eggcup—let alone
crawl across that marsh for upwards of a mile. They found
you beside the yacht basin, looking like a bundle of old
clothes."

"I didn't crawl, I flew."

"You Luftwaffe boys never give up, do you? Naturally you
flew, like I'm a belly-dancer and this is the Folies Bergères."

"What?"

"Never mind, just take it easy. You're on the way to Magdeburg in a hospital train."

"Magdeburg? But I don't want to go to Magdeburg."

"Why not?"

"Because I'll have to fly there."

"I thought you liked flying."

"I do, but . . ."

"Get some sleep now. Jowanski, hurry up with that
damned injection! Steady, man, nobody's going to hurt you."

The hand that forced my head back on the pillow exerted a
pressure of 20.5 psi—I gauged it exactly. I yearned to fly
again—to soar across the rooftops with Maryla. I didn't want
to go to Magdeburg.

"No need to worry either way. It'll be a good six months
before you're clear for takeoff."

The man's face floated down and out of sight. I was climbing once more. All around me I could sense brightness,
lightness, and the gentle soughing of a buoyant breeze.

Maryla, I'm on my way. . . .

"Glad to hear it," I said.

Epilogue

Lutz Wehrmann scraped a living as a carpet dealer, truck driver, and used-car salesman immediately after the war. He now heads the Middle East sales division of a well-known auto manufacturing company in southern Germany. Given half a chance, he will readily describe what happened on his last combat mission and how he acquired his scar. Engaging four Mustangs single-handedly, he shot down two and rammed a third with his airscrew. The resulting wreckage penetrated his cockpit canopy and wounded him in the face.

Universally popular, Wehrmann rates as a likable, straight-dealing go-getter.

Hans Ketsch became a lecturer at the College of Physical Education, Cologne. Braack has paid several visits to his home in neighboring Düren. Although their talks are friendly and animated, they never end in any deep or genuine agreement. (Braack: "No form of authority exists in its own right. It can't exist at all unless people are prepared to obey it." Ketsch: "I was an officer. I'd sworn an oath of allegiance—that meant I *had* to obey. Only a starry-eyed idealist like you would try to read some philosophical meaning into the war years.")

Martin Lenz crash-landed his Me 262 near Antwerp and was taken prisoner by the British. In 1955, after several years as a struggling jazz musician, he applied for a job with Lufthansa. He is now an airline captain.

Hermann Braack hanged himself in his office at the Reich Air Ministry, Berlin, in February 1945.

Michael Braack studied philosophy and educational theory after the war. He taught at a school near Hamburg but retired early and is now a free-lance writer in the German Federal Republic.

Maryla Brandys was caught up in the German retreat from Silesia in February 1945 and has never been heard of since.

Postscript

We now know that the United States Government did not ordain the dropping of atomic bombs on Hiroshima and Nagasaki to end the war quickly and prevent further loss of life. Its underlying purpose was to test a revolutionary new weapon.

Although the Japanese authorities had long declared their willingness to negotiate a peace settlement, this fact was deliberately suppressed. The bombing of Hiroshima was falsely represented as the only means of ending the war. In reality, it was carried out at the insistence of physicists and arms manufacturers.

When German fighter pilots like Adolf Galland and Johannes Steinhoff pleaded with Hitler for a bigger and better fighter force during the latter stages of the war, they were unaware of the possible implications of any such improvement in Germany's air defenses. Cities such as Essen, Hamburg, Frankfurt, and Munich might well have suffered the same fate as Hiroshima. With the benefit of hindsight, the Germans can count themselves fortunate that world-beating fighters like the Tank Ta 152, Dornier Do 335, and Messerschmitt Me 262, though urgently requested, were never produced in significant numbers.

Glossary

NB. All Anglo-American equivalents are very approximate because of basic differences in function and organization.

1. Luftwaffe fighter formations in ascending order of size:

Rotte (pl. *Rotten*)	Pair comprising leader and wingman.
Schwarm (pl. *Schwärme*)	Foursome comprising two *Rotten.* (Here translated "finger-four," the term by which it became known when adopted by the RAF.)
Staffel (pl. *Staffeln*)	Formation comprising three *Schwärme,* or approximately twelve aircraft, prefixed 1 to 9 in arabic numerals.
Gruppe (pl. *Gruppen*)	Formation comprising three *Staffeln,* or approximately thirty-six aircraft, prefixed I to III in roman numerals.
Geschwader (pl. unchanged)	Formation comprising three *Gruppen,* or approximately one hundred aircraft, followed by an arabic numeral.

2. Luftwaffe ranks occuring in text, in ascending order of seniority:

Gefreiter	(USAF) Airman Third Class; (RAF) Aircraftman First Class.
Obergefreiter	(USAF) Airman Second Class; (RAF) Leading Aircraftman.
Feldwebel	(USAF) Staff Sergeant; (RAF) Flight Sergeant.
Oberfeldwebel	(USAF) Master Sergeant; (RAF) Flight Sergeant.
Fähnrich, Oberfähnrich	"Ensign," Junior and Senior Grade. (USAF) Aviation Cadet or Warrant Officer; (RAF) Acting Pilot Officer. (These grades were supplementary to whatever noncommissioned rank the holder had already attained.)
Leutnant	(USAF) Second Lieutenant; (RAF) Pilot Officer.
Hauptmann	(USAF) Captain; (RAF) Flight Lieutenant.
Major	(USAF) Major; (RAF) Squadron Leader.
Oberstleutnant	(USAF) Lieutenant Colonel; (RAF) Wing Commander.
Oberst	(USAF) Colonel; (RAF) Group Captain.

3. Other unit designations, appointments, et cetera:

Jagdgeschwader (abbr. JG)	Fighter *Geschwader*.
Geschwader-Kommodore	*Geschwader* commander. Normally, though not invariably, a *Major*.
Kampfgeschwader (abbr. KG)	Tactical or bomber *Geschwader*.
Staffelkapitän	*Staffel* commander. Normally, though not invariably, a *Hauptmann*.
Sturmgruppe	Official designation of a volunteer *Gruppe* whose pilots were pledged to "storm" enemy formations and, if necessary, destroy them by ramming.
Sturmstaffel	Subunit of a *Sturmgruppe*.